MAVERICK

A DARK AND DIRTY SINNERS' MC: SIX

SERENA AKEROYD

Copyright © 2020 by SERENA AKEROYD

All rights reserved.

No part of this book may be reproduced in any form or by any electronic or mechanical means, including information storage and retrieval systems, without written permission from the author, except for the use of brief quotations in a book review.

❦ Created with Vellum

MAVERICK

DEDICATION

To Anne.
    Better than Henry Cavill.
    Who needs Superman when you've got the BA-EA?
    Thank you for putting up with me, darling x

PLAYLIST

If you'd like to hear a curated soundtrack, with songs that are featured in the book, as well as songs that inspired it, then here's the link:

https://open.spotify.com/
playlist/7howLKC9Qa2pgeNl7YSUWO

This might not be what you're used to from the Sinners. That's my fault. ;)

UNIVERSE READING ORDER

FILTHY
NYX
LINK
FILTHY RICH
SIN
STEEL
FILTHY DARK
CRUZ
MAVERICK
FILTHY SEX
HAWK
FILTHY HOT
STORM
THE DON
THE LADY
FILTHY SECRET (COMING NOVEMBER 2021)

ALERT! ALERT!

I CAN'T BE HELD responsible for damaged Kindles hurled during the reading of this novel.

;)

Please be mindful here. You're on book six of a series loaded with triggers, and this book is no exception.

That being said, buckle up, Divas, you're in for a ride.

Love

Serena

xoxo

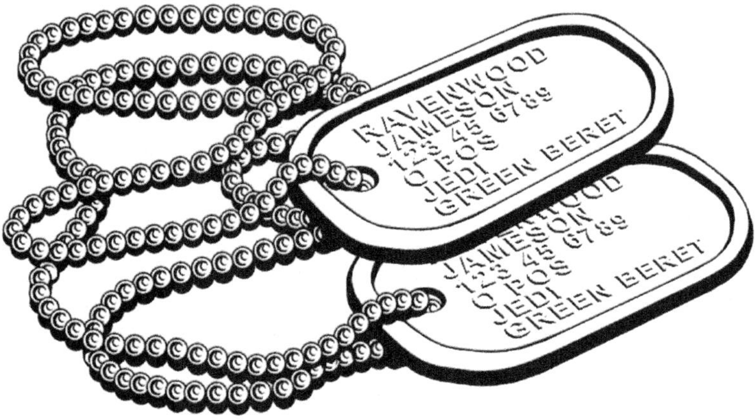
RAVENWOOD
JAMESON
123 45 6789
O POS
JEDI
GREEN BERET

PROLOGUE

MAVERICK

THE TIGHT SPACE of my bunk was no place for two guys to lie together, at least not in this fucking heat.

I thought I'd known the likes of this smothering inferno before, but nothing beat this summer in Kembesh. While we were up high in the mountains, sheltered somewhat from the outright blast of bone melting hell, the monsoons had been particularly bad this year. My insides felt like they were being stewed, and I was used to worse circumstances than this one. Used to the worst combat situations imaginable.

I blew out a breath, which made the hairs on Nic's chest shift under the breeze and, trust me, in these conditions, that was about as much of a hurricane as it got around here. I studied his pecs, abs, and the delicious divots where his muscles created a whole different plane of their own, and I was beyond tempted to rest my hand there, to let my fingers slide down to cup his dick.

But I couldn't.

We were bunking with our ODA, an unusually small one of ten members because we'd just lost Harrison and Wamba. They'd been blown up, and the rest of us bunch of Snake Eaters—Special Forces—were still coming to terms with their deaths. Wamba was the last fucker I thought we'd lose. He was neurotic all the way, following regulations left and right to his usual point of madness. If anyone should have died in that IED explosion, it was me.

I'd never been good at following orders, which technically made me a shit soldier, but I tried to follow rules as much as I was able to. Being raised with MC brats had me questioning shit I shouldn't really question, but along the way, I'd pulled some crazy stunts, saved some important people, and I'd managed to earn my place in the Green Berets.

Nic was older than me and I was his subordinate, and we definitely weren't supposed to be fucking, but the other guys turned a blind eye to all that when he had his hallucinations.

The whole team knew Nic should be back home, we all knew he should be retired, but he was too good at what he did, and our SOB of a colonel kept pulling shit, doctoring his reports, and making moves that saw Nic in the sandbox time and time again.

We were tight, brothers in arms who would die for each other, but for Nic, we wouldn't *just* die—we'd outright fucking kill.

That was the level of devotion he stirred in us.

We'd go into hell for him, would cross the Judecca to bring him back. Only trouble was, the river of wailing in Hades was where Nic's mind was half the time anyway. How could we retrieve someone from their thoughts? Rescue them mentally if not physically?

But our love for him was why our bunk was at the back. The others had adjusted theirs, made makeshift curtains to give us some privacy that was more for their benefit than ours. I'd go so far to say that Rodger and Ruby were homophobes, but they never said shit.

Never would.

Because I kept Nic going. I kept him lucid.

I had no idea why, but I did. Lying in this tight bunk with him, just breathing the same air, just relaxing as much as we could in this fucking shithole, it calmed him down.

I respected the others too much to try anything, even though I wanted to. Losing Wamba and Harrison was hitting us all hard, and knowing we were about to get two new team members wasn't helping. With what we did, we needed to trust our brothers, and that was tough when we had to bring two new soldiers in. More than that, we had to survive long enough to get those new team members—

"I've got a bad feeling about this place, Mav."

Those were the first words he'd said since he'd woken up from a fitful sleep.

"That's because you're paranoid," I replied lightly, even though he really wasn't. Nic had an inbuilt monitor for trouble that was usually spot on. But as unease filtered through me because I knew he was right, I tried to shift the tone. "You just know that the only MREs we have left are the goulash."

He pulled a face, but his smile peeped through. He was filthy—we all were. This combat outpost was in the middle of Bumfuck, Afghanistan, and it was barely functioning as we'd just recouped it from the Taliban two nights ago. Running water was a luxury right now, and we stank like dead pigs. Not that I cared. Didn't even care that my chest was sticking to Nic's thanks to the perspiration coating us that had dried where we touched.

I sometimes felt like I couldn't get close enough to him, so being glued in place was my idea of heaven.

"I don't think it's the goulash I'm scared of," he muttered dryly, but he turned his head and pressed a kiss to the crown of mine.

Closing my eyes at the touch, I rasped, "I know."

We all did.

We'd been outnumbered, but we'd won back the outpost. Somehow.

The odds hadn't been in our favor. Losing two of our team was lucky in the grand scheme of things, but lucky and loss didn't go hand in hand.

And luck this deep in the sandbox, this far out from communications with other COPs? Unlikely.

They were waiting.

Just like we were.

They were coming for us again.

We just had to maintain our position, just had to stay alive until the 10th Mountain Division, my old unit, finally got their asses here.

I rubbed my stubbled cheek against his chest, taking advantage of these moments of intimacy while my other brothers were out there, keeping an eye on things. We'd take over for Ken and Eagle Eyes in a half hour, because after sixty-four hours of active duty, they needed some fucking shut-eye.

He squeezed me, kissed my head again, and rasped, "Maverick?"

"Yeah, Nic."

"You know I love you, don't you?"

I clenched my eyes closed because that was the first time he told me that, the first fucking time, and I knew where his mind was at.

The PTSD was so entrenched in his brain it was like he had a ghoul in there.

Maybe he did.

I knew he was waiting.

Waiting to fucking die.

I could have railed at him, gotten angry. Told him not to tell me those words because he wasn't sharing them to make me feel better, to cement what we had together. No, he was using them as a goodbye.

"We're going to get out of this," I snarled. "We've been in worse situat—"

He shook his head. "Maverick."

His tone was the one I'd been listening to for years, the calm, steady melody of a man who somehow fooled the rest of the world into believing he had no demons. He was the best master sergeant I'd come across, but he shouldn't be here.

He should be home. And from his voice, I knew he felt like he'd never get back there again.

"I need you to make it, Maverick. I need to know you'll get home, that you'll get back to the real world. I love you too much to think of you—"

The tears that pricked my eyes shamed me, but the serene tone, the way in which he said my name... how his plea wasn't plaintive, just hopeful, I had no choice but to reach up and cover his mouth to stem the tide of his words. I couldn't hear any more.

"I love you too, Nic."

And the second those words fell from my lips, I wished them back.

I wished them to hell, because the moment they drifted from my vocal chords, formed intelligible sounds that could be understood, that was when things went FUBAR, and death embraced our team once more...

ONE

GHOST

TEN YEARS LATER

KATINA: *Is he awake?*

    Me: *Not yet. He will be soon though. Get some sleep, zayushka.*

    Katina: *I'm not a rabbit.*

    Me: *You are. My rabbit.*

    Katina: *I'm going.*

    Me: *Good. SLEEP!*

TWO HOURS LATER

KATINA: *Is he awake?*

    Me: *Katina! Why are you awake?*

    Katina: *I'm worried.*

    Me: *I know, kotyk. I'm worried too.*

    Katina: *Will he be okay?*

Me: *We won't let him be anything else.*

Katina: *Mommy wasn't okay.*

Me: *Maverick isn't Mama.*

Katina: *I want him to be okay. I like his smile and how he makes you smile. You don't smile enough, Alessa.*

Me: *He makes me happy. He'll wake up soon. I promise.*

Katina: *You can't promise that.*

Me: *Tak, I can.*

Katina: *I hate it when you speak Ukrainian.*

Me: *Tough. You're going to learn it. It's what Mama would have wanted.*

Katina: *o.O*

Me: *O.o*

Me: *Get some sleep. Please? You'll be the first person I'll call when he's awake.*

Katina: *Spasybi.*

Me: *You're welcome <3*

TWO

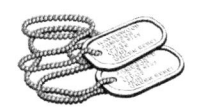

GHOST

TWO HOURS LATER

"WHO ARE YOU?"

Have you ever lived a nightmare?

My life was a nightmare for years.

I'd had things done to me that no one could begin to imagine, endured the evilness of mankind like few had, and yet one biker brought me to my knees.

"Who are you?"

One biker hurt me more than any of my rapists—or as they called themselves, owners—ever could.

He didn't mean to.

He didn't torment me physically or torture me sexually.

He simply looked at me like he didn't know me.

Like he didn't remember me.

And that hurt more than anything else that had ever happened to me, because, God help me, I loved him.

I loved this biker. This scarred, war-hardened man who had eyes like sparkling dimes, the most kissable lips imaginable, and hair that, thanks to the short spikes from the buzz cut he was growing out, gleamed like precious metal in the sun. This biker, whose real name I'd only come to learn when we married. Even knowing it, however, I just called him Maverick.

Either that or husband.

A husband who didn't remember me.

But this wasn't some stupid soap opera, wasn't a sitcom for people's entertainment.

This was my life.

I'd say my husband glared at me like he hated me, but it wasn't hatred. What he felt for me wasn't even that much. I was a nonentity to him. A nobody.

Which was what hurt most of all—to Maverick, I'd never been that.

I'd been somebody.

Always, somebody.

But now, I was back to being a nobody.

My throat felt tight and thick, itchy as the desire to cry hit me hard, but no tears fell. I knew it was some strange thing that had happened to me with my last owner. Crying was difficult. I'd taken to faking tears because they wouldn't fall for me anymore, not after what I'd been through.

So instead of getting some relief from crying, I just felt clogged up a little like our old toilet in my home in Mezyn, back in Ukraine.

"Where's Nic?"

He kept on asking that, kept on demanding for this Nic who I didn't know, had never even heard of, but his desperate tone hit my heart hard. If his desperation for a stranger didn't take me aback, then my disabled husband, a man who lived in a wheelchair, stunned me further by getting to his feet, standing on them, just as Link and Steel, two of his MC brothers, as well as a nurse, made an appearance in the room.

They tried to restrain him after they got him back into bed, yet the more they tried to keep him there, the more anguished he was. The more desolate.

I had never heard him mention Nic before, but he was desperate to get to him—whoever he was. His brothers didn't appear to know who this Nic was either.

"We'll find out who Nic is," Link vowed, his face sweaty with exertion as both he and Steel worked hard to keep him contained on the bed.

His words were the passcode that triggered a cessation of Maverick's struggling. As if they'd flicked a light switch, he stopped. Turned still.

"Until then," Steel told him, "Ghost is here."

Mav stared up at him. "Who's Ghost?"

I saw Link pass me a guilty look, but I didn't stick around to find out how else he could break my heart.

I loved him.

What a time to realize it.

Swallowing down the need to scream, I stared at the walls, at the floor, at the little skid marks on the linoleum. I stared at the set of two uncomfortable chairs where I knew Link and Steel had been sitting, leaving me inside with Mav so he'd wake up with me at his side, and wondered how everything had gone so wrong.

People passed me by, rushing in and out. Link and Steel were tossed into the corridor with me, and as they talked around me, time passed, but it was almost as if I was dead to its endless whirl.

Brain a blur, heart racing, out of nowhere, my lungs just wouldn't work.

I started to gulp down air, started to swallow it, but it wasn't the same as breathing. My skin prickled with the makings of a panic attack, and sweat beaded at the base of my back and dotted my temples. None of it compared to the sensation of claustrophobia that had me seeking fresh air.

"Leave her," I heard Link mutter behind me. "She needs some space. Christ, poor Ghost. Can you believe Mav—"

I didn't hear any more, was too busy dashing forward, heading down the corridor toward the doorway that would take me to the outer hall.

It was a maze here, and knowing I was trapped inside made me feel worse, but just as I reached the doors, someone cleared their throat, and through the fog of panic, someone called out, "Mrs. Ravenwood?"

They'd started using my full title here, and it was strange to my ears. Strange because I half expected to hear 'Mrs. Maverick' instead, but Maverick wasn't his real name.

Jameson was.

Jameson Ravenwood.

I'd heard it once on our wedding day. A hurried and harried affair that began out of necessity and, to me at least, had turned into more.

So much more.

He'd married me to protect me, to let me stay in the U.S. and to have some freedom to come out to the cops, to tell the authorities what the Lancaster family had done to me. How the father and son had enslaved me as well as three other women.

It wasn't the green card which kept me safe. While I knew Maverick thought that was why I'd gone ahead with the wedding, it wasn't. *He* was. With him, I felt safe, and that was a rare and precious thing in my world.

Hope aside, I was pretty sure that, at some point in the future, ICE would track me down and haul me back to Ukraine, married or not, but when he'd asked me to be his wife, a strange calm had overtaken me.

In all honesty, thinking back to that moment, when he'd proposed in the most unromantic setting imaginable, calmed me *now*.

It helped me breathe.

Helped me turn to the doctor.

Helped me feel like my skin wasn't too tight for my body.

I turned around slowly, trying to use the time to get myself back on track. The doctors didn't often talk to me because Stone, a doctor at the hospital but also Steel's Old Lady, usually did the explaining. Not just to me but to the council too.

These words... Old Lady. Council. They were new to me. Not to my vocabulary, just new to me.

I'd somehow found myself in a whole other subculture within a culture. It was both fascinating and terrifying.

Until now, I hadn't been scared. Because of Maverick.

Why did he have to go back to the clubhouse?

Someone had targeted the place where the Satan's Sinners MC lived and worked, someone had bombed it and destroyed it. In the aftermath, the place had been nothing but rubble, more wreckage than shelter, and Maverick had entered the building in his wheelchair, where the roof had collapsed on top of him, then he'd ended up here.

Out of a wheelchair.

So much was going on, so much made no sense.

A woman I'd been imprisoned with, enslaved with, had turned traitor on the Sinners. In the aftermath of the bombing, Tatána's body had been discovered amid the rubble, and Maverick had been injured and unconscious ever since.

I'd never imagined this was how it would have gone down.

Never could have foreseen him losing his memory.

Even knowing why he'd returned to the damaged clubhouse, I

still resented it. Would club business always take precedence? Even above his own safety?

I blinked at the doctor, mad at myself for failing to hear him talking to me. Gulping, I whispered, "I-I'm so sorry, sir, but I—"

He frowned at me a little, and I shrank back at his annoyance. Then he surprised me by asking, "Are you all right?"

Fiddling with my leather cuff, something Stone had given me in the early days so I could hide the slave brand on my wrist, I shook my head. "My husband just woke up. He doesn't remember me."

His eyes softened, even if they dropped to the cuff I was still messing with. "I've just checked him over."

"You have?" I rasped disbelievingly—exactly how long had I been out of it? My mind a blur?

"Yes," he murmured, reaching out, his hand going to my shoulder.

I stared down at it, the free and easy way he'd just moved to touch me...

Was he only trying to comfort me?

Maybe that's what people did here. Normal people.

Someone was distressed, they reached out to comfort them. But for me, the doctor's hand was like a bunch of spiders crash-landing on my shoulder.

I stared at the digits edgily, feeling as if each one was an insect that was going to crawl up my neck and into my ear, down my shirt collar and beneath my clothes.

Out of nowhere, my breathing began to grow worse once more, and the doctor, sensing that something wasn't right, backed off.

Not far, just a step, but his gaze was sharper now.

Meaner?

I didn't know. My brain was too frazzled to read his expression.

I wasn't used to being touched anymore. Not by anyone. Maverick could, but he wasn't just anyone, and that had nothing to do with him being my husband.

He'd been there.

From the start.

In my sick bed, he'd visited me.

When I'd hovered at death's door, he'd stayed with me.

He'd sat there and eaten with me as I struggled to get food down.

As Giulia and Stone had changed my bandages, dosed me up with antibiotics, he didn't leave.

He'd held my hair as I puked.

He'd let me hide my face in his throat when things got to be too much.

His arms, his touch, had become a haven.

And I'd just been locked out of the one place I'd never thought I'd lose.

Yes, *never*.

Hope was a drug I'd become addicted to, because even though I feared ICE would destroy the life I was building, I'd started thinking in terms of 'forever.'

What a fool I'd been.

I should have realized that forever wasn't something a woman like me would ever have.

"Mrs. Ravenwood?" the doctor asked, drawing me from my heavy thoughts.

"Y-Yes?"

"I've long since suspected that Mr. Ravenwood has been suffering with CTE."

"CTE?" I repeated, questioning my level of English because, at that moment, he might as well have been speaking Mandarin. "What is that?"

"Chronic traumatic encephalopathy is a neurodegenerative disease which causes severe and irreparable brain damage. Unfortunately, it's something that can only be truly diagnosed upon a patient's death, but there are signs, and those signs are what Jameson has been displaying for a long time."

"You know him?" I queried, confused. "How?"

"Well, back in the day, we attended the local high school together. Then, after he was transferred out of Bethesda, about three years ago now, he came here before he was fully discharged. I was his doctor at the time." He pulled a face. "The second he was out of the hospital, he never did as he was supposed to, never even bothered returning for checkups, but his recent scans merely confirm my belief. His Diffusion MRI and CAT scan—" He sighed when I looked at him blankly. "They're special ways to take photos of the brain."

"Oh." My brow puckered, and I thought about *why* Maverick was in the wheelchair. I'd thought about it before, but I'd never imagined he had a problem with his head, just with his legs. Hence the need for the chair. "You thought he had something wrong with his head before?"

"As I explained, it's not as simple as that. CTE is something that has no cure, no real way to diagnose outside of an autopsy. But his behavior, his moods, everything at that time indicated, to me at least, that he was a sufferer." He sighed. "This recent response merely confirms it in my mind. The amnesia after yet more trauma to the brain is—"

"Is what?" I rasped, terror filling me.

Maverick was the smartest man I knew. His life went down behind a computer screen, his brain whirred into action whenever he was on one of his investigations. How could that same man have brain damage?

Confusion had me doing the unthinkable.

My hand snapped out, and I grabbed the doctor's arm, holding it hard enough to gain his attention—which I'd had anyway, really. "Please, tell me you can help him."

"There's no cure, ma'am." He winced. "I'd like to run a PET scan—"

Was that expensive?

"Go for it, Barry," Steel rumbled, and I whipped around to look at him, relieved he'd made an appearance at that moment.

How was I supposed to approve a PET scan, whatever that was, when I didn't even know how any of this treatment was being paid for?

So many Sinners were in the hospital right now thanks to the bombing. As a foreigner, one who'd always lived on the less than legal side of the tracks, I didn't know how any of this worked.

The doctor cast a glance at Steel who was, I noticed, scowling at him. Biting my bottom lip, I flickered my gaze between them, then watched as the doctor nodded and bustled away.

"He shouldn't have come to you about this," Steel groused, twisting around to watch the other man leave.

"He's my husband," I whispered, clinging to that label because it meant something to me.

I knew it had meant something to Maverick too, at least before all this.

What was happening here? How had everything gone so wrong?

"You don't know his medical history, and you don't know what insurance he has," he said gruffly. "He should have spoken with all of us, is what I mean, Ghost. I'm not taking away from the fact that you're his wife."

"One he doesn't remember," I remarked bitterly, and then I shook my head. "I'm sorry, Steel. I have no rights at all to know anything about Maverick, do I? You're very patient with me, letting me sit in there instead of you—"

He grunted and reached out, then his hand hovered on my arm for a few seconds before he pulled back and muttered, "Ghost, you have every right to be in there, every right to know the nitty-gritty details of Maverick's shitty medical history and his current condition. You brought my brother back to life. Fuck, he was a living corpse before you came along. Only got up in the morning to do shit for the MC. Being treasurer was his only reason for being.

"Then you appeared and changed that. I can never not be grateful for you, Ghost. Ever. And I know all my brothers feel the same way. It's just there are legalities and shit you don't know about—yet. Which is the keyword." He reached up and rubbed the back of his neck. "It speaks to the man and his state of mind that he could hide from everyone who fucking loves him that he could walk, Ghost. That he didn't need that goddamn chair.

"Plus, I only just found out he served in Afghanistan because of this Nic guy, for God's sake. We only knew about his deployments in Iraq and Libya."

Nervously pleating my hands together, I murmured, "I never even imagined—"

"Why would you? None of us did either. I'm just confused as to what his game was." Then, he reached up to rub his eyes with a weariness I felt in my own bones. "It's not the first time we've heard mention of this CTE though. Stone was just explaining it to me the other day."

"She was?" I clung to that because I trusted Stone. This wasn't her department—she worked in the ER—but she came along to help liaise between the MC and the hospital staff as, to be frank, they wouldn't listen to anyone but her.

Being in this hospital was more of a clue than ever before that the Sinners ran West Orange.

I'd known it, partially, for a long while. When Giulia, my friend, had been raked over the coals by the authorities for murdering one of the men who enslaved me, and whose death led to the MC liberating me and the other girls who'd been trapped in that horrendous cabin in the woods, it hadn't been by the local sheriff.

Lancaster had brought in detectives from outside because the sheriff was in the Sinners' pocket.

Here, in the hospital, rather than being tossed out or laughed at for insisting on special treatment, the men got it like they were royalty, and I knew for a fact they weren't.

Steel grunted again. "I think Barry mentioned it to her before when Rex asked Stone to run interference on Mav. For a long while after he came back from overseas, he was in Bethesda, which is a military hospital, for, Christ, thirteen months, and then he was brought here. Rex would only deal with Stone, and she learned the ins and outs of his case back then." He sighed. "Ghost, this CTE shit, it's not good. It's a kind of dementia."

His sigh, the pity in his eyes, and the unhappy twist to his mouth all spoke louder than words.

"You don't think he'll ever remember me again, do you?"

His jaw gritted, and though I already knew what he was thinking, the slow shake of his head was like a death knell to my heart and, somehow, I was supposed to call my baby sister and tell her that Maverick wasn't okay like I'd promised.

Making me just another adult who'd lied to her...

THREE

GHOST

THE FOLLOWING DAY

"THIS IS FOR ME? Well, Maverick and me?" I spluttered, aghast and overwhelmed at the sight of the home Lily had guided me to.

We'd walked through her mansion that was like something a Tsar could live in, then we'd roamed over a manicured backyard that consisted of more land than what a communist leader would consider adequate for a palace... All of this had led me to a large building in the center of the plot.

It was like something from a dream.

A bad one.

Because I'd swap the luxury of this place for the crowded attic where Maverick had made me feel like a normal human woman again.

I plucked at my bottom lip as I twisted around, staring here and there as I tried to process what was actually happening.

I felt like I was standing in the middle of a golf course, only with a looming house at the back of me that overlooked this majesty. The rich green lawn was so plush that it seemed like velvet. Then there were the beds of flowers that, even though it was a dull day, seemed to shine and blossom to order.

I wasn't sure if money could make flowers grow or bloom, would have thought that was a biological impossibility, but I was looking at proof of tiny daisy-like flowers I didn't know the name of, that were unfurled and peering toward the day's meager sun.

These flowerbeds were ornamental, with expensive-looking urns amid them that tumbled water into the ground in a fancy way. If the velvet lawn and the flowers that defied biology weren't enough, then that was nothing compared to the pool.

I'd never seen anything like it.

In pictures, I'd seen the Grand Canyon, and I could only liken the pool to that. Except it was a miniaturized version. Bright red rocks were cosseted by a body of water that could have been a lake. The walls were built up, craggy as though nature had plunked them down there, shielding a pool that was majestic in the extreme. Amid that grandeur, amid the canyon-esque walls was a house.

A miniature version of the big house.

My new home.

Lily felt guilty. I understood that. But it wasn't like it was her fault her brother and father had done what they had to me, Tatána, Amara, and Sarah.

"I wasn't sure if you'd want to stay here, but I thought this way you could have privacy, could be close to Katina, and also have room for Maverick to—" She sighed. "There are a couple of bedrooms. I know Luke lived here," she said in a rush. "But you can totally tear it to pieces, Ghost. Like, I wouldn't blame you. I can even bring the sledgehammers and wreck everything he owned."

I shot her a look, but though my smile was small, my amusement wasn't. "How wasteful."

She crinkled her nose. "I just want you to be happy here. Link and I can move in if you want, and you can use the house—"

I moved around in a circle, eying the property that was funded on blood, sweat, and tears. Her mother's. Hers.

She was talking as if she hadn't been victimized as I had. As Amara had.

No, she hadn't been held captive in a cabin in the woods, made to do things a normal, sane man wouldn't ask of animals, but she'd been sexually abused. She'd witnessed her mother's murder.

So, yes, this house was built with blood money—not just mine and her mother's, but hers too.

Maybe I should be bitter, but Lily was such a sweet person. So kind and caring. She'd been through so much, and though I knew Tatána had been resentful, maybe Amara just a little as well, I didn't feel the same way. I just couldn't.

Was that because Maverick had given me security?

Perhaps.

I didn't know, could never know what had led Tatána to turn her back on the men who'd kept us safe, who'd taken us from hell, who'd saved us from the worst kind of death...

Had Amara been in on it? I wondered if the MC was monitoring her, maybe they were keeping their eye on me too. It would make sense.

I couldn't blame them.

I would even help them if I knew how, because they hadn't just saved us, they'd fed us and made sure we were healthy. This was, in my opinion, the worst kind of betrayal. For Tatána to be sneaking around in Rex's office, a place that was out of bounds for everyone other than the council, was tantamount to an admission of spying.

If she hadn't died in the blast, hadn't died at the site of her crime, they'd have killed her for it, and I couldn't fault them.

Her betrayal cut deep and left behind a lot of unanswered questions.

Who was she spying for? We didn't know anyone outside of the clubhouse... At least as far as I was aware. What had her game been?

"Ghost?" Lily asked warily.

"*Tak?*" Realizing I'd spoken in my mother tongue, I murmured, "It's okay, Lily. You don't have to look so guilty."

She bit her lip. "I don't?"

I shook my head. "No. You don't. And I don't need a sledgehammer." I grinned at her. "You Americans truly are so wasteful."

Her nose crinkled again, and the little wrinkle was so endearing that I reached over and tapped it gently with my finger. She was surprised by the gesture, and considering I didn't particularly appreciate people touching me, I was taken aback that she didn't slap my hand away.

I wasn't the only one with issues, after all.

Instead, she reached for me, entwining my fingers with her own, then murmured, "Ghost?"

"Yes, Lily?"

"I'd like to be friends."

Smiling, I shook my head at her. "Silly, we already are."

She shot me a sheepish look. "I felt that way, but I just wasn't sure, you know?"

Her father truly had ruined her self-worth.

Funny, wasn't it? How I could be standing on a property worth tens of millions of dollars and the owner of it all wanted to be friends with an illegal immigrant, and *she* was the one who was scared of rejection.

I tightened my fingers about hers. "Well, you have no need to doubt."

A bubble of noise exploded behind me, but I didn't jump

because I knew who it was. I'd slowly grown accustomed to Katina and her effusive ways. She was so American in some things, yet had little traits that made me wonder how Mama had taught them to her when she'd died when Kati was so young.

Ukrainians weren't the most effusive of people, not as boisterous as the Americans, moreover, among our families, we were close and affectionate. A man would think nothing of kissing his father, whereas here that was unheard of past boyhood. At least that was as far as I had seen among the MC.

Maybe they weren't the best cross section of society to learn things from?

I twisted just in time for her to rush into my arms, and when she did, I realized she was sobbing. Her dramatic antics almost had me smiling, but I understood. I wished I could sob too. In fact, her tears made me feel both better and worse. Worse because I wanted to share her tears, wanted to break down and let my feelings out. But better because she felt this for me. She was hurting for me.

I wasn't alone anymore.

"Whhhhyyy?" she wailed from a rat's nest of hair that covered half her features. "Why did he have to go into the clubhouse?"

Her sniffles made it very difficult for me to understand her, especially with her face shoved into my stomach the way it was, her arms tight around me to the point of pain. The hugging was a new thing. She'd been wary around me since her arrival at the compound, but the bombing seemed to have had a positive effect on us.

Every time she'd seen me ever since, she hugged me.

Like she was scared to let go. Like she was scared I'd disappear. She wasn't to know that only death would take me from her, but death was what I knew she feared the most—hadn't she already lost both her parents?

I hugged her harder. "He'll get better," was all I could tell her, because I couldn't tell her the truth.

Couldn't explain that Maverick had gone into the structurally unsound building to get his hands on some tech stored in a safe in there to make sure the FBI couldn't sic forensic hackers on them to learn more about the MC's activities—legal or otherwise.

How could I express any of that to a child? Especially when I felt bitter about it too? I couldn't, so I didn't bother trying.

Lowering my head, I pressed a kiss to her crown. "All will be well," I assured her, even though I had no way of knowing if that was the case.

By the time I'd left the hospital this evening, Maverick had endured so many tests that he'd been growling like a bear. I wasn't sure what the MC had done or how they'd pulled so many strings, but before I'd come to Lily's home, we'd had some results back.

The trauma was clear. Having seen the graphic imaging, there was no getting away from the fact that Maverick had been hurt in ways that no one could literally see. It was a wonder he was fully functioning. The doctors had spoken of the need to evaluate the level of tau deposition in his brain, but that was where my English had failed me.

All I'd known was that the brothers who gathered around Maverick's bed had looked grim.

I bit my lip at the thought, wondering what was going to happen to the man I loved as Kati asked, "You're staying here, aren't you?"

"I am," I confirmed.

"She's going to be in the pool house with Maverick," Lily said softly, reaching out to carefully stroke away some strands of messy hair that were glued to Kati's tear sticky face.

"Why can't she be in the main house with us? There are lots of bedrooms!"

"Because they need their privacy," was Lily's stalwart response, and I shot her a grateful look.

The smile she returned was wry, which told me Lodestar, who I knew was also staying here, had told her that I wasn't capable of dealing with Kati full-time.

That made me feel useless, and shame filled me with the thought, but it was only the truth.

I could barely look after myself, never mind her too.

Being close by, knowing Lodestar was there, as well as the rest of the MC family who were living in for the moment, filled me with peace.

She could visit but she could leave, because *pizda rula,* she was noisy.

Wincing at the treacherous thought, I reached down and kissed the crown of her head again.

I loved her so fiercely that I'd crossed an ocean for her and endured torments I'd wish on no one just to be by her side. I'd never imagined that when I could finally be there for her, I'd be letting her down by taking a step back.

I released a shaky breath as I inquired, "Lily was just going to show me around the pool house. Want to see?"

Kati's bottom lip popped out, but she nodded. "I wanted to stay here. It's so cool. At night, Lessie, you can hear the ocean."

My brows rose at that, as well as the nickname she'd given me —Lessie, that was a new one—but Lily snickered. "It's not the ocean, Kati. It's just the pool. There's a wave machine."

Eyes widening, I asked, "A wave machine?"

"Simulates the sounds of the sea. Father was nothing if not a poser."

I surprised us both by laughing at that. Kati had no idea who Donavan or Luke Lancaster had been to me, and that was how it was going to stay.

Not for the first time, I tasted their names on my lips, names I'd only learned in the aftermath of my rescue, as I wandered into the place where I'd be living from now on. I had no way of knowing for how long, but it was to be my home and I knew I could be happy here.

Maybe being under the roof of the men who had tortured me sexually should break me out in a cold sweat, but there was a delicious kind of justice here. They were dead, having been slain at the hands of people who'd served them their ends and delivered my new beginning, and I was alive.

I'd survived.

The thought was strangely buoying. It added a spring to my step, and that spring was definitely needed because the next few days, maybe weeks, were going to be tough—I was nothing if not a realist.

As Kati and Lily tugged me around the place, showing me the bedrooms and the kitchen and my beautiful connecting bathroom that looked like it was made out of one piece of marble, I was enamored with it. Especially when Lily told me I was welcome to redecorate.

The place was absent of character, enough that I knew she'd had all of her brother's possessions tossed out, and the blank space soothed me.

Filled me with satisfaction.

The best way to get back at those horrific human beings was to live my best life.

And to do that, I needed Maverick to be better.

For however long I had him, for however long I got to stay in this country, I wanted to be by his side. Even if he didn't want me there.

"Lessie, want to come and play a game with Star and me? She's grumpy. We need to cheer her up."

I shot her a cautious look. "Isn't Star always grumpy?" As far as I could tell, Lodestar's general status was harried, calculating, and ready for the shit to hit the fan.

She'd been the only person in any way expecting the blast that had triggered this nightmare. Maverick and she had argued about it the morning he'd been hurt.

She was why he'd gone to the clubhouse.

I bit my lip, because the desire to blame her was strong, but in her defense, both of us had pleaded with him to stay away from the clubhouse.

He was the one who hadn't listened.

"She is, but she's worse than usual," Kati grumbled with a sigh as she leaped onto the bed I'd told her I was going to use as my own and started jumping up and down.

I watched her, my head bopping with the movement, and had to rub my eyes at her enthusiasm.

Had I ever had that level of energy?

"A game will cheer her up."

"Which game?" I questioned warily, certain Lodestar would want to see me as little as I wanted to see her.

"Clue."

I frowned. "What is that?"

"You've never played?" Kati squealed, but finally stopped bouncing long enough to clap her hands, and then she did the damnedest thing... she somersaulted, in midair, off the bed.

"Whoa!" Lily burst out, her eyes wide at the display.

Mouth gaping, I managed to ask, "Kati, since when did you do gymnastics?"

Her eyes twinkled. "It was just something Cyan was showing me. Neat, huh?"

Neat?

That about summed it up.

FOUR

MAVERICK

"HE ISN'T DEAD."

I glowered at Link who was sprawled beside me in one of the uncomfortable hospital armchairs, trying to register that he was old now.

I mean, not decrepit. When I looked in the mirror, I was the same. Just as old as him. Scarred too.

What the fuck was wrong with me?

I felt like I was twenty-seven. In my head, I was back in Afghanistan at Nic's side as our A-team leaped from post to post, putting out fires before they had the chance to turn into infernos.

Instead, I was somehow approaching forty, had spent the past four years in a wheelchair when I was capable of walking, had married someone called Ghost—what kind of name was that anyway?—and the man I'd loved with all my fucking being was dead.

It wasn't possible.

It. Just. Wasn't. Possible.

"You know we wouldn't lie to you," Link grumbled, folding his arms across his chest, a peevish glower crossing his features as he huffed at my refusal to accept the truth.

"You would. You're pulling some kind of joke on me—"

He shook his head. "You know that isn't true. We wouldn't joke about shit like that."

That was the kicker.

I knew they wouldn't.

But I wanted to think they would.

Link, alongside Rex, Nyx, Storm, and Steel, were like family to me. They weren't blood, but they might as well have been. We pulled shit on each other all the time, but nothing like this.

Nothing about someone being dead when they were really alive.

"I can't handle him being dead," I said rawly, staring at my feet that were bare, exposed to the air because I refused to lie in this bed like I was sick.

The doctors weren't letting me out of here until they finished running their tests. I had a feeling, from that gleam in Dr. Beau's eye, that they were going to try to use me as a human fucking guinea pig, but they could back the fuck off.

"You have to handle it, Mav," Link murmured softly. "I'm sorry. I wish I could tell you otherwise, that he was happily married with two point four kids in Wyoming, but he ain't, brother. He passed a long time ago."

Steel, standing in the other corner of the room, grumbled, "There's a lot that makes no sense right now, Mav."

"Where's Rex?" I demanded, knowing he wouldn't lie to me.

"He's with Bear. He won't leave his side, and if you saw the state of him," Nyx replied grimly, "you'd get it."

Flinching, because if Nyx said it was bad, then it was fucking bad, I stared at my feet some more before I wiggled my toes.

Toes that, according to these guys, I'd claimed were paralyzed.

"Was I ever really paralyzed?"

Steel blinked. "Yeah. You were. For a while. You stopped doing rehab or things like that. Wouldn't come here, refused to do anything that would get you back on track. You've always been a stubborn fuck. Not surprised your brain shut down and restarted messed up to get some things out in the open."

The rancor in his voice had me shooting him a glare. "You obviously know nothing about computers if you think that analogy works."

He rolled his eyes, but Link was the one who said, "I can't believe you don't remember Ghost. Do you think if I hit you on the head again, you'll wake up and remember her? Damn, it killed me to see her the other day, Mav. You fucking annihilated her."

"Link," Nyx grumbled. "The idea isn't to make him feel like an even bigger pile of shit."

The gloomy shadow standing by the window was some men's idea of a walking, living nightmare. He brought death, and it wasn't the government sanctioned variety either. Not like with me.

I'd say the years hadn't been kind to him, because there was hell in his eyes, but the prick was as handsome as ever. The craziest shit of all was that, today, I'd learned he had a firecracker for an Old Lady.

A pregnant one.

Somehow, and I had no fucking clue how it was possible, Nyx was going to be a father.

Talk about mind-blowing. Shit, if that wasn't enough to make my mind force quit before restarting as normal then nothing would.

Certainly no little mouse called Ghost.

Okay, little mouse wasn't exactly being fair.

She was beautiful.

Stunning, actually, even if she was on the thin side. Frail too.

I'd never been the kind of guy who got off on the damsel in distress shit, but maybe what drew me to her was the fact she wasn't that. All day, she'd been sitting with me even though I'd thought about asking her to go because she didn't talk to me, and I had nothing to say to her. But it didn't stop her from coming in for a visit. She'd only left because my brothers had made an appearance, and Link, for whatever fucking reason, had pulled her into a hug before she went.

I mean, she was supposed to be *my* wife, but she didn't even talk to me. Sure as fuck didn't try to hug me.

Not that I'd have let her.

But wasn't that what a wife should do?

I'd watched so many fucking *telenovelas* with my mom that I knew how this shit worked. My wife should be sobbing at the foot of my bed, pleading with me to remember her, for God's sake.

Instead, she was the little mouse I'd just likened her to. Scuttling in, sitting in silence as she read a book, then scuttling out again.

Was that really the kind of woman the thirty-seven-year-old Maverick would marry?

Sure, she was a looker, but the stoic and silent type?

"I'm not trying to make him feel like a pile of shit," Link countered, forcing me to tune back into the conversation.

"No? Well, it sounds like it to me," Steel argued.

"You can't hurt me where she's concerned because I don't know her."

My words were harsh, but they were the truth. I had no reason to tell these guys anything other than that.

Their response gutted me though.

Even Nyx winced.

Fuck.

What was it about her that had these guys trying to shelter her?

Had they changed so much or was she just that good a wife?

I cleared my throat. "Where's Nic?"

"We told you already, he's dead, Maverick," Nyx muttered, pinching the bridge of his nose.

"I mean, where's he buried? Arlington?" I asked, the words feeling too thick to utter.

He couldn't be dead.

He just couldn't be.

"Yeah, he's there." Link sighed. "I can't believe we didn't know—"

My mouth tightened. "You knew I liked guys."

He flipped me the bird. "I'm not shocked about that, I'm shocked about you fucking falling for a man in your unit and us not knowing shit."

"You remember what he was like back then," Steel commented, folding his arms across his chest. "All stoic and silent."

Eyes flaring at the words I'd just used to describe the woman who was somehow my wife, I rumbled, "I wasn't supposed to say shit about us. I was his subordinate. We weren't supposed to be together."

Nyx snorted out a laugh. "Ever the rebel."

My lips twitched. "That's me."

"That *was* you," Steel pointed out softly, cutting Nyx a disapproving look. "You ain't been a rebel for a long time, Mav."

Nyx pshawed. "Just because he wasn't pulling crazy stunts anymore doesn't mean he hasn't been doing..." His voice waned, and I knew that was because he'd remembered where we were and that the walls had ears.

My curiosity was pricked though. "What have I been doing for the club?"

Link cleared his throat. "You were the treasurer."

It was my turn to snort out a laugh. "Now I know this is BS. Me? Treasurer?"

Nyx shrugged. "You were damn good at it."

Shooting each of them scowls, I rumbled, "This can't be real."

"It is, man. Wish it wasn't," Steel said with a grunt, even as he straightened up some as a knock sounded at the door and he pulled it open. When he did, in walked Barry.

This was why they were here.

Because they were family.

Because they stuck around for bad news.

When Barry glanced around the room, eying each of the kids who he'd treated like shit when we were in school, the audience of bitchin' badass bikers that'd fuck him over in an instant, I couldn't stop my mouth from running off. "Always thought you were a prick, Barry. Did you know that?"

The supercilious fucker's shoulders straightened and his smile, loaded with a smugness that made me want to smack him, grew a tad more shaken.

Back in the day, we'd been the outcasts. I mean, we still were. But we were a lot deadlier now.

Even with amnesia and ten years older than I was mentally, I knew of six ways to kill the bastard without hauling my ass out of bed.

That made *my* smile smug, and it only widened when Link started chuckling.

"Probably not wise to piss off the guy holding the clipboard, Mav," Nyx said wryly, but I knew he was fighting laughter too.

I shrugged. "I figure Barry knows I can break his leg without bothering to put on pants..."

The good doctor glowered at me, but he pulled on his professionalism like it was an uncomfortable shirt.

"Must be hard treating us with decency," I pointed out, "after all those years of treating us like shit when we were back in school. Gotta say, Barry, the years haven't been kind to you."

Barry Beau—what a fucking name. How the hell had it been *him* who'd picked on us?

His eyes flared wide as his spare hand automatically went to the place where his hairline was starting to recede. As my brothers snickered all around me, I raised my legs, grateful for the boxer briefs Link had sneaked in for me—kinky fucking nurses, wanting my balls hanging out—and topped my knees with my arms as I sat up.

"Come on then, hit me with it."

"You have the brain of a sixty-four-year-old," was not so beautiful Barry's sniped response.

"You don't say? Probably still smarter than you," I retorted, uncaring about his words.

My old nemesis growled under his breath, then the door opened and in wandered a couple of his colleagues, and instantly, his tone changed, turned softer, kinder.

Wasn't sure who he was trying to fool.

He was still a prick in a doctor's coat.

As words like tau deposits and brain trauma floated around me, I processed it all. Handled it.

What was I supposed to do?

It wasn't like I was scared. I'd spent half my life waiting to die, knowing I'd end up passing over a lot sooner than I should because of how I lived. Sure, this was a slower kind of death, but I guessed I'd be alive to see it.

I'd outlived Nic.

By two years.

Fuck, how was it that he'd died at thirty-five? How had I survived ten years without him?

My insides churned up something fierce, and my grief was a thousand times more powerful than the news the doctors were serving up like it was a side of BS on prime rib.

My brothers' faces spoke loud and clear—I might have changed, might have lied to them, might have somehow become the club's treasurer, but I was a good man.

They loved me.

I guessed I'd been doing something right even if I'd been hiding a ton from them too.

When the doctors wandered out, discussing prognoses and treatments and things they were going to do to try to slow down the extent of the damage, I had only one thing to say.

"I need to get out of here."

I kind of expected them to give me shit, to tell me I had to stay in the hospital, get treatment, do whatever I had to to get better.

But that was, I figured, the beauty of this situation.

I wasn't going to get better.

This was me.

Maybe I'd get my memory back. Maybe I wouldn't.

Maybe I'd lose my fucking marbles for real when I hit fifty, or maybe I'd be dead by then.

Who the fuck knew?

Who fucking knew anyway? Wasn't like everyone in this room wasn't a ticking time bomb too, was it?

That was what it meant to be human.

We lived. We died. Hopefully, as we lived, we brought something good to the fucking world.

At my declaration, Nyx merely sighed. "We're going to Arlington, aren't we?"

I nodded. "We are."

"You ain't ridden a bike in four years, brother," Link pointed out gruffly.

"Arlington's no more than four hours' ride, Link. I think I can handle that."

"You can if you ride bitch," Steel grumbled. "Fuck knows what's going on with your head. You can't BS me. I can see you're fighting a migraine."

My brows rose at his insight. Sure, I had a migraine—I'd had one since I woke up. That was what being a soldier meant. You got up, got on with shit. War didn't stop because you had a fucking headache.

"We could get Hawk to drive him down," Link suggested, waiting for Nyx to lobby it back.

"Think he should ride. Clear out the cobwebs," was his retort.

Even though it pricked my pride, I'd only just earned the right to start wearing boxer briefs again under this shitty hospital gown. I figured I shouldn't run before I could walk.

"I'll ride bitch. Who's ready to feel my dick at their back?"

Link snorted. "Forgot what a fucking pervert you were, Mav."

I grinned. "Sure, 'cause you've changed since I last met you?"

The shake of his head said it all, but his words gave me pause. "Weird as fuck when you say shit like that."

I shrugged. "In my mind, I just flew in from Afghanistan. Ain't seen you fuckers for a good eight months. And you sure as shit weren't these old cunts."

"Old but still pretty," Link countered, but even as he was teasing me, I saw the concern etched on his face.

Clambering off the bed, I stood up and stretched, aware that they were gaping at me and ignoring it. They'd been doing that ever since I'd gone to take a leak that first day, and Nyx had shoved me into a chair seconds after I got up, as though I was going to fall over like a toddling kid.

Somehow, I'd managed to gain back the use of my legs, somehow I'd managed to gain enough muscular strength to walk, and *some-fucking-how*, I'd managed to do all that without their goddamn knowledge.

Maybe I'd been bitten by a radioactive spider too.

That seemed to be how my life was rolling right about now.

Getting out of Dodge wasn't as easy as I'd have hoped, especially when Barry tried to have security take me into custody, but what was I? A fucking wimp? I went to throat-punch one of them, pulling back a bare inch from connecting with him. His eyes were wide as he shrieked, almost like I *had* hit him, but the move triggered the reaction I wanted—the pair of them backed off and left me the hell alone as Barry squawked behind me about shit I wasn't interested in.

Never would be either.

Whatever time I had left on this planet, it wasn't going to be spent in a fucking hospital ward. It was going to be doing the shit I needed to do.

Living.

In more borrowed clothes, even on borrowed hogs, because the blast that had half the club tucked up inside the hospital I was just leaving had taken out a lot of our rides, I clambered on behind Link.

It was weird for both of us, because we shared bikes with our bitches—no one else. And I knew for Link it had to be weirder because he had an Old Lady now, whom I certainly wasn't.

For four hours, I stayed close to him without trying to make shit creepy. Hugging him around the waist wasn't going to happen, so I monitored the road as much as he did, making sure I moved with the bends and stayed low and close as we maneuvered around tight spots.

For four hours, I dealt with the migraine that was getting worse under the heat of the sun, the roar of the wind blasting in my face. My skin was starting to ache too, and my actual skull felt as if it was throbbing under the weight of a borrowed helmet.

The honks of a hundred horns through the ear plugs Steel had shoved at me before we took off, the throb of the bikes, the rattle of the goddamn straight pipes, everything seemed to sink into my brain and shake it around as though it was being blended, but I coped with it.

I knew I wouldn't be able to focus on anything else, be it my recovery or the help the MC needed in the aftermath of this heinous attack on our territory, if I didn't see for myself that Nic truly wasn't here anymore.

It seemed like yesterday we'd been in that bunk, sharing it as he tried to get over a migraine by napping. How had things changed? How was I that person now? The one dealing with migraines and nightmares, and the one being diagnosed with abbreviations and illnesses that weren't possible to treat.

PTSD was a part of life for almost all soldiers, and I knew, just like a lot of the guys on my A-Team, I had it.

Ken was so wired most of the time that it was a wonder he could take a leak without managing to shoot his own dick off. Then there was Wamba—he'd stuck so close to the rules, to the fine line of orders, to an anal-retentive degree. Boggled my mind that he'd ever been able to get to sleep at night without a colonel giving him permission.

Ten years, man, ten fucking years. Gone. Without a trace.

I had time to think about it on that ride. While I didn't have silence, I had no means of communicating with my brothers who rode through two states for me, who helped me on, what was essentially, a pilgrimage.

A pilgrimage to the only person I'd ever loved.

Not like *love-love*. I'd adored my mom, and my brothers all took up prime real estate in my heart. But Nic? He was like my Romeo.

He couldn't be dead.

He just couldn't be.

Only, he was.

Those four hours on the road culminated in us managing to get into the cemetery just before it closed for the day. I had no idea how they knew exactly where Nic was buried, but they did. Which told me they'd expected this. Had anticipated my wanting to visit and had been prepared for the eventuality.

Section 60 was a marker most soldiers knew about. At least from my generation. We all had someone buried there, someone we'd served with who'd died in the wars in Iraq and Afghanistan.

I just never thought I'd be here for Nic.

The walk from the entrance to that sector was hard going. Proof that, even if I could walk, even if I was strong enough to do it on my own and without help, I wasn't used to it. I'd need to build up some strength, some stamina too, and get myself ready for anything, because even though the war was over for me, I knew the MC was deep in the throes of one on our home turf.

Still, those thoughts were shuffled aside as I passed fallen brothers, witnessed the tears of loved ones who grieved their lost as they visited their graves, talking to them as though they were alive, moms and dads tending to the pristine pitch of grass like it was ragged, kids standing solemn and bitter as they tried not to cry, tried to process what was impossible to process.

Through it all, I tried to come to terms with the prospect of coming across the one name I didn't want to see etched into white marble. It hit me that if I, a grown man, couldn't deal with this, then how the fuck could those kids who were visiting their mommies' and daddies' graves?

My brothers' surety made me want to hesitate. Run away.

They knew to head four rows deep, twelve across from the path we were on, and I followed them. Knowing they wouldn't steer me wrong—even if I wanted them to.

Dominic J Ellis
  MSG
  US ARMY
  Sep 8 1975
  May 17 2010
  Purple Heart
  Operation Enduring Freedom

THE PAIN that speared me was worse than the agony in my head.

For a second, I couldn't breathe.

For a second, I couldn't think.

For a second, I couldn't move.

And then, all three happened at once. As I gulped in air, my knees gave out, which had me plummeting, face first, to the soil.

Forehead to the grass that blanketed the man I loved, I wept.

For him.

For me.

For the past that was lost to me, the present that was tearing me to shreds, and a future we'd never have together.

Through it all, my brothers stood around me in silent sentry. Guarding me. Guarding the man I loved as I came to terms with a truth I couldn't remember.

A truth I didn't want to be real.

But one I'd have to come to accept because there was no denying what I was seeing.

Nic was dead.

And so were we.

FIVE

GHOST

AFTER A COUPLE of nights alone in the pool house, it was with relief that Maverick came to stay with me.

The place was big, larger than I was used to, and I rattled around it, unsure what to do, where to be, how to act.

Lily told me to treat it like this was my home.

But it wasn't.

Perhaps it was pathetic, but Maverick had come to be that.

He was my solid ground, which made things a thousand times worse for me when the day he returned to me, the day he walked through the door, he point blank ignored me.

I bit my lip as I watched him storm down the short corridor toward the room Link pointed him to. Without a backward glance at me, he headed in there, leaving me feeling breathless at the sight of him walking, which still came as a surprise, but also at the state of his face.

It was ravaged.

He'd been crying.

The pressure on my bottom lip had me wondering how the bit

of flesh hadn't given in to the force of my teeth, but as he strode away like I was the ghost Link had nicknamed me, I turned to him and asked, "Why was he crying?"

"We went to visit Nic's grave at Arlington."

Surprise hit me. "Is that nearby?"

He shrugged. "Four or so hours away in Virginia."

My lips parted. "Four hours? That's a long distance! Should he have been traveling so soon—"

Link stepped toward me, and as the brothers tended to, he made a move to touch me then froze when he remembered he wasn't supposed to.

Sighing impatiently, I demanded, "Link?"

He winced. "Truth is, Ghost, there was no way in hell we were going to keep Maverick from that place. He needed to see for himself how the land lay."

"He's devastated," I whispered, turning back to look at the now closed door.

"I wouldn't be surprised if this was the first time he really let himself feel anything for Nic," he admitted rawly. "We'd never heard of him before. He'd never mentioned him to us. Considering how he's suffering, that seem healthy to you?"

"Lodestar must have known—"

"Christ knows what she knows," he muttered grumpily. "She's a law unto herself." Because I could hardly argue, I stayed silent until he sighed. "Everything will turn out right, Ghost. Might not seem like it now, because things are so fresh, but we needed to know what was going on with him."

"Do we really know more now than we did before?" I countered, unsure if that was a lie Link was feeding himself or me.

He hitched a shoulder. "I don't know, but what I do know is that you need to give him some time. Some space. Some sympathy. To him, rationally, he knows we're no longer in our twenties, but he's fresh off the plane from Afghanistan, Ghost. Pushing him won't achieve anything."

I didn't bother to reply because if he thought I was the kind to push then he was wrong. It hadn't been in my nature before I'd been sold, so why would it be now?

Getting the feeling he was talking to himself more than me, telling himself not to push the friend who was like a brother, I let him go, watching as he lumbered back to the big house.

Amid the stylishly coiffured gardens and the grand pool, Link stuck out like a sore thumb in his jeans, leather cut, and boots. He didn't fit in around this place. Not like Lily did. Maverick and I didn't fit in either. Maybe not even Star and Kati. Tiffany did, I'd seen her yesterday when she came to visit her mom, who also looked well at ease around such luxury.

Evidently, Lily didn't care whether he fit in or not, because she was there, like they were on each other's radar, rushing toward him, not stopping until he was picking her up and hauling her into his arms.

The sight had my heart sighing, because I liked both Lily and Link—that had nothing to do with the fact that Link had been the one to get me out of the dungeon I'd been in—and wanted them to be happy.

That was the difference between Tatána and me, I thought. Not Amara, who was a little too focused inwardly—not selfishly, just her introverted nature made her different and difficult to get to know. But me, I wanted others to be happy. Wanted them to grab their slice of contentedness where it could be found before it was snatched away. As life, I'd learned, always snatched the good things away...

Tatána had begrudged people their joy, and that was why it was getting easier to accept that she could have sold out the MC.

It wasn't my fault—I wasn't responsible for her or Amara and their behavior, but oddly enough, it felt that way. I felt duty bound to understand why she'd done what she had, which was annoying because I didn't think I'd ever get any answers.

Reaching up, I plucked at my bottom lip as I watched Link laugh at whatever Lily had said when, with her legs around his hips and his arms supporting her, they retreated to the house.

A unit.

They were different somehow.

They'd always been close, always been affectionate, but I felt like something had changed since they'd gotten engaged. Intimacy... Could a diamond ring really change things that much?

As I pondered that, I also pondered the fact I couldn't bear to be staying here with a brooding Mav when all I wanted was to go into his room and sit with him, huddle into him and have him comfort me as much as I comforted him.

I'd never been the kind of person who'd dreamed of being able to lie in a bed with a man, just talking about dreams and wishes, hopes and prayers for the future. I'd always been a busy child with chores my grandmother had set as well as schoolwork.

There'd been no time for thinking foolish things. There'd only been time for doing.

I'd never complained because that was just how I'd been raised, but even though it hadn't been a week since I'd lost the Mav I knew, I missed him something fierce.

With nothing to do, nowhere to work, and time on my hands, I decided to go and sit with Kati. She liked my company, in fact, seemed to want to hover around me all the time, and I wanted to speak with Star.

I wondered if she knew anything about Nic, anything she felt comfortable sharing, because if she could tell me more about Nic and Maverick as a couple, then it would spare his feelings if she shared them with me as it wouldn't be a wound I'd need to prod to understand how I could help him more.

I refused, point blank, to think there wasn't a way to help him.

There had to be.

I couldn't just give up on what I had with him, even if it was barely anything in the grand scheme of things.

It wasn't like we'd done anything other than sleep together. We'd kissed a few times, pecks on the lips, gentle brushes of his mouth against my temple or on top of my hair, even a few deeper caresses, and what I knew Giulia called dry humping. His hands had clung to me in sleep. We'd shared secrets in the dark... but we hadn't had sex.

Was that why he'd forgotten me?

It was hard not to think that. Hard to wonder if I should have spread my legs so I'd be memorable...

Hadn't I been told so many times that the only memorable thing about me was my pussy?

The thought stung, and I drifted out of the pool house, leaving Maverick to his grief as I took the same path Link had to the main house.

As I moved, I happened to see someone standing in the window on the upper balcony. Recognizing Tiffany's mom, I didn't bother to raise my hand to her as I'd already established over last night's meal that I was a nobody to her.

That everyone MC related was a nobody.

It was why she stayed in her room, a little like Miss Haversham.

The whimsical thought of one of the characters from a favorite movie of mine had a smile chasing across my lips because I highly doubted the stylish and still fashionable woman would appreciate the comparison—even if she barely left her room.

I felt bad, but it didn't stop me from snapping off a frond of lavender at the head and crushing it between my fingers before raising it to my nose. The sweet floral scent had my memory pinging, because the last time I'd smelled it, I'd been back home.

A continent away and that smell didn't change.

I wished I was that way too. I wished I was the same as I'd been back then, but now I was Ghost. Not Alessa. *Ghost.* In more ways than one.

As I rubbed the little bud over my pulse points at my throat, letting it crumble between my fingers before I dropped the damaged flower into the soil to be at one with the earth, I carried on my way, entering the house by passing through my favorite room—what I'd heard Lily call the salon.

English was a strange language. A salon could be a place where women had their hair cut, but also a living room. I wasn't sure about the connection, but I was certain that I'd never been anywhere like it. Of course, I'd heard them call it a great room too, but I wasn't sure why. It wasn't 'cool.' It was just big.

Overhead, there was a chandelier that, when illuminated, looked like it belonged in a movie. Hundreds of glass baubles hung suspended in the air, looking like juicy apples that were ready to be plucked from the tree. Whenever I stepped into this room, my gaze always drifted upward to the beauty of the installation that had a magic of its own because it seemed so tactile even though I knew it wasn't at all.

The rest of the place was a little fussy, even as it screamed money. Expensive furnishings, the fabrics deluxe in a way that I'd never seen outside of magazines, and art and antiques rubbed shoulders with an ease that lit my humble beginnings up in sharp relief.

I'd always known we were poor, but this place made me realize the level of our destitution, which reminded me of my mother's fate—she'd sold herself into marriage.

Mama had flittered away to the States to marry a man she didn't know to pay for her mother's healthcare, to support me... She'd been young and beautiful, carefree and buoyant even if the local village had thought she was a slut for being a single mother.

It killed me that I'd lost her before I ever had the chance to know her as more than just a woman who sang lullabies to me at night, and who had shadows under her eyes from fatigue that came from working the farm as well as her shifts at a local factory. She'd been strong and dedicated, had loved her family enough to always smile through her exhaustion...

I hated that Kati wouldn't know any of this about her too. If I felt shortchanged, then how must she feel? I'd have to be the one to remind her, but whenever I did, it became clear that my mother and the one who'd raised her were different, and that always upset my sister. To the point where we'd barely spoken of her at all.

My mother danced in the kitchen barefoot, but Kati's version sounded—crazy though it seemed—brittle. *Delicate.* Always perfectly made up and wearing fancy clothes.

What had her husband done to her to make her like that?

I'd never know, would I?

Uneasy now with memories and regrets, heart aching with grief for both Kati and myself, I darted out of the room and into the hallway. The girlish giggles had me smiling as I followed Kati's noise down a polished marble corridor lined with more paintings and such toward a kitchen.

It fit, especially as I knew how much Kati tended to pack away.

I found her sitting at the kitchen table, eating what looked like carrots, cucumber sticks, and hummus, while Star glowered at something she was reading.

"Bad news?" I asked as a greeting.

Star shot me a look and shrugged, while Kati squealed and

flew out of her chair before throwing herself at me so she could hug me.

I wouldn't lie that being so freely touched came as a surprise in the aftermath of what I'd gone through, but it was a sign that we were closer than before, which was something I could never regret.

Ever.

I pressed a kiss to her dark blonde hair as I squeezed her tightly in a hug, and as I pulled back, holding onto her, I chivvied, "Are you making mischief?"

"Nope. I'm talking to Kyrian on Star's phone. He says his daddy is better."

Ah, Kyrian. Her crush.

She shot me a smile that came complete with a gap where one of her last few baby teeth—or so she'd assured me—had fallen out last week.

Before the blast.

Before everything had changed.

Again.

Why did things keep changing?

Tucking her into my side, I focused on Star. "You look tired."

"I'm okay, just in pain," she muttered, and I frowned at her.

"Should you be out of the hospital?"

Her eyes cut to Kati, and even though her grousing denied it, I knew she was back here for my sister. "I've already had Lily bitching at me about this," she grumbled, voice gruff. "I'm fine. Been through worse and I'll go through worse still."

Tension filled me at her words. "Just because you've been through worse doesn't mean this particular situation isn't bad. You shouldn't measure everything up to the past. If you do, where does it end? Well, I have a migraine," I mocked, "but I won't take any acetaminophen because I didn't need it when I almost lost my leg—"

Her scowl told me she didn't appreciate what I had to say, but deep in her eyes, I saw a glimmer of something that, shockingly enough, I took to be respect as she hadn't expected me to contradict her.

I wasn't sure why, but that had me swallowing down some nerves.

Lodestar was a soldier. It was in everything she did. In her behavior, how she held herself, the way she stared down the world like she wasn't afraid of anything.

By comparison, I was a nothing. A no one. Not a fighter or someone who took the world head-on. I was a victim. The only thing I'd done was survive, and even then, I hadn't done much.

Amara had been the one to escape the cage we'd been kept in. I'd just lain there, knowing I was dying, trying to hold on even though I thought I'd go insane with the need for water.

She'd managed to break free and had, growing weaker every day, tried to make noise so that somebody, anybody, could hear us. I'd thought it was futile when she was too weak to even stand on her own two feet, but like knights in creaky armor, the MC had swooped in and saved the day.

All of that had happened around me. To me. I hadn't done a thing to help myself.

So for this woman, this warrior to look at me with even a whisper of respect, even if it wasn't earned, well, it hurt. In a good way.

Kati moved over to Star and slung an arm over her shoulders. "Ghost's right, Star," she muttered, pecking her cheek with a kiss. "Can I get you those pills the doctor sent you home with?"

I wasn't altogether sure if I was happy my baby sister knew about these 'pills,' but it wasn't like Star would have been given a prescription of heroin, was it?

Still, the insight into their relationship was interesting. Star, by no one's ideals, was a mother. Kati wandered around the clubhouse with wild hair that didn't look like it had been brushed in a month, usually had dirt on her face, and, thankfully, was too young to really stink, but she'd get that wet dog smell after a few days which told me Star wasn't forcing her to shower.

But she never forgot Kati.

Somehow, she never did.

Not a day went by where I didn't see her hug Kati or Kati kiss her back on the cheek. Where Star didn't make her a sandwich or tell her to grab some 'green shit,' which I thought were vegetables —just like with her veggies and hummus today. She might be an unorthodox mother, but she was better than me.

We were blood, but somehow, I felt like I had no rights to Kati, and I was just relieved that though their relationship was unusual, it worked for them.

It took the pressure off me.

Which, of course, made me feel both guilty and relieved all over again.

Talk about a vicious cycle.

"Go on then," Star muttered, acceding to the whims of her daughter who giggled and skipped away like she didn't have a care in the world. I heard her feet thudding against the marble and knew, one day, she'd slip or fall, and should be told not to run in the house, but maybe Star knew that too, because her gaze remained watchful on the door Kati had just left through, yet neither of us said anything, until...

"She has to learn."

Star's mumble had me shrugging. "I know."

"You didn't say anything."

"Not my place." I knew she was wary around me, knew she probably thought I'd try to take Katina away from her. There was nothing I could do to diminish that fear, aside from shore up Star's rights.

"You're her sister," was her gruff retort.

"You're her mother." I shrugged again. "Even if she does run around like a crazy person, she's a good girl."

Star's chin jerked up. "I like her running wild. I never could. It's nice to watch her skip around the place, singing and shit. I mean, I never know what the fuck she's wailing about, but she seems happy."

I slipped into the seat opposite her at the dining room table where she was perched awkwardly, looking like she was in serious pain from the tight purse of her lips, the strain around her eyes, and the tension in her body that wasn't usually there. Both Maverick and Star acted like they had metal wires instead of bones keeping their shoulders and spine straight, but there was a fragility now that I wasn't used to seeing.

Come to think of it, when Mav had walked into the house, he'd had that same stiffness about him.

Was he in pain?

Aside from the head injury and the concussion which, of course, had to be painful, I didn't think there was anything else wrong with him. Did that mean the headache was that bad?

I hoped not.

"I like to see it too. I never had that either. We lived on a working farm, and there were always chores to do. It's nice to see her have her freedom. We grow up so fast. Too fast. I'm glad she gets to stay young."

Star shot me a surprised look. "You worked on a farm?"

I nodded. "A dairy farm. It wasn't fun."

"We had a ranch too, but not for dairy. For slaughter." She winced. "Then with Daddy being an all-out hunter, it's no wonder I'm so easy with death and killing things."

The instant she let out the words, I got the feeling she'd like to suck them back in again. I didn't let her be embarrassed or worried though. She was good at killing things—that meant she'd be good at keeping Kati safe, which mattered to me. When I was sent back to Ukraine, Kati would need someone to protect her.

So, I just said, "You're good with her. It makes me happy to see that."

Some howling started down the corridor. It might have sounded like a mother cow giving birth to a calf, but it was Kati singing something in a language I didn't understand.

Lodestar, taking pity on me, murmured, "It's K-Pop. She could be singing about slaughtering bulls too for all I know."

My lips twitched. "Not sure that would be a pop song if that was the content matter."

"It's a fucked up world. Who the hell knows what sells anymore?"

Kati wandered in, still skipping, but with each step, she rattled now too. She moved over to Star, dropped the bottle in front of her, then wandered over to the fridge. She didn't return until she had some juice in her hand as well as a little cake in the other. The cake she shoved at Star with the order of, "Eat it. You haven't eaten anything yet."

Star grumbled, "Heil, Hitler."

Kati giggled. "The brothers say that about Giulia." Her chest puffed up. "When I grow up, I want to be just like her."

"Jesus Christ," Star groaned. "Wait until you learn who Hitler is. I don't think you'll wanna be like him then."

Kati frowned. "He's a real person? I thought it was, like, something on Netflix."

"No, he was, like, real, like, you know?" Star huffed, grabbed the cake, tore open the packet, and took a large bite as she did something on her phone. Shoving it at her, she said, "Go on, read it. Tell me if you wanna laugh now."

Kati scrunched her nose up. "Is this a teachable moment?"

My brows lifted at that, and it was hard, so very hard, not to laugh. "Yes, it is."

"Is she supposed to know it's labeled a teachable moment?"

Star shrugged. "Don't know." Her lips pursed. "Don't care. Read, monkey face."

Kati sighed. "Okay," she grumbled, grabbing the phone, revealing the screen to me.

I watched as she scanned through the article as Star finished the cake and popped a couple of pills.

"She reads fast, doesn't she?"

Star nodded. "Taught her how to speed read. That stuff they make them learn in school is too boring to spend a lot of time over."

Using a cough to hide more laughter, I dipped my chin to shield my smile and simply watched Katina process a piece of world history that had escaped her this far.

When she was done, she shot Star a look. "I don't like him."

"No? Good. I'd need to take you to a child shrink if you did, and I really don't feel like paying six hundred dollars an hour for you to play with playdoh and pretend you're not a psychopath."

"Six hundred?" Kati tipped her head to the side. "We can come to a deal where you can give me that money and I'll play with toys all by myself."

Star snorted. "No can do, kid. Unfortunately for you, you're normal."

Kati heaved a disappointed sigh, then her fingers traced over a couple of the pictures on the article. "Why did he do that?"

"Why do people hurt each other ever?" Lodestar asked rhetorically. "Some folk are good, some are bad, but it's never that simple, sweetheart. Look at the Sinners. You know what Mary Jane Winslop told you about them?"

"That they are bad people? Scum?"

Inside, I tensed up, hating to hear that about men who were rough around the edges but damn good people in possession of big hearts.

"Yes. Well, would *scum* care for people the way they do? Look how they've watched over your sister, look how they helped Cyan and Keira when they were down on their luck and didn't have enough money to make rent. And then look at Stone. How they prettied up that bunkhouse so she could have someplace nice to stay while she got better...

"What sounds worse to you? Some judgmental little bitch who calls people who are like family to us scum, or her desire to hurt you, to make the family you care for seem bad in your eyes?"

She pondered that for a second then cheerily inquired, "Does Mary Jane need to visit a shrink?"

Lodestar smiled. "Yeah, I think she does. You should tell her that next time she's mean."

"Can I call *her* Hitler?"

"Well, I'll get called into the office for that, so no. We need you to stay under the radar because although your papers are good forgeries, the less trouble you cause the better."

Kati's shoulders straightened in umbrage. "The last time you went into the office, I skipped a grade! That wasn't my fault but yours."

Lodestar winced. "Yeah. That was accidental."

"I don't want to skip another grade."

"You won't. We're working on making you dumb down for the class, aren't we?"

I cleared my throat. "You are?"

"Yeah. Look at her, doesn't know anything about Hitler at her age. Disgusting." She heaved a sigh. "Not the teacher's fault or anything, it's this stupid new system they introduced. So I let her do what she wants in class, but at home, she does real studies, and then we have to work hard to make her look normal." She reached over and tugged on Kati's hair. "We don't want them to know how smart she is."

"Why?"

Kati tutted. "Because they'll make me skip a grade again, silly."

Because all of this seemed utterly logical to them, I merely shook my head. Maybe it was wrong, maybe it was bad, but like Star had said, those words were relative.

The meaning was not often as easy as black and white.

That fit for all of us, I saw. Not just me and Maverick or the rest of the Sinners, but for Lodestar and the Old Ladies and Kati too.

The thought, somehow, settled me. Made me feel better.

None of us were normal. None of us fit in with the Mary Janes, and for the first time, I recognized that I didn't *want* to be a Mary Jane. I didn't necessarily want to be Ghost, but I'd be quite happy to be Alessa again, so maybe that was something I needed to work on.

Not just for me, but for Kati and perhaps even Maverick as well.

SIX

ALESSA

"NO BACKUP. Pass it on. No medevacs."

My sleep wasn't the deepest anymore, not even when I'd rested in Maverick's arms had I slept a full night through, so it could have been the fact I was on the other side of the hall, or it could have been his volume that awoke me.

"No backup."

It was a mutter at first, one that had me blinking past the dazed state of dreams I didn't wish to remember.

"Pass it on."

A rumble this time. Louder. Deeper.

Angrier.

"No medevacs."

A snarl. Hissed out.

"No backup."

Again and again it went on. Mutters, rumbles, snarls. Over and over. Until I jerked in surprise when he screamed, full blast, like something out of a horror movie. A scream so torn up that, though it was just a sound, it was like it had torn edges that were studded with blades. Blades that could rip through me faster than a bullet ever could.

Jumping to my feet, I almost skidded on the rug that lay beside the bed as I hurried out into the hall. He sounded like he was terrified, and my only desire was to soothe that, but I hesitated outside his door, the depth of the shadows messing with my mind as I pressed my forehead to the cool expanse of wood that separated me from my husband.

A husband who didn't remember me.

A husband whose dreams sounded a thousand times worse than my own.

Anxious, I made claws with my hands, wanting to stop myself from invading his privacy, a privacy he'd made clear that he wanted to maintain because since he'd returned from the hospital this morning, I hadn't seen him.

Not once.

I knew he'd left the bedroom to grab some food, but that was it.

I'd left him to it, knowing he needed to settle in, reacquaint himself with the new normal, but his distance wasn't just metaphorical. It was tangible. As if there were bricks between us, solid and heavy. Impossible to break down. So maybe *not* bricks. Maybe concrete walls with steel rebar inside them.

His whimpers quieted down, the scream fading so I wondered if I'd imagined it, if I hadn't heard it at all, but then it came again.

"No backup. Pass it on. No medevacs."

On repeat, endlessly, until I felt sure I'd go insane with hearing it.

My breathing was ragged as panic hit me. I didn't know what a medevac was, but I could guess as to its meaning.

Wherever he was in his dream, he was in a situation where backup was needed but wasn't on its way, and his brothers in arms were being injured, possibly slain in action, with no incoming medical aid.

And he was stuck there.

Back in that time, that place.

My mouth worked when he screamed again, and uncaring about the walls he wanted to build between us, I shoved my way inside and rushed into the room. I thought the sound of the door opening was the reason for the scream breaking off, so I didn't run in, just took careful steps inside his space.

The scent of perspiration was heavy in here, like he'd been sweating buckets to the point where it permeated each breath I took, filling me with the essence of his terror. Through the windows, the play of the water from the pool, how it moved thanks to the wave machine, sent dappled shadows and lights inside, illuminating my path as I approached his bedside.

Moving closer, I whispered, "Maverick?"

I didn't want to touch him, not when his defenses were down and he was deep in a firefight, but he repeated those damn words again.

"No backup. Pass it on. No medevacs."

They were haunting him, terrorizing him and, in turn, terrorizing me.

When the scream came next, I was ready for it, ready because he was deep in some twisted cycle I needed to break, and I grabbed his shoulder, trying to shake him awake.

It worked.

His head jerked like I'd punched him, and one second he was deep in another world, and the next he was here.

But his eyes weren't. He was awake. Aware. But his eyes were dead. Vacant. Like he was staring a thousand yards away from me. Staring and staring, desperation oozing into the look. All of that hit me within a hundred milliseconds, and before I could plead with him to return to me, his hand was on mine, his fingers hard around my wrist.

One moment, I was standing beside the bed, hovering over him. Then, I was beneath him. His forearm went to my throat, the pressure so intense I gasped as the weight of it felt as if it could cave in my windpipe.

Choking and spluttering, I fought with him, but every time I tried, he snarled, "Bitch. Fuckin—Why won't you die? Why won't you goddamn die?"

The words would fuel a million nightmares if I lived that long, but I could feel the shadows starting to creep around my eyes as I struggled, kicking my legs out, trying to make him register that I wasn't an enemy.

Wasn't even a soldier.

I was just me.

A woman he'd forgotten.

A ghost even as she lived.

I let some words spew from my lips, words I didn't even register. Words I didn't recognize as my mother tongue.

But he did.

Somehow, as I pleaded with him in sputtered Ukrainian, he heard me. It penetrated the fog that had overcome him as if it was a noxious gas, and his eyes seemed to switch back into focus. When he stared at me, stared at us, how he was holding me, pinning me to the bed, he leaped back like I was fire and he was being scorched.

He reared back so hard and so fast he fell off the bed, rolling into a ball as he landed on the floor safely—was everyone around here a gymnast?

The stupid thought hit me even as I stared up at the ceiling, where the pool still made playful shadows as I gasped and coughed my way back to normalcy.

The pain in my throat was excruciating, but it was the pressure behind my eyes that hurt the most, and the stitch in my lungs that were starved of oxygen that had me rolling onto my side, curling into a fetal position. I thought it said it all that, instinctively, I didn't move away from him and face the wall so I couldn't look at him. No, I moved so I was staring at the other half of the mattress where he should be lying.

"I'm so sorry," he rasped, the words coming from my husband even as the voice wasn't one I knew. "I'm so fucking sorry."

Cat-like, he was back at my side again without the mattress even moving. I had no idea how that was possible when I knew he weighed a ton from experience, but he was there, his hand hovering above me, his heat a solid presence that loomed over me.

Was I just too drained to bat him away, to free myself from him?

I had no idea why I just lay there, why I just stared up at him, hurting emotionally and physically, aware he was in as much pain as I was.

"I'm so sorry," he repeated, his hand moving to my throat where, with delicate fingers, he traced the skin that was red and raw from his hold on me. "I-I didn't know it was you."

Was that supposed to be some consolation?

Swallowing down my nerves, an autonomous gesture that hurt as well, enough to feel like I was burning there, I rasped, "Who did you think it was?"

His sudden tension, the torment in him, hit me hard. I knew he was back there, even as he had one foot in the present.

"Someone…" He coughed. "In the Taliban."

My body still rebelling what I'd endured, half certain he'd attack me again, I dared to stare up at him and ask, "Who?"

"You don't need to know that."

"You thought I was him. You can tell me."

"It wasn't a him. It was a woman." He shook his head. "Please, I don't want to think about it."

Confused, I stared up at him. "The Taliban had female soldiers?"

"They used anything and anyone as ammunition," he said gruffly, flipping onto his back with an ease that stunned me.

Before, he'd always been careful. Like he thought his bones were made of glass. Even when he moved in bed, he moved slowly, like his joints were seizing.

Now, it was night and day, and it had me wondering if mentally he'd been more fragile than I'd realized.

"How do you move so well?"

"I don't know."

"Y-You were paralyzed."

"I used to be, according to the doctors, but I must have been hiding my recovery. Either that or I was avoiding it. They said there was no physical reason I couldn't recover. It wasn't like my spinal cord was fused. I just refused to go through the PT I needed."

"Refused the help, but did it in secret?"

"Must have," he rumbled, releasing a soughing breath that hit me hard.

Beneath me, his sheets were damp with sweat, and the scent of him was raw, filling my nostrils with the pure essence of him.

Maybe someone else would find it unpleasant, but it was actually comforting.

It was him. And, mere moments ago, I'd been in sheets that scented of tropical flowers.

I much preferred this.

Even as I carried on cupping my throat with the one hand, with the other, I reached out. Knowing it was stupid, that he was still touchy and on edge, I had to connect with him.

I was a stranger to him.

He was what I needed to sleep at night.

He flinched when my fingers brushed his skin, but he didn't attack me this time. "You shouldn't touch me," he said thickly.

"I-I need to."

"I don't know you."

"But I know you." Nerves hit me enough that I gulped, which brought with it a coughing fit as my abused throat protested the move.

He sat up, carefully helped me roll onto my back again, and then leaned over me. The pressure of him against my side, the feel of him so close made me want to push into him, hug him tightly, and have him hold me just as fiercely.

Only, he didn't do any of that. Didn't reach for me or try to hold me. Just grabbed the glass of water I realized was on his nightstand, the rim of which he pressed to my lips.

My skin felt tight and hot, red with the exertion of the coughing fit, and though I spluttered my way through, I swallowed a little that eased my suffering even as some trickled down the sides of my mouth, forming puddles around my neck.

"You should go back to your own bed," he said gruffly when I'd stopped choking.

"I find it hard to sleep without you."

He released a heavy sigh. "That was the Maverick of before. I assume he didn't attack you if you dared touch him while he slept?"

His tone was loaded with a sarcasm I wasn't used to hearing from him.

It hurt.

Everything about this did.

Not just from his attack, but that his dreams plagued him

enough to have him behaving like that... In his mind, it was clear to me that he was fresh from the war. Fresh from the torment.

What had he done over there? What had he been made to do?

"No, he didn't attack me, but sometimes we just slept together. It made it easier for both of us to drift off to sleep."

"You have issues sleeping too?" I heard the disbelief in his voice, the strange scoff that had me wondering why he'd think he was the only person here who had a reason for nightmares, then he drawled, "As if a pretty little thing like you has anything inside her head that'd keep her up at night."

Taken aback at his surety, I peered at him.

Pretty little thing?

What did that mean?

That my brain was vacant? That I was a doll who'd endured nothing in her life that was worthy of suffering nightmares?

To say I was offended was an understatement.

Then, the insult twisted around inside me.

I didn't know this Maverick.

He didn't know me either.

And... as much as I wanted him to be normal, to be the person I'd fallen in love with, he thought I was a 'pretty little thing.'

One without a past.

Without a future.

I was a nonentity to him because he didn't care about me.

Yes, that hurt. It stung so badly it was like a slash of a knife to my skin—and trust me, I'd had that happen to me more times than I could count—but more than that, I felt curiously free.

Free.

He didn't know me. I was a blank slate to him. A canvas that had yet to be painted. One that wasn't loaded down with lines which were shaped into images that spoke of a tragic past, a history that was to be pitied.

Free.

Though I could have answered, I didn't. I wasn't sure what to say. I needed to think about my next move. If I didn't share with him the truth of my past, what *should* I share with him?

The doctors had spoken with the brothers who, in turn, had explained to Lodestar and me today what was wrong with him. Lodestar, of course, understood immediately, and when I'd left the kitchen to return to the pool house, I'd seen her draw up sites that were related to CTE, and saw she was researching it.

My English was good. But it wasn't *that* good. As bad as I felt for not trying to look into what he was going through, what I'd learned from their serious expressions was that this Maverick could be the one who stayed with us forever.

That my worst fears might be realized—he might never remember me. I might always be forgotten by him.

Unless I suddenly became memorable.

And I wanted to.

I wanted to so much.

Not for a green card. That was irrelevant. If I had to return to Ukraine, so be it. But I needed to be the kind of woman this man remembered.

It mattered to me.

So, to buy myself some time, because I needed a moment to figure out what I could tell him about me that wasn't about being a part of the slave trade, I asked, "Would you tell me about Nic?"

He tensed up at that, and though the question was cruel after his dreams, it was pertinent.

He'd left his hospital bed, had traveled for hours on the back of a bike while he was suffering with head injuries, all to get to a cemetery to visit the site of one man's grave.

That meant something.

Nic meant something.

He was memorable.

I needed to learn why.

"I don't want to talk about him," he rasped stonily.

"No? Why not? Who better to talk about this stuff with? You don't remember me, Maverick, but I know you. You forget that. You stonewalled Nic away for years, never letting him see the light of day to the point that, when you were injured, this was the only way your brain could let him live again—"

"What are you talking about? Live again?" he growled. "He's dead. There's no more living for Nic."

"There is," I countered, and though his anger should have had me cowering, it didn't.

This was Maverick.

No, the Mav of before wouldn't have tried to crush my windpipe. No, he hadn't endured such violent nightmares, but I had to have faith in the man who had become the one I loved.

He wouldn't hurt me.

He wouldn't.

Not when he was in his right mind.

"How is there?" he snapped. "He's gone. Buried in Virginia, dressed in white marble, and trodden on every fucking day as someone moves over his patch to get to their loved one."

Maverick snarled under his breath, surging up into a sitting position as he raised his legs, dumped his arms on them, and buried his face there. His hair was a mess. He'd been growing it out ever since I met him, and now the short strands of silk had my fingers craving to reach for them, to stroke his head, to soothe him.

Stupid, I knew. He didn't want my touch period. Here I was, wanting to make him hurt less like he was a child who needed a boo-boo kissed better.

"When someone dies," I told him softly, my voice raw, "if you never think about them, never let them be free in your mind, they pass into the shadows. When you think about them, when you remember them, they live on. They can't die if they hold a place in your memory."

"I never forgot him. I just—it hurt to think of him," he said gruffly.

"How do you know? You don't remember who you are."

He snarled under his breath. "Are you trying to piss me off? I wouldn't have forgotten him, okay? Nic was too important to me to forget."

"Why?" I questioned carefully, hoping he'd talk to me. Goodness, I more than hoped—I prayed. Prayed to a God I'd stopped believing in a long time ago, one I'd believe in again if it meant Maverick and I had a chance at being together.

The breath hovered in my lungs as I waited for him to reply, as I wondered if he would, and when he did, disappointment hit because he asked, "Why do you care?"

"I'm your wife," I told him gently.

"So? Lots of wives hate their husbands, and vice versa."

"I didn't hate you. You didn't hate me." If I didn't want him to know about what had brought me into his life, then I knew I'd have to lie. I didn't want to, but I would—once I knew what to tell him instead of the truth.

The prospect of being Alessa, not Ghost, was too tantalizing a possibility. I wanted that more than I could say, more than I even wanted this man's love. Because I deserved the chance to be free from my past. I deserved the chance to be the woman I could have always been.

I just needed to figure out exactly who that was.

"No? I guess I wasn't a bad husband then."

"You were a perfect husband—"

He snorted. "The last thing I'd be is perfect."

"You were perfect for me."

"I was lying to you about my mobility. That seem like I was good people?"

"I don't care about that. You did everything for a reason."

"A reason I don't remember," he scoffed. "Essentially, you fell for a man who was lying to you."

How apt was it, then, that I was going to make him fall for a woman who was lying to him?

There'd be no malice in it, none at all, but I was taking the opportunity presented to me with both hands, and I wasn't going to take the high road.

I was going to take *my* road.

The one that liberated Alessa and let her be herself.

"I fell for a good man," I persisted. "One who comforted me when I had nightmares, who never rushed me into anything. Who held my hand when I needed him to, who made sure I ate when I forgot, and coaxed me to eat when the idea of food made me nauseous. One who was always patient with me, always gentle and kind—"

"That doesn't sound like me."

"Well, it was. Why would I have grown to love you if you weren't all those things?"

That seemed to give him pause. "You loved me?"

"I did. I *do*." I licked my lips at that, wondering what he'd say, what his reaction would be, but he didn't give me much of one. Instead, he kept his face turned away so I could only see his expression from the side.

"Why?"

"I told you why, Maverick."

"Did I tell you my real name?"

Uncertain, I stared at him. "Well, I mean, we got married. You used it at the courthouse."

"We got married in a courthouse?" He made an explosive

sound under his breath. "I think I sound like a selfish asshole. A beautiful woman like you should have all the white lace and meringue dress and wedding cake she needs."

"I was happy with the courthouse," I told him simply, and it wasn't a lie. "I just wanted to be married to you." Another truth, even if it was fudged a little.

Our marriage had a purpose, but I'd never have gone through with it if he didn't make me feel safe. Being his wife meant I was able to step forward and declare to the world how evil Donavan Lancaster was. He'd been thrown to the wolves because of my statement. Had arrest warrants hurled at him because Maverick had helped me shore up my legal position in this country, all while protecting *me*. Keeping *me* from harm.

Being his wife had given me wings... but only because he was there to catch me if I fell.

I knew, one day, ICE might come for me. They'd figure out that my marriage was a farce and I'd be ripped from the family I was coming to love, but that was in the future.

In the here and now, I was at this man's side, and he needed me.

Whether he'd admit it or not, he needed me. He had before, and he would again, because nobody, and I meant nobody, could understand what he was going through—but only one survivor could help another through the labyrinth I knew he'd woken up in.

So, I told him, "Maverick, you can paint yourself anyway you want, but I'm telling you now, I fell for you. You can't take away my feelings, and I won't push them onto you, but I'd like to help.

"Maybe it seems selfish to you—of course I want the old Maverick back—but I feel as though this *you* was always hidden from me. I'd like to learn about you, would love to help you get some peace if you let me." I cleared my throat when he didn't argue with me, and I carried on, "I've always had nightmares.

They're stupid ones," I lied. "Yet you never made fun of them, never made me feel dumb. You helped me get some rest, I'd like to help you too."

For the longest time, he was quiet. So quiet I wasn't sure if I should get up, if I should head back to my room and find a couple of packets of pain relievers because my throat was already starting to ache, and I thought a hot cup of tea would soothe it, but just as hope fled and I began to realize my words had had no effect, he murmured, "Nic was my rock."

I barely breathed as he spoke those words, and I barely moved because if I did, maybe he'd wake up and would refrain from sharing the hard truth with me. So I froze in place and let him talk.

Let him do what he needed to start the journey back to me, because no matter what, whether it was the new or old Maverick, he *would* come back. That was a promise I made to both of us.

SEVEN

MAVERICK

"NIC WAS MY ROCK."

I hadn't meant to speak, hadn't meant to say a word, but there was something about this woman who was somehow my wife.

Not just my Old Lady.

My *wife*.

I'd wifed her.

My ties to the MC had been unofficial from adolescence. I'd always remained on the outskirts of the club's boundaries because my long-term goal had been to serve in the Green Berets. But to be promoted into that elite band of brothers, there was a background check—one I'd have failed if I'd been patched in.

For all that, I'd never stopped being a brother to the council, to the rest of the club too. If I could help, I would. Just unofficially.

But the way I worked, even back when my brain was telling me it was 2010, I'd never have thought of wifing a woman. I'd have always branded her as an Old Lady.

She was different, and the ring on her finger, a simple gold band that represented much more than she could know, was proof of that.

Guilt speared me as I thought about how I'd woken up.

Her panicked, dilated eyes desperately peering up at me, her face burning bright red, her throat pinned beneath my forearm, her body struggling but those struggles were starting to die with her as she began to pass out from oxygen deprivation. Death had been too close at hand, and I wasn't even sure if she knew it.

Tomorrow, there might even be proof of it in burst blood vessels in her eyes and around her mouth, never mind in the bruising on her throat from the force of my attack.

I'd almost killed her.

Christ.

"How was he your rock?" she whispered softly when I fell silent.

Her voice was always delicate, raspy, but now it was worse. I'd done that to her.

Fuck.

"He helped me through some tough times, and we got closer together. He had bad PTSD, but he was so good at what he did, the CO kept signing him off for more duties when he should have been retired out."

She fell silent at that, processing my words. I'd noticed a slight accent to her timbre, but she spoke English perfectly. At least I thought she did. Had she not understood me?

Tilting my head a little so I could look at her without her knowing, I managed to catch a glimpse of her frown. But it wasn't of confusion. Combined with her wide eyes, I knew she wanted to understand. Was desperate to.

Had anyone cared that much about me ever?

Nic had loved me, but he knew I was a soldier. More than that, he knew I was a natural born killer.

This woman, this *Ghost,* she didn't look at me like that.

Nor did she treat me like I was an invalid.

Unable to pinpoint exactly how I felt when she was gazing at me, I cleared my throat and rumbled, "Aren't you going to ask what he was good at?"

"What was he so good at?" she parroted promptly.

"My team got all the shitty jobs. We each had our particular talents," I mused. "So we'd get shipped off to the far corners of hell by our CO. Nic could build a bridge faster than I could fix my hog." I shook my head. "I've seen some damn good engineers in my time, but Nic was spectacular."

"He built things?" she queried, her surprise evident.

"Yes. He was the weapons man, but his experience was varied. Sometimes we had to get a tank across a bridgeless river or…" I winced, not wanting to think about the less than innocent occasions when Nic's skills had come in useful. "He was good at *everything* he did. In English, we say, 'He was a jack of all trades.' Except, in his case, he'd been a master of much, not few."

"What was your specialty?"

"Computers."

She winced. "Of course. Dumb of me to ask."

Was it? It surprised me that she knew that much.

"Plus I'm very good at hand-to-hand combat." And sneaking into locked buildings where I could take out a target with no one being the wiser.

"We all had our place, and Nic wasn't their leader but we treated him like it because he was the eldest."

"What made you fall in love with him?"

"One day, we'd just seen this woman blow herself up with kerosene because she'd been forced into an arranged marriage, and Nic cried." I sucked in a breath. "We were used to seeing so much shit over there, so many things that belonged in a horror movie that we just got used to it. I'm ashamed to admit I didn't cry. Her screams haunt me," I disclosed, "but I didn't cry. Nic did, and it was like when you put a key in the door and turn the lock. It was a revelation."

"I'm sorry your story together has such a harsh beginning," she whispered, and the bitch of it was, I heard her sincerity.

Here I was, telling her about how I'd loved some guy she'd never heard of when she was my wife.

How fucked up was that?

"Everything about our beginning was harsh. That was why I stuck to him. If he was my rock, I was his glue. Especially toward the end."

"You remember the end?"

I shook my head. "I just remember Kembesh."

"What happened?"

"You don't want to know."

"Don't I?"

I heaved a sigh. "We were cornered in an outpost the Taliban forces had overtaken. We'd spent days getting it back under our command because there was a shit ton of weapons stored there that we didn't need getting into their hands.

"They holed up in a mosque, and we were waiting on backup."

She tensed. "No backup. Pass it on. No medevacs."

Eyes flaring wide, I whipped around to stare at her. "What did you just say?"

"You were repeating it in your sleep," she whispered miserably, and she rolled upright so she could press her hand to my shoulder. "I'm so sorry, Maverick."

My mouth quivered at her sympathy. "Why are you being so nice to me? If anything, you should hate me."

"I can't hate you. I love you." Her smile appeared, but it was twisted. Rueful. "I realized it the morning you woke up."

Now that surprised me. Brows soaring, I asked, "You didn't love me when we got married?"

Her wince was minute, but I caught it. Before I could ask her what that was about, she shrugged and murmured, "It was more of a marriage of convenience."

"Why?" Terror flooded me. "Are you pregnant?"

She cleared her throat. "No."

Relief washed the terror that had just hit me clean. "Thank fuck. Christ, I couldn't deal with that right now." Sweat popped out, beading on my temple, collecting down the length of my back. I could feel it, each droplet being squeezed out of my pores like I was a ripe lemon being juiced. "Why did we marry?"

"I'm surprised you can't hear my accent. I'm not American."

I'd heard the accent, but it was faint. "Where are you from?"

"Ukraine."

It didn't take much to piece things together. "You needed a green card?"

"Yes." She smiled at me. "Falling in love with you was something I started to do before you proposed, but I didn't realize it until the relief hit me when you woke up. Facing the fact I could have lost you was the short, sharp shock I needed."

More guilt hit me. "I'm sorry I don't remember you."

"I'm surprised you're sorry, but I thank you for it anyway."

"Why are you surprised?"

"Because you keep acting like you hate me," she said simply.

"I don't hate you," I said rawly, turning away from her. "I just don't know you."

"And that hurts more than anything else." A sad sigh escaped her. "Maverick?"

"Yeah?"

"Before the accident, when you found it hard to sleep, I used to sing to you. I know you don't know me, so you probably would just like me to leave, but if you want, I could sing to you now?"

I twisted back to face her. "You'd do that for me?"

"Of course."

Everything about her was facile. Not because she was dumb, but because she was so open. So guileless.

I wasn't used to that.

"Why do they call you Ghost?"

"It's just a silly nickname. My real name is Alessa. You used to call me that."

Something hitched in her voice that caught my attention, but though it sounded like a lie, I saw no reason why she'd lie about her name. "Alessa. That's pretty. Did you call me Maverick?"

"Mostly. Sometimes Mav. Never Jameson."

I pulled a face. "Good. Always hated my name. Mom had the shittiest taste in them. We had like eight cats and she called them all weird shit. Fabio, Clark."

Her lips twisted into a smile as I rolled my eyes. "Well, I like yours."

Grunting, I just said, "I can't promise I won't hurt you if you stay with me. I think it'd be best if you left. I don't want to wake up the way we did tonight again." I couldn't deal with the stain of her butchered innocence on my soul.

"I'll leave once I think you're sleeping," she offered.

Her generosity hit me, her selflessness too.

She really did care for me.

Only a woman in love would be willing to stay in the same bed with the nutcase who'd nearly killed her because he was stuck in a nightmare.

Scrubbing a hand over my face, I murmured, "If you're sure?"

"I'm sure."

I didn't really want to hear her sing—what was I? Five? But I felt obligated. She offered, and she was being kind when I'd done everything but be that to her. The least I could do was listen to a few dumb lullabies.

Only, that wasn't what happened.

As I lay tensely in bed, my muscles taut as I prepared myself to endure her singing, the first haunting whispers of her voice seemed to trickle around me. Call me crazy, because I knew I was halfway to losing my mind anyway, but as she sang, I closed my eyes at the lilting melody that had the nerve endings behind my eyelids pinging like a light was being shone against them.

Tension oozed out of me, slowly but surely, and gradually, I could feel the taut pressure in my muscles give way as I started to relax.

I didn't even know when she stopped singing.

Certainly didn't feel her leave the bed.

I just slept.

EIGHT

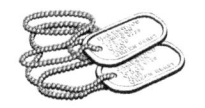

GHOST
TWO DAYS LATER

"JESUS CHRIST."

I winced at the blasphemy but didn't say anything. I was more than used to it, just wasn't accustomed to having it be related to me. Nobody had cared before if I was bruised—I'd forgotten that had changed now.

People cared about me.

I didn't look up as Nyx approached me, didn't say anything as he tipped my chin up so he could look me square in the eye.

"He did this?" was his gruff question.

"It was an accident." It sounded like a lame excuse but, really, it *had* been unintentional. Of course, that 'accident' had me feeling rough enough not to want to leave my bedroom in the past two days. Well, that and because I didn't feel like bumping into Maverick yet.

Giulia, wincing as she rubbed at her neck where her sling collided with her throat, scoffed, "Accident, my ass."

"No. Truly. I surprised him. He's hyperaware right now. You have to be careful when you approach him."

Nyx grimaced. "I remember that from before. It's like he thinks everyone's an enemy." His glance at me turned apologetic, like he was saying sorry in advance for not beating the shit out of the brother who was also a soldier who was also my husband.

There was no need for him to look that way though. No need because I didn't want Nyx to beat Maverick up, didn't want him to be punished for what had truly been an accident. It was nice to know, however, that Nyx would be there for me if things did devolve to that extent.

I was included in the circle because of Mav, and I was inordinately grateful for that. I didn't think I could handle losing him and being on the outside looking in with the brothers and their Old Ladies as well.

Giulia, having approached me at the same time as Nyx, slung her good arm around me, and I saw that Sin and Tiffany were standing in the doorway to the kitchen too.

Tiffany bit her lip at the sight of me, which irritated me a little. I appreciated her concern, don't get me wrong, but that lip bite was a reminder I was an object of pity right now. These women were with their men, their big, strong, manly men who'd go to war for them, kill for them, and mine? Couldn't remember me.

Because I knew she meant well, I swallowed the dab of irritation. To be fair, I was surprised I even felt it because I'd been trained a long time ago not to feel much of anything. Maybe it was a good sign I could feel irritated by that tiny gesture. Maybe it was a sign of growth and change.

Because that idea perked me up, made me feel like less of a puppy who'd been tossed into a pack of man-eating wolves, I shoved away my feelings and watched her move over so she could tuck me into a hug.

Wrangled between two strong women, I just let myself flow

into her, tensing as she murmured, "You can always call me. I'm here for you, Ghost."

I knew she meant it and was grateful for it, but what went on between Maverick and me was private. Personal.

They were his brothers, his family, but I was his wife. Even if that didn't mean all that much right now.

I tipped my chin up, determined to put a brave face on for his sake and mine, before I asked, "Anyone want coffee?"

Receiving a chorus of 'yes,' I headed to the coffee machine I'd turned on just as Mav's people made an appearance, grateful I'd made decaf because Giulia was pregnant. Setting the carafe, sugar, and milk onto a tray I found in a cupboard, I placed some cups and saucers on there as well.

The kitchen wasn't fully stocked, but it had basics, like coffee and milk as well as some bread and things like peanut butter. Lily said she wanted us to have whatever we needed, but didn't want us to think we weren't welcome at the main house.

If anything, I knew I'd need to do a grocery run because Maverick didn't seem to want to leave his room, never mind the pool house.

The kitchen was very sweet, in fact, the whole place was. If I wasn't an ex-sex slave, if Maverick didn't have amnesia and we were real newlyweds, this would be an incredible place to start off married life.

The bittersweet thought had me choking up as I twisted around, grateful I'd forgotten about spoons. As I dragged them out of the clean-cut, buttercream colored drawers that matched the caramel marble counter, I managed to paste a smile on my face before I returned to the table.

There was space for all of them, plus me and Maverick if he turned up.

If being the operative word.

Tiffany placed the cups in front of her and started pouring coffee for everyone, and I let her, because it put the focus on her and not me, which was the last place I wanted it.

As everyone grabbed a cup, with only Tiffany keeping her saucer, I wasn't surprised when Nyx muttered, "Where is the fucker?"

Giulia elbowed him in the side, then winced with discomfort—she kept forgetting about her dislocated shoulder. "It's early. I told you we shouldn't have come."

He jerked his thumb in Sin's direction. "We met them on the way."

Sin grimaced. "Just wanted to check in. It's been crazy for him, felt like I had to make sure he had everything he needed."

Tiffany's hand moved to cover his. "Padraig, we talked about this."

He pulled a face. "I know we did. It's just fucking hard, Tiff, to see him laid low. To head to that fucking section in the cemetery." His jaw tensed. "We could so easily be buried there."

My brows rose. "Of course, you were a soldier too, weren't you?"

"Nothing like Mav," he said gruffly, ducking his head. "I was just a grunt. Mav was special." His chin tipped up. "Was so fucking proud when he got that Green Beret."

"What is this?" I queried, peering around the table, looking for answers.

"Just a part of the Special Forces uniform," Maverick murmured as he slipped into the room.

Everyone tensed, but only the guys jerked to their feet. Tiffany and Giulia, not unsurprisingly, were gaping at the sight of a man they'd only ever seen in a wheelchair walking to the fridge.

"Christ, why's there no milk?" he grumbled under his breath.

Leaping to my feet, I told him, "I used it for coffee. I'll go get some more from Lily's place."

Giulia snorted, and before I could dash off, she grabbed my hand and pulled me back. "You ain't his slave, Ghost." She shot me a pointed look when she used that horrible word, and my cheeks flushed.

"He wants milk and I just used the last of it."

"Yeah, he does, so he can go and fucking get it. The bastard's legs work now, don't they?"

Maverick twisted around to scowl at her, and when he did, his gaze glanced over her face and—

Oh, God.

Was that recognition?

His chin tilted down and back, and in his eyes, those doubts and questions and the fog of uncertainty was still there, but I knew it like I knew my own damn face in the mirror, the face *he* apparently didn't.

But Maverick recognized her.

Jealousy speared me in the gut. Sliced through the tendons at the back of my knees.

The pain...

Pizda.

I started fiddling with the cuff on my wrist, which drew his attention a second before it immediately flashed back to Giulia.

"Where do I know you from?" he burst out like he couldn't contain himself.

The tension around the table soared as Nyx cleared his throat. "She's Lizzie Fontaine's kid, Mav. Giulia's my Old Lady."

He snapped his fingers. "That's it. You sound just like her!"

Relief hit me—of course he recognized her. He'd grown up around her mom and he'd known her when she was a kid.

"Great, I sound just like my harpy of a mother," Giulia grumbled, hiding behind her coffee cup.

"Harpy fits," Nyx teased, laughing when she pouted and he curved an arm around her, pretty much hauling her out of her seat and onto his lap as he sat them both down again.

Mav, seeing this, shook his head, then he returned his focus to the fridge like milk had made an appearance while his back was turned, before he peeked another glance at them.

"He's affectionate now, Mav," Sin said dryly, evidently understanding why Mav was taking a second glance at what was a pretty normal occurrence where Nyx and Giulia were concerned. "It takes some getting used to."

Nyx flipped him the bird even as he pressed a kiss to the side of Giulia's neck.

"Yeah, I can see that," was all he said by way of a response. He grabbed a cup of yogurt, finally settling on that, before he went through the drawers to find the cutlery.

It was hard, so hard, not to get to my feet and help him, but it was like she knew my nervous system better than I did, because every time I tensed, Giulia's hand would snap out and she'd pinch me.

Glaring at her didn't stop her, nor did it stop her from commenting, "Pretty shitty thing to do, Maverick, to pretend to be in a wheelchair for years on end. Were you ever disabled?"

Even Nyx tensed at that.

"Fuck you," Mav retorted, but there was no heat to the curse.

"My man does that very well," she countered smugly, a wry twist to her lips as she studied him.

"Don't push him, Giulia," Tiffany warned.

I bit my lip, feeling nervous when I didn't know why. This wasn't my Maverick, it wasn't like I had to excuse him. These people were his family, but I still felt on edge. Giulia, for all she was a walking nightmare sometimes, seemed to recognize my unease though, because she reached for my hand and squeezed my fingers, not to punish this time but to soothe. To comfort.

Gratitude spilled through me because I knew, at that moment, she had a reason for doing this. She was making waves on purpose.

"Who's pushing who?" was her retort as she cast a glance at Tiff. "I'm just saying it how it is. We came to visit him, and what do we find? Ghost looking like a walking punching bag—"

"I don't want to talk about it," Maverick snarled.

"It was an accident," I whispered.

"Sounds like it."

His mouth tightened at our comments before, with eyes like fire, he snapped, "I don't want this going outside of this room. For whatever reason, I kept my mobility a secret. Do I seem like the kind of prick who'd put his loved ones through shit to make them worry?"

"No," was Sin's immediate response, and he shot Giulia a look that had her sniffing.

"Well, just because you don't remember Ghost doesn't mean you can treat her like a fucking slave."

There was that word again.

I knew Giulia too well now to recognize that she was a smart little cat who managed to choose her words wisely when she looked like she hurled whatever at whomever just to get a rise out of them.

"I never asked for shit from her," Maverick snarled, finally whipping around to declare his outrage at her statement. "I don't even fucking know why she's here. Like what's she doing here? How the fuck am I supposed to even think about getting better with her here haunting me like I'm supposed to remember who she is?"

Just as my heart was shattering, Giulia snapped, "Thought you weren't the kind of prick who put his loved ones through shit, Mav? Just because your head's fucked up—which is entirely your fault because who the hell goes into an unstable building that'd just been bombed in a wheelchair?—doesn't mean you don't have a lot more people who are your family now.

"You don't remember Tiffany either, but she's sitting opposite me, remembers you, and she wasn't fucking you neither. Ghost has been the only bright spark on your horizon since she arrived at the compound. You've got no right at all to dismiss her when she was the reason for you waking up in the morning. So pull your head out of your ass."

Nyx smoothed a hand over his bristling mate's arm. "She's right, Maverick."

"Of course I am," Giulia said with a sniff and a toss of her ponytail.

Nyx's lips twisted a little, pride sparking with desire in his eyes before he focused on Maverick. "You were miserable before Ghost came. You barely ate, you *never* slept, and all you did was work. You wouldn't touch any of the clubwhores, never drank, and we couldn't get you off the goddamn compound. We were fucking terrified we were gonna lose you to the PTSD, man.

"Then Ghost comes, and all of a sudden, shit changes. You're going off the compound to marry her, and you're leaving to visit her in the bunkhouse, and you're eating and caring about the future instead of just the MC's profit margins." Nyx shrugged. "Your mind might have erased that, but we remember, and we're telling you, with love in our hearts because you're our fucking brother, that you can't fuck this up.

"When the Maverick we know comes back, when your memory returns to you, you're gonna be in a world of shit if you don't treat Ghost right."

A few pieces of my shattered heart came together at that, and my bottom lip quivered in the face of Nyx's defense. He meant it. And Giulia, when she looked at him like the cat who got the cream, agreed with him. A glance at Sin and Tiffany revealed the same thing.

"She was your reason for living," Sin concurred softly. "In such a short space of time, she became your world. It's a sick twist of fucking fate that you don't remember the one salvation you've ever had, Maverick. Nyx's right—you mess this up, you push her away, when shit does return to normal for you, you're screwed."

An explosive sound escaped Maverick, and in surprise, maybe a little fear and a dash of awe, I watched as he grabbed a few of the breakables from the table, an empty cup, the empty pot of milk, the dish with sugar in, and he hurled them to the floor.

Before he stormed out.

"That handed his ass to him," Giulia said smugly, as she calmly picked up her coffee like nothing had happened at all and took a deep sip.

The urge to go to him was strong. The urge to fix things was stronger. But I wasn't his Band-Aid right now. He was all alone, and that hurt me more than anything else could.

Yet as I stared around the table at the men and women who'd just defended me, who'd just gone to battle for me, I realized something important.

Mav's people weren't just his.

They were mine too, and even though Mav's loss was a gnawing ache in my stomach, that eased it some.

I wasn't alone.

Maverick, even in this, even *now*, had figured out a way to look after me—through the family who loved him, and because of his love for me, they had welcomed me into the fold. It was time I started remembering I wasn't a slave anymore.

I wasn't something someone could piss on.

Wasn't an object to be used and abused.

I had a voice.

I could act.

So even though, internally, I quivered with nerves, I found myself with no alternative. I got to my feet, ignoring the sudden silence as I left the kitchen, and headed toward Maverick's door.

It was closed. Everything about him was closed off right now, and though it made me nervous, I sucked in a breath, curled my hand into a fist, and knocked.

He didn't answer for the longest time, and though everything in me wanted to turn around, to head back to the kitchen and the people who cared for me, I didn't.

I stayed put.

I knocked again.

This time, he deigned to holler, "Go away!"

I gritted my teeth. "If you need me, I'll be in the kitchen."

It wasn't much of a stance, wasn't much of anything, all told, but to me, it was more than I'd have been capable of before.

Being passive was something that had been bred into me, so changing that wasn't going to be easy, but nothing about this situation was.

If, by the end of it, I had more guts than before, I didn't think that was a bad thing.

I'd never be like Giulia, which was fortunate, I thought wryly, because New Jersey could only handle one Giulia Fontaine, but they'd never met Alessa Shevchenko either. The *real* Alessa. The one who'd had a voice, who'd had guts, who hadn't been scared of her own shadow.

So when Maverick growled, "Why the fuck would I need you?" I didn't let hurt fill me, just tipped my chin up and retorted.

"You're the one with the degenerative brain condition. If you can't figure out why you might need me when you could suddenly fall ill, then maybe you're in a worse state than we thought."

I braced myself for a barrage of angry words, for rage and wrath to spill forth and to lash me like it was acid. I stood there, quivering like a flower in a strong breeze, but I didn't leave. I didn't run.

I stayed. Despite the fear, I stayed.

And the acid never spilled. The ire never came.

Instead, a click sounded, the handle lowered, and the door pulled inward. He didn't let me inside, just peered through the gap he made and rasped, "You're right. I might need you. I'm sorry I was rude."

I nodded. "Apology accepted." Then I twisted on my heel and headed back to the kitchen.

It might not be much of an accomplishment to some people, namely Giulia, but to me, it felt like I'd managed to climb Everest.

NINE

LODESTAR

THE ONLY PLACE in the house I seemed to get comfortable was the kitchen. Which was inconvenient because it was the place most people congregated and I rarely got any peace. Ordinarily, that would be enough to have me running for the hills, holing up in a basement, but as much as the noise pissed me off, being around people was what I needed right now.

Not that I'd ever admit it out loud.

I was still dealing with concussion headaches, the pain in my leg was excruciating, and it hurt every time I breathed, but I had stuff to do. Not just the usual either.

It wasn't often Nyx came to me, but come he had, and with a couple tasks in mind. Tasks he'd usually give to Maverick, I knew.

I also knew from what everyone had told me, from what the brothers had said of his current situation that, mentally, Mav had gone back in time.

He was twenty-seven, not thirty-seven, and to him, a year earlier, that was when we'd just broken up. Perfectly shitty timing considering the situation.

Still, Nyx needed to know if a local guy was a pedophile, and even if I'd been gutshot, there was no way in fuck I wasn't going to find out the truth for him. Not just because it gave Mav a break either. I needed to prove myself to these fuckers—I just wished I wasn't so goddamn exhausted that work was a chore.

As for the other task, the less important one in my opinion, I also had shit to find out about that cunt who'd been stalking Indy. The one who'd been monitoring the clubhouse through that Ukrainian bitch.

According to Nyx, the prick was dead now—I wasn't about to ask for details—and not only had I already taken his cloud accounts apart, but the surveillance gear in Indy's place was gone too. Plus, with the clubhouse gone and the stalker dead, there wasn't much spying to be done...

Unless he wasn't spying on Indiana for *fun*, but for business.

And there went my heart racing again, because if it *was* for business, then I needed to work on that situation. Fast.

So much to do, so little fucking time.

Grimacing, I got back to work, but shifted several times in my seat as I tried and failed to get comfortable. Only when the sun moved through the kitchen window and puddled me in a pool of warmth did things change. Instantly, my bones stopped feeling like they'd been run over by a Mac truck, and I could relax some. That was when Maverick made an appearance in the kitchen, of course, and he jumped so hard at the sight of me that I jumped in turn, which sent shockwaves of discomfort ricocheting through my system.

The horror on his face made it very clear that he was remembering our breakup, and I got it. I'd been the one to end things with him, so seeing me in the kitchen had to be like pouring salt on the wound.

Those final days had not been pleasant.

I'd tried, Lord had I, but pleasant simply wasn't in my nature. Especially not when he'd been the best boyfriend ever and had been impossible to split up with. I'd had to go to extraordinary lengths to break us up that he hadn't deserved. But love was dangerous, and I'd had to save us both.

"Maverick," I murmured softly.

"Lodestar, what the fuck are you doing here?"

I pulled a face. "You might not believe it, but we're friends now."

"Jesus Christ." He reached up and rubbed his forehead hard enough to make me wince. "This is starting to get fucking annoying."

"Only just 'starting,' huh?" I half teased, even though nothing about this situation was funny.

Of all the people I knew, of all those I trusted, Maverick was up there on the top of the list.

And because he'd gone back in time, I was the exact opposite to him.

The last thing I needed, with things as delicate as they were with the New World Sparrows, with things as wonderfully precarious as they were, was him back in 2010, but it wasn't like I had much say in how his brain worked.

I had no choice but to deal with his suspiciousness and wary glares even if, and I'd admit this to no other, it hurt like hell to see his level of distrust.

It had taken years for him to trust me again. Years of sowing careful seeds, of being there after Nic died, of always having the information he needed, and being useful for him to appreciate me.

Even worse, he'd only started to truly let me in after I disappeared.

As much as I loved Maverick, as much as I hated that he

disliked me again, I wasn't about to sell myself to white slavers for the privilege of his friendship.

He grunted at my attempt at humor, then moved over to the fridge where he pulled out a gallon of milk. Investigating the cupboards helped him discover the location of a large tumbler and a packet of cookies.

Was I surprised when he wandered off with both without bothering to cast me another glance?

No.

It hurt though.

Even as I was reminded of how much milk he'd drank in the past, how he could consume a gallon of it per pack of cookies... When we'd dated, I'd always made sure I had milk in my digs because it would be like running out of Coke or beer for another guy.

Crazy how I only just realized that I hadn't seen him drink milk in a very long time.

As I pondered that, watching his back as he left the kitchen, a little buzzing noise caught my attention. My gaze drifted down to the computer screen in front of me, and when I saw who'd overtaken it, I found myself smiling.

aCooooig was a nuisance to be sure, but the last time we'd chatted, he'd been helpful.

He'd shown me proof of a potential threat to the MC, and while I'd continue to keep my eye on Cruz, I trusted he had the club's best interests at heart. Especially now that I knew he and Indy were an item. It helped that he was the Sinners' Grim Reaper, tasked with cleaning up the DNA spilled in the line of duty. A man didn't pull stunts like that without being loyal to his brothers.

As dangerous as I was, my reputation was couched in shadows

as that was how I wanted it. No one in their right mind would want to make an enemy out of Nyx, whose rep was out and proud in the midday sun, so I knew I didn't have to doubt Cruz because Nyx would skin his balls for me.

ACOOOOIG: **Heard you got blown up.**

Me: **Not a question? Just a statement.**

aCooooig: **Well, few people lie to me. Especially when I'm truly interested in something.**

Me: **Should I take that as a compliment?**

aCooooig: **Most people would avoid my interest.**

Me: **I never claimed to be sane.**

aCooooig: **How are you?**

Me: **Broken leg, bruised hip, battered ribs. I'm okay.**

aCooooig: **Sounds it. *Not.***

Me: **I've dealt with worse.**

aCooooig: **When?**

Me: **Do you really want to know? Or have you already found out the truth and want confirmation your sources are on the money?**

aCooooig: **Your distrust wounds me.**

Me: **I'll bet.**

aCooooig: **Actually, I know a lot about you, but reading it from reports is never as interesting as hearing it from the horse's mouth.**

My lips twitched. Me: **So I'm a horse now, am I?**

aCooooig: **I haven't seen your picture yet, so you could be.**

I hadn't seen his picture either, and if he had 'reports' on me, that was more than I had on him. Details on aCooooig were surprisingly well hidden.

It didn't take a genius to figure out he was affiliated with the Irish, what with a name like that—*acuig* was the Gaelic word for the number five—but for me, I knew who he was tied to simply because of how I'd found him.

When I'd been throwing shit at the wall and hoping some would stick, I'd waded through various crime organizations, causing trouble among them, trying to find my way into their defenses.

Along the way, I'd found aCooooig, whose security system had impressed me, but it hadn't been good enough to keep me out. I'd had fun though, and in my line of work, few were ever good enough to entertain me.

Still, for all that I was busy, I kept my ear to the ground for anything aCooooig related, but he was as much of a phantom as I was.

Was he giving me BS about having reports on me? Not just one with a picture of a blank face with a question mark for features, but with actual information on me?

The notion was disquieting.

Mostly because if he had that on me, then I should have that on him.

aCooooig: **You there?**

Me: **Yes. Wondering why we keep on dancing around each other when we're on the same side.**

aCooooig: **You broke my code. Plus you keep wrecking my hardware.**

Me: **You've wrecked mine too.**

aCooooig: **Tit for tat. A man's hardware is sacred.**

Me: **Is that a euphemism?**

aCooooig: **In this instance, no. I prefer my hardware to my cock.**

Interest stirred in me. Me: **How true is that?**

aCooooig: **Sixty percent true. Depends. Is the woman I'm looking at hot in this hypothetical situation? If so, then forty percent true.**

I snorted. Me: **Like to look but not touch, huh? Are you ugly? Struggle to get laid?**

aCooooig: **Beauty is in the eye of the beholder.**

Me: **So says every momma to every unfortunate kid who ever was.**

aCooooig: **Well, my ma would say I had the luck of the Irish where my face was concerned. But looks aren't everything, Lodestar.**

Me: **Aren't they? Most men would disagree.**

aCooooig: **I'm not *most* men.**

Me: **Is that supposed to reassure me?**

aCooooig: **Or warn you to approach with care… more likely to be that than a reassurance. Never was good at that.**

Me: **Then I hope for your sake you never broke in a virgin.**

aCooooig: **ROFL.**

My brows rose, because I hadn't expected that to amuse him. That it did had my lips twitching.

aCooooig: **If I had, I wouldn't be New York's most eligible bachelor.**

Me: **Methinks the lady doth protest too much.**

aCooooig: **Now who's being mean? Play nice, Lodestar. Or are you just being crabby because you're in pain?**

Me: **:/ Probably. Sorry.**

aCooooig: **Heard the Sinners' compound is totaled.**

There was no point in tensing up at that. No point whatsoever. I knew from his code, from the A+ hacking he did on the regular that he probably knew my blood type by now, but still, that he knew my general location didn't sit well with me.

Especially as I'd yet to determine where he was.

NYC was a big fucking place. Lots of people. Knowing the city and a general neighborhood wasn't enough.

If he knew I was with the Sinners, then he knew how to get to me. I was okay with him being aware of my injuries because he could have come across a doctor's report. That was one thing. Knowing my current location was another.

aCooooig: **Don't worry, I'm not going to hurt you.**

Me: **I feel so reassured.**

Not.

aCooooig: **The Sinners are allies.**

Me: **Allies are just friendly enemies.**

aCooooig: **My, my, my. Such a cynic.**

Me: **If you're looking to chat with a naive ingenue, I'm not your girl.**

aCooooig: **Naive ingenues are boring. Why do you think I never fucked an Irish virgin?**

Me: **You only fuck women if they're from the motherland?**

aCooooig: **What do you think? o.O**

aCooooig: **Out of curiosity, where are you from?**

Me: **Originally?**

aCooooig: **Of course. I'm about as Irish as a potato.**

Me: **Meaning you're not?**

aCooooig: **Well, if you want to get into a philosophical debate on the rights of natural citizenship…**

Me: **I have better things to do with my time.**

aCooooig: **Thank fuck.**

Me: **LOL.**

aCooooig: **Go on then. Where are you from? Originally?**

I snorted. Me: **Delaware.**

aCooooig: **How disappointing. The very first Delawarian, huh?**

Me: **Actually… my mother was fourth generation Irish. Dad was second gen.**

aCooooig: **So… you're Irish?**

Me: **More American.**

aCooooig: **But your people came over on a boat and slinked through Ellis Island?**

Me: **Is this giving you a boner?**

aCooooig: **Might just be. You have potential, Lodestar.**

Rolling my eyes, I tapped out: **Your charm knows no bounds.**

aCooooig: **It's been an issue all my life.**

Laughing, I shook my head, amused despite myself.

Something about this fucker had gotten to me from the very start.

I could almost regret making ground beef out of his security system, but hey, better for me to hack it than someone truly malicious.

Well, I *was* malicious, and if he'd been helping the Italians or the NWS then I'd have done more than wreck his system... but aCooooig was a pleasant challenge.

Someone to butt up against.

There'd always been Maverick, of course, but he didn't work the same way I did. Not anymore. Becoming the Sinners' treasurer had changed his MO.

aCooooig: **Watch out for a gift from me.**

I narrowed my eyes at the screen. Me: **Already been bombed once. Don't want another present.**

aCooooig: **Friendly enemies might be what you consider us, but I prefer allies. Just one little token to a boss ass bitch from a boss ass bastard.**

Snorting out a laugh, I replied: **Thanks. I think.**

aCooooig: **TTYL.**

I didn't have a chance to reply before he cut the connection between us, making the chat screen disintegrate away like it had never existed.

We both had code on each other's hardware. No matter how many times I took it off, it popped up again... and vice versa.

I knew the bombing had done more than break a few bones and had rattled my brain too when the thought of his presence on my computer didn't piss me off, but felt more like a hug than a malicious threat.

Shaking my head at the thought, I switched programs and went through the manual stripping of my gear to delete his presence even though, by the end of the day, I knew it would be back again. And as I checked my code on his software, found it deleted and restored it, I smiled.

Then, when five PM rolled around and someone buzzed at the front gate and it was a delivery driver, I'd admit to feeling no small amount of excitement as I realized it was his gift.

As promised.

When I opened up the box to reveal ten pounds of candy corn, my smile made another appearance.

Allies, indeed.

TEN

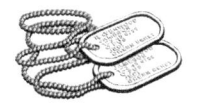

NYX

THE NOISE in my head wouldn't quit. It was there, an endless blast of sound that made it impossible to hear what Giulia was saying.

The day had been a crappy one.

First, the funeral. Saying goodbye to Jaxson had sucked because I'd promised his dad that I'd watch out for the kid, and I'd tried to, but I couldn't watch out for a fucking bomb. Watching him being returned to the earth, then women I'd fucked over the years too, had been as much of a headache as the night our compound had been destroyed.

Then, Cammie had persisted in blowing up my phone. Normally I'd have ignored her. I wouldn't even go through the bother of blocking her number, but we'd lost a lot of people along the way. We could have lost her as well if she'd been there, if she hadn't left because her father was sick.

I'd never loved her, had never really even cared for her. I knew I was a bastard for that when I was well aware of her feelings for me.

I wasn't sure how, looking the way she did, she'd come to me a virgin, and I'd never wanted to be her first, but she'd approached me on one of the few nights I drank and before I knew it, I'd been tearing through her goddamn hymen.

That had made me keep her around longer than most of the bunnies I boned exclusively, which I knew she'd taken to mean that I had feelings for her.

But I hadn't.

I never had.

And now, with Giulia at my side, our baby in her belly, I recognized what it was to *feel*.

If Cammie felt this much for me, how couldn't I have answered her call?

How couldn't I give her some semblance of peace so she knew I was okay? It wouldn't make things better, could even make things worse, but the need to give her some closure was real.

From my sister and Old Lady's reactions, I figured I'd fucked that up, but I'd tried.

That was more than I'd have done before Giulia came along.

After the call, things had steadily worsened.

All my life, I'd been chasing closure too. The need for vengeance was one of the only things that got me up in the morning. The need to make pedo cunts pay had been my reason for fucking breathing for so long.

Indy's admission, the revelation that she'd been abused by our uncle too?

The need to kill was there, a raging beast in my soul that wouldn't quit. The demons inside me, that I wore on my back, were screaming at me to let them out, to let them free so they could wreak havoc on any who thought they could harm the innocent.

But I'd just made a promise to Indy.

And she was right.

My first duty was to my unborn child.

"Nyx? You're frightening me, baby."

I didn't blame her for being scared. I was fucking trembling like a pussy. Hell, she *had* a pussy and she was stronger than this.

But Indy... God, had Quin been targeted by our uncle too?

Before the blast, I'd been scheduled to visit with him, but I'd canceled in the aftermath. Now I wished I'd gone because, once again, I'd let him down.

Fuck, when would I stop letting down the people who mattered the most to me?

My throat was clogged with tears and rage and the outlying urge to kill, maim.

I'd thought they were safe.

Indy hadn't been. Why wouldn't Kevin have targeted Quin? He'd told me he'd hurt me, so why wouldn't he approach my baby bro?

My hands were shaking as I reached for my phone, tugging it out of my jeans. We'd been standing by my bike ever since I'd staggered out of Indiana Ink, leaving my sister behind as I tried to cope with what she'd gone through.

I knew that was messed up. *She* was the victim, but she'd been the one to hug me, to try to make me feel better. Nothing she could say would ever do that. I'd killed Kevin. I'd stolen his last breath from him. I'd watched his brain explode like it was a watermelon falling from a one-hundred-foot drop.

I thought I'd known vengeance.

I didn't.

Nothing could make up for this.

Nothing.

And the depth of the betrayal made it hard for me to breathe.

I'd let her down.

I'd let Indy down so fucking badly it was a wonder she could look me in the eye, never mind have me close enough to ink.

"I-I need to speak with Quin." I scrolled down for his number. We'd managed to get a new cell into Rikers for him, one I didn't want to know where he kept.

"Why? What's going on? You and Indy were fine until I went to the bathroom, then I came back and it was like WWIII had just hit her shop."

Her brow was puckered, her expression one big mass of confusion as I stared at her beautiful face.

She got my crazy.

I got hers.

But while it had started as that, while we were both two insane fuckers riding and dying together, this went deeper now. It had nothing to do with the kid she was carrying and everything to do with her.

Indy's promise was something I would never have been able to give to her before Giulia.

Just the rage her revelation triggered was something that would have had me hauling ass out of the tattoo parlor and heading to—

Christ, it wasn't like Maverick was *compus mentus* right now. That was why I'd gotten Lodestar in on the hunt for Martin London. So even if I wanted to go off on a slaughtering sesh, I couldn't. I had no one to definitively slay.

But that wouldn't have stopped me.

I'd have done something stupid.

I knew myself too well not to know that, so if it wasn't for this woman, this crazy beautiful woman, who'd somehow agreed to tie herself to me, who didn't mind my demons, who fucked with them on the regular just as I did with hers, I knew my sanity would be compromised.

The thought had me pushing us forward, away from the borrowed hog I was using, and toward the side wall of a building that was at the mouth of an alley. I moved with her until her back was against the brick, and because she was perfect, so fucking perfect for me, she didn't say shit, just flowed with me until I stopped. Then, she pushed her forehead against mine the second I tipped my chin forward and our hands tangled, bridging us together, connecting us in another way.

If I could have been inside her, I would've. But this went deeper than sex. This was... fuck, it was just everything.

She was everything.

"Talk to me, baby," she urged, but she did so softly, carefully. Like she recognized how fragile I was.

Fuck, what a pussy.

I closed my eyes. "Kevin... Indy just told me he got to her as well as Carly."

The sharp indrawn breath, her tension, all of it transmitted itself to me. But the way she literally fucking throbbed in the aftermath of my confession spoke of a true rage that few could handle.

Few, read none. Because only *I* could handle this woman.

Only *I* could bring her peace, fuck with her crazy, deal with her rage.

I was born for this.

Born for her.

Just as she was for me.

There was no doubting her sorrow for Indy, but her response was what I needed to feel vindicated. A normal woman might have said, "Oh, Nyx, I'm so sorry." But Giulia didn't say shit. She just *reacted*. Viscerally. And that calmed me down like nothing else could.

Her fingers tightened around mine to the point of pain, but it grounded me, brought me a semblance of peace as the quiet flowered around us.

"You want to check if he got to Quin too, don't you?"

"She slipped through the cracks. Why wouldn't he?" My voice broke and I felt no shame for it.

My kid siblings.

Fuck, I should have protected them—kept them safe.

"What made her tell you now?" she asked softly, dangerously. I knew that wasn't aimed at Indy who, nuts though it was, she seemed to get along really well with.

"She said I could handle knowing, that she needed to tell me because she was trapping the truth inside her for my benefit and she needed to be free from 'the cage of her silence.'"

"What else did she say?"

God, this woman.

Fuck.

I pushed my forehead into hers before I angled my head and caught her lips with my own. She was there for me, right from the start until the very end as I thrust my tongue into her mouth and started to fuck her there, at the opening of the alley, uncaring if anyone could see us.

My dick hardened, rubbing into the belly that was shielding our baby, but it wasn't about arousal. That was just the response my woman wrought in me.

It was about connecting. About the link between us.

Because Giulia knew something else was affecting me.

Knew it because she knew me.

She groaned into my kiss, which was my cue to pull back. Her inky black hair made her creamy skin look all the more like silk, and as she stared up at me with glittering eyes, her body soft as it merged with mine, sinking into me as she let me support her, I knew there'd never been room in my heart, my fucking soul, for any other woman.

Cammie had never had a snowball's chance in hell of meaning shit to me.

Because I'd been waiting for Giulia.

Since the day I was fucking born.

"She made me promise not to—"

Her gaze softened at my hesitation, because I couldn't exactly confess to serial killing out on the sidewalk, now could I?

But she understood. "Why did she?"

"She said I needed to make sure no one hurt our kid. Needed to make sure that I wasn't locked up and that no fucker could get to them."

Her nostrils flared. "She's right."

"I know." I moved my head, pulling back so I could rest it against her shoulder. As I did, she pressed her lips to the only part she could really kiss—my ear. "I have to... hurt them," I admitted roughly. "I-I need to. It feels like the only thing that'll keep me sane some days."

A sigh escaped her. "Your sanity is as important as your freedom. Maybe we can find a happy medium?"

"What do you mean?"

"There's more than one way to destroy someone than by ending their life." She hummed under her breath. "Lodestar and Maverick would be able to help with that, I think."

"You're right," I said gruffly, as I processed the many ways in which torturing people was possible now.

Long distance.

But there was someone who was close by. Someone who had come to my attention and who needed handling.

If Martin London was a fucking monster, then I had to deal with him. I just had to.

Giulia, like she was reading my mind, murmured, "One last hurrah?"

"You been watching old war movies again?" I asked, amused despite the situation.

As I pulled back, I caught sight of her grimace before she shrugged. "Can't help the fact they're all that's on when I wake up at night."

My lips twitched at that BS, and I pressed my smile to her grimace, muttering, "Sell that to someone else. Or just bounce onto me and I'll get you back to sleep." She still had fucking nightmares. The second I died, I'd be shadowing Luke Lancaster in hell and making him pay for what he'd done to my woman.

"How do you think I got the way I am? Too much bouncing."

Her snicker fucked with my heart, and I pulled back, pressed a hand to her stomach, and connected my forehead with hers again. We were going to be fucking parents. That was a duty, a solemn one, that few respected, but we weren't 'few.' And that was the only reason I could contemplate giving up my version of therapy.

"Indy—"

"What, love?" she prompted when I hesitated.

"She believes Cyan is being groomed."

Rage flared in her eyes like a match to a puddle of gasoline—it lit up her soul, called to the demons in mine. This woman. Perfect for me. As always. "What are you doing about that?"

I loved that she expected me to be on the case. No judgment that another bastard was on my shit list. Just expectation that I'd be ready and willing to take out the fucking trash.

"Got Lodestar on it. Hunting out his secrets."

"Any news from her?"

"Not yet."

"You should contact her. See what she's found out." Her fingers squeezed mine to the point of pain before she untangled one of our hands so she could reach between us and grab the cell I'd shoved back in my pocket when I'd moved her toward the mouth of the alley.

Within a minute, with her backup, I was on the line. Not with Quin, who I'd thought I'd be speaking with, but Lodestar.

Maybe it was fate. Maybe it was destiny that was finally working on my side, because when I asked her, "You got any information on Martin London?" Lodestar answered.

"Preliminaries look okay. He was a pastor up in Salem and was renowned for working with kids affiliated with gangs. He's retired now. Helps out at the local schools with underprivileged kids—gets them into extracurricular activities to keep them on the right side of the law."

Giulia stared at me. "Could he have been trying to get her 'clean?'" She pulled a face. "Not that she's dropping baggies of coke around the schoolyard, but these fucking evangelicals—you know how they roll. Probably think she's Satan's spawn because her daddy is a Satan's Sinner."

My brow puckered as I thought about that, thought about what I'd heard from Indy as she talked to Cyan the day she'd drawn her away from a potential predator.

"Maybe. She was sullen and defensive when she spoke of him."

"He made a lot of friends in the community in Salem, Nyx. Lots of people who speak very highly of him, especially with his work with underprivileged kids."

Giulia heaved a sigh. "Cyan isn't exactly on the streets, but…"

"No, but perception is everything," Lodestar concurred. "And to pastors, like you said, a life in an MC isn't ideal for a young, impressionable girl."

"So, you're saying he's legit?" I rasped.

"I'm saying that I need more time to truly investigate." She grunted. "I'm slower than I'd like, Nyx. I fucking hate it and don't like to admit it, but I'm not going to let Cyan down. It's just, for every two hours I can work at the moment, I'm sleeping eight. It's messing with my output. Just give me a couple extra days to dig deeper than what he wants the world to see."

Giulia nodded at me, urging me to answer, so I just replied, "Okay, Lodestar. I know you'll push it as far as you can."

"I wish Maverick was able to pull his weight," she mumbled. "Damn inconvenient both of us being out of play right now."

She wasn't wrong.

I cut the call on a short goodbye, and Giulia's hands slipped around my waist as she drew me tighter into her. The feel of her, the heat, it melted the ice that was starting to overtake my soul.

"We'll know soon," she promised me.

I nodded, but when I *did* learn the truth, what was I supposed to do?

I'd already let Indy down, was I going to break a promise I'd only just given her?

"Indy would understand," she soothed.

"Would she? I don't think so," I disagreed.

"Someone has to—"

"I know," I breathed. "But in this case, London is Storm's—his little girl, his to kill—so I'm okay. For another day."

Her exhalation encompassed just how hard this was going to be for me. "Maybe you should speak with Quin?"

Understanding her hesitance, as well as the change of subject, I whispered, "I seriously don't think I could deal with that right now. I know that's fucking selfish of me—"

She squeezed me. "He's stuck in a jail cell, Nyx. He's not going anywhere and the conversation isn't either. But," she reasoned, "I don't think it's something you should do on the phone.

You already promised me you'd go visit him. I think something like this should be talked about face-to-face."

My jaw felt like it had turned to stone as I nodded, because she was right.

I'd never tell her this, but she usually was, and rather than be pissed at that, it was a weight off my shoulders. I never wanted her to bear a burden so big it broke her, I wanted to be the one who caught her demons and helped her lay waste to them. But that, in this moment, when my worst nightmare had come to pass, she could be there for me?

It made me love her all the more.

ELEVEN

CYAN

"YOU'RE SUCH A GOOD GIRL, CYAN."

My cheeks pinkened at Martin's tone. "Thank you, Martin. I don't know why Daddy is being so mean to me right now."

"If you were my little girl, I'd never be so cruel. I can't believe he left you, Cyan. I'd never do that."

Tears pricked my eyes because Martin was right. Daddy *had* left me. It didn't even matter that he was back home now, I'd barely seen him.

Fairness had me realizing that he was busy, that with Uncle Rex in the hospital with *his* pop who was badly injured from the incident, Daddy had to take charge of the clubhouse.

Why had he come back for them though and not for me and Mom?

I gnawed on my bottom lip as I whispered, "Remember when I told you Mom and Dad were arguing on the phone? Before Mom tried to get me to stop talking with you?" She'd taken away my phone and had dramatically reduced the time I was allowed in front of a screen, but Martin had managed to get a tablet to me.

I missed him so badly and hated Indy for getting in the way of our friendship.

He made me feel good. Made me feel like I was more than an MC brat.

Everyone at school hated me, said I was scum. Harry Jenkins had even managed to break into my locker and had tagged 'MC SCUM' all over my stuff. Mom had gone to the office about it, but it never worked.

How were we the scum, how were we the criminals when these idiots from the town could do these things to me?

"I remember, honey. Did you forget to tell me something?"

The hairs at the back of my neck pricked at his tone as I registered he was mad. Martin liked for me to tell him everything. Sometimes I did, sometimes I didn't. Some things he asked made me feel weird inside, and I couldn't always share with him. I just wanted him to love me though, and when I told him the truth, he always told me he did.

This wasn't one of the things that made me feel weird, but that made me upset. I knew what he'd say, knew what he'd think, and I didn't want to hear him say it. But he was my best friend, and he knew most things about me and my family.

Just not this, because I'd only discovered the truth recently myself.

"What is it, Cyan?" he demanded, his tone hard with his annoyance.

I bit my lip, nerves fluttering inside me as I sought a way to appease him. "I overheard Mom say that Daddy cheated on her when she was pregnant with me."

He grunted under his breath. "He doesn't deserve you, Cyan. You're too good a little girl for him."

I was mad at my father, mad at him for things I didn't even understand. I felt like, when he'd gone to Ohio, he'd abandoned me. It didn't matter that he called me every day, he wasn't *here*. He wasn't stopping Harry Jenkins from ruining my things. Didn't stop the girls in my class from being horrible to me.

Mom tried, but she wasn't Daddy.

It was *his* fault I was an MC brat, after all. He'd always called me his princess, but it was only when I'd started middle school when I realized we were everything the kids in my class accused us of being.

Criminals.

And to learn that he'd treated Mom so badly?

My head was all over the place.

I loved him. I missed him. While he was in town, I missed him so badly because everything had gotten so much worse since he'd left, and I needed him to ground me again. Martin couldn't compete with him, but Daddy wasn't even trying to help me. He was just doing stuff for the MC. It was like I didn't exist anymore. Like I wasn't here.

But for all Martin's voice had me tensing up because I knew he was angry, I couldn't stop myself from defending Daddy. "H-He was young when he had me. We all make mistakes."

"You could never be a mistake, Cyan."

I blinked at that. "I didn't mean—" Did I? I meant that everyone made mistakes, but Martin's words made me see things differently. Was I a mistake too?

Was I the only reason my parents had gotten together?

Nausea churned in my gut, making me feel like I could puke.

"It's okay, Cyan," Martin told me, his words softer now, kinder. He wasn't mad anymore, and the relief that hit me stopped the churning in my gut. "I'm here for you. I'll always be here."

I closed my eyes, the sense of security his words gave me had me releasing a shuddery breath.

And when he asked, "Can you take a picture for me, baby

girl?" I didn't even get hot and flustered. "In fact, you can take two. You're so pretty."

He loved me.

He wasn't going anywhere.

He wasn't going to abandon me like Daddy had.

That was all that mattered.

So I took the pictures even though I knew I shouldn't, even though it was wrong.

I loved him.

Enough to please him.

Enough to help him when he asked me.

That was all that mattered.

TWELVE

MAVERICK

IT WAS COLD OUT, but that fucking pool had been beckoning me for days now. What with the headaches and the flashbacks, the hallucinations and the nightmares, I was turning into a zombie. The only consolation was I didn't feel like eating brains and I hadn't hurt Alessa since that first night.

Not that I felt any better about that.

For a couple of days, she'd walked around with smudge marks on her throat from the force of my assault, and in the whites of her eyes, there'd been those broken blood vessels I'd predicted. She displayed no signs of anger, no signs of anything.

Did I hit her on the regular?

The thought had plagued me ever since.

I didn't know the man I'd become, had no idea what kind of person he was, but she'd fallen for him so that had to mean something, didn't it? The only trouble was I couldn't hide from how she wore her bruises with ease, no shame or bitterness tangling up those pretty features of hers.

She was used to abuse.

It killed me to admit it, but I knew domestic violence could be common among soldiers who came back from a bad deployment overseas. There was no excusing it, but we weren't animals. We were men. With thoughts and hopes and dreams that were wrecked every time we saw the worst kind of shit humanity was willing to do to one another.

You couldn't toss us into that quagmire of hell then expect us to come back like perfect tin soldiers. This wasn't a fairy tale.

Knights who went away with their armor gleaming returned with it creaking and in need of oil.

That was how I felt. Even if, rationally, I knew I hadn't been in the sandbox for a long time, there was no avoiding what my mind believed.

Having lived with her for a few days now, I understood why she was nicknamed 'Ghost,' because it was like living with Casper. The trouble was, I wanted to talk to her and just didn't know how.

I slipped into the water with a sharp gasp as the chill immediately hit me like a slap to the face. When I surged back out, I jerked in surprise as I found Link sitting on one of the loungers by the side of the pool. He had a beer in hand, his cut was off, and his booted feet were crossed at the ankle.

"What are you doing out here?" I asked, not altogether happy about having his company.

"Wanted to talk to you."

"Well, I ain't in the mood for chatting."

"Tough shit. I let this crap go on long enough—what the fuck did you do to her, Maverick?"

I cut him a look, my mouth tightening with regret and anger at being questioned. "It was an accident."

"Like she accidentally walked into a door? Or how about she fell down some steps? Shame the pool house has no goddamn steps, you fucker."

Jaw tense with agitation, I managed to bite off, "I didn't mean to hurt her."

"Wife beaters never fucking do."

Rage hit me then, and I almost leaped out of the pool and went for the bastard, but as I surged forward to act, it was like someone had taken an ice pick to my fucking head. I crumpled, sinking down into the water like I was made of paper, and only the fact that I clung to one of the massive decorative rocks stopped me from going under the surface.

Grabbing on tight, like my life depended on it, I waited for the hammer blow to disperse. My ears rang with sound, my brain felt like I'd gone three rounds in the ring with Tyson, and I didn't even feel Link grab me and haul me out of the water until my body collided with the ground as if I was nothing more than a bag of bones.

I lay there, gasping for air, excruciating agony making it seem as though the walls of my skull were caving in, and through it all, Link was there. I felt him, his heat, his solid presence, and when, after Christ only knew how long, the agony abated, I managed to turn my head and see he was lying next to me, I gasped, "Thanks for not letting me drown."

"Dumb fuck," he rumbled softly, his words quiet, telling me he knew my head was hurting. "Why would we go to so much effort to save your scrawny ass if we didn't love the shit out of you? Brothers to the end, Mav. I don't think you ever got that, not really. You were overseas, and you had brothers in arms, but we're the same. We'd die for you—just like they would."

Throat choking with emotion, not just from his words but from the pain, I managed to grind out, "I did know that."

"Well, you hid it real well, along with the fact you didn't need a wheelchair anymore."

I blew out a breath. "I have no idea why I did that."

"I know it's irrational to be mad when you're not even that fucking man right now, but I am. We fought for you, you piece of shit," he grumbled, moving slightly so his ankles were still crossed, but so he could rest his hands on his stomach as he stared up at the night sky. "We were the ones who got you out of Bethesda when you called, not your goddamn A-Team."

"They were deployed," I countered. "If they made it out at all. I don't even remember that." I could have researched my old unit, but I hadn't had the heart. So much so I hadn't gone near a computer since the hospital.

Link grunted. "This is all kinds of fucked up."

"I know. I swear, I didn't mean to hurt her, Link." Of all the brothers, even more than Nyx, Link was protective toward women. Sure, he was a hound dog, or had been until he'd taken up with the woman who owned this mansion, but he'd always been good with them. I figured that was why Alessa actually managed to relax when he was around, enough to laugh.

I'd heard them in the kitchen—talking and shooting the shit.

How were things so normal for them when it was the exact opposite for me?

She was my wife, but she whispered around me like we were dancing a silent tango. There was no laughter in her eyes whenever she deigned to glance at me, only hurt.

I didn't blame her, but it still messed with my already messed up head.

"What happened?"

"I was having a nightmare."

"Shit, she came in and tried to wake you up?"

I shot him a surprised look, one that had me rolling my head to the side to glance at him, which triggered a wave of pain that took me to the brink of consciousness.

I barely heard him as he rumbled, "We had an issue with the

clubwhores after you got back. They kept thinking a BJ was the cure for PTSD. One bitch, Lacey, kept on trying, only this time you had a fucking knife. Nearly sliced and diced her. It warned the others to back off though."

"Jesus," I rasped. "I don't remember any of that."

"Why would you? Meant nothing in the end."

"Surprised you of all people would say that."

He shrugged. "We told them, they didn't listen. You can't help stupid."

My lips curved but though I wanted to laugh, I wasn't a fool. My head wasn't ready for anything with that level of exertion.

"She sang me to sleep, even after I did that to her."

Link cleared his throat. "She's a keeper."

"She told me we married so she could get a green card."

"Something like that."

"What aren't you telling me?"

He shrugged. "Nothing. You didn't do it for that. You did it because she was the first person in what felt like a goddamn lifetime to make you smile. It was nice actually, seeing you be normal again. I didn't realize how much I missed you." He released a shaky breath. "Now, here you are, back again, and I wish you were the new old Maverick. Fucker, you always had to do shit the hard way, didn't you?"

Managing to laugh a little, I rumbled, "Guess I fucking did."

"She loves you, Mav. Whether or not you remember her, don't treat her like shit, okay? Tell her to go, and we can move her in with us. Just don't hurt her. She's gone through enough already."

Before I could ask what she'd gone through, what 'enough' entailed, he rolled into a standing position.

"Let's get you back inside."

"No," I retorted. "I want to stay by the pool. The fresh air feels better out here. It's stuffy inside."

He moved around me, squatting down again as he plunked a cell at my side. "This is yours now. Your old one didn't survive the accident. Call me when you're ready to head on in. You're in no state to be doing shit on your own."

Wincing at how goddamn true that was, I muttered, "Thanks, bro."

"It's an honor, Mav."

And I knew he meant it.

He trudged off, boots thudding against the uneven stone surface surrounding the pool until he hit the grass. Then, he might as well have been Casper like Alessa. No wonder I hadn't realized he was there until he made himself known to me.

Staring up at the sky, with its inky black hue and the twinkling stars that had always grounded me when I was deployed, I let myself sink into the uncomfortable stone floor.

My back hurt where it connected with sharper edges, and my body was one big ache as the pain in my head started to drift down to my toes. But the cold was bracing. It reminded me I wasn't dead. That I was alive.

Somehow.

"Maverick?"

I closed my eyes at the sweet tone of her voice. There was just the gentlest difference in intonation between how she said it—my brothers pronounced it 'Mav-rick,' but she enunciated what was a silent 'E' to them.

She padded toward me, evidently not put out by my lack of an answer, and laid a towel over me, which took off the chill.

My eyes popped open again, and I told her, "Thank you."

"You're welcome." She hovered, then moved over to the lounger where Link had started off our conversation. I almost expected her to start one up herself, but she didn't.

She stayed quiet.

In the distance, I could hear something coming from the big house. Childish laughter, little gurgles of glee that even a monster would be hard-pressed not to smile at, and I rocked my head over the ground as I studied the mansion.

How had Link, one of the poorest of us with the hardest background income-wise, come to live here?

It'd have boggled my mind if said mind wasn't already scrambled like three-week-old eggs.

"He loves her. She loves him."

"You a mind reader now?" I didn't bother to look at her, just stared over the property that made a basketball star's mansion look shoddy.

It was bigger than the last post where I'd been stationed, for fuck's sake. Had so many windows and doors that it made the White House look like a girl's playhouse.

I'd wandered through those halls, come across authentic pieces of art, rooms that reminded me of something from a fancy bordello, and more bedrooms than Buckingham Palace. But that grandeur, for all it was impressive, was nothing compared to the land around it which was manicured yet somehow tactile.

Money had never been the be-all and end-all of my life, that was what came from being an MC brat, but the truth was, even I was slightly overwhelmed by what the property's size represented.

Lily Lancaster wasn't just rich.

Neither was she *just* wealthy.

This was more than just one percent territory, and I wasn't talking about the MC variety either. Hell, I was thinking it might even be one-hundredth of a percent.

"I'm not a mind reader," she inserted gently, "but it was clear to see what you were thinking."

"It wasn't, actually, because I didn't doubt Link loved her.

None of the brothers are poor. They all make great bank, Bear is —" My brow puckered. "He isn't the Prez anymore, is he?"

"No. Rex is," she informed me softly.

I released an irritated breath. "Goddamn this."

"You almost drowned before. I saw you."

"Would you have left me to die?" I choked out bitterly, not even finding comfort in her shocked gasp.

"Of course I wouldn't! I only didn't come rushing because I saw Link get to you first. I-I thought it might be wise to let you two talk. You've been hiding away in your room. I don't think that's good for you. Even before, while you were stuck in the attic a lot, your door was open for your brothers. Especially the council."

Sensing an opportunity, because this was the first time since *that* night she'd spoken to me so freely, I asked, "Who's on the council?"

"You, Link, Nyx, Steel, Rex, and Sin. Storm used to be, but he left to go to Ohio."

"Why?"

She clucked her tongue. "It's club business. How am I supposed to know?"

My nose crinkled. "Damn, I forgot about that too. I haven't lived in the MC for a long time."

"Why not?"

"Because I had goals, and I knew having entanglements with them would prevent them. So I never hung around the clubhouse after I hit sixteen, and the guys" —a smile creased my lips— "used to come to my place after school so I could keep my rep clean.

"Bear still gave me a cut though. It was an honorary one to get me through my service until I came home for good. He let me wear it at funerals and weddings and shit when I was back home on leave." When her lack of reply felt loaded, I knew I'd perplexed her, as I'd thought that would trigger more questions not this loaded silence, so I murmured, "To be in the Special Forces, you go through a background check."

"They truly care when they're throwing you onto battlegrounds like you're pawns in a game of chess?"

I snorted, which made my ears ring—reminder to self: don't do that again.

"The Special Forces are special for a reason. Let's just leave it at that."

"I know of the SEALs—"

"Everyone knows the fucking SEALs. Bunch of show-offs," I grumbled. "We're just as capable as those fuckers, but we don't hog the limelight like they do."

A soft chuckle escaped her, and I couldn't blame her. Not really. Christ, what a stupid goddamn conversation to be having when my brain was mush thanks to those 'special' years as a Green Beret.

I reached up and pressed my forearm to my eyes, covering them as I asked, "Who sits where in the council?"

She muttered, "I don't really know."

"Bullshit. Women always know more than they let on. The brothers are stupid if they don't think their Old Ladies are well aware of every aspect of club life."

"Well, I know some, but not that much," she retorted on a huff.

My arm hid my smile. "Some is more than nothing."

She sighed. "Nyx is the VP now. Lily and Tiffany, who is Sin's Old Lady—you met her the other day in the kitchen—well, they were kidnapped, and Storm saved them. However he did it, though, it meant he had to move to Ohio. Ever since, Nyx has taken his place."

"Can't imagine Nyx as VP."

"I don't think he can imagine it either," she said drolly, "and he's living it."

Almost smiling again because Nyx was all about the action, not the admin, I rumbled, "Sounds about right. Sin... what's his place?" I'd always liked him. He was a soldier too, or, I guess, a vet now. He'd been good people despite being Grizzly's kid.

Fuck, I'd never liked that bastard. How the hell he and Bear had been brothers was beyond the laws of logic.

"He's the enforcer. He took over for Nyx when the council was shuffled around. You're treasurer—but I'm not supposed to know that," she whispered. "But Lily is going to be helping you with the club books, so I found out that way."

Bitches... never could keep shit quiet.

I wasn't mad though, more grateful for the insight into the MC that was my life now.

I'd gone from avoiding the clubhouse at all costs to somehow being integral to the running. Of course, that avoidance hadn't run as deep as I let her believe. Even though I wasn't affiliated with the MC back when I was a teenager, it had only been unofficially so. I'd gone on most of my brothers' first runs with them and had gotten into shit I really shouldn't have. I'd been a brother in everything but a patch.

Link was right—they were as important to me as the guys who served with me. More because we'd come up together and we'd go down together. From the beginning to the very end.

"Is Storm the VP in Ohio?"

"No, he's the Prez."

I grunted. "That's good. He was too smart to be Rex's VP. Probably got him into a world of trouble being bored."

She cleared her throat. "You know Keira?"

"Yeah, he wifed her."

"They're getting divorced."

That came as no surprise. "She found out about his cheating? Scarlet always warned him about that. Said he'd never be able to keep shit from Keira. She was too much of a good girl to turn the other cheek."

"Who's Scarlet?"

My brow puckered. "Storm's sister. Where is she?"

Ghost shrugged. "I don't know. I've never heard anyone talk about a Scarlet before. Scarlet like the color, right?"

Frowning, I nodded. "Yeah, like the color." She'd always been as colorful as her name. "I wonder where she's at. Wouldn't surprise me if she left. Most women can't handle the life." I pursed my lips at the thought. "Seems like Keira is another one that bit the dust."

She sniffed. "A clubwhore told her he screwed around on her when she was pregnant—talk about humiliating for her."

Fucking snatch.

Anger hit me hard enough to make my temples throb, but I let out a rough exhalation and tried to calm myself down.

It didn't work.

"Dumb fucker," I growled.

"I would say so, yes. He hurt her and his daughter very much."

"I can believe it. Amazing how someone so goddamn smart can be as thick as pig shit sometimes." I heaved a sigh. "Scarlet wasn't the only one who knew his addiction would get the better of him one day."

Alessa tensed. "Addiction?"

I grunted, but rather than answer because it wasn't my business so it sure as fuck wasn't hers, I asked, "Link and Steel—what are they?"

"Link is the road captain and Steel is secretary."

"That fits. Link still a mechanic?" I questioned, even though I knew the answer already because I'd smelled engine oil on him when he'd lain beside me.

"He is. He works at the MC's new garage."

"We have a garage?" I queried, rolling my head to the side.

"Yes. And a diner, a bar, and a strip joint." Her lips twisted. "You were working on a microbrewery. We talked about it quite a bit."

"A microbrewery?" That came as a shock. "I don't even like beer."

She snorted. "Apparently that changed too."

I knew why she was laughing, but Christ. Talk about a one eighty.

Perplexed, I murmured, "Alessa?"

Confusion further hit me when she sucked in a sharp breath. She tended to do that whenever I used her name—and I had no fucking idea why she had such a visceral response to my using her goddamn birth name.

Another question I needed to ask, one I instinctively knew she'd shy away from.

"Yes, Maverick."

"I don't think I'm going to get better. I think this is the new me." I'd always been good at reading people, and I sensed a gentleness about her that resonated with me deeply.

I didn't want to hurt her more than necessary. Either emotionally or physically.

What was the point of putting her through this when I either wouldn't remember or I'd end up blowing my brains out when everything grew to be too much?

Too many brothers, my fellow soldiers, had taken their lives, and for the first time, I understood.

Death was peaceful.

At the moment, there was no peace for me.

When I heard the lounger creak as her slight weight shifted, I expected her to leave me alone, to head back into the pool house, but she surprised me. She moved toward me, crouching at my side even as she lifted the towel and moved beneath it. Uncaring that I or it were damp, she pressed her face to my arm, and it spoke to how guilty I felt, how cruel I'd been, that I didn't flinch away.

I didn't know her.

I didn't want her touch.

But she deserved that kindness.

"The new you is someone I want to get to know."

The question was, however, did I want to get to know her?

My love for Nic was a powerful force inside me, an entity of its own that beat with a pulse. But he was gone. Dead. Had been for years even if my brain was only registering that now.

Alessa was here.

She hadn't run away.

She wasn't making me feel like a pile of shit even though I deserved it.

So many of my men had received 'Dear John' letters, to the point where mail wasn't something to look forward to when you had a girl, it was something to be wary of. Something to fear.

We'd bitched about those feckless cunts, had called them out, yet here Alessa was. Doing the exact opposite of running. How could I fault her for that when I'd judged those other women?

How could I turn her away when she wanted me?

Me, a wreck of a man. My head like stew. Suffering with something that made me collapse like a pansy in a pool, and who was lying shivering under the sea of stars because the prospect of getting up, of moving, was enough to make me sob like a little girl.

"What if I'm not worth knowing?" I rasped. "Alessa, I don't have good odds. This CTE is degenerative. It's not going to go away, and it isn't going to get better."

"Are you going to kill yourself?"

The question should have surprised me, but I'd taunted her with the label of mind reader earlier, and I'd done so for a reason.

She tended to appear when I wanted a coffee and disappear when I wanted to be alone. She knew when I was hungry and seemed to sense what I was going to say before I even fucking said it.

In all honesty, it was irritating as fuck, but it told me how much she studied me. How much I meant to her.

"I see this ending that way," I told her gruffly, expecting harsh words and bitter recriminations. Instead, I felt the warmth of her tears against my arm, and her silence was more painful than the ice pick to my head of before.

"I would like to be there for you to help you see that it doesn't have to end at all. You're still young, Maverick."

"Not as young as you. What are you? Twenty?"

"Twenty-four."

Jesus.

Talk about robbing the cradle.

I sighed. "Why the hell do you want to be tied to an old man like me for, Alessa? There has to be another brother who can help you get your residency—"

"Maverick, don't you see yet? The residency doesn't matter. Whether I stay here or not is irrelevant. Before the clubhouse crashed, I somehow thought you'd come with me to Ukraine. Maybe I was wrong, but I could see you coming with me if I was tossed out." She released a shaky sigh, one that sounded choked from her tears. She wasn't the only one who felt choked up. "Whether we're here or there, it didn't matter to me. All that counted was you, me, and what we had together."

"Fuck, Alessa, I'm so sorry," I vented on a long exhalation. "I'm so sorry I went into that clubhouse."

"It was important to you," she whispered, once again not letting me beat myself up over this.

Proving, yet again, that this woman was solid gold, whereas I was just fool's gold.

"Do you know what I was doing?"

"Lodestar, she—"

Tension hit me at that. I found it hard to believe we were friends after how she'd treated me during our breakup, and seeing her sitting at the kitchen table every morning was irritating as hell. Especially when I saw my MC family talking to her. Sure, I didn't know half of that MC family, but the principle didn't change any, did it?

"You don't like her, do you?"

Her question didn't exactly come out of the blue, but I muttered, "It's awkward."

"Most things are now."

Well, she wasn't wrong, so I admitted, "*When* my head is at, we only just broke up."

"You were together?"

"For quite a while. We served in the 10th Mountain Division together. That was how we met."

"I didn't know that."

The tension in her voice told me she didn't like knowing it either.

Amused that she could be jealous when being in the same room as Lodestar made my skin crawl, I shoved that aside and asked, "What were you going to say? What about Lodestar?"

"What have the brothers told you about that night?" she hedged.

"Not a lot, to be honest. I haven't given them much of an opportunity to talk to me."

She sighed. "I don't know if I should be the one to share this with you, Maverick. I don't have all the facts."

"You have more facts than I do, and you can tell me what you know. I'm a big boy, Alessa" —another sucked in breath— "I know what I can and can't handle, and I can always talk to them once I have some foundations down. The worst thing is knowing that there's a whole conversation going on around me and I'm not allowed to hear it."

"Yes," she said softly, "that must be awful."

"It is. It's more of a handicap than you can imagine." I cleared my throat. "I'd appreciate you telling me what you know. Be it a little or a lot, I'd appreciate it either way."

I turned my head so I could look at her and found myself entangled in her gaze as she was staring right at me. The pain between my ears disappeared some as my focus shifted, ensnared by those beautiful jade eyes peeking at me.

She reminded me a little of a fairy, her features diminutive but ethereal. Fragile but high cheeks, rounded brows that gleamed gold no matter if it was under the sun, the moon, or just a lamp. Her hair was wispy, somehow, but it looked like it was getting thicker. As if she'd been sick for a while, which fit because she was crazy thin. I'd watched her eat a sandwich, and it had taken her a painful amount of time.

With her delicate bone structure, she might have seemed childlike, but there was something about her that got to me. Maybe it was the kid in me who'd had a crush on Tinkerbell, but she was life-sized and definitely an adult.

She was also the direct opposite of me. I was rough and jaded where she screamed a sweet innocence that made me want to protect her even as I wanted to push her away, which made things damn complicated.

Sighing at the thought, and wondering if I'd been sent this fairy because I wasn't supposed to die just yet—it wasn't as if I had a death wish, but I figured what I was going through would make a saint curse until the air was blue—I murmured, "Are you going to help me, Alessa?"

For a second, she bit her lip, the plump pad compressing under the firm bite, then she appeared to come to a decision because she whispered, "Lily's father was an enemy of the club. It caused issues with the Italians because he worked with them."

"The MC's at war with the *Famiglia*?" I queried, brow furrowing. Fucking Italians.

She nodded.

"They're who blew up the compound?"

"I mean, I think so. Who else would do something so crazy?"

I hummed under my breath, thinking she'd be surprised at how many fucking nutcases there were in this world.

"Either way, Lodestar appeared to know something was going to happen that particular night. She was on the roof, and when the blast hit, she was hurled to the ground."

"Hence her injuries." I pondered that. "She's lucky to be alive." Even with our training, specialized deployments and landings in rough terrain, the clubhouse was fucking high off the ground when you were being hurled into the sky and were landing with no parachute.

"You asked her why she was on the roof, and she told you things that I probably shouldn't have heard." She dipped her chin. "She said the gate to the compound was open, that someone had opened it, and that a sniper was waiting out in the distance. He was the one who set off the blast."

"That conversation prompted me to return to the clubhouse?"

"You wanted to make sure the hard drives were destroyed so the FBI couldn't get any data from them."

"As well as find out if there was any CCTV footage of whoever opened the gate?"

"Yes. Lodestar also gave you a guesstimate of where the sniper's—" She broke off.

"Sniper's?"

"I can't remember the word. I want to say where a bird makes its home, but that can't be right."

My lips twitched. "It can, actually. A sniper has a nest." Allowing my mind to drift for a little while, I murmured, "Did any of the brothers know this?"

"No, and you told Lodestar not to say anything because you told her she'd get tossed out of the MC if the council learned she'd been aware of a potential threat to the compound and she didn't keep them in the loop."

Mouth tightening, I rasped, "She's as treacherous as ever."

"No, she was trying to protect the compound, but she said the intel she had wasn't reliable." She cleared her throat. "To be honest, Mav, she appeared quite truthful and you believed her. I don't think you'd have told her to stay quiet if you didn't think she was trustworthy."

I understood why she thought that, but it still baffled me to believe that I gave that bitch any trust whatsoever.

The harder I started thinking, the more the dull throb in my head pounded, so taking it as an equation that thinking caused me pain, I rumbled, "I need to get some rest."

"You do," she agreed.

"Tomorrow, I need you to help me."

"Me? Why?"

I sighed. "Apparently, Future Maverick likes that cunt, and even if I don't, I'm going to have faith in him and in you—"

"Oh, dear," she muttered miserably. "Please don't. I don't want to get into trouble."

A surprised laugh escaped me. "Trouble? We're not in school, Alessa. Even if you did mess up, what do you think I'd do? Make you stand in the corner?"

Something darkened in her eyes, and it wasn't arousal.

I tilted my head to the side, which had a lightning bolt of pain spearing me to the quick. A breathless moan escaped me as I reached up and cupped my skull, supporting it as much as I was able.

I couldn't say a word, couldn't even take a proper inhalation as she somehow got me into a sitting position then helped me onto my feet. I wanted to tell her that Link said he'd help, but even though I managed to choke out my brother's name, she ignored me, seeming determined to help me do this by herself.

By the time we were staggering toward the pool house which, thank fuck, was only a short walk down a small path, she was breathing hard and her skin was dewy with perspiration. As for me, I was barely breathing period, because if I did, it hurt.

Jesus.

Feeling like fucking crying when we made it inside the small building, I let her guide me into the bedroom. As we arrived at the side of the bed, she stunned me by letting go of me before dragging down my wet boxer briefs and dumping them on the ground. Then, she deposited me with as much care as she was able—and that wasn't much—onto the mattress. Not that I could blame her.

As the agony lit my nerves on fire, I curled into a fetal ball. In my misery, I didn't even think about her, she didn't even enter my head, until I felt her warmth at my back.

She curved herself around me, fitting every line of her form against me so she touched me from head to toe. When her arm moved over my stomach, I didn't flinch away. Maybe I'd have preferred for Nic to be the one holding me, to be the one soothing me, but not only could I not have him, I was just grateful not to be alone.

Maybe I deserved for her to abandon me, but she didn't.

Which was the exact moment when I knew Alessa Ravenwood, for all that she was a stranger to me, was a keeper.

And the MC brat in me took whatever he found in true finders keepers fashion...

THIRTEEN

ALESSA

"WE SHOULDN'T BE OUT HERE," I grumbled, as I'd been grumbling since Maverick had first woken up this morning and urged me to pepper Lodestar for information on the exact location of the sniper's nest.

I'd always known he was stubborn, but this was taking things to another ridiculous degree.

He was in pain, his face was drawn with it, but here we were, in the middle of a field on the Sinners' compound.

In the distance, there were construction noises as the place had been cleared of rubble from the blast and brothers from all over the country had come in to help the original chapter.

It was, to my mind anyway, proof that the MC was just an unorthodox community, with everyone pulling together no matter the distance between each 'family.' I liked that, and it confirmed once more that the brothers were good people.

Even good folk got their hands dirty, didn't they?

Overhead, the sky was a bright blue, and the clouds were like cotton, wispy and filmy, not enough to give much cover from the heat of the sun. I knew that had to be hurting Maverick's eyes because even though they were decidedly feminine in style, he had asked me if he could borrow my shades. It meant I was squinting but he was in agony, and I couldn't bear to see that, so I gave them to him.

I almost wished I was a girly-girl and had picked ones in the shape of flowers or something because that would have been worthy of a photo. My big, dark, mean biker of a husband wearing flower-power sunglasses. Ha.

Technically, I didn't have a license, but that hadn't stopped Maverick from urging me into a pickup truck this morning. It had been outside in Lily's front yard, and as usual, there were keys in the ignition.

I'd noticed that before. The MC guarded their bikes like they were the lost treasure of the Templars, but their cages, as they called them, they barely secured at all. Their way of storing the keys was just to leave them where they were needed, uncaring that each truck was worth a small fortune.

At least, they were to me.

Apparently not to the brothers.

I wasn't used to driving automatic, having driven manual back in Ukraine before, well, before when I'd lived there, and though it was easier, it was also harder because though the signs were universal, they were different, and I was out of practice, not having been behind the wheel since I was nineteen. At least the U.S. drove on the right like back home, otherwise it would have been a nightmare.

It had been made a thousand times worse when, with every bend I took, or every stop light I braked at, Maverick had bitten off a tight groan. He'd attempted to haul it back in, to withhold his pain, but I'd heard—it was too late.

But Maverick was a forceful man, and I simply wasn't trained that way.

Compliance was rewarded with less pain.

Outright rebellion was rewarded with agony.

How was I supposed to go against five years' worth of training, training that was tied to corporal punishment, to save Maverick from himself?

As he bent over, his hands on his knees as he tried to get his breath back, I accepted I'd have to do something.

He was, after all, a man.

And men were stupid sometimes.

Moving over to him, I stepped through the low brush that scratched my calves with every step.

"We need to go back," I told him, trying to add some power to my voice, but he ignored it and me.

"I'm fine."

"Yes, you look *fine*," I retorted, and if I sounded waspish, then so be it. "Bent over at the waist like that, you're lucky I don't want to kick you because you'd be flat on your face if I did."

He twisted a little to peer at me over his borrowed sunglasses. "You'd do that?"

That he was wary amused me.

As if I could push a man of his size and stature over. Even though he was quite lean, what there was of him was muscle. Hard and packed. Hadn't I felt the proof of that against me last night when I'd curved into him?

I'd done it for selfish reasons.

I needed to sleep, and he smelled like Mav even if he wasn't actually *my* Mav.

I thought he'd rested too, because I hadn't awoken with a forearm clamped to my throat, neither had I suffered a random assault thanks to whatever nightmare he'd endured.

Both of us had slept, but he'd awoken first as he tried to

clamber off the bed, before he'd fallen back, panting, sweat popping out of every pore in response to the dumb move.

I'd had to help him use the bathroom—well, I mean, I hadn't had to touch him—more like just maneuver him into a standing position all while trying to avoid glancing at his penis.

Why was it when you tried to avoid something, you ended up seeing more of it than ever?

He hadn't had an erection at any point of the exercise, even though that was how men woke up, and I knew he could get them because I'd felt them before when we slept together. He'd tried to hide his response, but he was quite big and there was no hiding *that*.

When he refused to sit down which made far more sense in my opinion when he could barely stand, I'd given him some privacy. Only, when I'd returned to find him standing with both hands braced on the wall, leaning over like even that was too much for him, I'd maneuvered him into the shower where there was a bench.

After, I'd put some of my training to good use, and I'd cleaned him then I massaged his shoulders and back, carefully tending to his head as well.

As I worked, I found far too much pleasure in touching him when I'd always been revolted by massaging past owners, and when I'd come across a large tattoo on his shoulder, in the center of his back, I didn't have to wonder how I'd missed it. Well, missed *that* on top of all the various others that decorated his spine including a portrait of a beautiful woman whose tragic eyes had been portrayed to perfection, as well as a very dark design that reminded me of a paisley pattern on a scarf my grandmother used to wear for church.

Seeing how he pretty much lived in his cut, it made sense I hadn't seen these as the leather vest kept that wall of flesh hidden from sight. I was used to seeing his defined torso with all its scars and ragged flesh that had fused together badly, but the tattoo fascinated me because I knew what it represented.

There was a kind of knife that reminded me of those bowie knives hunters used. It thrust upward with two crossed arrows behind it. Then, in a kind of ribbon that swirled around it, there was the declaration, '*De oppresso liber.*'

Ever since, I'd been thinking about it, thinking about having the right to touch his back, to touch him, but even as I'd found pleasure in the act, I regretted easing his pain now.

Not only because the feel of him beneath my hands was delicious to the point of agony, but because it had made him feel better, which had led to this moment.

Him being a fool.

As I thought about his long, strong body, the pressure of his hard muscles against my palms, I decided that the only way to help him was to give him another massage. It was awkward with his position, and I knew it couldn't be helping his head to be dangling over the way he was, so I tried to get him onto his knees.

He was desperate enough that he managed to help me help him, and he stunned me by pushing his forehead into my stomach and wrapping his arms around my legs as I started to give him an Indian head massage.

It was wrong of me, but when he moaned, his breath burned me through the thin cotton of my shirt, and the vibration of it set my skin alight in response. As I rubbed his temples, making gentle circles as I tried to ease his pain, I attempted to focus on anything but those moans which made me feel like I was going to leap out of my skin.

I'd feared that any sexuality I might have had had been robbed from me by the men who'd owned me, but as I stood there, in the middle of a field, construction work in the distance, the scent of smoke still in the air from the blast, and my husband driven to his knees from pain, I realized there was a kernel of *something* deep inside me.

A *something* that Maverick held the key to.

And if now wasn't a terrible time to realize that, when Maverick wasn't the man I married, when he was in agony and I was trying to soothe him, well, I didn't know if there could be worse timing.

Talk about selfish.

"Oh, God," he said thickly, and I tilted my head back and closed my eyes, trying to ignore how my nipples budded in reaction to his plea which reminded me of something a man might say as he was about to orgasm.

Shakily, I released a breath he didn't hear because he was moaning again, a low-level vibration that worked on me better than a Sybian.

Biting my lip, I tried to focus, tried to push through the delicious sensations he was inadvertently gifting me with, and moved my hands down to his neck. He tensed up, pain hitting him with me approaching new territory, but he placed more pressure on my stomach as he gave me more of his weight.

That level of trust from a man I sensed wasn't trusting at all, a soldier who was, at least in his head, fresh from the battlefield, gave me hope.

Hope was dangerous, I knew that. But what other choice did I have?

I loved Maverick.

Loved him when I'd thought those feelings were going to be dead to me from now on.

He was my light at the end of the tunnel. A glimmer in the distance that I could cling to even if it wasn't forever.

He was a destiny I'd never dared believe I'd have, and while I was right, while he'd been taken from me just as I'd feared, here he was, lowering his barriers.

I'd massage him twenty-four seven if it meant he'd stop locking me out.

Then my pleasure, my relief in what I'd thought was his softening toward me, turned to sawdust because the groans mumbled from his lips morphed into sobs, and I felt his wretchedness. Felt it and recognized it. I felt it every day in some shape or form.

It was a black hole, something you could never get out of, something you could never escape, could only avoid for so long before it would always rear its ugly head again.

I knew why he was crying. For his Nic. Someone I'd never met, a stranger who'd helped forge Maverick into the man he was today—the man I loved. I mourned him as Maverick did, shared his pain, and just carried on holding him because in all the years since Nic had died, I knew, without a shadow of a doubt, that Maverick had never been held while he mourned his lost love. I knew that, maybe, just maybe, he'd never even cried either.

It was awkward and unwanted, he didn't want my touch, but I couldn't stop myself from bowing over him and pressing my lips to the crown of his head. He didn't feel it, didn't register the touch, but my heart did. My heart needed to help him get through this— not just so it would lead him back to me, but because Maverick had given me the support I needed when I'd been dying, he deserved as much, if not more, from me.

So I held him as he cried, said nothing as he wept for his Nic, and was there for him.

Like he'd been for me.

Today, that was all I could do.

But maybe tomorrow, there'd be another opportunity. Something I could do to help ease his burden, his woe, because in my arms, Maverick was burning through ten years' worth of grief, and that wasn't healthy.

Not at all.

"Maverick?" I whispered, hating to hear his sorrow, hating that I felt it.

He tensed up some, but otherwise didn't respond to me, so I plugged on, knowing I needed to speak, knowing he had to understand something.

"You don't know me. To you, I'm a stranger. But if you don't trust me, and you don't trust yourself, then you need to trust in your brothers. They know what I am to you. They know what we were coming to feel for each other." His tension transmitted itself to me, and rather than give up, I carried on regardless. "So this morning in the shower when I said you weren't ready for this, you heard those words come from a woman who means nothing to you... But I love you, Maverick, and I want what's best for you.

"If you respect nothing else, respect that. You're sick right now," I mumbled. "Let me care for you."

When he maintained that abyss-like silence, I wanted to weep, and then he nodded, his forehead rubbing against my stomach, and it felt like I'd won a major battle when, really, all I'd won was the right to tell my husband when he was on track to killing himself...

Not much in the grand scheme of things, but more than I'd expected this morning.

Which was saying a lot.

FOURTEEN

MAVERICK

"I JUST SENT IT PRIORITY," I rasped as I stared at an old comrade in the camera, an old comrade who, to me, was someone I'd seen that morning I'd woken up in the hospital—when the nightmare that was my life had begun.

That morning in Kembesh, he'd been young. *Normal.* Now he'd grown a shocking pelt of hair, all of which was white instead of the dark brown I was used to seeing.

At first, I'd wondered if he'd doused it in that paint you used for a Halloween costume, but it was natural. He'd gone gray.

"I need the results ASAP," I said uneasily, trying to reconcile the past and the present and, as per fucking usual, failing.

"I still can't believe—" Ken shook his head. "Six years, man. Ain't heard from you in six fucking years!"

I winced. "I'm sorry about that, brother." A breath escaped me. "I don't know what the hell I was thinking cutting communication like that."

"You being serious when you say you can't remember shit?"

"Wish it was a lie, but it isn't." My throat tightened. "I didn't even know Nic was dead."

Ken's gaze softened. "Goddamn Kembesh. Still have nightmares about that mission. I got out a few months after. Liam did as well. Got to be too much, you know?"

I really fucking did.

"Nic, man. Been a long time since I thought about him."

"That's what the living do, isn't it?" I said tightly. "Forget."

Had I forgotten Nic? Had the Maverick Alessa loved stopped thinking about him every damn day? Was there light at the end of this tunnel—one that pricked the gloom of the abyss of grief that was choking me?

"Sometimes, but every Memorial Day, I go through my list. Too many brothers gone, Mav. Too many fucking brothers gone. We're lucky we got out in one piece."

If you could call this one piece.

I blinked at him. "Do you have any idea why I'd pretend to be in a wheelchair?"

He frowned. "No. You mean, you weren't disabled?"

Embarrassment hit me. What I'd done was fucking shameful. It didn't even matter that I'd needed a wheelchair in the early days of my recovery, it left me feeling like I was letting down the brothers who genuinely needed them.

Reaching up, I rubbed at my eyes and muttered, "No. I wasn't."

When he cleared his throat, I knew he was embarrassed too. "This is all kinds of messed up, Maverick."

I dipped my chin but refused to let our gazes bridge. "Damn right it is." A sigh rumbled from me. "I really need your help, Ken."

"Figured as much since this is the first time I've heard from you in over six years," he said dryly, "but I don't work for the—"

Before he could finish, I raised a hand and said, "I know, man,

I know. No one is where they used to be. Trust me, I get it. But I'm pretty sure you have contacts still." His grimace confirmed it. "I need the samples to be matched against the database of veterans, active duty soldiers, cops, fucking firefighters... you name it."

He snorted. "How about we throw in CIA agents too, huh? Just for shits and giggles."

"If you've got their NOC list, go for it," I told him, my voice utterly serious.

His eyes bugged out a little. "You shitting me?"

"Do I look like I'm shitting you? I need to know."

He pursed his lips before he asked, "Long time ago, I'd have done this without question. But it ain't a long time ago, brother. You gotta tell me what's going on."

Though inwardly I cringed with yet more shame, I murmured, "You remember my family?"

"Your ma died—"

"They're not blood, but they're still family."

"The MC?" He nodded. "I remember them."

"Well, their compound was bombed. They sent in the father of one of my brothers, had his bike hooked up with the bomb, and then had a sniper detonate it."

His brows rose, but it was a testament to the crazy shit we'd had to do in the name of Uncle Sam that he didn't do much else by way of a reaction. "You want me to identify the sniper then?"

Bowing my head, I said, "Yeah. Remember Lodestar?"

Ken laughed. "How could I fucking forget that crazy-ass bitch? Thought you and she weren't on speaking terms."

"Seems like the Maverick pre-blast got on like a goddamn house on fire with her."

"Apparently the bomb doused those flames."

"It sure as hell did. But she managed to find the nest, and though the bastard was clean today, where he'd set up is a major pain in the ass for anyone trying to make a spot for himself. There's bristle and bush every-fucking-where."

"It's a blood sample?" he guessed.

"Well, it's a part of a bush but there's blood on it, yeah. As well as a tiny piece of fluff from what he was wearing that he thought he collected before he left."

"Dumb prick," he muttered.

"No Green Beret," I confirmed drolly as the pair of us shared a grim but satisfied nod.

"I'll see what I can do, Maverick, but I make no promises."

"I expect none, and am grateful for what you can do. Whatever that might be."

His hum was disbelieving and dissatisfied. "Is it gonna be another six years until I hear from you again, you prick?"

My lips curved into a rueful smile. "Naw."

Maybe something in that smile caught his attention because his head tilted to the side a little. "Maverick? What's going on?"

Gaze darting from his again, I rumbled, "Nothing, Ken. Nothing. Aside from the craziness that I just told you about."

"Yeah, you told me some fucked up BS, but there's something else going on." He grunted when I kept my attention averted from the camera. "Fucker, tell me what's going on."

It was the 'fucker' that did it.

The fucker that took me back to that day at Kembesh, and it pierced my memory, reminding me of the last time I'd heard him call me that.

Or, at least, the last time I remembered him calling me that.

He'd hollered at Nic and me to get our asses out of bed, told us that the Taliban were starting to mobilize—like we hadn't figured that out ourselves with the goddamn bullets tearing through our tent.

He was a bridge, at that moment. A bridge that joined me to Nic.

"It's like this," I told him gruffly, sharing the whole sorry fucking tale of the state of my brain, of my life right now. Offloading onto him like I'd never offload onto my MC brothers because they'd never understand.

Would never truly get what it felt like to feel this way.

Having served, Sin might understand, but *this* Maverick didn't know him. Wasn't close to him at all, so opening up simply wasn't going to happen.

"Just like Nic before he died in Kembesh," Ken rasped after I finished telling him all the shit I was going through, and that right there was why I'd told him.

Confirmation.

I'd needed it.

Nic had been a dead man walking long before that battle, and it seemed like fate was destined to fuck with me too. Only, my death wouldn't be honorable like Nic's.

"You're not thinking of doing something stupid, are you?" Ken rumbled, tension gripping his features. His café au lait coloring had blanched a little at my recounting of my symptoms, ones that mirrored Nic's, and he leaned forward, closer to the desk like he could urge me that way to stop myself from doing something I might regret.

He'd done well for himself. His desk was fancy, a rich mahogany beast that suited him, that came complete with ornate photo frames that housed pictures of his wife, Tameka, and some kids that I'd never met because when I knew him, he and Tameka were newlyweds and weren't pregnant. The wall at his back had molding around the walls, and in the center was an oil painting I knew was an original.

He'd gotten out of the army, and unlike some of our fellow

brothers who ended up on the streets or who lost everything, he'd made something of himself, and I was proud of him for that. The street rat who'd enlisted because he had no family, no home, and no future had turned his life around.

Picking up on that, I mumbled, "I'm surprised you still have this number."

He blinked, not anticipating that as my response. "I kept it for my old army buddies. Glad I did now. Never thought I'd be hearing from you today, or ever if I'm being honest."

I grimaced, and yet again, guilt hit me hard. "To me, I saw you the morning I woke up in the hospital. It was before that final showdown in Kembesh."

He sighed. "It's fucked up, man."

"Sure is."

"Please, Maverick, don't..." His mouth puckered up, twisting into a hard line that told me he was trying to fight his emotions and failing. "Mav, don't reach out like this only to take *you* away from me. I don't think I could—"

"I don't know what the fuck I'm doing, Ken. I don't know what to do, where to go, how to be. I'm still a soldier in my head, but I'm not, I'm a biker for an MC.

"Somehow, I'm married and I have a wife who looks at me like I'm breaking her fucking heart every time I glance at her and don't remember her. Then the people who are like my family are under threat—that's the only thing I can focus on right now. That's what's keeping me going."

His jaw tensed, and he rumbled, "If I get you this information, do you think it's going to resolve the problem with your MC?"

"Meaning you won't help me out just in case?" I shook my head. "Please, Ken, don't. We need to know who did it."

"You going to kill them?"

It was my turn for my lips to twist. "Ain't gonna admit to shit over WhatsApp."

He snorted but reached up and pinched the bridge of his nose. "I'll get the results to you, Maverick."

"I appreciate that, brother." Then, softly, I murmured, "Congratulations on the kids."

His smile appeared, and he picked up the frame. He didn't turn it to me, didn't move it so I could see it better or so he could point out the kids' names. He just looked at it and said, "Some days, they're the only reason I get out of bed. We're all still fighting, Maverick. Don't forget that when you're questioning why you're sticking around—it ain't for you, it's for the people you'll leave behind."

And with that, he cut the call, leaving me reeling, because I knew he was right, and I still wasn't sure if I cared either way.

FIFTEEN

ALESSA

I SHOULDN'T HAVE LISTENED to his phone call.

I shouldn't have.

Not only because it was private, and the two men had been reconnecting, but it had also been business.

One thing I'd learned in my time in the States was that men didn't like it when women heard them talk about their business.

But when you were treated like a piece of furniture, nothing more than something to rest your feet on like a footstool or to be ignored like a coat stand, you got used to hearing things you weren't supposed to.

You also got used to eavesdropping because a pissed off owner was an owner to be wary around.

I'd been beaten bloody too many times not to take advantage of whatever information I could get, so I listened. It was a habit. One I needed to break, especially as how disheartened I felt at the end of the conversation, which told me the old adage was true.

Eavesdroppers never heard good of themselves.

In this instance, it was proof I hadn't gotten through to him. Him weeping against me meant nothing.

Or, as Giulia would say, bupkis.

But his conversation triggered something in me, something... fatalistic.

My eavesdropping had taken place by the small patio that overlooked the pool. With its comfortable table area and loungers where I'd been enjoying a pot of tea, unable to help myself from appreciating the landscape of a home that had once belonged to a man who had pissed on me because he could, because I was worth less to him than a toilet. But after the conversation, my appreciation withered and I moved away, heading across the manicured yard toward the main house.

I slipped inside the great room, knowing Kati hated that room and was less likely to see me in there. I could hear her squeals around the house, and despite myself, had to smile. Tiffany's mother had already complained to Lily about it—I'd overheard that conversation too—but Lily didn't appear to mind, and it was she who was keeping us all.

The level of wealth that took, especially when I thought about how often the Prime van was here for Tiffany's mom, and the fact that there were so many of us staying here, boggled my mind.

I'd never had much, and somehow, I'd been transported into a world where whatever I wanted could be purchased in the blink of an eye because I knew that if I wanted something, an expensive trinket or a speaker from Amazon, Lily would buy it for me.

That was the level of her guilt.

Maybe I should capitalize on that, but it wasn't in my nature. I didn't need much.

I just wanted Mav.

Could she Prime him overnight for me?

If that was in the cards, then I'd definitely do it. A Maverick who looked at me with love and affection, the burgeoning hope that spoke of a promise in the future where there'd only been shadows before. A Maverick who held me with tenderness, who curled up to me in sleep where we chased each other's nightmares away...

No, I didn't think Lily could overnight that to me.

If only she could.

The tears pricked my eyes yet again, and I wondered if Maverick was going to reap another miracle in that he'd make me cry when I hadn't managed that feat in years.

"Ghost?"

The soft utterance of my name had me freezing as I crossed the marble-lined hall with its checkerboard floor. Peering over my shoulder, I blinked at Lily and murmured, "Hello."

Her smile was wary. For some reason, since the bombing, she'd grown more hesitant around me. The strides we'd made toward friendship as Tiffany made all of Donovan Lancaster's victims discuss what they'd endured at his hands had disintegrated into dust.

I didn't like that.

Lily was nice. Kind. Good people. My grandmother would have liked her. She'd have called her a *bila vorona*—a white crow, or in English, the black sheep of her family.

And thank God she was too.

"Is everything okay?"

I shot her a tight smile. "Not really."

Distress appeared in her eyes, and I watched as she reached down and twisted the ring that was new to her ring finger. "Can I do anything to help?"

"Would you please drive me somewhere?"

She perked up, shoulders straightening. "Of course," she said eagerly. "Where to?"

I hesitated, but admitted, "Two places if that is not too much to ask."

"It isn't," was her quick response.

Nodding at her, I murmured, "If you say so."

I watched as she dashed down the stairs to meet me on the ground floor. Before she reached me, she diverted to a closet that was tucked under the staircase, one I'd been in and that was larger than the entire first floor of my childhood home, a closet which housed only coats and shoes and gloves...

She returned with a light cardigan hanging over her arm, one that perfectly matched the smart white blouse and tailored pants she wore, and which offset the navy bottoms. On her feet, she sported high heels with enough of a spike to remind me of the days when I'd been forced to wear such shoes.

Yet she had no owner forcing her to wear them... I couldn't see Link asking this torture of her. He loved her too much. Although, men often did things that counteracted what they said, but I didn't believe this was the case with him.

He was patient with her. That patience was clear for anyone to see, and always took my breath away because Lily blossomed around him.

It was strange to think that when she looked so put together. So pristine. She dressed for a magazine shoot and was always ready for anything—case in point now. Yet she was like Pinocchio. A doll. Then he came around and she turned into a woman.

That made me happy for her. I knew what it was to be a doll.

"A guilty pleasure," she told me, dragging my gaze from the shoes to her face. My cheeks heated as her nose crinkled. "I love them."

"Can you drive in them?" I queried warily.

"Of course. I wear them often enough," was her cheerful retort as she shrugged into the slim wool cardigan that finished off her outfit, making her catwalk ready and not prepared for the chores ahead of me.

As she moved toward me, she gestured a little, indicating I should go with her, and together we headed to the garage that was more of a stable for mechanical horsepower.

There were supercars here, names that would make small boys weep with the desire to sit behind the wheel of these vehicles. But as we moved deeper into the garage, I noticed that the first ten or so were severely damaged.

They weren't wrecked, not like they'd been in a car accident, but they were scratched and battered. It took me aback to the point I was gaping at each injured vehicle and trying to cover my surprise because I had no idea what on earth had happened and it wasn't my place to judge.

I trudged behind Lily as she took me to a car that was low to the ground, a bright yellow, and after she grabbed the keys from a placket on the wall, the doors surged up off the ground at the click of a button on the fob. This one wasn't damaged.

"I hate this car," she told me frankly, which had unease slipping inside me. "If I didn't think it'd kill me, I'd crash it."

My brows rose at that. "You'd crash it?"

She hummed. "One of the bastard's favorites," she said mirthlessly as she headed for the driver's seat then, stunning me, she traced the key along the side of the car, scratching the paintwork of the priceless vehicle.

Choking, I dashed around to see what she'd done, and felt like hyperventilating at the devastation she reaped, devastation she'd evidently been reaping on the first ten or so cars in the garage! "Lily! You should not do this!"

Her smile was wicked. "It feels good. Go on, you know you want to." She shoved the keys at me, prompting me to back off like she was handing me a pile of cow dung. "Honestly, Ghost, it'll feel great. Donovan loved this car. It was his pride and joy. He'd come in here and run his hand over it after he'd had it waxed. He always smiled like a little boy when he sat behind the wheel."

The words were too similar to the ones I'd thought mere moments ago, and I blinked at her, accepting she wanted me to do this...

Mouth working, unsure of myself, I hesitated, but she didn't let me. She reached for my hand then folded my fingers around the fob. "Go on," she urged. "It's really cathartic."

Throat thick, I thought about her words and registered that today was a day where I really needed this.

I needed catharsis.

I'd just never thought to start it with this.

With the fob in hand, I measured the weight of it, thought about those times when I'd been picked up by Lancaster's security from the pit of hell, thought about how they'd dragged me into their van like I was a pig ready for slaughter, and thought about the house where I'd been taken, where I'd been abused, where I'd been raped, where I'd been *hurt*.

My jaw clenched, I turned the key around, and very carefully, I pushed the tip into the paintwork just above the door handle.

A shaky sigh escaped me, but it burst into a full breath as I ran the tip of the key around the side of the car, making swirls here and there, going into spiral shapes as I made it all the way to the trunk. When that happened, I went back, scoring deep lines into the bright yellow monstrosity that had been a beloved item of the sadist who'd once owned me.

"Told you it felt good."

I peered at her, aware I was overheated and sweaty, much like I'd been running or something, but it was just... well, I didn't know what it was. Didn't know why I was perspiring like I'd just worked out, but here I was, clammy and sticky, in need of a shower, but that wasn't going to happen.

Not yet.

This was just round one.

"*Tak.*" I nodded abruptly. "It felt good."

She smirked at me. "You sure you can't drive?"

"Not legally. In Ukraine, yes, but not here."

"Shame." She winked at me, then her smile turned wary. "Maybe you'd like to crash it too. Maybe, one day, we can drive it off a cliff together?"

I tilted my head to the side. "Lily, why are you so different than when we were in the bunkhouse?" I reached out and curved my hand around her arm. "There is no need to be. You are not to blame for your family's flaws. We told you this, didn't we?"

She licked her lips. "Yes, you did, and then..."

"Then what?"

"Tatána was found spying. She must have truly hated us to do that. She had to know what she was risking."

"More fool her. I am not like her, and I would appreciate your help in ascertaining that Amara isn't either." My mouth tightened with determination. "If she knows anything, I'll make her talk."

Her eyes widened and she cast me a quick look. "That's where you want to go? To Rachel's place to visit Amara?"

"That's my first errand, yes."

"What about the second errand? Assuming you've got a list."

"I do. Indiana Ink. I would like a tattoo." I tipped up my chin. "It is time."

I sensed her surprise, but she shrugged. "Sounds good to me."

"Do you speak Latin?"

More surprise from her quarter. "I learned it in school. Unfortunately." A smile danced around her lips though. "The teacher was cute." She snorted. "Actually, he looked a little like Link."

It was my turn for my eyes to bug. "No way!"

"Yes," she said with a giggle. "He was blond and rugged... wasted on Latin, IMO."

"Sounds like it."

"Why do you ask?"

"Because I want to know what something means." I hesitated a second as the words were hard to pronounce. "*De oppresso liber.*"

"Let me see... something like, from being an oppressed man, to being a free one."

The breath caught in my lungs. "Truly? This is what it means?"

She nodded. "Yeah. If you translate it word for word. Sounds like a motto to me—maybe for his unit in the army? If it is, then it might translate differently. Where did you see it?"

"Maverick has a tattoo on his back. I've seen his other ones, the bird on his chest, the Native American headpiece on his shoulder, you know? But not that one."

"Must have been the motto of the division he served with. Google it."

I winced. "I have no phone."

A hiss escaped her. "Shit. We need to rectify that. We will after we head to the ink parlor. What are you getting done?"

More unease filled me. "You don't need to buy me things, Lily."

"Sure I do. Everyone needs a phone. What if there's an emergency? I swear, if Tiff hadn't had a phone, we'd never have had our asses saved that day we were almost kidnapped." She shuddered. "You need a phone. And now that Maverick is so sick, what if he needs an ambulance real fast?"

I heaved a sigh. "You said that on purpose."

She smirked. "Sure did." She handed me hers. "Look it up. There's no pin."

I did as she asked. "Special Forces."

"It fits."

It did. I thought about what the motto meant and couldn't help but draw a parallel to me.

Hadn't the MC freed me? An oppressed woman?

I said as much as to Lily who agreed, "It's true. It's uncanny. Before this whole clusterfuck, too, you were both freeing each other from oppression. Sure, it was of a different variety but that doesn't matter, does it?"

"No," I told her softly. "It doesn't."

Her smile made another reappearance as, in a singsong voice, she whispered, *"De oppressae libera."*

"What does that mean?"

"Instead of being about a man, it's about a woman instead. You."

Shivers danced down my spine. "I love it."

"You want that on you too?"

"Yes," I whispered with resolve. "I do." And it felt right. *Bozhe mir*, it felt right. Fitting.

I was a slave freed from her masters.

A shudder replaced the shivers, but she snatched the horrible memories from me by murmuring, "After we go to Indiana Ink, we're going shopping, Ghost. It's about time you got some new clothes. We'll get you the phone then too."

"That isn't necessary. I'm fine with what I have."

She sniffed. "You deserve more than the stuff Giulia bought ages ago."

"You don't need to buy my loyalty, Lily," I told her softly, meaning every word.

Her shrug was dismissive. "I'm not."

"You are."

"I'm truly not." Her smile twisted her lips. "Let's prove that

Amara isn't like Tatána, hmm? Then I have something for both of you."

"What is it?"

"Freedom." Then she moved toward the driver's seat and climbed behind the wheel.

I gaped at her. "You can't just tell me that then say nothing more."

Something gleamed in her eyes that looked suspiciously like amusement. "Sure I can. Hop in, we've got shit to do."

Curious, I obeyed—something I was good at—and headed for the passenger seat. Climbing into the low vehicle was a task in itself. Remembering that Donovan had been in peak physical fitness, he'd still been quite old.

"You should have seen him getting in and out of it," Lily said with a laugh, like she knew where my mind was running. "He had a bad back from weightlifting too much—he was obsessed with looking and staying young. Some days, he'd flop out onto the floor, crawl on his hands and knees, then use the door to get to his feet." She snickered. "It was hilarious. Such a prick. Always interested in appearances and nothing else."

I cut her a look. "Was he never a good father?"

"No. Not before or after Mom's death." Lily grunted. "It is what it is. But I take malicious pleasure in destroying what he loved."

Reaching over, I pressed my hand to her knee. "I understand."

"You will soon enough." She smiled at me, then hit the ignition button. It roared to life and she reversed out of the parking space before we surged out of the garage, down the driveway, through the gates, and onto the Orange Hills subdivision.

This house wasn't part of the massive estate Tiffany's father had built, it was just off to the side, but the access roads to West Orange itself took you through it.

Back home, this kind of place would be like something from a dream. Row after row of mansions, each one set in a prime spot with more land around it than a farm. Behind the high walls that guarded them, you could only see the roofs peeking through the trees, that was how private it was.

And I lived here.

Whether it was temporary or not, I lived here.

Me.

The sex slave.

The victim.

The ghost.

I blinked, taking in the sights because they still impressed me even though this wasn't the first time I'd been down this street. Lily had the radio on semi-loud, which left me and her to our mutual thoughts, but I was okay with that. I was quiet by nurture, and I had a feeling she was too.

Sure, I was curious about what she'd said, but she would tell me in good time. She wasn't a tease. But her words did stir me.

Freedom.

What did that look like?

What did it taste like?

I pondered that, wondering what to expect, what to think. I couldn't imagine being free. Not entirely. The freedom to speak, to eat what I wanted, to use the bathroom without making a special request, the right to move freely around the house, the ability to wear clothes—all of those things were what freedom looked like to me.

But I knew that wasn't how the rest of the world worked.

Those were things they took for granted.

I reached up and tweaked my bottom lip, pinching it as Lily drove us into town. She headed somewhere first, pulling up at a drive-thru before she ordered a coffee and tossed me a look. "What do you want?"

"I don't know."

Her smile turned pained. "Would you like something sweet? Milky? Strong?"

Hesitantly, I asked, "Sweet?"

"You don't have to ask, Ghost." Her eyes were warm. "What do you feel like drinking?"

I thought about it, thought about what I wanted, but I didn't know. Behind us, a car pulled up and tooted the horn, which had me jolting.

"Ignore him. Do you want a water, Ghost?"

Water would be easy.

"Is your drink sweet?"

She smirked. "Sure is."

"May I have what you're having?"

"Of course." She patted my knee, then turned to the intercom to place her order. When the car behind us honked their horn again, she slipped her hand through the open window, raised it high, and I saw her give the driver the finger.

Amusement warred with shock and had me covering my smile as we swung around to the next window where we retrieved large containers filled with mostly whipped cream.

At least, it seemed that way.

As I stared at the mountain of sugary cream, she muttered, "I never realized, until recently, how little you guys went off the compound."

"Some of us more than others," I said grimly, thinking of Tatána. "Have they spoken with you about her? About what she was doing?"

Lily shook her head as she pulled into a parking space. Taking a sip of her drink, she hummed with delight at the concoction which had me wondering how she stayed so slim, before she said, "You know what they're like. They don't talk about these things."

"She wouldn't have been in the office if she wasn't spying."

"I know. Trust me. I asked Link but he won't say anything. Even if I ask nicely." Her bottom lip popped out in a pout. "I'll admit, it gets wearing hearing, 'It's club business, babe. You know I can't talk shop with you.'" She rolled her eyes. "But I guess that's the compromise you have to make to be with these guys."

"I wouldn't really know," I said uncomfortably. "I mean, Maverick used to talk about things in front of me, but the others would ask me to leave the room."

"I think Maverick was born beating a drum to his own particular rhythm," was her wry retort. "I'm not surprised he bent the rules for you."

"I miss him," I said simply, nipping a fleshy part of my bottom lip between my teeth.

"I can only imagine," she whispered sympathetically. "I'm here for you, Ghost, you know that, right?"

"I do." I cleared my throat. "Would you please call me Alessa?"

"Of course." She twisted in her seat. "Why aren't you telling Maverick about your past? Giulia and Tiffany mentioned it, then Link said something that made me realize you're keeping him in the dark..."

"I'd like the chance to be me without the past clogging things up."

"Is that wise?" she rasped. "Lying to him isn't the best way to start anything, Alessa."

"I know, but I-I can't tell him, Lily. I just can't." I fiddled with the lid on my coffee. "He already looks at me like I'm nothing, if I tell him what I went through, I'm terrified I'll see disgust in his eyes as well. I don't think I could deal with that."

"Maverick isn't like that," Lily protested.

"Maverick *wasn't* like that," I corrected. "This Maverick is new to all of us. I don't think even the men really know him. I-I heard him and Link talking the other night when they were out by the pool. Maverick, when he was a soldier, wasn't that close to them. It's only when he returned home that things changed. He's a wild card, Lily, and I can't risk him thinking that I'm dirty."

"You're not dirty."

My jaw tensed. "I am."

"No, you're not," she snapped, and her hand grabbed mine before she squeezed it. "You didn't ask for anything you endured, Alessa. You're a victim, but you survived. You're here and you're in that bastard's car and you just keyed it, and you're going to spend a shit ton of that fucker's money on clothes you don't really need but just *want* today."

"That doesn't make up for what he did to me." I swallowed, and I knew my eyes were raw with remembered pain as I looked at her because her mouth trembled at the sight of me. "What *they* did to me," I corrected softly. "I was like an animal to them. They didn't care, they didn't... I wasn't a human to them, and they treated me as such."

"I didn't kill him, Ghost."

"But you wanted to." Pity for her filled me. To want such a thing was a terrible admission, and yet no father had deserved it more than Donavan Lancaster.

Her mouth tightened. "I know I did. It just didn't work out like that."

"As long as he's dead, that's all that matters," I told her calmly, before I took a sip through the sugary swathes of cream to finally reach coffee.

"You're right, but I wish I'd been the one to do it. I can't ever regret—" She grimaced. "But I kicked him for you. I don't know what they'd done to him, Ghost, but they..." A breath escaped her. "You said they didn't treat you like you were a human, well, I can promise that was served back to him."

"It was?"

Our eyes clashed and held. "It was."

A soft smile played around my lips. "Good."

SIXTEEN

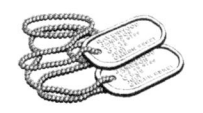

HAWK

THE HANGOVER from hell had me moaning as I flopped off the bed in an effort to go for a piss. When I face planted, I didn't even groan, just crawled on my hands and knees to the john before somehow managing to get to my feet so I could use the bathroom.

Head banging all the while, I didn't even manage to regret the amount of tequila I'd consumed at the bar last night. The Sinner-owned establishment had seen a lot of my ass since the bombing, and it'd be seeing a fuck ton more before this whole mess was over.

I didn't have it in me to be ashamed about that.

Dad was dead.

North, the fucker, had run off with our stepmother.

Giulia was pregnant.

The clubhouse was gone.

I'd nearly died too.

Five facts. Each of them, on their own, difficult to handle, but en masse was just more than anyone could deal with.

The least worrisome was Giulia, but fuck, as a mom? I wasn't sure how that was going to roll, especially not with Nyx as the baby daddy. Should I expect Junior as a nephew? The ultimate problem child? Or would things somehow turn out for the best like I hoped they would for her sake?

Then there was North. My twin. The one person I'd shared everything with, yet the cunt didn't even tell me he was boning Dad's Old Lady, and he didn't even say good-fucking-bye when he went AWOL.

I hated that my eyes welled up at that. Christ, such a pussy, but North was my shadow. And I was his. We were a team. His dumbass got us into shit, but he was the charmer. I was the fixer. We worked well together, always had and, I'd thought, always would.

Acting as a single entity was harder than I could say, and I was struggling. So if I drank more tequila than was wise, so fucking be it.

When I'd finished in the bathroom, I didn't return to bed. Jonesing for something to drink, I trudged out of my borrowed bedroom and into the hall.

We were staying at the club's lawyer's place. I was pretty sure that wasn't a part of her retainer, but there was something funky going on between her and Rex anyway.

I remembered Rachel from when I was a kid, from when I'd lived here before Mom had taken us away from Dad. She'd been a scrawny thing then, all big eyes and bitter smiles. Even though I was younger than her, she was still smaller than me, and I knew that was because she'd been malnourished as a little girl.

To this day, she was small-boned, but fuck, it looked good on her. If the Prez wasn't boning her, he really fucking should.

Scratching my balls as I strolled into the kitchen, I came face-to-face with a scenario that had me jerking to a halt.

Christ, my defenses were way too down if I hadn't registered this clusterfuck.

My baby sis was standing by the counter, wearing an evil smirk as she watched Ghost, whose face was stern with resolve and whose hands were fisted in Amara's hair, slam Amara into the kitchen table. Beside Giulia, Lily hovered, her nerves plain to see even if she wasn't stopping this...

I frowned, then barked, "What the fuck is going on here? Giules?"

They all froze, whipping around to stare at me, and, no word of a fucking lie, I came across one of the most surreal moments of my life.

In the country farmhouse kitchen, complete with scrubbed oak beams that I'd no idea where they'd come from in the middle of fucking West Orange, a matching table that looked ancient, and a dresser loaded down with china dishes, as well as a host of counter space and cupboards, it was like watching a *Sons of Anarchy* episode in an *Architectural Digest* photoshoot.

"I'm too hungover for this," I muttered under my breath, regretting the bottle of tequila I'd had because I should have had twice as much. When dealing with Giulia, it was always wise to go in with double the recommended dose of anything.

Rubbing the back of my neck, I headed deeper into the kitchen as my sister muttered, "Carry on, Alessa, you've got some extracting to do."

To punctuate that, Ghost immediately obeyed by slamming Amara's face into the table once more.

My brows rose. "Extracting? You don't need to do shit. Link already talked to her yesterday." Then, as an afterthought, I asked, "Who the fuck is Alessa?"

"Me," said Ghost.

I blinked. "Oh." I mean, it didn't take a fucking genius to realize that Ghost wasn't her real goddamn name. Still, in my hungover state, it felt like a massive leap.

Dumbly, I peered at Amara who, I noticed, wasn't struggling.

"She wouldn't betray us," I rumbled easily, before striding over to the fridge where there was OJ I badly needed to consume.

"How the fuck do you know that?" Giulia groused. "You a mind reader or something?"

I flipped her the bird because it was either that or get mad about her sass. Fucking women—I swear, we only bred them insane in my family. Mom was just as bad... Hard to believe I missed her.

This year had been the shittiest of my life.

Mom dead, Dad dead, North gone...

How were Giulia and I the only ones left standing?

Blowing out a breath at the thought, I muttered, "She's got a crush on you, ain't she? Why would she jeopardize that?" And what a tragedy that was.

Amara had the finest tits a man could wish for in a fuck buddy. I'd seen pornstars with smaller racks than hers. They'd been unimpressive when she'd first arrived, but that was what happened when you starved a woman, I guessed—their tits disappeared first.

After all this time with the Sinners, she'd filled out again, and she'd filled out fine. It wasn't the first time I'd noticed either.

She and that bitch, Tatána, always scurried around the place like frightened mice. That was why we were all reeling from the fact that Tatána had betrayed us with that cunt David—the prick who'd worked for Nyx's sister at her tattoo parlor.

When had shit become so complicated?

Had it always been that way or was there some author out there, some divine being that was deciding to fuck with our lives?

Talk about goddamn cruel.

I grunted at the thought, mentally flipped that unknown being the bird as well because they deserved it as much as Giulia did, and ground out, "You can't be serious? Sure as hell I'm not the only one who noticed it."

As tragic as it was that Amara was gay because those tits were wasted on another woman, it fit. I knew the 'girls' had all been through things that Satanists would consider cruel, so why wouldn't they be anti-men?

Alessa/Ghost whispered something in Ukrainian, the hand she had in Amara's hair tightening to the point where her knuckles bled white. I winced in preparation for the woman's face being slammed into the table yet again, but even I jolted in surprise when Alessa dragged her back and tipped her so she was peering up at her, her head perpendicular to the floor.

Amara squealed before quickly gushing, *"Tak!"* I didn't have to speak the language to hear the misery in her voice. And now that I thought about it, Amara wasn't even scared by the firm grip Alessa had on her hair or the way her face was being smashed into the table.

I frowned at that because even though I knew what they'd gone through, how bad did it have to be if this kind of treatment didn't illicit much of a response?

Uneasily, I stared at the scene once more. Giulia was a sicko, so I disregarded her reaction, Lily was definitely nervous which told me she knew they shouldn't be doing this as it appertained to club business. As for Alessa, she was calm. So was Amara.

Weird.

With a carton of juice in my hand, I leaned back against the fridge and said, "Leave her alone. She didn't do shit."

"You didn't think Tatána did either, and this isn't *Old Man* business," was all Giulia said, but her eyes were mean. "This is Old Lady business."

I scowled at her. "Since when is that even a fucking thing?"

"Since I became an Old goddamn Lady." Her chin jutted out,

and I got the feeling that if I'd been nearer, she'd have gladly head-butted me.

Wouldn't be the first fucking time.

"If you think I'm gonna be like Ma and am gonna let you fuckers treat me like I'm a walking pussy and womb, you've got another thing coming."

I rolled my eyes. "As if anyone would even dare."

She smirked. "That's how it's gonna stay. Bitches deal with bitches. How it should be."

Staring at Alessa whose hand was still firmly clasped in Amara's hair as they muttered shit to each other in Ukrainian, or was it Russian? I didn't have a fucking clue. To be honest, it was kind of hot though. All those guttural sounds, the way Alessa held her, how Amara submitted...

Shit, now was not the time to get a boner. Mostly because I needed all the blood in my brain to deal with Giulia.

"She ain't scared," I pointed out. "How you going to get anything out of her?"

"He's right," Lily said softly.

"Tells you what they've been through, doesn't it?" Giulia retorted, but her cheeks were pinched, and in her eyes I saw the shadows Nyx had mostly chased away.

Boggled my mind that the club's enforcer turned VP had done that.

Trust Giulia to find comfort in a psychopath's arms. Ma'd be proud.

Not.

"It does," Lily agreed, her tone sad.

We all knew she'd been through as much shit as the girls. Not that it was a competition. Although, where the women had been stored was a thousand times worse than the mansion Lily lived in, but gilded cages still required the prisoner shit and piss in them, didn't they? From what I'd heard, though, the girls had literally had to do that.

Link had told me once that they'd been covered in it. Mostly it fucked with my mind that the girl we'd buried, on the same day as my father, had been left to die in her cage, while Amara, Alessa, and the now dead Tatána had lived alongside her.

Shuddering at the thought and deciding I really needed to watch SpongeBob after this, I muttered, "What does she say, Alessa? Does she know what Tatána was doing?"

At my words, she took a step back and relinquished her hold on the other woman's hair. I had no idea why my question was the trigger, but she muttered, her tone still thick with an accent I wasn't used to hearing from her, "She says she knew Tatána was sneaking around."

I frowned. "Why didn't you say something?"

Amara didn't move from her place at the table. She rolled her head on her forehead though, so she was face down against it. Her hands, neat and tidy things, with clean, short nails, were pressed on either side of her. It was kind of like looking at a drunk mime artist.

"Tatána said she was looking for her own Maverick. What was I supposed to say?"

My brows rose at that, and I cast my sister a look. "She was screwing around with a biker?"

Amara shook her head, rocking it from side to side against the oak table. I wished she'd stop, to be honest. It was weird, and if I said that, then it really goddamn was.

"No," Alessa translated for her. "I didn't think so. But I wasn't sure. The bikers scared her, but she was jealous of Alessa. Said she wanted that kind of security."

"She was the kind of woman who coveted," Alessa concurred, but a flash of grief splashed across her features, settling in to darken her eyes, making her mouth turn down at the corners. Who the fuck could blame her?

Tatána had coveted what she had, and now it was clear to see from her devastation that Alessa coveted what *Ghost* had.

I'd never really known Maverick that well, what with him practically being glued to the attic and my being a prospect, so I had all the shit jobs in the clubhouse. But I knew enough to see a man in love, to see that he was head over heels for his girl...

I couldn't even imagine what Alessa was going through, and though I was sure she wouldn't want it, she had my sympathy. Loss like that was impossible to get over especially if what I'd overheard Nyx telling Rex was true—the doctors didn't know if he'd ever regain his memory.

How fucked up was that?

"Are you gonna bring out the corkscrews now?" I asked warily. "Dig 'em under her nails, make sure you squeezed all the information out of her?"

Giulia huffed. "We're not the Spanish Inquisition."

"No? Just looks like it to me then, huh?" I strolled over to the table, dumped the juice on there and gently, carefully, so I didn't scare the shit out of her, rested my hand on Amara's shoulder. She jolted like my fingers were connected to a live wire, then she sat up, her gaze darting to mine.

It was my turn to react like there was a live wire connecting me to her.

Jesus.

Those fucking eyes.

How had I never noticed them before?

How had I never goddamn seen them?

They were like ice. Smoky gray with hints of white, making the black of her pupils pierce me like a knife to the goddamn gut.

The flashbang had me rearing back like she'd shocked me with a cattle prod, and I twisted away from her and snarled at my sister, "Whether this is bitches' business or not, leave her the fuck alone. The council vetted her." And then, though I wanted to storm off, to return to my bed, to fall back into the misery of my hangover, I couldn't. I knew those fucking eyes would haunt me.

I had a feeling they always goddamn would.

So, crouching in front of her, taking note of how she watched me warily, her lack of trust evident despite the fact I'd just ordered the other women to leave her the hell alone, I pressed a hand to the back of her head, ignoring her wince as I gently stroked my fingers through the tangled locks of her hair. She blinked at me, those snowy eyes of hers shielded by sooty lashes that were so thick I had to wonder what they'd feel like whispering against my skin if she kissed me, and I asked, "Let's get some peas for your forehead."

Her brow furrowed. "Peas?" she asked thickly, repeating my words and vocalizing them like a child would.

"Frozen ones. For the swelling." I knew she didn't speak English, but this close, with her eyes pinned on mine, I got a different feeling.

Did she understand more than she let on?

Who could blame her for trying to find security in hiding how much of our language she spoke?

I cut Ghost a look, annoyed at her for having put Amara through this. Christ, after what they'd both been through, how could she have done that to her?

Then, as shitty as it was, I recognized what she'd done was actually good for the club. She cared about the Sinners' interests, and that mattered. It mattered a hell of a lot, especially in the face of their 'sister's' betrayal.

"Translate for me."

If Alessa recognized my irritation, she ignored it and did as I asked. The look in Amara's eyes didn't change, and I knew that a 'look' was something that could easily be interpreted. How did anyone show an emotion through the striations in a pupil? But I just knew... call it some sixth goddamn fucking sense, but she understood me.

She didn't need the translation.

I surged to my feet once more, retreating to the freezer where I grabbed two bags of frozen carrots as there were no peas to be found, and I returned and pressed it to the back of her head even though she'd taken the cautious step of sitting up. Pushing the other against the goose egg on her forehead, I murmured, "It's okay to settle back as you were. I'll make sure they don't hurt you."

Giulia snorted at that, so I shot her a glower. Her quirked brow had my scowl darkening, but there was no frightening Giulia. She hadn't been born with the necessary brain cells to find fear in dangerous men—if she did, she wouldn't be Nyx's Old Lady.

Giving her up as a lost cause, I graced Lily and Alessa with a gimlet stare. When it didn't work on either of them, I had to give the fuck up.

Trouble was... much as I hated what Alessa had done here, what my sister and Lily had been involved in, each of them was a victim. They knew what it meant to be on the other side of a man's fist, but Lily and Giulia, Ghost until recently, were secure in the protection of their men's arms.

Even as it impeded my ability to threaten them into compliance, I couldn't be anything other than glad for them and sad for Amara.

SEVENTEEN

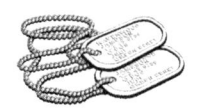

ALESSA

I SHOULD PROBABLY FEEL bad for hurting Amara the way I did, but I didn't.

The feel of her hair in my grip, the rush of power as I forced her to talk was intoxicating. But for all that, it wasn't something I could do again.

I'd done it this time because only I could comprehend what Amara had been through, only I knew how to get to her. Violence wasn't the way, domination was, and I knew the brothers would never understand that. How could they? Link still hesitated to put his hand on my shoulder whenever he approached me. Even when they were mad, when they were furious, reeling from the devastating blow that had been dealt them, I knew they'd never really take things to another level.

Not without outright proof that she'd done something wrong anyway.

She'd thought we weren't being serious at first, that was when I'd grabbed her by the hair, forced her to take a seat, and slammed her face into the table. That was as aggressive as I'd been, but it was plenty enough.

I wouldn't want to repeat the action, but would for Maverick.

He needed to know the truth? Needed to know who was conspiring against his MC? Well, I'd help him with that endeavor.

Hearing him tell a friend he'd served with that was the only thing he had to get up for in the morning, I realized I had to act. Once the threat was neutralized, perhaps he'd make an attempt on his life. Before that happened, I needed to prove to him that he had more than the MC to live for.

He had me.

Hearing Amara say that Tatána was jealous of me, that she'd wanted what I had with Maverick, had reminded me of the keening loss I was dealing with.

Maverick lived. But my Maverick seemed dead to me. He was in there somewhere though—I had to believe that—and that side of him was what I needed to appeal to.

The one thing that hadn't changed was his love for his MC brothers, so that was where I'd start.

If they were his Achilles' heel, then that was where I'd aim my attention.

"Storm? What the hell are you doing here?"

Giulia's caustic question had my lips twitching, and Lily choked out a laugh as we walked into the tattoo studio where Giulia was working now, and where the ex-VP of this Sinners' chapter was hovering at the front desk she'd recently begun manning for her sister-in-law.

Indy snorted. "See, this is why I hired you, Giulia. For you to greet my clients."

She snickered. "Then you got the best employee ever. But seriously, Storm, what the fuck are you doing here?"

"Getting fucking ink, Giulia. What the hell's it got to do with you?"

She and Indy shared a look, and though I was curious, my interest stirred deeper when Indy shook her head and Giulia's nostrils flared like she was angry.

Wiry, like he was coiled with energy he couldn't burn off, Storm jiggled his keys, drawing my attention his way. He was a handsome brute, slightly leaner than the other brothers and with a mop of hair that was longer than the last time I'd seen him, tangled waves that bobbed around his ears and dipped to his shoulders.

For all that he was good-looking, he was also a perennial cheater. Which made him quite, quite ugly in my opinion. Especially as I'd grown close to his wife, Keira, when she'd had to move back to the compound because she was saving up for nursing school.

"Look, should you really be wasting time?"

"Why? What's my time got to do with you? I can't work twenty-four fucking seven."

"You should be spending time with Cyan and Keira," she argued.

Indiana heaved a sigh. "Giulia—"

"No. He has a right to know." Her chin jerked up. "Some truths need to be liberated."

Indy blanched somewhat, and I'd admit to being totally confused as to what was happening here. There was definitely an undercurrent that Lily and I weren't involved in, and to which we were helpless bystanders.

"What are you talking about?" Storm snapped, his patience wearing thin.

Giulia had that effect on most of the brothers. Well, apart from Nyx. He was the only one who seemed to find her amusing. I'd often watched their dynamic and wondered how a man like him—one who wielded respect and power around the club like it was a scepter and he was king—allowed this pocket rocket to wrap him around her finger.

Indiana cleared her throat. "Hasn't Keira mentioned it?"

"Mentioned what?" Lily chimed in, her interest piquing as mine was.

I'd only come in for ink, but now this was happening, I wanted to know more too.

"Lodestar's still looking into it, isn't she?" Indy retorted. "Her initial findings were innocent."

Giulia's eyes narrowed. "And you and I both know you wouldn't overreact."

Indy scowled right back. "He told you."

"Course he fucking told me." Giulia hissed out a breath as she slid her hand over her hair. The gesture was explosive, like she was trying to stop herself from doing something more violent.

I wasn't sure what was going on, aside from the fact that the already bloodthirsty woman appeared angrier than usual. To be honest, I'd thought she was simply hormonal. Some pregnant women craved candy, maybe Giulia was a true vampire...

But apparently not.

Apparently, something had happened to make her that way.

"Would you stop talking in circles? I've got places to be," Storm rumbled, his gaze slipping between the two women.

Indy and Giulia were similar in nature. Both of them strong, both of them the kind of people who head-butted their problems rather than avoid them. *Govno*, why couldn't I be more like them?

"If you don't tell him, I will," Giulia rumbled. "Nyx should have said something when it was clear Keira hadn't."

"Not our place," Indy pointed out.

"Yeah, it is. If you want Nyx to keep his promise to you."

A hiss escaped her. "Jesus, Giulia. Low blow."

"You can't ask Nyx to stop doing what he does best and not expect him to find release somewhere."

"This is getting annoying," Lily complained. "Storm's right. Stop talking in circles, dammit! What the hell's going on?"

But Storm's eyes had sharpened at Giulia's comment. Even I knew that Nyx had an addiction to torturing pedophiles... that Indy had asked him to stop was enough to make the ex-VP cease his bristling and gain his full attention.

"Why would you ask him to stop with his crusade?" Storm asked softly, his attention on Indy.

"Because he has a baby on the way, and he needs to make sure that child is safe. That's his number one duty."

Storm scowled. "He can do that and burn his demons at the stake at the same time."

"Not if he's serving life in a federal prison," Giulia growled, her booted foot tapping against the floor as her patience thinned.

"I asked him to protect his child from what I went through." Indy tipped her chin up, and in her eyes, there was a fire, one that threatened to raze Storm to the ground if he wasn't careful.

"Kevin got to you?" Storm choked out, his hands dropping to the front desk as he leaned over it and into Indy's space. "Jesus fuck, Indy. Why the hell didn't you tell us?"

Before she could answer, his cell buzzed. I thought he was going to ignore it, but Indy grumbled, "When Metallica plays 'One' on your phone, we both know that's Rex."

He frowned. "This is important—"

"The bastard's dead," she rasped, but her gaze tangled with Giulia's again, and even I felt the scorch of the warning in that glance. "He can't hurt us now."

Storm hissed under his breath, but he picked up his cell.

"Rex?" He winced at whatever he heard, then he covered the base of the phone and muttered, "I gotta go. I'll be back, Indy."

"Can't wait," she grumbled. "Remember the aftercare? It's been a while since you last had ink," she called out as he headed to the door. "Enjoy," she tacked on with a wicked cackle.

Waving her off, he growled, "I remember. Bye, ladies."

Before he could leave, even though his glower would make a demon wary, and even though it was clear Indy needed us, I had to ask him something, so I grabbed his arm and watched as he stared down at my hand with a frown.

"Ghost?" he queried, his tone polite.

"Maverick asked me about someone, and I didn't have an answer... He wanted to know where Scarlet was."

Storm's nostrils flared at that. "She ran off about four years ago."

"You don't know where to?"

He shook his head. "If he remembers her at all, he'd know trying to keep track of her was like trying to stalk a butterfly." His mouth pursed. "Christ, been a long time since someone asked after her."

"I'm sorry," I said softly. "I didn't mean to hurt you."

He just grunted, carefully detached his forearm from my grip, then headed on out.

As I watched him go, Lily shuffled over to me. "Who's Scarlet?"

"His sister. Someone Maverick brought up the other night."

"She was a bitch," Indy called out.

Giulia snorted. "You think everyone's a bitch."

"Nah, I ain't that dismissive. She was no better than a club-whore, but she got away with murder because she was Storm's sister and used to bat her big eyes to get out of shit. Never liked her. Stone and I used to hang around with the guys, but she didn't —she was the high school bike."

My mouth dropped open. "That's a mean thing to say."

She winced. "Yeah, it was. We've all got pasts. I shouldn't judge, I just... well, I never liked her."

Because I understood that, and just because you were cut from the same cloth as someone didn't mean you had to get along—case in point me with Tatána and Amara—I murmured, "Indy? What you were saying earlier..."

"I know you mean well, Ghost, but I really can't deal with you being sweet to me."

I reached over the desk, much as Storm had, then placed my hand on her arm. "I'm here if you need me."

Her jaw tensed. "Thank you. I appreciate that."

Lily whispered, "I'm here too, Indy."

"I could kill you for bringing this subject up, Giulia," Indy snapped, scrubbing a hand over her face. When she did, the new tattoo on her arm was clearly visible. A little pink, just starting to scab over.

"What happened?" I asked softly, watching as she peered down at where I was pointing.

She blew out a breath. "Cruz branded me."

"No way!" Lily said with a laugh. "Oh God, that's amazing news."

"It really is," I agreed with a soft smile when I saw the war going down in her eyes. I knew how she felt—like a bull caged in a ring, one that wanted to tear some matador's head off, but the guy hadn't shown up for the gig.

Indy shot us both tight smiles. "Stone was pissed at me for not telling her immediately, so thanks for not giving me shit, guys. She hasn't answered a call from me in at least five days."

Giulia moved over to the desk and sat on the edge of it, all without saying a word. She just stared at Indy, then murmured, "I want to help Nyx stick to his promise, Indy. You deserve blood, but I think him knowing you and Cruz are together will help." She hitched a shoulder. "Aside from that, I'm just glad you and he are an item."

"Why?" she rumbled warily.

"Because if he's what made you finally speak up about what you went through then that's a cause for celebration."

"Thought you'd be mad at me for telling Nyx, for breaking down his guard."

"He's not the man he used to be," Giulia said simply. "He's *my* Old Man now, and I protect what's mine. That includes you, sister-in-law."

"God help me," Indy said with a groan, but I sensed she was reluctantly amused by Giulia's claim.

Lily cleared her throat. "What were you talking about with Storm?"

"Indy caught Cyan with this guy... she thinks he's grooming her." Giulia twisted to look at both Lily and me. "Lodestar's been hunting the bastard down, and apparently he used to be a pastor, worked with underprivileged kids."

"No fucking way," Indy growled. "That's not happening. He's no pastor. You just have to look at him to know he's bad news."

"I haven't seen him," Giulia said with a shrug. "Either way, you can't judge on appearances, Indy. You know that better than me, and look at Nyx. We know what he's done, but you wouldn't think he was a psycho looking at him, would you?"

Indy's lips twitched. "No, you wouldn't."

"You do know you just admitted to loving a psychopath, don't you?" Lily asked wryly.

Giulia shrugged. "He's mine. That's the only label I need to know."

"What are we going to do about this man?" I interrupted. "I'm not sure I know what grooming means. Isn't that what happens with a dog? Where they get shampooed and brushed?"

Three sets of eyes turned to gawk at me, but it was Indy who, with a shake of her head, said, "That's exactly what it isn't, Ghost."

"She wants to be known by her real name," Lily tacked on softly, making me smile despite the concerning nature of this conversation.

Indy shrugged. "Fine with me. Never did understand it. You're not a fucking ghost. You're alive. You're a goddamn survivor. Trust Link to come up with that bullshit for a nickname—"

"Hey!" Lily protested, evidently about to stand up for her man.

"Ladies!" Giulia grumbled. "We're getting off topic. Alessa, it's hard to remember you're foreign with how well you speak English, but we're talking about when an old pervert talks to a young child and makes them think the pervert is good people when they're not. Makes them trust him, gets into their confidence."

"So he can abuse them?" I asked warily.

Giulia, her expression ripe with disgust, nodded. "Bastards."

"*Khuy na ne!* We have to stop this! We can't let this carry on. We must do something!"

I felt like my face was bright pink with rage, my heart was pounding, and disgust was crawling through my system like a million centipedes had overtaken my body. The rage consumed me, firing me up as if I had a bunch of embers under my feet that my bare soles were walking on.

Lily reached out and grabbed my hand. "Alessa! Calm down!" she barked, and I jerked back, surprise hitting me at her sharp tone.

I turned to look at Indy and Giulia, both of whom had wide eyes.

"You were speaking in Ukrainian, honey," Lily said gently. "Are you okay? You kind of went crazy on us there?"

"I-I did?" I rasped, staring at the other women, reading their concern and surprising myself by finding comfort in it. Lily's touch didn't repel me, not like a strange man's might have, but I reached up, cupped her wrist, and squeezed her gently. "I'm okay."

She shook her head. "No. You're not. What happened? You just kind of..."

"Exploded into Ukrainian and did some ranting and raving?" Giulia inserted dryly, but I could see she was worried for me too.

"I-I don't know what happened." My head was buzzing though.

One time, I remembered walking up the stairs in front of Donovan Lancaster. He'd pushed me because I wasn't walking fast enough in the device he had me in, and when my knees had collided with the stone steps, my brain had just turned to mush. I remembered waking up on the floor in a pile of limbs, having passed out from the pain. It was strange because I'd endured worse at his hands, but for some reason, that had pushed me into unconsciousness.

Feeling shaken, wretched at the thought of Storm's daughter being groomed, I whispered what I'd said in Ukrainian, "We have to do something."

Giulia dipped her chin. "We do."

"But what? What do we do?" Lily asked, and I saw her eyes were pink. She'd been abused as a child, so she knew what it felt like.

I prayed to God that her father was being raped in hell by demons. That was the fate he deserved.

Indy licked her lips. "We could threaten him?"

"How?" I asked, but I saw Giulia's eyes light up with interest.

"We can discuss it while you get your ink, Alessa," she said brightly.

So we did.

And by the end of the ink being completed, we'd cried, sworn, and plotted together.

Lord help me if that didn't make them feel more like sisters to me than Kati did.

EIGHTEEN

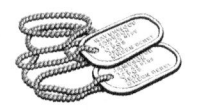

MAVERICK

"WHERE THE HELL HAVE YOU—"

Before I could finish, I watched as Alessa lifted a baseball bat high and let it collide with the mega expensive Lamborghini Veneno. As I stood there, she did it a few more times, destroying the bodywork of a car that probably cost two or so million, *used*, and didn't stop until the glass of the windshield was smashed, and the mirrors were hanging like limp lettuce on either side of the car.

When she was done, she was panting, her hair had come loose from the high ponytail she'd been wearing, and her breasts were heaving with the effort of wielding the baseball bat with the intent to cause as much destruction as was physically possible.

It was the first time I'd really seen her be out of control. Even in the aftermath of my waking up and almost choking her, she'd been gulping for air, but there'd been a calmness about her, an acceptance...

The thought put me on edge because I knew that meant she was used to abuse.

Accustomed to mistreatment.

Here, now, however, she looked like a warrior. Like she wanted to destroy, and though a man joined the army for many reasons, to make war wasn't one of them. To fight for peace, sure. But that didn't mean the soldier didn't get a boner when Wonder Woman came running toward him. One who was intent on wreaking chaos on a harmless supercar that, even my biker self, could drool over.

Her gaze was defiant as she stared at me, like she was expecting criticism but wasn't going to take it. Who could blame her? She was a grown ass woman, who, somehow, was my wife too.

It was a surreal thought.

Surreal because, at that moment, she became more than just a label. More than just a weight around the neck of a man who was drowning, a man who happened to be me. She became a woman.

Flesh and bones. Blood and muscle.

Tits and...

Christ.

Now was not the time to recognize just how fine she was in her dishevelment.

Because I had to look away or I'd get a hard-on, and I was in no state of mind to deal with that, I switched focus and came across about ten or so supercars that were as wrecked as the Lamborghini.

"What the fuck?" I rasped, taking in the ruined vehicles that would probably cost more than this palatial house did on the real estate market.

"It's therapeutic," Lily told me, her voice prim. I twisted around and caught sight of her over by the doorway to the garage where I realized she'd been standing, watching Alessa destroy one of her cars.

"You told her to do that?" I rumbled.

"Why are you speaking around me?" Alessa demanded, dumping the bat which clinked a few times as it collided with the ground. Christ, I felt each clink in my skull. Though the pain was more manageable after her help, this wasn't making it better. "I have a voice," she snapped.

I firmed my lips into a line I knew was loaded with disapproval. "I know you do. I'm just not sure if I trust that voice when you've obviously lost your mind."

"I told her to do it, Maverick," Lily countered. "I wanted her to do it. But you might be right. She *has* lost her mind."

"*Pizda*, Lily. Don't bring it up."

She shrugged. "Who in their right mind turns down a bank account with ten million in it?"

My eyes bugged out. "Huh?" I whipped around to face her. "Ten million? What the hell are you talking about?"

Lily straightened up but her arms moved around her stomach like she was comforting herself. From what, I wasn't sure. The past, the present, Alessa's rejection? Who the fuck knew? These women were obviously insane.

I was definitely bisexual, but men were so much more fucking rational that I'd spent a good chunk of my sex life burning off my needs with other dicks. This just confirmed why guys were easier lays.

"I want her to have independence from you, from the club too. I want her to know that she can do whatever she wants. Even if she has to return to Ukraine—"

My brow furrowed and tension hit me. My ribs felt constricted, and suddenly, it was really hard to choke out, "What the fuck are you talking about? Return to Ukraine? Why would she do that?"

"I don't know if I'll be allowed to stay here, Maverick," Alessa answered grimly, her cheeks still pink from exertion. Fine strands of gold clung to her forehead where sweat beaded. They also clung to her throat, and I'd admit my fingers itched to release the locks from their inadvertent prison.

Christ, she was beautiful.

The name Alessa suited her actually. It was a pretty name for a woman who was so much more beautiful than pretty could even begin to describe. There was something about her that was frail and delicate, but the golden blonde hair, and the angelic features with their slightly pointy edges that made her look like a fairy—I had to admit, she was gorgeous.

In a weird way, she reminded me of my mom. Which sounded skeevy and positively oedipal considering Alessa was my type, but skeevy or not, I shoved two fingers up at Freud. I hadn't wanted to bone my mom, and I wasn't sure if I wanted to bone Alessa, no matter how hot she was.

Not that my dick was on board with that statement. Not with her looking like a warrior angel intent on finding justice—

"Why won't you be allowed to stay here?" I parroted before my mind could be swept out from under me by thoughts of *her* under me.

What the hell was going on with my head? I didn't think I could blame this on the CTE either.

"Because they might think we only married for a green card," was her patient reply. "If we were hauled in now and they questioned you, they'd think our marriage was fake, wouldn't they?"

That had Lily huffing. "Which is why I want Alessa to know that she can do whatever the hell she wants. With that amount of money, she's free to buy her green card."

Unease swept over my wife's features. "I don't want to be like them."

Lily shrugged, appearing to know exactly who 'they' were. "If you can't beat them, join them," she retorted. "I'm sure as hell not about to throw their money out. I want to use it for *good*. You can too, Alessa. You can do whatever you want with it.

"Donate eight million to a charity, use the other million for Kat and her schooling, then secure your future with that final million and know that you never have to bow down to any man again." She sniffed at that, then shot me a defiant glance that had my hackles rising.

Like I was doing any of this on purpose, for fuck's sake.

"Look, Lily—"

"No, Maverick, I *won't* look. You've treated Alessa like shit. Maybe that's because she's a stranger, and I understand that she is to you, but the guys you love like brothers have told you what she is to you, and you still aren't treating her the way she deserves. Why the hell would I want her to think she was tied to you forever when this you isn't whom she tied herself to, hmm?"

Her snarled retort had me gritting my teeth.

She had a fucking point.

Goddamn her.

Before either woman could say another word, I stormed off, not wanting to deal with Lily or Alessa, not wanting to deal with how hot under the collar she'd made me, or how Lily was right— why would Alessa want to stay tied to me? Why, when I was as much of a stranger to her as she was to me?

But the thought of her leaving... No, that didn't sit well with me either.

I wasn't sure why when she meant nothing to me, even if her kindnesses over the past few days had brought some relief to my life, but I didn't want her to go.

As the shadows of the garage, with its harsh lighting that messed with my eyes, gave way to sunlight, I winced as spots danced around my vision. I wanted to run back inside the house, but my head wouldn't let me. Just crossing the neat courtyard was enough to make sweat pop out above my top lip, and I nearly fucking wept when I finally made it to the front door.

Pressing my back to it, I took some deep breaths, trying to calm down, trying to stop that strange throbbing in my head from overtaking me, and just when I was sure I was about to lose the fight, I felt a hand on mine.

"Can I help?"

The voice was soft, childish. I peered down, way down, at a little girl who was Alessa's image—if Alessa didn't brush her hair and had constantly filthy cheeks.

"There's no helping me," I told her rawly, then because there was way too much emotion in that statement when she'd only been trying to be kind, I managed to force a wobbly smile before rasping, "Thank you for offering though. That was sweet of you."

She narrowed her eyes at me for a second, then murmured, "If you don't let me help you, I'll tell Star on you."

I sniffed. "What kind of threat is that?"

"A big one," she retorted. "Star's the best at punishments. She knows exactly what you don't want to lose and will take it away."

She'd always been a bitch.

Maybe my distaste was clear in my expression, because Katina sidled up to me and said, "I can tell you've been in her bad books too."

"Yeah," I said gruffly. "A few times. What did you do?"

"Nothing. Yet."

My pounding temples couldn't put up with this much longer. "Meaning you've done something she hasn't found out about yet?"

"Exactly." She heaved a sigh. "Anyway, I can talk to you all day or I can help you. Which do you prefer?"

I let my fingers fold around hers. "Lead the way."

She beamed a smile that was brighter than the sun and just as painful to behold because it was the spitting image of her sister.

A sister I really didn't need to think about just now.

"Star doesn't want me to know, but I'm not stupid. You're different now than you used to be, so I mean, how couldn't I tell?" she groused. "She knows I'm smart, so she should have told me the truth instead of me having to poke through all her things."

"I'm okay," I lied.

Her snort was derisive. "Yes, Maverick, you look it." Then, her derision disappeared and a flash of vulnerability overtook her expression. "I was glad you were going to be my big brother."

"You were?" I asked, surprised by her remark.

"Yes. But then you turned into a big jerk." Her mouth twisted, and a pugnacious cast creased her expression. "Now I don't want you to be my big brother until you start acting like one."

"How are they supposed to act?"

"Protective, of course." She huffed with disgust. "Don't you know anything?"

Not about being a goddamn big brother when I was an only child. "How old are you again?" I grumbled.

"Why does everyone always ask me that?" she muttered. "Don't you know it's rude to ask a lady how old she is?"

"It'd be rude to puke on a lady too, so if you don't want that, I'd hurry the hell up."

Her eyes flared wide at that, but she managed to hustle us forward. I didn't put much weight on her, but for some stupid reason, the feel of her small, sweaty hand in mine gave me the drive to stagger through the hall like I was coming off a ten-hour bender. When we made it into the great room, she didn't lead me to the doorway that would take us into the yard, she aimed for the sofa.

It was a long black thing, more cushions than made sense, and it looked better than my bed ever could.

Accepting the wise decision not to push it much more, I let her help me down onto it, let her grab my feet and lower them onto the cushions, even fucking let her take off my boots.

"Your feet stink."

"They don't," I retorted numbly.

"Well, they do to me," she complained, before she fell silent.

Thinking she'd left, I placed my forearm over my eyes and tried to think about anything other than passing out. If I could just relax, maybe nap, then that would stop the inevitable from happening.

To some people, there might not be much of a difference between the two, but to me, there fucking was. Thirty goddamn years, that's what.

"Do you need Lessie?"

The soft whisper almost had me leaping out of my skin, which made my brain rattle, but I rasped, "No. I'm okay."

She grunted. "You don't look okay." Her small hand patted my shoulder. "Don't worry, Maverick. You go to sleep. I'll guard you."

And even though it was stupid to think that a kid could guard me, maybe that was all I needed to goddamn hear, because getting to sleep stopped being a struggle and started being inevitable...

NINETEEN

QUIN

I FELT a little like a kicked puppy trying to earn the way back into his owner's good graces when I took a seat at the table and waited for Nyx to show.

I mostly expected him not to turn up, even though logic dictated he was here otherwise I wouldn't have been brought into the visiting room. Of course, Indy might be here in Nyx's stead...

I could easily see that happening.

She'd have found out about Nyx rescheduling the visit and would have told him to fuck off and leave the baby of the family to her to look after.

That was my sister all over. Protective of those she loved. Defensive to the point of self-annihilation when it came to making sure the people she cared about weren't hurt.

I was a lucky guy to have Indy as flesh and blood, but it didn't really have anything to do with good fortune. I'd saved her once upon a time, and she'd gotten it in her mind to save me.

Over and over.

I was such a fucking mess.

Fitting, I figured, that I'd learned that in Rikers.

Maybe it was the constant threat of a beating, of getting raped, of having murdered a prisoner for my MC in here, or simply the slow passage of time that was making me introspective, but Rikers had shaken some sense into me.

If the parole board was kind, I had eleven months left in this hellhole... some days, I wasn't sure if I'd survive another twenty-four hours, never mind a week or a month. But something would happen. A letter would come in, or I'd get a visit, and that would see me through.

My hand was shaking when I lifted it to rub the back of my neck because today was one of those days. One where I felt like grabbing the shiv I kept in my boxer briefs—which I was getting sick and tired of using as a purse for carrying all my contraband—and slicing my wrists wide open.

I needed this visit.

And as much as I wanted to see Indy, I needed to see Nyx more.

He was like a father to me rather than a brother. Dad had been around for most of my life, but he'd been deadbeat. That wasn't me casting shade either. After Carly, things had gone to crap in our family, and I didn't think we'd ever really recuperated from it. Maybe we never would.

Maybe we were destined just to go around and around and around in a constant, vicious circle. All of us self-destructive, all of us just trying to find a peace that had been denied to us for decades.

The thought had me bowing my head.

I had to think of the future. I had to think of a year from now, when I'd be free. Fucking free, at long last.

Releasing a shaky breath, I heard the clanging of the doors, the clicking of the goddamn endless locks, and peered up, trying not to hope too much that Nyx was here.

It wasn't just that he might have had to reschedule—he could have been pulled aside. After all, he was an MC affiliated with me. He wasn't supposed to be allowed to visit. But 'supposed to' and 'could do whatever we fucking wanted' were synonymous in my world.

Unless we got caught.

There was no 'getting out of jail free' card once we were locked up.

I rubbed my chin, unashamed to admit my palm was sweaty as I watched the family tumble in through the doors. Kids and sisters and wives and girlfriends, baby mommas and mothers, they were all here. Their eyes lit up like they were heading for a day trip to the New York Zoo and not a trip to this shithole.

As much of a fuck up as Dad had been, at least we'd never had to visit him here.

Thank Christ for small mercies, eh?

When my brother stormed around the corner, looking his usual growly self, the relief that hit me was instantaneous. Another shaky breath escaped me, this one loaded with joy because, fuck, it felt so good to see him. So fucking good, especially after the news driving around the joint.

I didn't want to believe it, but this place was worse than a fucking hair salon in a two-bit town. Gossip spread like chlamydia. If I could have hurled myself at him for a hug, I would've, but my limbs weren't exactly mine to control right now.

Instead, I stared at him, willing him to see me, willing him to not give me shit. Ever since I'd been sent up, he'd barely spoken to me, hadn't written, had never visited. Only Indy had passed on the gossip, and she hadn't been by in a while even if she called every couple of days.

I felt like a parched desert in need of rain.

I needed more information, I needed to keep going, to stay alive.

Eleven months was nothing compared to what I'd already served, but the prospect of another fucking week was killing me.

I needed Nyx to give me some fucking reason to carry on.

He wasn't wearing his cut, which was so strange to me because since I was a kid, I'd never really seen him without it. He wore a pair of boots, some jeans, and a thick Henley because it was getting cold out—something else to dread, another winter in this fucking place—and looked so normal that it had me blinking a few times.

The cut didn't make the man, but he looked like a guy. A random guy walking into a random prison visiting room to see a random sibling.

It was weird. And nice.

I was used to thinking of him as both a brother by blood and by MC, even though I'd barely been a member of the Satan's Sinners before I'd been tossed in here. Since I knew what the MC was, I'd been waiting to be patched in, and then I'd gone and screwed everything up.

Story of my life.

When his eyes finally met mine, I was surprised by the lack of distaste in them. I'd changed since I came in here. The signs of youth had all gone now, replaced with a man who had to fight to survive, who had to fight to stay intact.

His lips parted, but he didn't miss a step, just strode toward me, as powerful as always, as sure of himself as always, and didn't stop until he was taking a seat opposite me.

Nearly all my childhood, I'd wanted to be like him when I grew up. Instead, I was a fucking patsy.

Goddamnit.

Anger lit up inside me, but I contained it. Just like I had to contain everything else that involved feeling in this shithole.

Eleven months.

That wasn't so long, was it?

"Hey, brother," he rasped as a greeting, and I swear to fuck, my throat choked up.

I bowed my head, breaking the eye contact, and squeezed my hands into fisted balls. When I got some composure, I looked back up at him and noticed his mouth was turned down as he studied me.

"You've bulked up some," Nyx mumbled.

"No alternative." My smile was tight. "Let's just put it this way... Link'd have a whale of a time in here."

Nyx snorted, but there was no humor in his eyes. "Fucker only likes butt play with chicks, not a hundred fucking serial killers."

"He has some taste then."

"Some. Although, you should meet his Old Lady. Lily's class."

"Still find it hard to believe how many of you are getting tied down," I said a little sheepishly. "Starting with you. I'm looking forward to meeting Giulia."

He cleared his throat. "I'd have brought her with me today, but I wanted to talk to you about something, and I didn't want her here, not in this place. She's... You're going to be an uncle, Quin," he rumbled, his smile tight as he imparted that bombshell, and what a fucking bombshell.

My eyes bugged wide. "You're shitting me?" It was rhetorical, because I knew he wasn't, but fuck... Then, I looked at him. Properly. And I saw there were shadows around him, shadows I knew meant his demons were haunting him even if he was happy.

I saw that too.

I was used to a Nyx whose mouth looked like an asshole because it was puckered so tightly with displeasure. I was used to a scowling Nyx who made a sourpuss appear cheerful. I was used to a Nyx who hunted down sick fucks because that was the only way he could get to sleep—and he was constantly exhausted. Bowed down with the weight of his self-appointed mission.

This wasn't *that* Nyx.

Relief for him filled me. I loved my brother, was proud to admit it, but I'd never thought he'd be happy. He seemed to be though. There seemed to be less edginess around him. Like this Giulia, the mother of my niece or nephew—goddamn, I was going to be an uncle—was mellowing him out.

I hoped so. For his sake, I really fucking hoped so.

"That's great news," I told him after a few seconds of processing the truth. "Absolutely fucking great." I didn't really know if this was true or not, but from what he'd been like with me, I knew I wasn't far off when I told him, "You're going to be a badass dad, Nyx. I just know it."

A breath escaped him. "That's what Indy said." He released a rueful laugh. "But I don't know how true that is. I just... I wanted to see you before because I wanted to check in on you. Indy's been giving me shit about not visiting, and she got Giulia to work on me." He scraped a hand over his jaw even as his shoulders were bunching. "I didn't want to. You know I'm fucking pissed at you for getting caught."

Not for committing the crime. Never that in my family, I thought wryly.

Not wanting to talk about it, I just grumbled, "I know."

"Well, I had no choice but to cancel the visit—"

"Why?" Before he could finish, I leaned in and demanded, "They're saying the Sinners are at their weakest in here, the cunts. Making out there was some kind of bomb, but I ain't heard shit from any of you." I pulled a face. "My phone ran out of credit so I couldn't call."

"Shit. I'll get it loaded up. The burner still working? I know those things are old and clunky as fuck."

"It's fine." I wafted a hand. "Is it true?" I demanded.

"We're never weak," was his arrogant answer, then he winced. "But the compound... we were bombed, Quin."

"What?" I snapped, jerking upright in surprise.

"Keep it down," he hissed, and I immediately slouched in my seat, reacting to his command like a soldier on patrol. "You know I'm not supposed to talk about shit like this, but I wanted to keep you in the loop."

"Christ," I whispered back. "Who the fuck would even dare?"

"We're working on it. But..."

"How is everyone?" I interrupted. "What the fuck is going on, man?"

"We lost Jaxson, Matty, Kingsley, Jingles, and Jojo. As messed up as that is, Bear's..."

My eyes flared wide. "Please tell me he's okay." Rex's dad was like my fucking grandfather. "Jesus, please tell me he's okay, Nyx."

"I can't, Quin. I can't. He's in a bad way." His chin tipped up. "Look, we can talk about that after—"

"After? We're talking about my fucking family here, Nyx. I need answers!"

But he plodded on. "I have to ask you something. Maybe even tell you—" Another hiss escaped him. "Indy's gotten together with a biker. Remember Cruz?"

"Course I remember. It ain't been that long." Plus, that fucker had the coolest negative ink going.

"Well, they're together."

"Shit, and she didn't tell me?" I complained, pissed again.

"She's coming to terms with it," he said wryly. "When the blast happened, I knew she was one foot out the door. We found out at the hospital that night that Giulia was pregnant, so when I heard her about to leap out of the life, I just... man, I couldn't let her go back to New Orleans."

My mouth turned down at the corners. "Agreed. That place wasn't good for her."

"No. It wasn't," he said with a nod. "Anyway, I told her, and she stuck around, but you know..." He cleared his throat. "You know my hobby?"

I frowned, but it didn't take much to figure out what he was talking about. Nyx wasn't exactly the kind of guy to knit, nor was he the type of man to whittle in his spare time.

He meant the pedos.

The killing thereof.

"Yeah, I know."

"Indy pleaded with me not to do that anymore. She said I needed to stick around to protect my kid, because..." He gulped, then closed his eyes like he was about to reveal something horrendous, where I was just clutching in the dark trying to figure out where the fuck he was going with this. "Because," he repeated, chasing down air like it was tequila, "I needed to do for my kid what our mom and dad didn't do for her."

For a second, the words hung around me like a toxic gas. They didn't disperse. Didn't disintegrate. They just hovered there, choking me, poisoning every breath I took.

Then, as the realization of what he was saying hit me, I rasped, "No."

He dipped his chin. "Yeah, Quin. Yeah. Kevin got to her."

In my ears, I could hear a kind of howling that I was too self-contained to allow past my lips. But inside my head, the screams were there.

Fuck, was this what Nyx had to cope with?

This endless scream?

I stared at him blindly, blankly.

"Not Indy. No." I shook my head, needing to believe that fucker hadn't gotten to her, but Nyx's eyes were goddamn wet.

Fucking wet.

He was crying.

Jesus fuck.

It was true.

My skin prickled with tingles of sensation as I stared at him, willing him to take it back, to say it was some kind of messed up joke, but it wasn't.

He started talking, but my ears weren't listening. My head wasn't on the conversation. It was on my older sister. The one I was closest to. Who had been there for me when I'd been sick, who'd watched over me before and after my transplant operation. Who'd protected me, who'd defended me...

Then I thought of the time I'd caught her using bleach on her skin like it was body soap from Bath & goddamn Bodyworks—

Was that because of Kevin?

A hundred other things filtered through my memory banks, and the cascade of memories only came to a halt when a guard barked, "No touching!" and I realized that Nyx had grabbed my wrist and jerked me forward.

Nyx's hands popped up to break the connection, but when I stared at him, dazedly, he demanded, "Did he get to you?"

"Kevin?" Slowly, dumbly, I shook my head. Then, because I couldn't cope with this anymore, because this was the last thing I could fucking handle, because I needed out and the walls felt like they were closing in, and because I needed to get to my sister and to fucking hold her and to tell her that she was insane for keeping this from me, I hissed, "Nyx, Indy told me James Lacey was running for mayor? Was she right?"

"Yeah, we had the other tossed out on corruption charges. He won." He scowled at me. "What the fuck does that have to do with anything, Quin?"

"Listen to me," I snapped, and for the first time, Nyx actually did. He straightened up, his head tilted to the side, just so, and I knew I had all his focus. "About two days before I was arrested," I whispered, ducking my shoulders, "the cops came to me. They gave me a file of information, and they showed me how I'd committed a crime that I hadn't committed." His eyes widened, but I raised my hand to stall him. "It was all there in black and white. Where I was, when I was, how I was. By the end of the file, with the pictures there in front of me, I thought I'd blacked out and had gone for a fucking ride, but I hadn't. Nyx, I hadn't."

A breath escaped me, and for the first time, it felt full.

Whole.

Like a weight off my shoulders. Like my chest was no longer being compressed.

I tipped my head back, just appreciating the sensation, before Nyx ground out, "Quin? What the fuck are you telling me?"

Slowly, I rolled my head back down so I could look at him, and I rumbled, "I'm innocent. The cops, those fuckers, they told me if I didn't do as they instructed then they'd have me thrown in jail. If I behaved and complied with their wishes, I could go on my merry way, but they'd expect some 'thing' from me."

The scowl I knew had pedos pissing themselves made an appearance. "What?"

I shrugged. "I don't know. They wanted me in their pocket, I guess. I was new to the Sinners. Maybe they thought they'd get an in with me. Well, I wasn't about to have that. I'm many fucking things, but I ain't a snitch. So here I am. But I can't be *here* anymore. Not when—" I closed my eyes, trying to avoid the howling in my ears. With a shaky hand, I tapped my temple. "Nyx? There's a... Christ, it's like a scream in my head."

My elder brother hissed. "I know, Quin. I know what that feels like."

That wasn't good news.

"I can't be here. You have to get me out."

"I'll figure something—" He snarled under his breath. "Why didn't you fucking tell me?"

"And get you into shit too? No goddamn way. If I can't be in prison, how the fuck can you be? You need your freedom even more than I do!" I sliced my head from left to right, unable to even comprehend the notion of Nyx behind bars. If I was close to slicing my wrists with a sharpened plastic spoon, he'd just bash his head against the wall until he fucking died.

"What does Lacey have to do with anything?" he whispered, hunching his shoulders as he leaned closer to me.

"His kid was one of the cops who framed me," I snarled, feeling like I was grinding my teeth into dust as I spoke. "I need you to get Rachel to figure something out, Nyx. Can you do that for me? Please."

He swallowed at the sight of my desperation. "I can, baby bro. Give me a couple of weeks. I'm going to work on this, and in the interim, you maybe need to get tossed in the hole. There, you'll be safe."

"Okay. But please..."

"Second I'm out of here, I'll be on the phone to Rex, Quin."

Nodding, I caught his eye. "I ain't doing good in here, Nyx, and I sure as hell ain't gonna do good in the fucking hole."

"No fucking wonder." He shook his head, his eyes loaded with guilt at his lack of faith in me as he breathed, "You're innocent."

Mouth pursed tight because I felt like sobbing, I just gave him another brisk nod. "I am."

TWENTY

AMARA

GROWING UP IN UKRAINE, poverty was too common. Some days, it felt like we all lived hand to mouth, and even that seemed like a luxury.

I knew there were those who didn't live that way, but in my tiny corner of the country, where everyone was a farmer and where the weather dictated the state of our stomachs for upcoming months, being poor was as normal as going to bed cold at night.

I'd come across the American version of luxury before.

Whenever Sir would take us from our pit and would have us brought to his home where we serviced him, I'd get a taste of how the rich lived.

That house belonged in a fairy tale. It was something a king would live in. With marble floors everywhere that gleamed like mirrors. Often, that was the only time I saw my reflection, when I was on my hands and knees, staring into the tiles. My dead eyes looking back at me as I recognized that escaping home, escaping poverty had given me exactly what my father had warned me about—a fate earned with the hole between my thighs.

A future dependent on a man's whims.

I'd just never anticipated how bad those whims could be. To be stored like a loathed hunting dog... a nightmare in itself. To be fucked and abused, beaten and punished—no dog should endure what I had. What Alessa and Tatána had.

That was why I was here.

Standing in front of a house my owner had once lived in and recognizing that this place was even more of a palace than the one he'd taken us to.

It was the size of a government building back home, and the driveway alone was majestic. The fountain was the size of a pool, and the statues looked as though they belonged in a museum. When a maid answered the door, it was surreal to be welcomed into the house. Not to be forced to crawl in, not to be made to beg for a shower, not to be raped, not to be tormented...

I entered like a human being.

Because I was a human being.

Not an animal.

Not something to be mistreated.

Slowly but surely, Tiffany and Lily had proven to me that despite everything I'd endured, I was worth something.

It was what had given me the courage to be here today.

"May I take you to the kitchen, ma'am? That's where Miss Lily is."

Ma'am.

Pizda.

Me. A ma'am.

Lancaster, if he'd been buried, was probably rolling around in his grave.

His staff calling me by a polite title.

I hoped he heard from wherever he was. I hoped he'd be doing the *hopak* dance in his six by four earthly prison that could never be as horrendous as where he'd stored me, Alessa, Sarah, and Tatána. Never mind the other girls who'd perished before us.

"Ma'am?" the woman asked with a gentle smile.

I swallowed, and though I rarely used English, rarely wanted anyone to know I could speak it, I softened at her smile, at her gentle and calm demeanor, and whispered, "I'd like to speak with Alessa please."

"Of course. She's in the pool house, not in the kitchen. Would you like me to take you to her?"

"If you don't mind."

"It's my pleasure. Please, follow me."

Her pleasure.

Truly?

Was it really her pleasure to walk me across a hall that practically sang with every step I took as the click of my heels echoed harmoniously around the chamber?

To take me through a room that looked like it was fit for a queen before we headed outside into a garden that was as big as my father's farm? That was neat and tidy and completely useless, all of it fertile soil that was being used to grow things such as flowers and grass. One didn't grow potatoes in a backyard like this...

Then there was the pool, with the property that perched beside it which was clearly the 'pool house,' yet in Ukraine, it was large enough to fit a family of six.

The wealth here was perverted. Disgusting.

Which, I supposed, meant I was disgusting too because I'd accepted Lily's offer a second after she'd made it. It wasn't enough to buy me happiness, to clean my past or my body or my soul, but it was a security I needed. *Craved.*

Ten million.

Lily gave it to us as if it were pocket change.

It almost amused me to think of what Tatána had done. With all her sneaking around, she'd tried to make herself a better life, when all she'd had to do was wait. She didn't have to spread her legs for a man who was more interested in the clubhouse than her, she didn't have to be beholden to anyone to have more security than we could ever have imagined...

She just had to wait.

Impatience had always been her problem. As had stupidity. It was why her nose had been broken so many times by Sir.

The maid drew me back to my thoughts as she knocked on the door to the pool house, and when it pulled inward, revealing Alessa to me, I tipped my chin up in greeting.

"Thank you, Mary," Alessa told the woman who bowed her head, accepting the dismissal with yet another small smile that she beamed at me before she made her way back to the house. To me, Alessa questioned, "What are you doing here?"

"I wished to talk to you." Since the blast, and since she'd come to the house where I was now staying, this was the most I'd talked. As a result, my throat felt a little rusty.

"What about?"

"Alessa? Who is it?" Maverick called out.

I cast a look at the hall behind her, then returned my attention to Alessa. We'd never been close. Sir had never encouraged us to be that. If anything, he'd rewarded us if we stood firm, dependent on only him. The other one, the younger one, had actively pitted us against each other, and when it came down to survival, we'd all thrown each other to the wolves.

That was why, after all we'd been through, she'd been able to come at me the other day. There was no love lost between us, but... I wanted that to change.

I was alone.

She was alone now, whether she realized it or not.

If only she'd accept Lily's offer—she wouldn't have to depend on a man for support, and she'd have money of her own. Just like me. We'd be able to do as we wished, go where we wished. Lily had given us freedom. She'd liberated us. With that new freedom, I found that I wanted to be with someone who understood where I'd come from and how it affected me. *Us.*

"It's Amara," Alessa said in English. "I'll be back in a few minutes."

"He has you at his beck and call?" I queried in our mother tongue, my gaze drifting over the shadows under her eyes, the misery in them.

She wasn't happy.

Neither was I.

But for different reasons.

And I was finding that I didn't have to be happy to feel at peace. Apparently, the two didn't come hand in hand.

"No, of course not," was her brisk reply. "If anything he wants nothing to do with me."

"Charming."

She shrugged. "It's the nature of his illness."

I'd heard about this 'illness.' "You believe it?"

"Believe what?" she demanded, scowling at me. "That he can't remember me? You think he'd make that up?"

"Tatána betrayed his brothers, the club. Maybe he remembers what you are, what *we* are, and he wants to be rid of you. We're used goods, Alessa. What use are we to a man?"

Pain flashed in her eyes, telling me she felt the same way as I did. How couldn't what we'd been through affect us? Affect our dealings with men?

"Maverick wouldn't do that. He knew everything before and

he was the one who made us—" She gulped. "He encouraged the feelings between us to develop. If you came here to punish me for the other day by besmirching his character, then you can just go. I did what I had to do. I needed to know if you were like that bitch."

Her words were spat out, but I heard her insecurity, and though we weren't friends, I had no real desire to play on her vulnerability as, in the past, I might have done.

Instead, a little tired, I murmured, "I understand why you did what you did."

She squinted at me. "You do?"

I shrugged. "In your position, I'd have done the same. You had to establish that you weren't involved with Tatána, you had to make them know you were innocent."

"And you didn't?"

"They spoke with me. I told them the truth. As much as I know of it anyway. You beating me was unnecessary. I had no desire to lie for her or that odd man of hers." I straightened my shoulders. "Before you say anything, I only saw him once and I told Link about it. Anyway, I didn't come here to make you feel guilty or to accuse you of anything. I wanted to know if you were going to accept the money Lily offered."

Unease creased her features. "I don't want to be like them."

I heard and understood her defiance, but it was futile—we'd both learned that at the end of a man's fist. "Then you probably shouldn't have come after me the way you did."

"I thought you weren't going to guilt trip me," she groused stonily, her hands balling into fists.

"I'm not. You have anger issues." I let my gaze drift from her to the hall where her husband was—somewhere in the vicinity anyway. "I understand that, and I understand why, but it doesn't give you the right to dominate me—that's what *they* did."

Her gulp told me my words had hit home.

Again, I shrugged. "The money will enable you to do anything you wish."

"It's tempting," she admitted, "but sometimes you have to avoid temptation. It isn't good for you."

"Neither is being poor and being beholden to a bunch of bikers." I pursed my lips. "I'm grateful to them, Alessa, there's no discounting what they've done for us, but we almost got killed because of them. What happened—that's crazy."

She winced. "It is. It *was*."

"Tatána didn't deserve to die for being an impatient fool," I tacked on.

"Better to die that way than to earn the wrath of the Sinners," she muttered, leaning against the doorjamb.

"Maybe. I can only imagine what they'd have done to her." I shuddered a little. "I get the feeling they'd make Sir and Master look kind."

"They kept us alive. The Sinners wouldn't care if Tatána died."

The thought had me hunching my shoulders. "Do you really want to stay around this place? With men like that? We've experienced too much violence in our lives. We deserve better than that."

"When she transfers the money over, do you intend on leaving?" she queried, and her surprise was clear.

"Why does that shock you? I don't have the ties here that you do, and if Immigration finds out about me they'll toss me back home anyway. Rachel already told me that the Visa processing time for my case could be four years, and in that term, I could be deported at any moment." I grimaced. "I have no desire to return to Ukraine."

"No? I thought that was where you'd want to be."

I snorted. "No. Shows how much you learned about me while we were stuck together."

Her expression as she pulled a face said it all. None of us had ever grown close. It wasn't possible in those circumstances, but that didn't mean I wanted that to continue.

If I'd learned anything since my escape from captivity, it was that friendship helped. Being around survivors like me helped. I might not like it, but I needed Alessa, and I thought she needed me too.

Alessa swallowed. "You want me to come with you?"

"I'd like you to think about it," was all I said. Then, I decided to be candid. "There's no place for me here now."

She frowned. "Why?"

"Hawk..." I gritted my teeth. His interference had probably spared me a harder beating, but equally, he'd revealed things I wanted to keep secret. "When he told Giulia about my feelings—"

"He was right?" she asked, surprised.

"Maybe." I reached up and rubbed my forehead where the bump she'd given me, the one Hawk had iced, was starting to go down. As kind as Giulia and Stone had been to me over all this time, they hadn't touched me like Hawk had. With a gentleness that belied his strength. "I think it was more like I imprinted on her. She was the first woman we saw, she cared and helped us... it was stupid."

"Nothing we feel is stupid," Alessa rasped, and when she grabbed my hand, I wasn't sure what she was going to do until she pulled me into a hug that was awkward, but for all that, felt good. She tucked me tightly into her arms, and I slipped my hands around her waist and clung to her as much, I realized, as she clung to me.

This wasn't just for my comfort. It was for hers too.

And when I looked over her shoulder and saw the man watching us from the end of the hall, a brooding frown marring his brow, standing when I'd only ever seen him in a wheelchair, I knew why Alessa needed the comfort.

Men... they were more trouble than they were worth.

TWENTY-ONE

MAVERICK

"DO YOU KNOW WHERE LILY IS?"

I cut my brother a look but shook my head. "Why would I?"

"Was hoping she was with Alessa. They've been hanging out together these past couple of days."

"Have they?"

Link grunted as he plunked himself down on a pool lounger. "You're back to being a prick again, I see."

I sniffed but didn't answer, just took another sip of the beer I shouldn't be drinking as I stared up at the night sky.

The stars didn't ask me questions and expect answers.

They just left me the hell alone, and I thanked them for it.

"You sit out here a lot," Link remarked.

"It's quiet," I retorted pointedly, making him snicker.

"Well, it'll be quiet after I fuck off again, but I'll only do that in my own good time."

"Jesus. Is this going to be another lecture?"

"Maybe." Link shrugged, his cut rustling with the move.

I took another sip of beer, wished it was something stronger, but even I wasn't dumb enough to mix hard liquor with the meds I was on.

"Say what you have to say and then fuck off."

"This is my home, you know? I don't have to fuck off anywhere," was his smug retort, in fact he was so smug that I had to snicker.

"You letting money go to your head?"

"I quite like being a sugar baby."

"Ain't you about ten years too old to be that?" I queried, shooting him a look.

His nose crinkled. "Probably older than that to be fair. Heard you could be one too."

I grunted. "I don't think so. Alessa doesn't want the money."

"Can't blame her, but I bet she'll come around. Ten million is a lot to turn down."

"I'm surprised Lily can afford to be so generous."

Link snorted. "That's Lily being restrained," he said with a chuckle, and I heard the hiss and pop as he opened up a beer of his own. "She asked me if fifty million each was too much. I told her ten was enough and to spend the rest on her charities."

He had to say that as I took a deep sip, which I promptly sprayed everywhere. "She has fifty million just hanging around?" I sputtered. "Wait, a hundred million?"

"Lily's got money coming out of her ears, Mav," Link replied with a laugh. "Most of it's her mom's, but the shit that's her dad's, she's shedding like a whore'll spread her legs for a four-hundred-dollar tip."

I sniffed. "Nice imagery there."

"Oh, I forgot, you're gay at the minute, aren't you?" was his cheerful retort.

"I ain't gay. I'm fucking bi." I grunted. "Sheesh."

"I know some gay guys who'll say the difference between a bi guy and a gay guy is five beers."

"What gay guys do you even know?" I snapped.

His chuckle told me he was just trying to rile me up, and I was pissed off that it worked.

I flipped him the bird which only had his laughter deepening. Bastard.

"You'd have to be gay not to get a hard-on at their victory dance the other day," Link pointed out, his voice a low, satisfied rumble. "Lily drives better than one of those cars."

"Don't need to know this," I retorted.

"Well, I need to share. You and me always talked about this stuff, Mav. Remember?"

I groaned, because I did. "I know way too much shit about your ass."

"Yeah, well, my ass is a sanctuary now."

My brows rose. "Why?"

"Because it's Lily's to play with."

I snorted. "Please tell me she pegs you."

"I'm working up to it."

Unable to stop myself, I started laughing. "A big pink dick?"

"Nah, I'll get one of those massive Hulk cocks. Ya know? Be a real man."

"'Cause only real men take big, green dicks?"

"Exactly." He held out his bottle for me to tap with mine, and I had to. I just fucking had to.

With them having clinked, he rumbled, "It's funny that you don't remember Ghost. Even back when you were nutso from the last deployment and your memory was all over the place, there were snippets that used to come to you."

My laughter and any and all amusement in this conversation died a short death. "I don't want to talk about this."

"No? Tough. Got something to tell you."

"Make it fast so you can fuck off and leave me in peace."

His grunt told me I'd scored a hit but not a deep enough one for him to fuck off as I'd requested.

"You know that leather cuff she wears?"

I frowned. "The red one?"

He snickered. "So you have noticed."

My eyes narrowed at him. "I've got eyes, don't I? It's just my brain that's mush, not my eyes. Well, most of the time."

"You getting those headaches again?"

"Yeah. They're fucking killer."

"Got one now?"

I could have lied to him, because that was one way of getting him to go, but this was Link. I just couldn't bullshit him.

It helped that he knew when I was lying too...

"No," I told him grumpily. "Wish I did though. At least you'd leave me alone."

"Dunno about that. This shit needs to be said. Lily's been wanting me to talk to you about this since you got back home, and to be honest, I've been hesitant to because it's clear to me that Ghost doesn't want you to know."

"Alessa," I corrected as I scraped off the wet label on my beer bottle with my thumb nail.

"Alessa," he concurred, "is keeping it from you for a reason, and I don't know what that is."

"You doing your usual 'Link'll fix it' gig?" I queried.

"Maybe. I just don't want to break something before it needs fixin', you know?"

Unfortunately, I did.

"What's the cuff mean to her?"

"It hides a slave brand."

For a second, I thought I'd heard wrong. Then, I twisted

around to stare at him and saw he wasn't joking. Link, the ever-fucking-jokester, wasn't joking.

I blinked. "You're shitting me."

"No. Wish I was, man."

My nostrils flared as I tried to process what the fuck he was telling me. "A slave brand?" I repeated.

"A slave brand. She was a sex slave until we saved her."

The silence that fell between us was ripe with a conversation neither of us wanted to have. It didn't take Einstein to conceive what she'd endured, what she'd gone through. I didn't need to know, even if I was compelled to.

How had that fragile, beautiful angel survived that?

How was she here, still standing, just hovering on the sidelines waiting for me to metaphorically kick her while she was already down?

A groan escaped me as I reached up and covered my eyes with my forearm. All the things I'd said, how cold I'd been, all the fucking—

Jesus.

"Your head bad?"

"No," I rumbled, even though it was a lie. Like a hammer to the skull, the migraine was back in business, but that wasn't the reason I wanted to puke.

That was all Ghost. *Alessa.*

"Tell me... how did she get her nickname?"

At my rasp, Link hesitated, then he admitted, "So, before Giulia and Nyx got together, they were just banging. It was funny as fuck because he wanted more from her, but either she wasn't willing to give it to him, or he didn't know what the fuck to do with her. I mean, you've seen him with her. I'd say he was whipped as hell, but it goes deeper than that. It's like..." He paused. "I mean, she's got him wrapped up in her but not in a bad way. It's as if, with her, his demons give him a break. Like he can think clearly, you know?"

I did, actually.

All the time I'd known him, Nyx didn't have an angel on one shoulder and a devil on the other. He had two devils, and they didn't just whisper in his ear, they yelled. Constantly. Like a demonic kind of tinnitus.

"I get it."

"Anyway," he said softly, his tone changing like he knew I was straining to hear through the pain, "one day, he's at the bar. We own a bar now. You know that, right?"

"Alessa told me."

He grunted. "She worked there, behind the bar, and this guy comes onto her, won't take no for an answer. Nyx dealt with him in his usual way, but the bastard came back for her when Nyx was on a run. Almost raped her, managed to get a finger inside her, but —" He grunted. "It's crazy how your perceptions change. Until Lily, I was just glad he didn't get his cock in her, and now, I realize that a finger is just as fucking bad." He released a breath. "Anyway, she killed him. Stone dead. But he was a Lancaster, and his dad owned all this. So the fucker manipulated the laws, got in some detectives, and tried to accuse Giulia of murder. It was working too. We were worried about her, and then one day, Lily goes to the bar, braves it, and manages to get a message to me."

When he quieted down long enough to make me realize he was lost in the past, I whispered, "What kind of message?"

"Some coordinates. Steel, Nyx, Giulia, and me, we headed to them, and we found three *living* women there. I swear, Maverick, I've never been anywhere like it. It was this shed in the middle of nowhere, the creepiest forest ever, but they were underground, kept in cages, shit and piss all over 'em. There was a dead body in one of the cages too..."

A sharp cry escaped me, one that made me feel as if someone had stabbed me through the fucking ear, but with the pain came a name.

A goddamn name.

"Sarah," I breathed.

"Shit!" Link sat up. "Mav, yeah. Sarah. She was dead when we found her." He gulped. "Rotting away—" He shuddered. "It was horrendous. Enough to give *me* PTSD. But one of the women was Ghost. We saved her, but I called her that because she was as light as a ghost, as pale as one, and as quiet. Her voice was so low—"

"Still is."

"Stone says she damaged her voice box screaming."

Gutturally, I grated out, "Fuck." Like I hurt for her too, the pain was hitting me on all quarters. "Fuck, Link."

"Yeah, I know." He swallowed. "Her story is bad, man. So bad. We made him pay though. Fucker suffered before he died."

"Where did he take them?"

Link stilled. "Huh?"

The nausea was still rumbling through my system like I'd just eaten tacos loaded down with ghost peppers, but for some reason, my brain was focused on one thing only.

"Fucker with this much wealth might store his goods like that, but he ain't gonna fuck them there."

A hiss escaped Link. "Jesus."

"Assume that means you don't know?"

"We never—Well, I mean, I never thought. Maybe Rex did. I didn't."

"You should find it," I rumbled. "Fuck knows if he's got other women there."

My face was slick with sweat to the point where I felt like I'd just been doused in water. Might as well have had someone flush my head down the goddamn toilet with how soaked through I was.

"Christ," Link rasped, and within seconds, he was dragging out his phone and shooting off a text.

"I hate to admit it, but the only person who'll be able to find something like that is Lodestar," I muttered grimly.

"I'll go talk to her." He leaped to his feet, but a few steps into striding away, he paused, hovered, and asked, "Mav?"

"I'll be kinder to her." It was all I was capable of saying, but it didn't begin to describe the metamorphosis going down in my brain.

"Good."

He walked off, leaving me like I'd hoped, but my mind was a thousand times more active than it had been before he darkened my door.

The excruciating pain was nothing compared to the guilt I felt, to the shame.

She loved me.

Whenever she looked at me, I saw it. Felt it. She'd admitted it, but words were one thing and seeing them in the flesh was another. Even so, I'd turned her away. I knew the pain of rejection—who the fuck didn't? But this was something else entirely.

I'd wifed her.

Made her mine, even if I hadn't branded her yet.

Unless this Maverick, who'd been strong enough to protect a sex slave from ICE, who'd somehow made her fall for him even though she had to absolutely *loathe* men, had preemptively branded himself?

Somehow, it felt like the kind of thing that Maverick would do.

I had no idea why, but the need to know if I had was as strong as the urge to find the place where Lily's father had fucked his merchandise.

The bastard.

I hoped the club had made his death as painful as possible.

Clambering to my feet was hard with my ears ringing, but I staggered across the poolside, almost falling into the fucking water—which was all I needed, to die *now*—before I eventually made it inside.

I walked into my bedroom, deeper into the closet where I'd noticed the door had a mirror on it, even as there was one on the front wall so someone could see themselves from all angles.

Switching the light on had shadows dancing across my eyes, and for a few moments, I just stood there, quivering like a feather in a storm, like a fucking pussy, until the dots abated and I felt like I could look into the light without going blind.

Squinting through the discomfort, I twisted my head slightly as I shrugged out of my cut then carefully unbuttoned the shirt I'd started wearing. It felt weird not to wear a wifebeater, but it was getting colder, and I didn't feel like dealing with frostbitten nipples as well as everything else.

When both were gracing the floor, I peered over my shoulder to see if I could get a glimpse of my spine, and I found a myriad wall of ink that I did and didn't recognize.

The Special Forces' insignia I'd had done after my first mission took center stage in between my shoulders, but there were all kinds of tattoos there now. Anything from a Chinese dragon to a portrait of my mom that sat on my lower right hip. I moved closer to the mirror on the door, angling it so I could see the ink, and the resemblance between her and Alessa wasn't as strong as I'd mentally thought.

It'd been a long time since I looked at a photo of her, because it hurt to do so, and it fit that I'd have her memorialized on my body but in a place I couldn't see every day because I'd loved her. So fucking much.

It'd been us against the world after my dad had fucked off. But it spoke of how special she was that she'd gone from being a clubwhore to an Old Lady—a miracle in our world. And my ma was that fucking special she'd been an Old Lady twice over. Because when my dick of a father had done a disappearing act, one of the council, Indigo, had wifed her.

I bit my lip at the memories, not really wanting to deal with them just now, even as I was relieved she and Alessa weren't at all alike. They had similar hair, but Alessa was a little more elfin, more delicate. Mom had been strong, her body filled out after she'd had me. Whereas my wife was like the feather I'd just likened myself to.

Reaching behind me, I carefully touched the ink, wishing she was here, wishing she'd give me a fucking hug and would tell me to get my sick ass in bed before she kicked me into it...

She'd been an angel with a potty mouth.

My lips twisted at the thought before I moved on, turning to look at the one I'd been avoiding.

The one that was just below my insignia.

For me to put anything there, well, it meant something. There was a blank canvas of space around both that and my mom's portrait, but the rest were a mix of badly positioned designs that made me wonder what I'd been thinking or if I'd been drunk when I had them done.

But the mandala was so unlike anything else on my body, and its patterns were so different that even with my head as messed up as it was, I saw the symbols for what they were.

Hope.

A fletch of arrows with a series of inverted 'L's were the pivotal part of each symmetrical piece. A little like a snowflake a kid would draw, a fancy one, half was done in black, the other was forged out of a negative space, so the white of my skin gleamed brightly.

I knew what the old Maverick had been doing.

He was the dark.

Alessa was the light.

His light.

I gritted my teeth at the thought, then for want of nothing better to do, I slammed my fist into the dry wall.

It hurt, but what didn't about this goddamn motherfucker of a day?

TWENTY-TWO

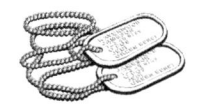

LODESTAR

THE FOLLOWING DAY

ADJUSTING my weight in my seat was starting to piss me off.

How a broken leg could hurt worse than being shot, I wasn't fucking sure, but I just knew that it did.

And it was making me grumpier than usual.

Enough to growl, "What the fuck are you all doing here anyway?"

The low-level chatter in the kitchen quieted at my grouching, but it was Giulia who retorted, "You don't own the place, Lodestar. You should remember that."

I grumbled under my breath. "When you've got me working harder than a fucking workhorse, bet your ass I own some of the place. This table, this chair, my territory. You're sitting at it. Fuck off."

She sniffed and flipped me the bird, which I didn't even bother glowering at, just shot her one back in turn. A lot of the brothers had gone on a run a day or so before, so they were hanging around Lily's place more than usual and it was starting to piss me the fuck off.

Didn't they know I had shit to do? Evil cabals to tear down Raymond Reddington-style? Houses of ill repute to destroy? And, somehow, a fucking mob family to tear to shreds?

It didn't happen by its goddamn self.

"Anyway, as I was saying before I was rudely goddamn interrupted, Rex hugged me this morning."

While I wasn't interested in the inane chatter from a bunch of Old Ladies, that caught my attention. Rex wasn't an affectionate kind of guy, and certainly not with a brother's woman.

I speared Giulia with my focus. "Did he say anything?"

She shook her head. "Just hugged me." Her eyes narrowed on me. "Why are you interested? Eavesdropping on conversations that have nothing to do with you?"

I sniffed at her. "Because it's weird, is why."

"I know it is. That's why I brought it up."

Alessa pressed a hand to Giulia's good shoulder. "Calm down, Giulia. She's in pain."

Damn right I was, but I didn't appreciate the whole fucking kitchen knowing it.

Because she meant well, I refrained from giving her shit. Instead, I focused on Giulia once more. "What did he do then?"

"What's wrong?"

The deep voice still had the power to send shivers down my spine, but because he remained a visitor in La-La Land, Maverick barely spoke to me now. Seemed he remembered me well enough to know when I was in red alert mode though.

"Giulia said Rex hugged her."

Maverick frowned. "He hugged you?"

"It's not like he poisoned her," Tiffany pointed out wryly before she took a sip of her coffee.

"Might as well have. He'd never have touched another brother's woman like that," was Maverick's reply, and it amused me because our trains of thought were along the same lines. As usual. He shot me a look. "What are you thinking?"

"I don't know. Yet. Giulia, what happened after he hugged you?"

"He headed off on his hog."

"Do you know where?"

"Do I look like his secretary?" she retorted waspishly.

"This is fucking important," I snapped back. "Did he say anything?"

"No." She bit her lip, seeming to finally pick up on the severity of my tone and the potential ramifications of what had happened this morning. "But when I drove past the clubhouse, I didn't see the red hog he's riding there, and you know that sticks out like a sore thumb."

I cast each of the women a look. "Call your men. Ask if Rex is with them."

"What's going on, Lodestar?" Lily asked uneasily, but she was obeying, her cell in her hand as she started the call to Link.

"I'm not sure. But—" I reached up and rubbed my forehead, wishing the concussion headaches would stop already.

This week had been a son of a bitch.

Last night, Link had charged me with tracking down the house where Lancaster might have played with his 'toys,' and I wasn't sure if it was hard because of my health or if it was that well hidden it was difficult to trace—I should have found it already, so I was pissed that I hadn't.

On top of that, there was the blast and the whole host of complications that triggered—finding who was at the top of the list, but so was determining whether a pedophile had access to one of the brother's daughters...

All of that when I was down to two hours' work capacity with eight hours napping in the aftermath.

If the bomb had been meant to slow me down, it was working.

And fuck if I didn't hate the physical proof I wasn't Wonder Woman.

When I was faced with a bunch of grim expressions and head shakes, I tuned back into the conversations going on around me.

"Rex isn't with any of your men?" I asked, seeking confirmation, and I received a chorus of 'no.'

Goddamn that man, because with the bad vibe churning in my gut and Maverick's distrusting self looking on, I was going to have to burn my ace in the hole.

Motherfucker.

TWENTY-THREE

REX

BY THE TIME I was in Brooklyn Beach, any agitation, deep in my soul, had gone. Dissipated. Disappeared even.

I was at peace with myself.

Whatever happened today, however it ended, I was happy with how I was going out.

I'd hugged Rachel this morning before she headed into work. I'd bumped fists with Rain, her kid brother, and I'd even slung an arm around Giulia—the only woman who'd ever leveled my psycho friend out—not that she'd appreciated the gesture. I swore, the reason they suited each other was because they were both so fucking prickly.

I hadn't texted the council, mostly because I knew they'd head into NYC with me, and I didn't need them to sacrifice themselves for me.

What I was about to do… it might mean my end.

For my mom, it was a risk I was willing to take.

She deserved more than she'd gotten, she deserved to rest in peace knowing that the people behind her murder were in hell. So, like the true Satan's Sinner I was, with the devil himself on speed dial, I'd deliver them.

Personally.

And I'd smile as I did it.

I just needed my brothers to keep the MC going no matter what happened today.

The warehouse loomed in the distance, exactly where Declan had said. It belonged to a businessman who had no ties to any of the Families, who didn't even know it was being 'borrowed' today, and even from this far away, I could see the men on the roof. Covering security from that angle. Even saw where there were men dotted around the courtyard.

It'd be hard getting in, but the truth was, I knew God was on my side.

I'd either die before I made my way to the summit, would have my ass hauled in and reamed before the four families, or I'd get to fulfill my purpose.

When I climbed off my bike, I felt the pressure of the pair of guns against my lower back, and I jerked my chin to the side to make it crack, bunched my hands into fists as I made my way down the path Declan had told me about.

There was a side entrance that was blocked off which, as a result, was going to be the least secured of them all.

I just needed to make it through a hole in a fence the Five Points were going to cut for me today, and then get to that side entrance, before I'd find a window that'd lead to the basement. After that, once I was inside, I had to make my way to the main floor where the summit was being held.

That didn't sound too mission impossible, did it?

Good thing I'd always fucking loved Ethan Hunt.

The tune to Mission Impossible in my head, which I'd admit messed with my focus some, I found the hole in the fence, which was there as promised, and I knew from that moment on, Declan would have men looking out for me. Not to kill me, but to make sure I reached the summit.

I knew he'd have an ulterior motive, knew he must want the same thing I did for the *Famiglia*, but so long as we were both on the same page and he was on my side, I'd take it, no matter his reasons.

My cut snagged on the chain-link, and I grunted when it snapped. Twisting around to collect the piece, I held the worn leather that had seen me through far too much and hoped it'd have the chance to see me pull more crazy shit.

I was too young to die.

But I was too old to let the disrespect to my parents go unsung.

I caught the eye of a Five Pointer, one I recognized from the initial meetings with the Irish. He dipped his chin and the AK he was carrying tilted down to the ground, like he was reassuring me that he was friendly.

I nodded back, grateful that my logic was right thus far, then I headed deeper into the courtyard where it was most dangerous. If someone on the roof saw me that wasn't Irish, I was fucked.

Hell, who was I kidding?

I was fucked anyway.

TWENTY-FOUR

MAVERICK

I DIDN'T TRUST Lodestar as far as I could throw her, but her concern was real.

Why, I didn't know, but she'd always had a strange kind of sixth sense where things like this were concerned. Just like Nic. Both of them had that spooky shit down pat.

"What are you thinking?" I snapped at her, both of us heading straight into military territory we'd been bred to exist in.

We were soldiers at that moment, and I was her CO, and she was my subordinate.

She cracked her knuckles as she refrained from answering me, instead called out, "Kat? I need you to go into my bedroom, and in my nightstand, there's a phone. Can you go and get it for me?"

Alessa's baby sister who appeared to go by two names, Kat to everyone but Alessa, and Kati to Alessa only, cast a look at Lodestar, but even the precocious kid seemed to sense that things weren't right because she darted off. Not even skipping away like she'd ordinarily do, just outright running.

"After the blast," she admitted gruffly, "I thought it was prudent to...clone Rex's phone."

The last part of the sentence was mumbled so quietly that over the ringing in my ears, I didn't hear it. But Giulia, who was at her side, did.

"You cloned Rex's phone?" she gasped. "Jesus, Lodestar, you got iron balls or something? Fuck, even I ain't brave enough to do that. Not that I could... but still. Christ."

Then, Giulia being goddamn Giulia, she lifted her fist at Lodestar who ducked back like she was about to be punched.

"I think she wants to fist bump you," Lily said wryly, her eyes amused as she took in Lodestar's reaction.

"Oh." Star blinked then bumped fists with Giulia. "Thanks. I think."

"When he finds out, he'll kill you," I warned her, not as impressed as the women were with her fucking antics.

This was Lodestar all over.

Unreliable, untrustworthy, disloyal. Fucking bitch.

Christ, I'd been a fool to get tangled up with her. I just didn't understand how I'd ever gotten over the past enough to be friends with her again.

Before I could reply, Kat came sliding into the room, a phone in her hand, her cheeks bright pink from exertion, and her breathing hard.

"We've got the next Usain Bolt before us, ladies," Giulia cheered, which had Kat flopping forward, her hands on her knees even as she wriggled her butt in a celebratory dance that had most of the women laughing through their nerves.

With the phone in hand, Lodestar tapped away, hunting down clues for Rex's whereabouts.

Not only was it not like Rex to go off without telling anyone where he was going, in fact, he rarely left West Orange. To the point where he was close to a hermit, subsisting in the clubhouse unless—well, this was the Rex of old, I figured. Maybe he'd changed. But before, he'd only ever really gone on a run when it was time to meet with new chapters in his dad's place, when Bear was Prez, or for Nyx's fun and games.

Though I wasn't as freaked out as Lodestar, I had to admit his behavior was odd. Odd enough to cause some concern.

"Shit, he called Declan O'Donnelly two days ago." She peered up at me. "You know why?"

I shook my head. "No. I've been out of it. Slept through most of the past two days anyway." He winced. "Nyx asked me to do some shit for the club, but I just haven't been up to it."

She waved a hand. "I dealt with it for you."

Though I was grateful, it choked me to give her my thanks. Alessa, catching my eye, arched a brow and murmured, "We're grateful for your help, Lodestar."

My ex grunted. "He always was a shit patient. I'll be glad when he gets his memory back though. I'm sick of being looked at like I just abducted and anal-probed him."

Kat giggled at that, then hurled her arms around Lodestar's neck. "You said 'anal,' Star."

Lodestar grumbled, "You're all sweaty."

Kat smacked a kiss on her cheek which had Star hiding a smile even as she was tapping away on her computer.

"I'm in touch with someone who's a part of the Five Points," she muttered, even as Kat kept her arms around her neck and was clearly reading the conversation that was going down on the screen. "I wanna know why Rex would contact Declan O'Donnelly when, as far as I know, Sin's the point of contact."

Tiffany commented, "He is, yeah. They're in touch a lot. Especially with the run going down later than planned."

Lodestar hummed under her breath, but it wasn't a short hum, more like a song. My brow puckered as I tried to think about what the song was, and it came to me with a flash.

'Firestarter.'

I remembered us at a rave in goddamn Prague, slipping and sliding against each other because it was so fucking hot in that club. For all she'd been grinding into me, I'd ground my dick into her just as much...

Good times.

Before shit had derailed.

Before life had changed.

Before Nic.

I gritted my teeth as she muttered, "Oh, fuck."

"What is it?" I demanded, rounding the table and her seat so I could read the screen too.

My nostrils flared when I read words I hadn't heard in fucking years.

"Jesus," I rasped.

"What is it?" Giulia snapped. "Don't keep it from us. What's going on?"

"A summit. Today. Brooklyn Beach," Lodestar rasped, and like that, I was no longer Maverick pre-Nic. No longer the Maverick who was fresh from the sandbox.

I was here.

In the now.

And as the past collided with the present, I dropped to my knees as I realized the man I loved like a fucking brother had gone on a one-way mission where his end destination was finite.

Death.

Only that could bring me back to life...

TWENTY-FIVE

REX

I MADE IT.

Barely.

My boots didn't even get the chance to clomp against the ground—that was how fast and how quietly I moved—and within seconds, or at least that was how it felt to me, I was away from the hole in the fence and kissing the warehouse wall.

Twenty or so feet from the point of my collision with the bricks, I found the promised basement window, and when I was inside, I sucked in a sharp breath of air as adrenaline whacked me in the gut.

Hands to my knees, I propped myself up, trying to calm myself down, well aware that this was only a third of the journey done.

Today would either end with me in a body bag or in handcuffs, I was well aware of that, but the sacrifice was worth it.

My family had been torn apart by the Italian cunts sitting in this building, discussing gang wars when they had no business to be discussing shit. I had to end them before they took any more from me, because if I didn't, then who would have the guts?

The New World Sparrows sounded like some kind of football team that was trying to rebrand themselves after having a racist name for a century, but they weren't a football team. They were a bunch of dirty alphabet agents, scratching each other's backs, getting each other out of the shit and making their people money in the interim. Worse still, they had links to the *Famiglia* and only the fuck knew what else.

I'd be doing humanity a goddamn service, and while I'd never been into lamb before, I'd be the sacrificial variety any day of the fucking week if it meant purging my country of this scum.

As I peered around, I knew this had to be a section the Irish secured, because I saw no one. Not a single soldier of any nationality. In fact, the next person I heard was from within the summit itself.

Several persons, in fact.

When I wended my way through the warehouse, I eventually discerned four different accents arguing and bickering, and I used that as a guide to reach them.

Though I'd heard about these meetings before, I'd never imagined what they'd look like.

Recognizing Aidan Sr. and his son, Aidan Jr., who were seated north on a compass, I took note of Finn O'Grady who stood at their back.

East held the Russians, west the Chinese, and to the south, as expected, were the Italians.

Each unit had two people seated at the table, and one person at their back.

Studying them from behind a door, I watched the argument continue, but as I listened, watched, learned, in the distance, I heard something.

The sound of thunder.

The unmistakable burgeoning roar of bikes.

They were getting closer too. Closer, closer. Until the snarl of their straight pipes felt like they were rumbling in my ears, making the ground beneath my fucking feet throb as if an earthquake was heading my way.

My lips quirked up into a smile, especially when I felt my phone give off a constant vibration against my ass as a ton of messages poured into my inbox.

I had no idea who'd figured this out, no idea how they'd gotten here in time other than the fact it must have taken me longer to get into the warehouse than it felt like, but someone *had* worked it out.

Somehow, they knew exactly where I was.

Sinners—even if one of us wanted to be lost, we'd never not go hunting for a brother.

I should have remembered that.

My gaze drifted back to the table where I caught Finn O'Grady's eye. His mouth curved into the faintest smirk before he arched a brow—telling me to move the fuck on.

So, with an army of my own at my back, one that had to be outside the warehouse, one that had the leaders at the summit, everyone apart from the O'Donnellys, peering around as if they could see the bikers from their seats, I strode forward, raised both arms, pointed one of my guns to the left, uncaring which it was, just needing for the *Famiglia* to feel the fucking pain of losing not just one, but all three of their Dons within sixty days, and took my shot.

Then, with the other gun, I fired again.

And again.

Until all three Italians were dead.

That was when all hell broke loose.

TWENTY-SIX

ALESSA

"GHOST?" he rasped, the words so weighed down with agony that I immediately moved across the kitchen to go to him. "I-I need my chair."

I immediately froze. And all around me, as Lodestar mobilized the troops, somehow hijacking Rex's cellphone to call in brothers to head his way, everything seemed to move at hyper speed. But for me? I was stuck.

Hope was a painful thing to possess. In fact, it was so beyond painful it was dangerous.

Every step I took toward him, I throbbed with hurt. With hope. With need. With resolve.

I dared to breathe even though my lungs felt choked, and I dropped to my knees beside him, feeling his pain.

"Maverick, you don't need a chair. Don't you remember?"

I let the chaos whirl on around me, well aware that Lodestar would make sure this was in hand, but I cast her a look and saw that even as she was working hard, even as her face was lined with the discomfort from her injuries, even as she spoke to someone called Digger, she was watching Maverick too.

I bit my lip before I gave him all my attention and in Ukrainian, I rasped, "Lord, please let him remember who I am to him."

It was the first prayer I'd made since I'd been sold to my second owner who made Attila the Hun look gentle.

Reaching out, I ran my hand over his head, moving to his neck where I quickly started the massage that had soothed him before. The tension in him began to abate, dripping out of him slowly but surely as I lifted my other hand and tried to calm him down.

He slouched, rocking forward into me, until I wasn't surprised when he was laying on the kitchen floor, curled up on his side while I worked on him.

By the time I looked up, I recognized I was alone with Lodestar and Kati. Both of whom were watching me care for Maverick.

I sensed Kati's curiosity, and wasn't surprised when she murmured, "You really love him, don't you, Lessie?"

Swallowing thickly, I whispered, "I really do."

He groaned as I worked on a knot in his shoulders, and even though my fingers were starting to ache, I persevered because he needed me.

Because he was close.

Because he pushed his face into the side of my thighs, and his arms weren't around his legs like they would have been before—they were tucked around me. The position was so awkward that it couldn't be anything other than intentional. But it felt different than the field beyond the clubhouse. This wasn't him using me as a prop, a means of hiding from the bright sun. It was for comfort.

Pure and simple.

"What's happening?" I asked softly, not wanting to stir him but needing to know what was going on.

Lodestar cleared her throat. "I called in Digger—he's one of the bikers en route to the Canadian border. Nyx messaged Rex last night to say there was a delay in the warehouse with the shipment, so they were still stuck in the city."

"Why did you call Digger and not Nyx?"

"Because MaryCat's getting due and her mom is insisting she gives birth at the Cedar Sinai clinic... that means he always picks up his phone. It's early in the AM, Alessa. You know these fuckers don't usually wake up before eleven."

I let my teeth dig into the inside of my cheek. "He's rounding them up?"

"Yes. I sent Nyx coordinates of Rex's location through 'Find My Friends.'" She tapped her fingers against the table. "Goddamnit, I hate being out of the action."

I frowned at her. "You're in the middle of the action—just at a distance. Someone has to coordinate things, don't they?"

Lodestar shot me a disgusted glance which told me she wasn't happy about being the coordinator.

"Where did everyone else go?" I questioned, deciding to change the subject. With anyone else, I'd say they couldn't get involved, but Star wasn't exactly a rational kind of person. I wouldn't put it past her to try to ride a bike with a cast on her leg and everything.

Apparently the U.S. Army taught their soldiers to be kamikazes when injured.

"I told them to get out. They were clucking around like pregnant hens," she muttered disgustedly, before she let her glance drift over to Mav. "Can you get him functioning? I need his input."

"He isn't a computer and I'm not a programmer," I retorted, thoroughly disgruntled. "He's in pain. Can't you see?"

"You gotta buckle up and get through the pain," she said unsympathetically. "What do you think I've been goddamn doing since the blast? Managing the work of three people, that's what." She harrumphed, then muttered under her breath, "If you want something done, do it your fucking self."

"She's right," Maverick rasped as he started to surge to his feet, wobbling as he did so. "I need to get to the city. I have to help Rex—"

Lodestar snorted. "You're about as much use as GI Joe like this."

I glared at her, then snapped, "Maverick, you're in no state to be going anywhere, never mind to the city. You need to relax. Your mind is clearly at war. You must take it easy!"

"Don't think he could take it much easier," Star grumbled.

"Shut up, Lodestar!" I snarled, for the first time in a long while, God, *years*, raising my voice. "You're not helping!"

She arched a brow at me, her surprise clear, but I ignored her and let her focus drift back to her work and returned mine to my husband. Taken aback to find he was staring up at me, I swallowed nervously. He wasn't looking at me with that vacant stare that terrified me because it represented how little I meant to him, but neither could I translate what that stare meant.

"I didn't think I'd ever see you again," he rasped, and his words floored me.

Mouth working, I whispered, "I don't know what you mean."

"When the ceiling came down..." His brow puckered. "All I could think was, 'Ghost isn't safe.'"

Ghost—again. Not Alessa. When he'd been making a concerted effort to call me by my true birth name.

"I'm safe," I countered thickly, trying not to get my hopes up and utterly failing. "The Sinners kept me safe."

"They couldn't protect you like I could."

Star snorted. "Hiding in a fucking wheelchair doesn't make you Hannah goddamn Montana."

My eyes bugged at that, and I swore I could feel a nerve under the right one start to tic. "He never claimed to be."

The other woman just scoffed under her breath, while Maverick set my heart alight by reaching up and touching my face with the tips of his fingers.

Dear God, the reverence in the caress was enough to make my eyes water when they hadn't watered in so long.

How had I—

Pizda. How had I lived without this?

How had I coped this long?

A choked cry escaped me even though I tried to contain it, and I wanted to scream and rail because I'd thought I'd never see this again, but here I was. Basking in his love.

It *was* love too.

He loved me.

It was clear in his eyes, in his touch.

Just not his trust.

But now wasn't the time to make demands. Now was the time to feel relieved over the fact he was with me, even if it was for only a handful of moments.

Unable to stop myself, I leaned forward, and while it was clumsy and difficult, I didn't care. I needed to kiss him, to reconnect with him.

As I pressed my lips to his, I imbued it with every ounce of feeling inside me. All the emotions I'd denied and hidden and avoided, I pushed past them, pulling back only to whisper, "I love you, Jameson."

His eyes were closed, but his smile made a swift appearance, and when he opened them again, the love in them burst out like a ray of light through a wall of gray clouds. "You promised you'd never call me that except on our wedding day."

I nipped a bit of my bottom lip with my teeth. "You remember that?" I asked, trying not to feel slighted that he didn't tell me he loved me too. It was still early days, and...

"Course I do." He released a breath. "Alessa, I love you too."

My jaw ached with how hard I clenched it, but I reached down and trailed my fingers along his chin and over his cheek. "Do you remember what happened after the clubhouse collapsed?"

His eyes fluttered closed again. "No."

"Do you remember why you went in?" Star queried, her tone clinical. Too clinical. I scowled at her—he wasn't some lab rat in an experiment. But of course she ignored my scowl.

He reached up and pinched the bridge of his nose. "I think I do. I had to make sure I grabbed the hard drives in the safe in Rex's office. But..." He flinched. "Something to do with you, wasn't it? You needed something from there too?"

Lodestar and I shared a look.

"Did you manage to get it before the clubhouse collapsed?" I rasped.

Releasing his hold on his nose, he swiped his thumb over to rub his eye instead. "I don't know. Were you given my personal belongings from the hospital when I left?"

I blinked. "I don't think so. The day you came home was a little crazy."

"One of the brothers will have grabbed that stuff and put it in your room, Mav," Star stated urgently. "Alessa, can you go look for it? See if the USB drive is there?"

"Maverick? Will you be okay while I'm gone?"

His smile was weak. "I've been better—"

"He's a goddamn soldier," Star rumbled. "Doesn't matter if he's been retired for years or not. Leave him alone, Alessa, and stop fussing around him."

I scowled at her, but when Mav patted my leg, I got to my feet with a huff and did as Star asked.

Not for the first time did I register the hard truth—Lodestar was a pain in my ass.

TWENTY-SEVEN

REX

THE MOMENT the sound of the silenced bullets rang free, I grabbed everyone's attention.

When, the second after I'd disposed of two potential Dons and a *consigliere*, I placed the weapon on the floor, only the Triads got to their feet, their unease clear.

According to O'Donnelly, when you sat at this table, when you entered this room, you were stripped of all weapons. That was why I was here—I was the gun for the Irish. For Declan. I wasn't the only one who wanted those bastards dead, who wanted to pour grief on the Italians.

They were like Hydra—you cut off one head and two sprouted up, so today, there'd be repercussions, but any stories about the Sinners being weakened had just been put to bed.

For good.

I raised my hands high, even as I turned my focus from the conference table where the Triads' leader, the Dragon Head, Zhao was starting to mutter orders to his vanguard, his deputy, but the Triads aside, all was calm.

Uncaring if I lived or died helped matters as, still with my hands high, I moved around the table. The Bratva eyed me warily, but they were clearly in on this, which meant the O'Donnellys had shared the information with their allies—not that I blamed them. It was a clear indicator that the Triads were very much tolerated but weren't friends with the Westies—the Irish.

Staring down at the sightless eyes of one potential Don, and seeing the other had already died too, I smirked before I caught a glimpse of the last sputtering moments of the *consigliere's* life. His mouth curled into a sneer as our eyes tangled, so I decided to end it by grinding my booted foot on the gushing chest wound.

As he groaned out his pain, his arms and legs buckled as he tried to avoid me, but there was no avoiding this.

I'd hit the Dons with better targeted shots, but had failed with this fucker. Still, three kill shots in under ten seconds—hardly bad. Dad would be proud of me.

My jaw tensed at the thought of my father whose future was uncertain, who might as well be on the ground with these cunts for all he'd want to survive *if* he managed to wake up, and I dug my heel in harder, not stopping until the hate in the *consigliere's* eyes was frozen forever in place.

Only then did I back off, wiping my foot on the cunt's suit as I moved away, which was when I realized there was silence outside in the hall, no sound of bikes, and there wasn't much talk going down in here either.

"Gentlemen, who is this person?" Zhao asked, his English clearly accented.

"He's an ally," Aidan Sr. rumbled, his voice amused as he peered down at the corpses on the floor.

"That I managed to discern," the Triads leader rumbled back. "This is clearly a targeted attack and goes against the laws of the summit—"

"There are no laws when we're at war," Vasov, the Bratva Pakhan, retorted, his hunched shoulders straightening as outrage had him sitting up in his wheelchair. "Those Italian bastards shot out my kneecaps—"

"Targeted my grandson," O'Donnelly snarled.

"And blew up my fucking compound," I growled, staring Zhao down. "If none of that doesn't deserve a takedown in your eyes, Dragon Head, then I'm not sure what will."

The leader narrowed his eyes at me. "Who are you? Aside from an Irish ally?"

"I'm the Prez of the Satan's Sinners MC. The mother chapter."

Zhao arched a brow. "I've heard tales of you. You target pedophiles, do you not?"

Though I was surprised news had spread about that, considering Maverick worked hard to keep things on the downlow where our kills were concerned, I didn't let it show. Because Zhao sounded impressed, I cautiously replied, "We do."

At my confirmation, he hummed under his breath and began tapping the table with his pointer finger. His two subordinates spread out, but as I tensed up, they moved over to the dead bodies, and shoving on gloves they retrieved from the inside pockets of their black Fendi suits, they dragged the corpses away.

The chair in which one of the Dons was still sitting, slumped over, a Bratva goon hauled away, tipping the body onto the floor like the trash it was, as O'Donnelly murmured, "Might as well take a seat, Rex. We have business to discuss still."

"You want me at a summit?" I repeated, surprised by the offer.

"As he said, we have business to discuss," O'Grady concurred.

"I expected to leave this room in a body bag, gentlemen—"

O'Donnelly snorted. "Oh, ye of little faith, Rex. Why would we willingly dispose of an ally?"

"Because it was worth it to dispose of an enemy?"

O'Donnelly Jr., for all that his pasty face was beaded with perspiration like he was coming down off a high, snorted. "You killed two potential leaders. There are five families, don't forget. Just because the three at the top of the triangle are missing heads doesn't mean there won't be potential Dons coming out of the woodwork."

I'd known that, but it still pissed me off.

O'Donnelly Sr. murmured, "Yes, son, that pisses me off as much as it does you. Nothing we can do about that. Cockroaches, the lot of them." He spared Zhao a glance. "Now that the devious cunts are dead, it's time to discuss the real reason I called this summit into being." His mouth tightened. "The New World Sparrows."

Zhao frowned, his confusion clear. As was Vasov's. "What are these New World Sparrows?" he asked, even as his security man leaned down and muttered something in his ear.

"They're a bunch of dirty cops," O'Donnelly Jr. rasped.

"No, it goes deeper than that," I intercepted as I moved into the newly vacated seat at the table. My phone buzzed as a reminder of what was going down in the outside world, and though this wasn't ideal, I still had a pulse so I'd sit in if I could and maybe effect the kind of changes required to take this scum out.

Quickly retrieving my cell, I saw Nyx was threatening to storm the building and shot him off a text telling him I was okay and that I had business to discuss. Once that was done, and because I was genuinely interested now that O'Donnelly had raised the topic of the fuckers who'd helped ruin my family's life, I gave the meeting my full attention.

"It has to. There has to be judges and court officials involved as well, even prison guards... Everyone taught to look the other way for certain specific cases."

"He's right," Finn O'Grady confirmed, folding his arms across his chest. "It's only logical."

"Who are these New World Sparrows?" Zhao asked, but something about the tone of his voice made me wonder if this wasn't the first time he'd come across the term.

"We've managed to ascertain that their MO is to haul someone in, someone with a sketchy background. They proceed to threaten them with a fabricated case where they're the guilty party even if they're innocent. The person in question then has two options—do as the officers say and be released, or refuse and serve time for a crime they didn't commit."

"To what end?" Zhao queried, making me scoff.

"I highly doubt that a Dragon Head as skilled as yourself can't figure it out. Weren't you the one who masterminded the Relain Bank Robbery back in 2019?"

A gleam appeared in the Triads leader's eye. "They have an army of soldiers willing to act to stay out of jail."

"Exactly," O'Donnelly Sr. obliged. "This is a problem, as I'm sure you can imagine. Especially when they create close ties with our mutual enemies."

Zhao's gaze flickered over to the corpses. "They were in bed with the Italians?"

"More than in bed," I rumbled. "I have a feeling they were outright fucking."

The other leader hummed under his breath. "And what do you propose we do about this?"

"Well," O'Donnelly Sr. stated, "that's why I called us here today. To discuss the NWS and how we're going to eradicate them."

Vasov arched a brow. "There's a way when they're entangled with law enforcement?"

I ground my teeth together. "There has to be a way—"

Vasov scoffed. "I have no idea who you are, neither do I understand why you're sitting at this table with us, but clearly the Westies believe you bring something to the discussion. I, however, can see you're personally involved in this and that's bad for business."

"Whether it was the Italians or the NWS, my club was targeted. My father's in a fucking coma, shredded into pieces because of those scumbags. I want justice, and I want it now. I have to figure that justice is something a man like you understands, Vasov. Or aren't you pissed about your kneecaps?" I asked, eying his wheelchair.

The Pakhan grunted under his breath, but he seemed to concede the point. At least, he did after he scowled at me like we were in the middle of a pissing contest.

The fucker was a fool if he didn't realize that I'd win that competition hands down against him.

When he conceded that too, and we eventually got down to business, I'd admit the entire meeting came as a surprise. And when, two hours later, O'Grady pulled me aside, I was even more astonished. With barely a chance to catch my breath, we shifted from business to personal, and where my mother was concerned, there was nothing more personal.

"Declan wanted me to give this to you," the Irish's money man informed me.

I frowned down at the folded piece of paper he held in his hands. "What is it?"

"A drawing." His jaw worked for a second. "As part of his therapy, they're trying to make their son describe the nightmares he's currently enduring. This is a cleaned up version of the woman he sees being hurt. They're trying to—" He sighed. "Well, I don't know what they're doing, but I guess they want him to see her whole rather than as the victim he remembers."

"Jesus," I rasped.

"He was only a kid. It's going to fuck with his head for life." He cleared his throat. "It's cleaned up," he repeated. "But Declan told me to tell you that his wife's a world class artist, and that if you'd like a painting, she'll do one for you as a gift."

My nostrils flared at the prospect, and I reached for it, muttering, "Thanks," as my fingertips took note of the paper's texture. My throat felt thick as I moved to open it, to reveal my mother's face as a child remembered her.

Moments before her death.

Half expecting a grisly sight, to see my mother's features beaten and bloodied despite O'Grady's reassurances, I unfolded the paper with shaking hands.

But when I looked into the rich blue eyes on the drawing, the velvet-like golden hair, and the delicate chin, anger unfurled inside me.

Because this wasn't Rene—*this wasn't my mom.*

This was a face I hadn't seen in four years. A name I hadn't whispered in that long because it always hurt Storm to talk about his AWOL baby sister.

"This is the woman who was killed?" I demanded, leaning into O'Grady's personal space, willing him to tell me the whole truth and nothing but.

Scarlet had been like a sister to me too. To all the council. She'd been a massive pain in the ass, and had been incapable of keeping her legs together, but shit—she was like her brother. Just with tits.

We'd been raised together. I'd given her her first kiss by accident when she was thirteen and I was fifteen. Nyx had popped his fucking cherry with her.

Christ.

Scarlet.

It was only then that I realized timelines had never been mentioned. I'd always just taken it as read that it was my mom's passing, which meant so much in the scheme of things. After all, without her, Bear had almost gone off the fucking rails. We'd nearly gotten into a war with the Lone Riders over in Philly because of her death.

"Yeah," O'Grady confirmed. "That's who Seamus saw being hurt. Apparently, four years ago, he and his mom were living in West Orange, working on a house for a client. That's where he saw the woman being murdered." He paused. "Declan seemed to think it was your mother—"

"It isn't," I said woodenly, peering down into the face of an angel with the mind of a demon. God, she'd been so much fucking fun.

"Who is she?"

"A woman who was like a sister to me." Which was why our kiss had ended with me backing off, even if she'd tried to give me a hand job to keep me by her side. Even at thirteen, she'd been a little nightmare.

"Christ, I'm sorry, Rex," O'Grady muttered, scraping a hand over his head. "I never imagined—"

"Why would you?" I folded the piece of paper back together and asked, "If the offer's still open, I'd appreciate the painting."

"Of course. I'll tell Aela."

I dipped my chin. "Thanks." Mouth tight, I rasped, "Can you do me another favor?"

O'Grady's wariness surged. "Depends?"

"I have a man in Rikers. I need to get him out. Whatever you need, I'll get you by way of payment."

"He's important?"

I shrugged. "Wouldn't ask for help if he wasn't. He's young, and he's a councilor's brother. With him in prison after what just happened, there's no way they're not going to try to use him as retaliation." I pursed my lips as I thought back to that convo with Nyx after he'd visited Quin, and the subsequent discussions with Rachel on the matter. "Brother or not, I have it on good authority that he's innocent of the crime he was imprisoned for."

O'Grady's gaze sharpened with interest. "The New World Sparrows?"

Dipping my chin, I told him, "I believe so, and I have a name... Lacey. Craig Lacey. He's with the 42nd Precinct."

"Those fuckers—"

"Exactly," I said with a grimace, because they were notoriously corrupt in that precinct. "He arrested Quin, got him hauled in on carjacking charges, then the judge went and threw the book at him even though he's a first offender. Had been only eighteen and serving time with goddamn serial killers and pedos... I'll admit to thinking the judge was just racist because Quin's a Native American. But now?" I shook my head.

"You think otherwise. Of course." He reached for his cell and murmured, "Craig Lacey is a start."

"I was thinking the same thing."

"Why not investigate this yourself?" he queried, his tone puzzled.

"Because I'm not exactly equipped for much of anything right now. The club isn't weakened, but we're definitely reeling. According to Declan, we're allies. If I can't trust you with this, then who can I trust?"

Then, with the drawing burning a hole in my cut and without waiting on another word from him, I retreated to the door where I knew a bunch of my brothers would be waiting, on the knife's edge, in concern for me.

One of whom didn't realize the sister we'd thought had run off years ago had, in fact, been slain under our noses by the Italians.

Those fuckers were going to pay, but how many more would we lose along the way?

That was my biggest fear, and something I couldn't even voice out loud. I had too many people relying on me. Too many people depending on me for answers I didn't have.

I'd walked in here today expecting to die, not plead Quin's case to men who had the ear of the governor... yet here I was, walking out again and of my own volition.

Maybe Satan really did watch over his Sinners.

TWENTY-EIGHT

MAVERICK

THOUGH MY HEAD ached like a bastard, I sat up and clambered to my feet. I rolled with a motion I was free to express now that it seemed like people knew I was able once more. I'd forgotten at first, to the point where I was sure my legs didn't work again, but they did.

My lies, my fears, were coming back to haunt me in a big way.

Hobbling over to Lodestar's chair, I placed one hand beside her on the table, then looming above her, demanded, "What's happened while I've been out?"

She cast me a derisive look that sheltered a world of hurt. I'd done something to slight her.

Christ.

She was one of the biggest babies I knew.

"A lot's happened," she muttered, "but not enough. I've been down too. Incapable of working at full capacity."

I reached up and rubbed my forehead. "Any news on the sniper?"

"The other day, Alessa asked me for the exact location of the nest I saw in Sinner territory—I gather you picked up something worthy of DNA testing, because you contacted Ken. We should be hearing from him any day now."

My mouth twisted. "You and your goddamn cloned phones."

"Like you haven't cloned mine."

I had to snicker. "Sure I have. Not that you call or text anyone on it. Boring fucker."

"Takes one to know one."

I grunted. "Not that I have a clone of your phone anymore. Crap, I guess I need to buy new gear as well." The thought was depressing. I'd spent a long time building my gear to my exact spec. Losing the computers was like losing family.

"I duplicated my order for you. You have everything I have."

Touched, I nonetheless jibed, "That's love."

Her grimace said it all, but when she peered into my eyes, clearly seeking something out, whatever she did or didn't find had her releasing a shaky breath. "It's nice for you to look at me like you don't hate me."

"I stopped hating you a long time ago," I said with surprise.

"Well, unfortunately for me, your head decided to go back to that year after we split up."

My nose crinkled. "Oh."

"Yeah. Oh."

Her dry retort had me nudging the side of her hand with my pinkie finger. "You're the one who was a bitch when we broke up."

"You'd never have let me go otherwise," she said sadly.

"Finding you in bed with your lieutenant wasn't the way to go." Goddamn Baldrick. I'd hated that fucker's guts before, so after I'd found them together in our fucking bed, it hadn't predisposed me to like him in the aftermath.

"You and I both know how possessive you are. You loved me. Nothing else would have broken us apart."

"I still do," I said with ease. "Love you, I mean."

"I know. I love you too." She shrugged. "But I know you're *in* love with Alessa. We're like siblings now."

Because I agreed, I just tapped her shoulder. "You need to let me in, Star. You need to stop keeping me out of the loop."

"Like you're one to judge," she retorted, her gaze drifting back to the computer screen. "You're the one standing here like you didn't live in a wheelchair by choice for four years."

"Yeah, I never said I wasn't a hypocrite."

She clucked her tongue. "If you think you're not going to tell me why you decided to hide—" Star grabbed my hand. "Are you in danger? Is that it? Do you need me to help you?"

A sigh escaped me. "I wish it was something as brave as that, Star, but it wasn't. I wasn't in danger. I was just scared, I guess. Scared to live again."

"You were hiding out in the chair?"

"Pretty much."

"You had to have been training in secret."

"I was."

"Why? Why keep it from the brothers?"

"Because they'd have made me do shit." I shrugged. "They'd have wanted me to live again, and I wasn't ready for that. In all honesty, I don't even know if I'm ready for that now."

"You love her," she told me, and I heard the fervency in her voice. "You've been pushing her away since you got out of the hospital. Honestly, Mav, if you'd treated me like you'd treated her, I'd have fucked off on day two."

"That's because you're not as kind as she is."

"There's kind and there's being eligible for fucking sainthood," she grumbled. "You have a lot to make up for."

"I know."

"If you could walk, why the fuck did you go into the clubhouse in that goddamn wheelchair?"

I sighed. "Habit, I guess. Stupidity? It was a crutch. Just because I could walk didn't mean I ever did. That's why I feel as shaky as a newborn lamb now."

"You've been walking around since the hospital," she pointed out.

"My brain says otherwise." Grimacing, I stopped looming over her and reached up to rub my forehead. "I have a motherfucker of a migraine."

"That's going nowhere," she muttered, her tone borderline sympathetic. As sympathetic as she got anyway. "You've got CTE, Mav. It's only going to get worse."

"Christ. Isn't that what Aaron Hernandez had?"

"Yeah. They said that's why he killed his wife, didn't they?" She hummed under her breath. "Fucking sucks."

My brow puckered. "Is Alessa in danger?"

She snorted. "Of course. She's married to a Satan's Sinner. But I figure she's been around worse cunts than you lot. She can deal with this. Plus, I heard she's pretty wicked with a baseball bat."

"A bat?" I winced. "Should I be scared?"

"Probably. Maybe you being out of it has been what she needed to grow a set of balls. You'd have gotten bored of her always jumping when you asked her to. Now, at least, she's got a bit of fire." Her nose crinkled. "You brought that on yourself though. I'd remember that when she surprises you with something."

"How would she surprise me?"

A smile danced on her lips, a smile that had unease filtering through me. "I'm sure you'll find out." Her head tipped to the side. "I'd move away if I were you. She's uncertain about you as it stands. Let's not add to it, huh?"

"She knows you mean a lot to me, Star," I countered.

"Yeah, she does, but she's just spent a long ass time being treated like Satan himself by you. Since you got out of the hospital, you've been fixated on Nic again. I figure you can soothe her ruffled feathers for a while." She shoved me away, and I complied, even though I dragged out the seat beside her so I could stare at her laptop screen.

The backlight hurt my eyes, made little flashes of strobing light dance around the periphery of my vision, but I squinted at the screen, trying to make out what she was doing.

"You need to bring me up to speed," I rasped at her. "I don't have time to lay low. The club needs me."

"I won't mother you, but let me state for the record that I think you're an idiot if you push it. Who the hell knows if you might drift back to that time again? You've got brain damage, Maverick. You have to take it easy."

I gritted my teeth. "I can take more rests—"

"Yes. You will take more rests," Alessa intoned from the doorway, the hint of Slav in her voice making my dick stir even though the throbbing in my head should have done away with any and all functioning of my cock. "You shouldn't even be looking at the screen. The doctor advised against it."

"Rules were made to be broken," Star murmured, but she was smirking as she spoke, her gaze drifting over lines of code that made her face gleam green in its illumination.

"Certain ones for sure. Not when it means the difference between being unconscious and conscious from a headache," was Alessa's waspish retort.

I wasn't sure why everyone was calling her that and not Ghost, but I liked it. I'd always loved her name. Since the day I'd heard her say, "I do."

Reaching out for her, I sighed a little as she slipped her hand into mine. "Any joy? Did you find anything in my personal effects?"

"No. Nothing."

I frowned. "Wonder if the council has something in their possession. They could have checked my stuff before they brought it back here."

She cupped the back of my neck. "There's time to think about this later. It's barely eleven AM and you must need to rest."

There was no hiding that my brain felt like it had been shoved into a Vitamix on high, but I knew there were things I had to do. Though it had been beyond my control, I'd wasted a lot of goddamn time. Whispers of memories of the past weeks merged into my consciousness, but mostly all I was aware of was the gaping great hole where Ghost should be. I remembered the gnawing ache of Nic's loss, of the grief I'd experienced, but I could also feel how I'd been pushing her away...

It was no wonder the weight I'd worked hard to encourage her to gain had begun to drop off. She looked drawn, too, but maybe not as drawn as I could have expected.

What was it Star had said? She'd grown some balls?

Intrigued despite myself, I tugged her closer, pulling her down onto my lap. "I'll go get some rest soon," I promised. "But first, I need to catch up."

Star peered at the phone in her lap, and a sigh escaped her as she flashed me the screen.

Rex: *Wait for me outside. All's well in here. I'm in no danger.*

Nyx: *The fuck were you even thinking?*

Link: *He wasn't thinking—*

The council began bickering, blowing up Rex's phone with messages which he clearly ignored as he didn't reply, but all three of us relaxed a little, knowing he was safe and well. He'd never have sent that text if he wasn't.

I read a couple more lines of the text convo between my brothers before looking back at Star's screen. With a couple of flourishes, she muttered, "There, that got the bastard off my computer for another day," before she switched onto another program.

Frowning, I studied the frames on the screen and asked, "CCTV footage?"

"Of the night of the blast," she confirmed, lips pursed. "I'm going to fast forward a lot of this shit because I've been bored enough weeding through it without having to watch it all again."

There were four screens on the top, in the middle, and at the bottom.

"Going to show them to you in sequential order." She tapped the middle screen. "Clubhouse. The party starts. The gates open forty minutes later."

My eyes flared wide when she zoomed into the screen, revealing a hooded figure who kept their shoulders hunched. They knew where the cameras were, because they kept their body twisted away from them, and I watched as they opened the gates, allowing a small truck with no plates to ride into the opening of the driveway.

The passenger door opened, the hooded figure climbed in, and that was where Lodestar froze the screen. In flashing increments that made me feel like I was at a disco because the strobe effect fucked with my senses, I saw a slither of a face revealed inch by inch.

"Christ, it's Tink!" I blurted out.

"Tink? The clubwhore?" Alessa sputtered, peering into the screen to get a better look.

"How long have you been sitting on this?" I snapped at Star, who shrugged.

"A couple of hours. I wasn't lying when I said it's been taking me a lot more time to get shit done, and this wasn't a priority."

"Getting a play-by-play of the night's events wasn't a priority?" I snapped, and when her eyes shifted to the screen, I hissed out a snarl. "When will I remember that you put your goals first?"

Her jaw tightened, but she pointed to the screen again. "Look, they veer off the driveway and head to the location I gave you."

"We saw no car tracks," Alessa murmured softly.

"They must have set up the nest on foot."

"Tink left recently, didn't she?" I muttered to myself. "She was—" The memory was there, just a little vaguer than I'd like. I wasn't sure if that was the CTE or if it was just attic theory. I rarely let anything the clubwhores did penetrate my brain too much.

I had more important shit to think about than those pains in the asses.

"She attacked Stone," Alessa prompted. "The night of Sarah's funeral."

"That's right," I whispered, the memory coming to me. "I wonder if she—"

"I haven't been able to ascertain the identity of the sniper," Star told me. "I don't know if they were working together long before this or if Tink decided to get some revenge on the Sinners by teaming up with a mutual enemy." She cleared her throat. "That's the last time we see the truck because the cameras were destroyed in the blast—"

"Bullshit," I snapped. "You and I both know you set something up somewhere else."

She sneered at me. "Like you haven't?"

I arched a brow at her. "I'll show you mine if you show me yours."

A sigh heaved from her. "Okay, but I've already been through the footage on my cameras." Grumpily, she tapped the keyboard and three more frames made an appearance.

"Why must you always lie?" Alessa remarked, sounding perplexed, and I couldn't blame her.

"Because treachery is my middle name?" was Star's mocking retort.

"She learned not to trust along the way," I countered, unwilling to accept her bullshit reply. When my ex's cheeks turned pink, I knew I'd scored a hit.

Grunting, she set the cameras rolling again. "See, I'm setting up on the roof—just there."

I nodded, still pissed at her over that.

It was strange how it felt as though our conversation in the hospital seemed a mere handful of hours ago when I knew it was weeks past...

Like the reminder was a prompt, a shard of pain sliced over my nerve endings, making my vision turn black for a few seconds. When Star spoke, it felt as though my head was buried in sand and then, out of nowhere, Alessa's hand began to rub the back of my neck, gently palpating the skin. A shaky breath escaped me, whispering from my lips as the pain edged away from sharp enough to make me wish for sleep to allowing me to concentrate just a little.

I shot her a look, saw a strange resolve in her eyes, one that warred with disapproval, but before I could say a word, Star snapped, "Am I talking to myself here?"

"No," Alessa answered for me. "But he needs to rest. You need to hurry up if you want to clue him in on what you've learned."

Lodestar grunted. "Key him in on weeks' worth of information in a handful of minutes? Yeah, that doesn't sound impossible, does it?" she groused under her breath. "Okay, double time." As she spoke, she tapped the screen. "I set up here, then I saw the sniper, there.

"A few minutes later, Bear rolls up the driveway, he climbs off the bike, the sniper targets his hog, triggering a detonation." She hummed a little. "Not enough to trigger red mist but enough to slice off a couple of limbs. Most of the damage to the clubhouse came from the gas tanks in the hogs parked outside." Her brow puckered. "Interesting, that. Like a warning shot almost."

"Why would anyone do that?" Alessa whispered, her voice loaded with horror.

Star and I shared a look, but she answered, "He's a Trojan horse."

I nodded. "They wanted Bear out of the picture and with maximum damage."

"Which means Bear knows more than they'd like." She frowned at the footage. "They didn't want the job to look like a hit. That's clear to see."

"No, they wanted it to be an outright assault on us."

"Why send the sniper at all? Why didn't they just shoot Bear if he was the target?" she ground out. "Why not just set a bomb off if attacking the clubhouse was their aim?"

"None of this makes any sense," I said with a sigh as tension clawed at my temples. "It feels like two MOs."

"Or one body of people trying to misdirect shit," she said grimly.

I worked my jaw, shaking my head at Star as I knew where she was going with this. "Not that hokey theory again."

She sniffed. "It's not a theory."

"Whether it is or isn't, can someone please explain?" was my wife's brisk retort.

"She's got it in her head there's this cabal of officials who—"

Lodestar scowled at me. "I'm telling you this is a cover up. Or a frame job. The Sparrows exist." She cut Alessa a look. "They're everywhere. The alphabet agencies, the army, the navy, the fucking Green Berets," she sniped. "The courts, prisons, goddamn town halls, even the fucking Italian mafia... when I say everywhere, I mean it. Their network's reach is insane." She pointed to the screen. "This is the New World Sparrows' handiwork, I'm telling you."

I just shook my head. "More like it's a Sinners' enemy wanting to weaken us."

"They wouldn't target Bear, would they? He isn't a brother anymore," Alessa pointed out weakly.

"He's a Sinner, even if he's not active. He was only allowed to roam because of who he is. Otherwise, we're tied in for life," I explained gruffly, patting her hand when I saw she looked peaky.

Alessa cleared her throat. "Star?"

My ex looked at my wife, her brow arched. "What?"

"*Horobchyk.*"

Lodestar shrugged. "No idea what that means."

"It's what we call the people who bring us to America," she whispered, her eyes wide with fear. "Sparrows."

Star tensed. "Jesus."

"That doesn't mean anything. Christ, when South Americans want to cross into the States, they call them coyotes. Doesn't mean Wile E.—"

"Maverick, get your head out of your ass," Star snapped. "I told you a long time ago about the New World Sparrows, but you wouldn't believe me. Well, they've come to your fucking door and blown it to hell so it's time you started fucking listening." Her mouth tightened and she went back to tapping the screen. "After the blast, the truck returns and barrels down the driveway and out onto the road. A handful of seconds later, close enough to make me wonder if she saw the driver, Rachel makes an appearance."

"She'd have said if she had," I argued.

"She isn't exactly pro-Sinners," Star pointed out.

"She works for us," I grumbled.

"So?" Lodestar huffed. "Too fucking trusting. That's always been your problem."

I grunted under my breath, but didn't have the chance to say anything as I watched the scene unfold from a distance. It was a lot different from when you were in the middle of the chaos.

"How did any of us survive?" Alessa rasped, her fear clear, and I wrapped my arms around her waist and tugged her close.

"Because they wanted us to," Lodestar rumbled softly. "They wanted to cause havoc, wanted to tell us we weren't safe even in our own HQ, and that they can get to us whenever they want, wherever they want."

A part of me wanted to scoff at that, wanted to tell her she was crazy, and I knew to some extent, she was nuts. But the Sparrows were something she'd been talking about for a long time. Before she'd gone to ground—or, at least, what I'd thought was her going to ground, and what I'd recently learned was…

I gritted my jaw. "You think the Sparrows were who sold you, don't you?"

Alessa tensed. "Sold you?"

Star shot her a look. "You're not the only ex-slave sitting at the table," she mumbled, but her chin tipped up and she glared at me. "I told you, years ago, they existed. That's why they tried to shut me up."

"Why didn't they kill you?" Alessa whispered. "Back where I'm from, we all know the Sparrows are deadly."

"They should have picked a different fucking bird, shouldn't they? What's scary about a sparrow?"

Alessa gulped. "You'd be surprised."

"Yeah, you would," Lodestar concurred. "And the reason they didn't kill me is because white women sell for a pretty penny in the Middle East." Her top lip quirked into a sneer. "Maverick, you ask me why I don't trust and why I do shit my own way, why I don't share things with the club... this is why. Because you think it's penny-ante cops and robbers shit.

"It ain't, Jameson. It ain't." She gritted her teeth. "This has been going on for a long ass time, but I'm going to be the one who ends them. Do you hear me?

"They put me through hell, and I got out by the skin of my fucking teeth—I won't let them take me again. I'll die first, but I'm going no-fucking-where until I take them out with me. I'm the most expensive mistake they ever goddamn made, and I'll make them die regretting that they let me live."

TWENTY-NINE

ALESSA

I WOKE up with a storm of heat at my back. All down my spine, along my legs, even the soles of my feet were cocooned in warmth.

It wasn't the kind of heat that came from a blanket, even one of those electric heating pads my *babusya*, my grandmother, had sworn by during the final years of her life. It was Maverick.

Any sense of sleepiness soon disappeared as I recognized what was happening.

Whenever I'd gone to sleep with Maverick and had woken up with him, I'd been curled around him. I'd warmed *him*.

That he was warming me was a reminder.

It hadn't been a dream.

This was real.

He was back.

The tears that refused to fall made my eyes ache, and I turned my face into the pillow, burrowing into it, adoring that everywhere smelled of him, that everywhere smelled safe again. I felt like an unripe orange being squeezed for juice, but my eyes burned as the tears longed to fall and when a slight trickle of moisture escaped, the relief was almost as powerful as knowing Maverick was behind me.

My Maverick.

Not Nic's.

I bit my lip at the uncharitable thought.

I hadn't known it was possible to be jealous of a dead man, but I'd admit to growing that way over the past few weeks. The strength of his memory in Maverick's mind had overtaken everything else, overwhelmed his world until I was erased from existence.

Was it strange that it was only now when I could accept how angry I was about that?

Like a lost puppy, I'd accepted every kick Maverick had hurt me with, every blow, but now that he was back, I knew something had to change. Something had to give.

Nic was gone. But I wasn't.

I was here.

I didn't begrudge Nic Maverick's love. I just resented the foothold he had on his damaged mind, and I knew I had to do something to mark my place in his head because I wasn't a fool. As quickly as his memory had resurfaced, there was no saying that it wouldn't disappear in a flash again when something stressful happened.

I was well aware my husband was a ticking time bomb, but I wasn't a coward. I'd stay by his side, uncaring if it was with his permission or not—I just needed to make sure he wouldn't forget me again.

I needed to be his link. A tangible connection that bound him to the present.

It sounded impossible, improbable. Unscientific and probably ridiculous. But a woman didn't endure what I had, and a man didn't survive what Maverick had, to come out, find one another, and for them not to fit together like two puzzle pieces.

We called it *dolya* in Ukrainian. Fate.

That was Maverick and me.

We were fated to love and to hurt and to lose and to remember. To endure... that was our destiny.

Tragic, perhaps. But less so when we were together.

My eyes flickered open when I heard a slight creak in the door, and when I saw Kati standing there, peering at us through the crack she'd made, I frowned at her.

A part of me wanted to shoo her away because I knew Maverick was still resting, had been ever since he'd allowed himself to relax after we'd heard news Rex was returning to Jersey in one piece, and there was no way I was going to let him wake up yet when he needed as much rest as possible. But she was my baby sister. Wild hair, what looked like soup down her shirt, and odd socks on her feet and all.

So instead of shooing her away, I raised a hand and beckoned her forward. She stunned me by complying. I fully expected her to dart off, to run away, but she didn't. She drifted forward on whispered steps, carefully pressed one knee to the mattress, then with a care I didn't think she was capable of, rolled herself against me.

"Is he really back?" she whispered, the words almost noiseless.

Rather than reply, I tucked an arm over her waist, and nodded. She huddled into me and stunned me further by relaxing. Kati, my overactive, loudmouth sister, *relaxed*. Actually calmed down, stayed quiet, and didn't even fidget.

She fell asleep too, only when I next woke up, she'd gone. Maverick hadn't though. He was still there. A bastion of heat.

That I'd needed the rest was a given. That he needed it was a foregone conclusion. Even knowing that, the desire to wake him was heady. I wanted to make sure he remembered me. His body appeared to, but did his mind?

For several minutes, I lay there, worrying. Then he mumbled, "Love you, 'Lessa," and I felt like sagging into the mattress.

Twice in two days?

Because I knew we'd somehow slept the day and a night through.

That was how exhausted we were. How much we'd needed the rest.

"I love you, Mav."

His face burrowed into my nape, and he released a sigh that sent hot air blowing over my throat. It was uncomfortable considering how warm I already was, but I wouldn't swap it for the world.

I turned slightly in his arms, moving so I was half facing him. It took some wiggling, but I managed to hook one leg over his, opening myself up to him in a way I knew he wouldn't register. He wouldn't know how big a deal that was, but I did.

A woman in my position made moves like that on command. Not by choice.

But I gave Mav that choice, and I appreciated that he didn't even know it.

I didn't want him to remember me for what I was—dirty. Used.

I wanted him to want me, not be disgusted by my past.

Cautiously, but needing more than just the words to reassure me that this was real, I pressed my lips to his. We'd kissed before, dry humped each other in the past, but I craved a different kind of connection. One I prayed would bind us together.

Even as I longed for that, inwardly I felt like ice.

Questions rolled over each other in my head—would I be able to do it? Could I really go through with it? Did I truly want him? Was I only doing this to bind him to me?

But as my lips brushed his, they started to fade. As did all other background noise.

I'd learned that before... funny how I'd forgotten it though. Strange how I hadn't recalled that, in the crowded attic of before, with the pounding music from the bar below, he'd kissed me and we'd drifted into silence. Into a haven of our own making.

But he welcomed me back by parting his lips and softly returning the kiss. He embraced me into that silent paradise by holding me, by letting me relax into his tender touch.

Maverick wasn't a gentleman.

I knew that.

Just because he was my protector, that didn't mean he was perfect.

He wouldn't be happy with gentle kisses and soft touches forever, but that he gave me that now had me hoping I'd be able to handle more in the future.

Sex meant pain to me. In my mind, that was all I knew it as. I'd been a virgin when I'd been sold, and my hymen had been torn away, ripped into shreds as much as my hope for a brighter future in America with my sister had been.

But I had hope again.

I had a future where I hadn't before because of this man, because of his family.

I wasn't a victim.

I wasn't a ghost.

I was Alessa, and it was time I took back what was mine—my identity. My sexuality. My personality. Me.

It was time I owned *me* again.

With that desire bolstering me, I slipped my arms around Maverick's neck and tugged him closer to me. I didn't realize the ferocity of my hold until we were plastered against each other, and I felt his response to my being here.

An erection.

One he didn't bother to shield.

It was...

Pizda.

Could I do this?

Could I?

I truly didn't know.

Penises represented so much—all of it bad... and then, he rubbed his lips over mine, pulling back so he could look at me, stare into my eyes like he could see all my secrets, and wanted to know each of them.

He stared at me as if I was his Ghost again.

I wasn't a stranger.

I was his.

The tension that had been inherent in his frame since the clubhouse's collapse had dissipated. He was lax in bed, and that made me wonder if he'd stop suffering with so much pain because such internal stress couldn't have been good for him.

"We don't have to do anything—" he started to say, but I moved so I could press a finger to his lips.

"Maverick?"

"Yes," he rumbled around my pointer finger.

"Why did you stop having sex?"

His brows rose at the question, and slowly, I moved my hand away so he could talk without any encumbrance.

"It wasn't physical," I pointed out, knowing it wasn't because today wasn't the first time I'd felt his dick harden in response to what we were doing.

"No, it wasn't," he agreed, his eyes darkening. "Have you been in love before, Ghost?"

My nose crinkled. "Alessa."

His lips twitched. "Sorry. That's going to take some getting used to."

"I know. And the answer is no. Not before you."

He lowered his head. "Before Nic, I'd loved people, but I hadn't been *in* love. He made me realize the difference. I-I figure you know who he is now?"

I wanted to scoff at that—know him? He'd been haunting us for weeks!

But I didn't.

How could I?

It wasn't Maverick's fault.

"I do," was all I said, and I kept my gaze on his lips because I didn't want him to see and misunderstand my resentment.

"Well, before him, sex was easy come and easy go. After Lodestar and I broke up, I slept around a lot," he admitted. "I was single, had a dangerous vocation, and could die at any given moment when I was deployed, and I was deployed more often than I wasn't back then. I fucked around whenever I could. Man, woman. I didn't give a damn.

"Then I met Nic, and he made me realize what sex was."

"What is it?" I whispered, curious now that I heard the dreamy quality in his voice.

"I've never told anyone this," he admitted sheepishly, a hint of self-deprecatory laughter gleaming in his eyes.

"I can keep a secret."

"I know you can," he said immediately. "But it's not something guys admit to. At least, not often." He released a deep breath. "I realized that sex with someone you didn't give a damn about was as unsatisfying as jacking off, so when Nic died, I just...stopped."

My eyes bugged out at that, because Maverick was a beautiful man. In fact, he was so handsome he could have been in a movie. The tiniest indent in his chin, the stubble that was the same gilt color as his shorn hair, the most stubborn jaw imaginable... he was gorgeous. And somehow, when he looked at me, I felt like I was just as beautiful to him in his eyes.

"You mean to tell me you haven't had sex in ten years?" I whispered, utterly agog.

"Well, off and on. Probably five. Before the accident anyway. My body wasn't broken," he muttered, "my head was." He tapped his temple with his finger. "And I don't mean this CTE crap. I just mean I couldn't get over Nic." He shrugged. "Before Lodestar, who fucked her CO in our goddamn bed, there was Lesley.

"She was my high school sweetheart, and she screwed me over during my first deployment, slept around like crazy and just broke my fucking heart in the process... so I kinda treated women like shit for a while, fell in with guys, and it just rolled on with that. Carried on fucking everything that moved, and then Nic came along.

"He was the only person, until now, who ever got me where it mattered. In all honesty, it wasn't—"

When he broke off, his unease clear, I murmured, "It's okay, Maverick. I'd prefer to understand. My feelings aren't hurt."

"I think they are, and I think they have every right to be," he countered, his eyes darkening to pewter. "I know I must have treated you like shit these past couple of weeks."

"You did," I told him, deciding it was best to be honest. "But you weren't you. It's not like I could blame you."

"I'd have blamed me," he said bitterly. "I blame me now." When I just sighed, he winced, but reached up to tuck a strand of hair behind my ear, and murmured, "I loved Lodestar. Even loved Lesley. But I recognized that what I felt for Nic was a once-in-a-lifetime kind of love."

The pain of his words was like a knife to the throat. I could feel my lifeblood spilling from me, only he didn't notice. His gaze was lost to the past again. That thousand-yard stare I'd come to loathe overtaking him, so I knew he wasn't lying here with me, but back then again.

"I lost hope," he whispered. "I lost all sense of self. I poured myself into my work. I dedicated myself to causes that Nic thought were worthy of our fight. And then I got tangled in something I didn't even understand. Not until Lodestar found me again three years ago. That shit she was talking about today—"

Because he didn't know I was lying in a pool of blood from my shattered heart, I just whispered, "The Sparrows?"

He hummed. "Yeah, well, she's been spouting it for a long time. I never believed the crap about the cabal, but by that point, I didn't give much of a damn about anything. She cared enough to try, so I figured laying low was for the best." He winced. "Between Kembesh and the IED blast that took me out of the game, those six years weren't great for me. I had a death wish. Went wherever I was sent, did as I was ordered—no questions asked. Got a rep for doing the jobs few would.

"I'm not proud of what I did," he muttered with a sigh. "But someone had to do the dirty work, and that was me for too long. When the IED..." He grunted. "Well, *after*, I hoped it'd kill me but it didn't. Only the good die fucking young, don't they?" He reached up and rubbed his eyes. "When I was shipped into the U.S. again, I was stuck in Bethesda for over a year. Couldn't seem to get any desire to live, didn't have much reason to get out of bed in the morning.

"My brothers, fuck, they tried, but I was a stubborn cunt. Until Lodestar sneaked into my room one night and told me to hurry the hell up and get better. She said I needed to get out of there because I was in danger, and I needed to disappear. She worked hard to make certain people think I was dead...and maybe I believed that, because for a long time, I felt it."

"Why were you in danger?"

"By that point, I had half the Middle East baying for my blood. This time, my A-team was involved in a mission in Benghazi that went wrong. Another one." He grunted. "It put us in contact with some people who we should have never met. I was the only one who got out of there alive. The IED explosion I was involved in"—he pressed his hand to his chest where there were scars on his torso, mostly on his lower abdomen and sides—"it was supposed to kill us all."

A sharp breath escaped me. "*Khuy na ne!*"

"I don't know what that means, but" —he smirked— "yeah, *khuy na ne!*"

My nose crinkled at his accent.

"So, there I was, supposed to be dead, feeling like the living dead, then I heard about you and what you'd been through. Then I went into that goddamn bunkhouse, and I sat in your bedroom and saw you struggling to live, but somehow staying strong enough to not let go... and I just—" His eyes flared wide. "It was like *I* came back to life too. Watching you grow stronger, watching you get better, making you eat, encouraging you to drink those shakes, winning a smile from you... Every day that you improved, I seemed to improve too. Slept a little deeper, could breathe a little easier.

"Until, all of a sudden, my day felt incomplete without seeing you." My shattered heart began to pulse with hope as he met my gaze once more. "Until, out of nowhere, I had to feel your hand in mine. Needed to feel your lips grace my cheek. I had to be closer to you—had to for my own selfish needs." He shook his head. "You brought me back to life, Alessa. You did. I was a dead man, dying even as I was living. Then you came along and you made me realize what it was to feel again." He licked his lips. "I'm not sure what I've done in my life to deserve two loves like this, and it terrifies me. *You* terrify me—"

"Me?" I burst out, unable to comprehend that.

"Yeah, you," he said with a soft laugh. "Ghos—I mean, Alessa, you have the power to decimate me." The simplicity of his statement resonated with me like nothing else could. "I-I somehow survived losing Nic. I had a purpose back then, and though the Sinners gave me a reason to get up in the morning, that wasn't enough to make me feel like living again. It wasn't enough to make me leave that fucking chair, to lead a regular life. You did that. You. And there's no one out there like you, so..." His jaw tensed, and I sensed he was gritting his teeth. "Alessa, you can't leave me. Please," he whispered, but it went deeper than that.

It was a plea.

He was begging me.

"Please, Alessa, don't leave me." His lips quivered as he pressed his mouth to mine, just resting there, not letting me speak, just holding me in place as he slipped his arms over my waist, tangling me up in him.

"I won't, Maverick, I won't," I mumbled against him, then annoyed, I jerked my head back so I could speak unheeded. "I didn't let go when you weren't mine. So I won't let go now that you are."

He swallowed. "What if it happens again?"

"It's likely." I bit the inside of my cheek to stop the prickling onset of tears. "There's no cure, but there's treatment—treatment you refused." He winced. "I had no hope of you coming back to me, but you did. So I'm going to take every day that comes, I'm going to hold you for as long as you'll let me, and if I lose you to Nic again, I'm going to pray you'll come back to me. I'm going to pray that God, or whoever it was that brought us together, will keep on doing that."

"If there was a God, he wouldn't tear us apart," he rasped, his lips turning down at the corners.

"I don't want to think of it that way. If I gave you a reason to live, *kokhanyy,* then it's the same way for me." My smile was shaky as I reached up to press my fingers to his unhappy mouth. "We've been given a gift. Sometimes, the path to enjoying that gift isn't smooth, but nothing about this life is smooth, and in the interim, we need to make sure that we enjoy every day we're blessed with."

His eyes fluttered to a close. "If I was a good man, I'd make you leave me." My brow puckered at his words, then that shattered heart of mine, the one he liked to fracture so frequently, finally merged back together for good when he rasped, "I-I can't leave you. I'm not strong enough to do that. Not *good* enough or selfless enough, but I could make you leave me."

Because that was foolish talk, I whispered, "You forgot me, Maverick. I didn't leave you. Lily offered me a bank account swollen with money, and I didn't go anywhere. I won't. You're stuck with me. Forever.

"Whether you forget me again or not, I won't ever forget you.

"That's a promise, *kokhanyy.*

"My vow to you."

And then, because he had a habit of putting his foot in things, I pressed my lips to his to shut him up.

That was, I reasoned, the safest thing to do.

THIRTY

MAVERICK

MY HEART HURT. It hurt. Not just because of how much I felt for this crazy woman but for what I'd put her through, for what I could put her through again in the future.

There was pain ahead of us, none of it physical, but she was still so strong. Still a thousand times stronger than I was, because she wasn't going to leave me.

I saw it in the resolve in her eyes.

Saw it in the shadows of hurt I'd etched into her soul.

I'd done what Lancaster and all her previous owners hadn't.

I'd left marks there.

That was the power of what she felt for me.

That was the depth of it.

That was the level of the feelings I inspired in her.

I was lucky.

I was selfish.

I wasn't going to let her go, but more importantly, I saw she wasn't going to let *me* go, and that meant more to me than she could know.

She'd cling to me as hard as I clung to her, and that liberated me. To love like I did wasn't fashionable. To love with your whole being was to welcome a world of hurt, and after Nic had passed, I hadn't thought I was capable of it again—in all honesty, hadn't wanted to be capable of it. Yet she'd proved me wrong, but more than that, she accepted this.

She accepted what she could see I felt.

She wasn't scared, not like Lodestar had been. Lodestar who'd only ever seen a fraction of the love I felt for Alessa from me. She'd run away, had run scared. Alessa, with all she'd been through, was strong enough to take what I had to give, to return it.

This woman, this soul who'd been sold, who'd been betrayed, who'd been used like no one should ever have to be, who'd endured acts of torture that I, a trained soldier, probably wouldn't have been able to endure, was whole enough to accept all I had to give.

And that was like letting the floodgates open.

Before the blast, I'd contained myself. Gifted her with chaste kisses that I imbued with my feelings. Held her until she slept, finding solace in her presence.

But now, the truth was out.

She knew what I felt for Nic.

If I didn't allow her to see what I felt for her, she'd forever feel as if she was second best.

But she wasn't second anything.

My heart had never belonged to me.

The two halves had always been meant for two people.

Nic—who'd made me into the man I was. Who allowed me to see that to love like I did, just as my mother had, wasn't wrong. That someone could accept that love and live with it and love me back.

And Alessa—who accepted my flaws, accepted I was broken,

accepted I could never be fixed and who wanted me anyway. Who took my love into her keeping, and cherished it as much as I'd cherish her.

My mouth trembled at the thought, and I found myself with no alternative other than to press mine to hers to stop that tremor.

She sighed into my kiss, sighed enough to part her lips, to slip her tongue into mine, to graze ours together. She sampled me, tasted me, doing what she hadn't really done before—explored me. She was hesitant, naturally, because this was a kiss imbued with love. With her feelings for me. And I basked in it.

I wanted to gift her with the same, but I couldn't.

Her past wouldn't let me.

For all that she blew my mind with her strength of will, she *did* have history. I refused to be like any of the other fucking bastards she'd lain with. I refused to force her in any way.

She had to come to me when she deserved for me to kneel at her fucking feet.

Anger spilled into me, but I refused to let it leak into the kiss. I just let her find her way, let her take what she needed from me and slowly, I felt the change in her.

Those exploratory caresses, like how it was when you first learned to kiss, morphed into something else. Growing tenser and wilder, hungrier as her need grew.

Need she felt for me.

My dick pounded, the ache so strong, so overwhelming that I wanted to groan in her mouth, but I was terrified I'd trigger a flashback. I knew how those felt, and the last thing I wanted was for her to remember what it felt like to be in another man's bed.

The rigid composure I imposed on myself was a small measure of self-punishment. It was the least I deserved for the shit I'd put her through, for the hell I'd made her endure.

As her tongue thrust against mine, her breathing became

choppy, and I closed my eyes as the sweet torment of her finding her passion in me overtook everything else.

It was there in the sweet flush on her cheeks, the bright gleam in her eyes when they opened to reveal a stark wonder that let me know she'd never been this turned on from a kiss like this before, to the jiggle of her tits with each panting breath.

When she rubbed those sweet mounds against my pecs, a groan escaped me—I couldn't help myself. Talk about heaven and hell all at the same fucking time.

Somehow, I managed to keep my hands down by my sides, but it was too late.

She'd heard.

She stopped.

She moved away.

Wanting to curse under my breath but concerned she'd take it as my being mad with her, I opened my eyes, half expecting to watch her move off the bed. But she didn't. If anything, she was peering down at me with a confused frown.

"Maverick?"

I blinked up at her, adoring the tousled state of her, the way her lips were pink from our kisses, the way she was flushed and bright and so fucking alive that I wanted to drown in her.

"Hmm?" I rasped, my gaze glued to her mouth. Which started to smile. Revealing white teeth that gleamed in the low light of morning, and which had the tiniest crooked slant to her front, bottom set.

Even that was perfect to me.

"Aren't you enjoying this?"

I blinked again. "Huh?" That had our eyes tangling.

"You're lying there like I've tied you to the bed." She frowned. "Do you need me to? I know everyone has their kinks."

Christ.

I cleared my throat. "No, I don't need that."

"Are you sure? I've done it befo—"

"No!" I barked, then quickly muttered, "I'm fine. I'm just trying not to lose control."

"Ah." She winced. "You have issues with control?" Her gaze glanced over my dick. "Is that it?"

Despite myself, I had to laugh. "You're doing that on purpose, aren't you?"

Her grin peeped out. "Well... you've been waiting a long time for sex. I'd imagine you're close to bursting."

I grabbed her hand and rested it over the covers which were tented by my hard-on. "I can handle a bit of teasing."

"Good to know," she retorted, but I could feel her amusement and was warmed by it.

She wasn't scared.

I'd figured she would be.

Like Alessa had read my mind, she whispered, "I was frightened at first."

"Not anymore?"

"You love me. Physically, you won't hurt me. I know that."

I wanted to flinch at her addition of the word 'physically,' but hell, I could make no promises about mentally or emotionally, could I? Not when I was dealing with something that made me flicker between the past and the present.

"Later on, we'll go to the hospital," I promised her.

"I was going to suggest that before we rested yesterday, but I knew you needed the sleep. You don't seem to like your doctor."

If it was Barry Beau, then she was right on the money.

Fucker was the cunt Lesley had cheated on me with—they'd even gotten engaged at one point.

"I don't wanna talk about that," I muttered. "I just want you to know that I'll get treatment. I'll do whatever to make sure I don't hurt you again."

Her gaze softened. "See? *Ya shchaslyva z toboyu,* Maverick." When she danced off into Ukrainian, somehow, I felt like we'd turned a corner, and she confirmed that by sliding her hand underneath the covers, flipping her fingers beneath the waistband of my boxer briefs, then letting them come around my dick.

A sharp breath escaped me because it had been a long time since anyone else's fist had been around it, and when she started to jack me off, speaking to me all the while in Ukrainian, I wasn't sure whether it was good or bad to have her talking to me with words I didn't understand.

Then, words didn't matter. Shit, I didn't give a fuck about them because what she did with her hands?

Holy fuck.

I hated how she'd gained the experience, but sweet, sweet, sweet Lord... George Harrison started serenading me because she squeezed and teased and rubbed and did something with her fucking thumb that had my eyes blurring. In a way I assumed had nothing to do with the CTE either.

My hips started to jack up and down, rocking in time to each flick of her wrists, and with every drop of pre-cum spilled, with every groan that whispered from my lips, with every clench of my fists into the sheets, she took me to the brink.

Not of arousal—I was already so far past that I was in another fucking state.

Not of need—she'd had me wrapped around her fucking finger since the first time I'd met her. Even when she'd been sick, I'd needed her. It had just been a different kind of need.

This was what a man felt for his woman.

What a man craved from his other goddamn half.

Even as I felt the leash on my control start to snap under the pressure of her fingers, I clung to it, needing to remain calm, needing to remember that being gentle with her was imperative, but with each goddamn twist of her fist, of her thumb over the glans, working her magic with every fucking stroke, I felt the beast inside me claw free. I couldn't contain it, just... God help me, I couldn't.

I snapped.

I let go.

I broke.

Surging upward, I rolled into her until she was flat on her back and I was on top of her, her legs were high around my hips, my dick was against the soft heat of her covered pussy.

I expected fear in her eyes, a stillness to her that stemmed from shock, and maybe both were there in the tiniest of increments, but mostly I saw a reciprocal fire that burned for me.

A thirst so deep for me that I knew it'd take a lifetime to quench.

More Ukrainian spilled from her, and I knew what that meant —she'd lost her English.

And I took that for the sign it was.

I reared up so I could shove my boxer briefs down, just far enough to grab a firm hold of my cock and to release it from the cage of my underwear. With my knees digging into the mattress, I used the space I made to shove her panties aside, and when I encountered glistening, creamy flesh, I groaned.

Fuck.

Just...

FUCK.

I gritted my teeth as the need to taste her warred with the need to fuck her.

I thought I'd have to go slow. That I'd have to walk her gently through the process.

But she was ready for me.

She wanted me.

And I knew that was the depth of her love. Of her trust.

God, this woman. She gave and she gave and she fucking gave.

I didn't deserve her.

But she was mine.

And it was time I proved that to her.

I notched the tip of my dick against her slick folds, rubbing it through her juices, getting myself wet, torturing myself with the first pussy I'd had in years, and as my eyes fluttered into the back of my head, I pushed into her.

With enough wherewithal to stay calm, I didn't thrust as hard as I wanted to, I gently surged into her, filling her up with me. With the only dick she'd ever know again. One that'd erase every other fucker's presence she knew.

I'd get her so cock-drunk on mine that she'd forget her past. She'd remember it only in her nightmares, and I'd spend a fucking lifetime erasing those too.

If I had to endure CAT scans and Dr. goddamn Beau's thermometer up my ass, if I had to go to Bethesda again, if I had to endure treatment after treatment, I'd torment myself on the hunt for a solution so that my Old goddamn Lady never had to know a moment's pain from me.

Because the space between us was too much to bear, I moved atop her, covering her slim frame with my weight. She clung to me, her arms coming around me, her legs cupping me, and I stared into her eyes, not letting anything come between us, not allowing it, vowing to never allow it again as our noses touched, and our breath brushed the other's mouth.

Slowly, I rocked my hips.

Carefully, I moved into her.

Gently, I made love to her.

Showing her what that felt like, knowing from what she'd told me before that she'd been inexperienced before she'd been sold.

And then, as her tension began to leach out of her, being replaced by a different variety, she stopped simply accepting what I gave her.

She started taking.

She rocked back.

She moved into me.

She made love to me.

No longer pliant in my arms, no longer just a doll beneath me.

Her nails dug into my back, her heels pressed into my butt. She tightened her cunt around me, she held me so close I knew that two people had never been this close before, and as I ground down into her, making sure that with every thrust my pelvis rocked against her clit, I watched her fly.

For the first time in a man's arms, she flew.

She experienced freedom.

Something I'd spend the rest of my days giving her.

Her orgasm triggered my own—my self-control was good, but it wasn't *that* fucking good. Within seconds of her cunt throbbing around me, I exploded into her, and as I let out a sharp cry, she moaned, sobbing something in Ukrainian as she clung even harder to me, holding me tight, so tight that I knew she'd never let go.

Ever.

And that was a promise I needed to feel, not just hear.

THIRTY-ONE

ALESSA

TIREDLY, I rubbed my eyes as I crossed my feet at the ankles, staring at the same damn piece of wall I'd been staring at for hours.

My phone buzzed beside me, and I picked it up when I saw that Giulia had created a group chat. One she'd labeled 'Giulia's Posse.'

Lips twitching at the sight, I entered the chat, and laughed some more.

Stone: *Why's it named after you?*

Giulia: *Because I started the chat. If you'd started the chat, then you could have called it Stone's Posse.*

Stone: *I'd never be so egocentric.*

Giulia: *No? Well, you snooze you lose.*

Lily: *This is handy, actually. I'm surprised one of us didn't think of it before.*

Indy: *This is all I need. You bitches talking all day, blowing my phone up with notifications.*

Stone: *Did someone talk? I didn't see anything.*

Indy: *Grow up, would you? I'm sorry I didn't tell you first about Cruz and me, but it wasn't like I could call you up when I was inking myself.*

Stone: *Can someone tell Indy that she's full of bullshit?*

Giulia: *I'll tell her! Indy, you're full of bullshit.*

Tiffany: *You know she's your boss, right? o.O*

Lily: *Like Giulia would care about that.*

Giulia: *I know. *whistles* But I'm armed with more needles and catheters than a doctor now. She's afraid of me.*

Indy: *Hardly. Frankie didn't even let you pick up any equipment when she came in.*

Giulia: *I know where it's kept. That's half the war won.*

Indy: **snorts**

Giulia: *Alessa? You there, honey?*

Me: *I'm here. Just reading. It takes me longer to understand like this.*

Giulia: *Huh, I never thought of that.*

Me: *Don't worry. I can catch up. Is everything okay?*

Giulia: *I thought it was time we were all on the same page.*

Tiffany: *Sounds ominous.*

Giulia: *It is. We're not like our mothers. I think we can all agree with that. Whether they were MC or not, we're not like them.*

Giulia: *We're stronger, and we're not going to take any BS. Amirite?*

Me: *You're right.*

Indy: *Yeah.*

Tiffany: *God, no, I'm not like her.*

Lily: *I refuse to be like her.*

Stone: *I sure as fuck ain't like my mom.*

Giulia: *Music to my ears. Well, now that we're definitely* agreed on that, I think we have to get together to stop our fucking Old Men from thinking we're like the last gen of bitches. They ain't about to ride over us.

Me: Maverick doesn't ride roughshod over me. If he did, I don't think we'd be here today.

Stone: I'll be by shortly, honey. To help explain everything. I hate that prick Beau.

Tiffany: If ever there was a man who didn't deserve the name.

Me: Why? What's it mean?

Lily: It's French for handsome.

Me: Oh dear, yes, that's a very poorly fitting name.

Giulia: Hahaha. Dude got burned by Alessa. That's how you know he's an ugly motherfucker. Don't think I've ever heard you insult someone before, babe.

Me: Well, I'm no angel. I'm sure me and Maverick will be insulting each other before the day is out. He's getting tired and I don't blame him. He's starting to snipe. I'm going to try to keep him calm but I don't know if that's doable.

Me: He's been in and out of different scans all day. Dr. Beau is really taking this to the limit.

Me: I'd say he thinks Maverick will change his mind before he gets all the data he needs.

Stone: Probably. This is his pet project. I know for a fact he's been working with the Jets, trying to create some kind of special helmet or something.

Stone: It's all the talk around the wards.

Giulia: You guys really know how to live it up.

Stone: Sure do.

Me: What are the Jets?

Tiffany: Football team.

Me: *Oh. Why?*

Stone: *Football players suffer with CTE a lot. Didn't Beau explain that? I thought he had.*

Stone: *Anyway, they get it a lot from all the trauma to their heads during the game.*

Stone: *He's trying to figure out how to pay off his student debts before he's forty, I think.*

Indy: *She's being sarcastic, Alessa.*

Stone: *Actually, I wasn't. I meant it.*

Indy: *So you're talking to me again?*

Stone: *Only to tell you you're WRONG.*

Indy: **flips two birds at you**

Stone: *I take your two fingers and snap them. Without setting them after. >.>*

Indy: *That's mean.*

Stone: *I know it is. It's a BETRAYAL. Seeing how you're good with betrayals, figured you'd be okay with that too.*

Indy: *For fuck's sake, it isn't like I haven't told you everything else!*

Giulia: *Just wait while I grab some popcorn. This sounds interesting.*

Indy: *Fuck off, Giulia. Stone, you're really starting to piss me off.*

Stone: *Tough shit.*

Me: *Tink opened the gate for the sniper who helped detonate the bomb.*

Okay, so that wasn't the best timing for revealing such a sorry piece of information, but I liked Stone. She'd helped me and the others back at the start, and she was always working right now. I'd barely seen her since the blast, and I knew she was doing too much because she was still recuperating from her own injuries while working long shifts.

As for Indy, I didn't know her so well, but I knew that both women were old friends. Old friends shouldn't be at each other's throats like this.

Giulia: *Say what?*

Stone: *Are you fucking kidding me, Alessa?*

Indy: *Those goddamn clubwhores. I hate the fucking bitches. I shit 'em all.*

Giulia: *I'd say that sounds uncomfortable, but now isn't the time for laughing matters.*

Giulia: *Alessa, how did you figure that out?*

Me: *Lodestar was showing Maverick a rundown of what happened the night of the blast.*

Me: *Tink opened the gate to the compound, let the sniper in, then got into the truck with him.*

Stone: *Holy fuck.*

Lily: *Jesus. This isn't going to end prettily.*

Tiffany: *She must have had a death wish.*

Stone: *She had one of those when she tried to fuck MY man.*

Giulia: *True dat. Hmm. You know we can't leave this to the brothers, don't you?*

Me: *Leave what? It isn't like we can do anything.*

Giulia: *Fuck that. There's plenty we can do.*

Giulia: *This isn't council business, this is bitches' business.*

Indy: *I wish you'd stop calling it that.*

Giulia: *Why? Why shouldn't I call it that? It's the truth.*

Giulia: *This kind of crap needs to be dealt with in-house. We need to teach the fucking skanks a lesson they won't forget.*

Me: *What kind of lesson?*

Giulia: *She needs to x.x.*

Me: *What does that mean?*

Indy: *Something that isn't repeatable on a device that isn't encrypted I'd guess.*

Lily: *I think it's time we had a party at my place. We can talk about things there.*

Lily: *I have to go because Rex is coming to talk to me about the books.*

Me: *Which books? Anything I might like?*

Lily: *No, LOL. I mean, the accounts. I'm starting to work on the MC's business accounts for them. Trying to take some of the load off Maverick's shoulders.*

Me: *Oh, sorry. I feel stupid. :/*

Giulia: *Don't you dare. As if you're stupid. It's English that's stupid.*

Giulia: *I like the sound of this party, Lily. When and where? Needs to be before Nyx is back, or he'll have crawled up my ass to make sure I'm safe.*

Tiffany: *That sounds like it'd be more Link's area.*

Lily: *Shut up, you. :P*

Tiffany: *Sorry, it was too perfect to resist.*

Giulia: *Ladies, let's keep this PG.*

Indy: *Because going all 'eye for an eye' isn't R-rated?*

Giulia: *Hey, I don't make the rules.*

Lily: *How about tonight then?*

Me: *I could probably do that. Maverick's going to be asleep for the rest of the day. I don't think he'll be home tonight.*

Stone: *I'll kill that fucker Beau if he put him through too much. You only just got him back!*

Giulia: *How's it been, Alessa? Everything okay?*

How did I begin to describe how perfect this morning had been?

In the face of how shitty today was turning out to be, it shone a brighter light on how perfect things were when it was just me and him. Alone. Together.

God, how he'd felt inside me was too difficult to explain.

There'd been no disgust, no revulsion. No pain. Just pleasure. Delight.

I bit my lip at the thought.

Me: *Once we found out Rex was on his way home, we spent most of yesterday and last night asleep.*

Stone: *Maverick's likely to need more rest than before, Alessa. There's no need to worry.*

Me: *Oh, I wasn't worrying. :) I know I needed the rest, so why wouldn't he after all he's gone through?*

Giulia: *If he treats you like shit—he'll have me to answer to.*

Warmth filled me.

Giulia's Posse... I quite appreciated being a part of it.

Smiling, I tapped out: *I'll be sure to tell him.*

A squeak sounded down the corridor, and I looked up and saw Mav being wheeled back on a gurney. His hand was rubbing his temple, and I just knew he'd need me.

Me: *Have to go. Mav's just come back. Speak later x*

Shoving my phone into my pocket, I rushed over to him and darted down the corridor at the same speed as the nurse pushing the gurney.

"Are you okay?" I murmured softly.

When he just shook his head, I knew words were beyond him. His eyes were loaded down with a misery that could only come from pain, but there was recognition there, so that gave me more relief than I could say.

I wasn't sure if there'd ever come a time when I looked into his eyes and wouldn't seek out that lack of awareness I'd grown accustomed to of late. Maybe in time, I would, but I doubted it.

Someone like me appreciated everything they had, and mourned everything they lost.

When the nurse wheeled him into the private room, leaving us alone with the proviso that the doctor would be on his way, I climbed onto the gurney the second he'd gone, and I whispered, "Go to sleep." I wanted to tell him that I'd protect him, but that was ludicrous... Didn't stop the words from whispering through my mind though.

He raised his arm with a grunt, let me snuggle into his side, and I pressed my head to his chest, uncaring that within ten minutes I'd regret the position when my entire body went numb from pins and needles. I felt the tension in him though, situated as close to him as I was with nothing between us except for a blanket, my shirt, and his hospital gown, so I reached up and gently rubbed his temple.

It wasn't a miracle cure, just a simple caress, but he slowly, increment by increment, relaxed, and for some reason, that made me feel more like a wife than ever before.

THIRTY-TWO

MAVERICK

"HEY, KEN. JUST GOT YOUR MESSAGE."

That was partially a lie. I'd seen I had a couple of missed calls, and that he'd sent a text, asking me to phone him when I had a minute, but Alessa had been with me.

Because of the extent of the tests, which were going to carry on into the morning, that fucker Beau had decided I needed to stay overnight. I wasn't happy about it, and when I'd seen Ken's messages, I knew I had to get rid of Alessa. She already knew far too much than was good for her.

It wasn't even about spousal immunity—knowing too much was bad for her. Our enemies weren't always legit alphabet agencies.

So I'd told her to go home, even though I didn't want her to take a fucking step outside the hospital without me. Didn't matter that I was as much use as a coffee mug made out of chocolate, didn't matter that she had a prospect guarding her ass, only when I had my eyes on her did I know she wasn't in danger.

"Hey, man! I have some news—"

"A heads-up first. I got my memory back." I winced. "Most of it. I don't remember our call, and if you hadn't told me in the message that the test results had come in, I wouldn't even know I'd asked you for something. As it stands, I don't know what I asked you about."

Ken's sharp inhalation said it all. "Jesus, Mav. Someone upstairs ain't cutting you much slack, are they?"

A laugh escaped me. "Nah. But after all the shit we pulled, maybe that makes fucking sense, huh?"

"Probably. If we don't land our asses in hell, I'll consider us lucky."

"You? Laughing about hell?" I arched a brow he couldn't see. "Stopped being a Methodist?"

"Take me out of the sandbox, stop aiming a gun at me, and apparently I chill the fuck out."

Snorting, I muttered, "Good to hear. Apparently, I didn't get the same memo."

"Apparently goddamn not." Ken cleared his throat. "What's with the beeping?"

"I'm in the hospital. Getting some tests. My memory came back yesterday, but the headaches are fucking killer."

"Shit, I'm sorry, man."

"Not your fault. Anyway, how are you doing?"

"You know we already had this conversation, yeah?"

"That Maverick did, I didn't."

When he told me about his wife and kids, I'd admit to being glad. If ever there was a man who needed to be settled down, it was Ken.

"Anyway," he said after a little while. "Figure it's time to let you know what you got in touch with me for... Your clubhouse was involved in a blast, and you found some DNA samples from the guy who detonated the bomb."

Surprise hit me. "Shit, I did?" And I hadn't told the council?

Hell, what the fuck had Star got me wrapped up in?

Whenever she came back into my world, I had to lead two lives. I got sick and goddamn tired of playing Janus because of her.

"Yeah, you did," Ken replied, but he sounded amused.

Rubbing my eyes, I grumbled, "Okay, hit me with it. You find out who our sniper is?"

Ken hummed. "Guy's a pro. Got a streak of blood that zigzags all over the nation. Interpol tagged him as a pro as well, what with a few kills taking place over in Europe. His jobs vary—nothing too standard. Anything from an adulterous housewife in Atlanta to a businessman who was close to retirement. No standard kill method either. Hit and runs, shootings, knifings... you name it."

"Christ. How the fuck did we get on his radar?"

"No idea. Got an ID for all its worth considering he changes them like he changes his dentist. Guy Paris."

I snorted. "Fake much."

"Yeah, not the first either. Andrew Moscow. James Madrid... guy's got a thing for capital cities. There are a fuck ton more IDs out there." Ken cleared his throat. "Something did roll up when I ran his details though."

"What?"

"It isn't the first time he's been in your area."

I scowled at my blanket covered feet. "No? When?"

"Eight years ago. It's unusual because he's a kind of 'one and done' guy, but for whatever reason, he's visiting West Orange again."

"Who did he kill eight years ago?"

"Well, that's just it. It was an unsolved hit and run. Apparently, the driver got out and left a fingerprint on the victim's throat."

"Why the fuck would he do something asinine like that?" I growled.

"A marker. That's how each of these cases are tied together. It's his signature. He always leaves *something* so that people know it's him. Maybe that's how he gets paid?"

"Jesus," I muttered.

"Anyway, it's someone from your club. Woman called Rene Banks."

Rene.

Rex's mom.

"Fuck. Ken, thank you so much for getting this info to me so quickly—"

"You need to spread the word. Get it, man. Totally get it. But hey, please don't be a stranger? It was good to hear from you."

"Agreed," I told him firmly, meaning it. "I won't let it be long before I'm in touch again. Thanks for everything, brother."

"You're more than welcome."

No sooner had I cut the call with Ken did I connect another one.

I hadn't seen any of my brothers since I'd regained my memory. This morning, after making love to Ghost, I'd known I had to act before, like a chicken shit, I cut and ran. I fucking loathed doctors, but for her, I needed to make sure that I was doing all I could to get better.

My health, right now, wasn't a priority.

For whatever reason, a so-called 'one and done' sniper had made a visit to West Orange again. This time, he hadn't just killed the Prez's Old Lady and triggered an episode that had almost destroyed the Sinners, he'd blown the clubhouse apart. Killed brothers, destroyed lives...

I hated to admit it, but it was starting to look like Lodestar was right.

There was a bigger picture at play, and it was time my brothers knew the whole story.

Before they died because of it.

THIRTY-THREE

ALESSA

FULLY EXPECTING for the kitchen to host our little party, I walked in only to find Stone and Indy sobbing in each other's arms. The second I was inside, I was hauled out again, Giulia shoving a glass of wine at me as she grabbed my arm and dragged me out.

"Leave them to it," she muttered. "Indy's been trying to explain about Kevin, you know?"

I winced. "*Na khuy.*"

"No idea what that means, but it sounds as bad as the situation merits." She squeezed me. "I think they'll be a while."

As we headed for the great room, I immediately walked over to one of the plush sofas and sank into its depths. When I was settled, I took a deep sip of wine, and afterward, grinned at Lily who laughed pointedly at the now half empty glass.

"Needed that?"

"Badly. Maverick was a pretty good patient, but it's been a hell of a day, and seeing him in pain was hard."

She winced. "I never realized seeing the person you love in pain could hurt so much."

"Probably the sign of true love," Tiffany remarked. She was sitting on the same sofa as me, but she had her feet tucked under her, and a pair of bright pink fuzzy socks which just peeped out from under her butt. In her hand, she had a can of White Claw she was nursing.

"Love equals pain?" Giulia released a disgruntled sound. "That's bullshit. With Nyx at my back, I know I can handle any-fucking-thing. That seem like a bad thing?"

Tiffany shot her a look. "You're all riled up. I wasn't trying to piss you off."

Giulia grunted. "Sorry." I watched as the smaller woman bounced on her feet. "Got a lot of energy."

A smile played on my lips. "Are you missing Nyx, Giulia?"

"I hate that I am, but yeah." She winced. "I'm one of those women now."

"What? In love?" Lily said dryly. "You think I don't miss Link? It's weird going to sleep without him now." She shrugged. "I figure we should embrace the 'old' in Old Lady."

Huffing, Giulia grumbled, "We're still in our early twenties."

"So? Love is ageless." Lily grinned, then burst out laughing. "You should see your face."

"Maybe it's the baby that makes her look like she wants to puke," I teased, amused to note that Giulia did look a little green around the edges.

Giulia's nose crinkled. "Nah, I'm surprisingly barf-free... very horny though. *Very* horny."

"So it's not Nyx you miss, just his dick?" Tiffany mused, laughing when Giulia threw a pillow at her.

"I'm almost tempted to ask Link to get a piercing just so I

know what it feels like. It's on my bucket list of things to do before I die."

A snort escaped Giulia. "If you think Nyx would let me handle his brother's dick, then you're crazy."

"Never said I wanted you to handle my boo's family jewels, now did I?" Lily retorted.

Amused even though I understood roughly eighty-five percent of what they were talking about, I noticed a wistful expression on Tiffany's face as she watched Giulia stride back and forth in front of the massive fireplace.

Having miscarried recently, it made sense that she'd be feeling nostalgic. By now, she might even be ready to give birth.

What was it about us, I wondered, that attracted torment and distress?

I had no answer for that, not when whatever 'it' was had also brought the men we loved into our worlds, but did one truly have to experience so much pain to appreciate the joy of the love we'd been granted?

I knew that I, for one, could have coped without the last couple weeks. I'd endured hell, been treated worse than if I were a pig, and yet, somehow, this past month was worse than it all.

Emotionally, I couldn't cut myself from it. Whereas in the past, whatever my owners had done to me, I'd managed to maintain distance. I'd spent a good chunk of eighteen months totally unaware of where I was, in a kind of fugue state that enabled my mind to be in a whole different place than where my body was. I'd only woken up from that when I'd been purchased by Luke Lancaster at an auction.

That was when a whole other episode of my nightmare had commenced.

Before, I'd been kept in a house. One with a bed. With a functioning toilet.

Lily's brother had stored me in a cage like I was a dog to let out at his whim.

A shudder rushed through me as I thought about those times, thought about the filth, the stench, and how much worse it had become when the other women had gradually been added to his stocks since his father was using us too.

"Alessa?"

Lily's soft voice drew me back into the conversation. I shot her a weak smile. "Yes?"

"Are you okay?"

Tiffany sat up slightly. "You had a funny look on your face."

"Maybe I was born that way," I teased, raising my wineglass to hide my expression.

"BS," Giulia rumbled. "What gives?" When she stopped pacing and folded her arms across her chest, I knew none of us were going anywhere until she got answers.

And seeing as I fully intended on returning to Maverick's bedside tonight, I didn't have time to waste.

"I was just thinking of before, is all."

As a one, the women winced.

"I didn't mean to bring the mood down," I said softly. "That's why I didn't want to talk about it."

"Maybe you *should* talk about it," Tiffany told me, her tone gentle. "We've stopped having our group chats. It's not good for any of us."

I was almost surprised when Giulia didn't scoff at that. She hadn't been a part of the chats as much as the rest of us had, but she'd always found her way to them whenever we got together. Maybe she hadn't been there from start to finish, but she'd always popped by.

After what my tormentor had done to her, who could blame her?

Giulia was not the kind of woman who was easy with being a victim. She couldn't simply accept her fate, switch her mind off, lie back, and take whatever someone wanted to dole her way.

She was a firecracker, only this time, she'd been burned. It was clear to me that loss of control was something she'd never forgive herself for, even though her attack was completely Lancaster's fault and not hers.

"You're right," Lily muttered, biting her lip a little before she continued, "Without Link here, I've been having nightmares again."

Giulia wriggled her shoulders. "I haven't been having nightmares per se..."

"No? Bad dreams then?" Tiffany questioned, her lips tilting up in a smile. "A rose by any other name would smell as sweet."

That had Giulia grunting. "I miss Nyx is all. I miss how he makes me feel."

"How is that?" I asked softly, curious about what she'd say.

It took a few moments for her to reply, but when she did, her words had warmth filling me. "He makes me feel invincible."

Lily released a choked laugh. "It's funny you should say that because Link makes me feel *visible*. It's so strange. I'm valued not just for my hymen or my name or my family's reputation... I'm Lily. That's all I am to him. Lily. His Old Lady."

Tiffany's eyes were watery as she confessed, "When I'm with Sin, it's like I can take a deep breath when, before, I was hyperventilating or something. He makes me feel strong, but more than that, he helps me be stronger. He believes in me. Believes I can do anything I set my mind to." She swallowed. "It's a wonderful feeling."

"It is, considering we were bred to be walking wombs," Lily said bitterly. "Crazy how the men we're with are the exact opposite of what our families would want for us, but they lift us up instead of tearing us down like our kin would and did."

"I wasn't a walking womb before," Giulia muttered, "but I know what you mean. Mom would roll in her grave if she thought I was with a biker. She'd tell me I was a stupid little bitch who didn't learn from the lessons she'd had, but Nyx... he's nothing like my father."

"He's whipped, is why," Indy remarked as she wandered into the room, her arm slung around Stone's shoulders as they headed to one of the empty sofas. With three large ones set around a coffee table that overlooked the fireplace, it was easy for all of us to find our own space, to get comfortable.

"Nyx is not whipped," Giulia scoffed.

Indy snorted. "Yeah, he is. You snap your fingers and he comes running."

Giulia's lips twitched, but there was a fire in her eyes that flickered as she murmured, "That's because you don't see what goes on behind closed doors. He comes running because he thinks he can bend me over the nearest surface." She raised her hand and blew on her nails. "And he'd be right in thinking that... Safe to say I'm usually bent over something by the time he rolls around."

Indy groaned. "I didn't need to know that."

"You brought it up," Stone said with a laugh. "You don't wanna hear about your bro's peen then don't talk about it with his woman. You know for a fact we're all curious as hell about his cock. No offense intended, Giulia, but he had some of the clubwhores dick-drunk for a looooong time. Before he started going all weird and fucking only one bunny for a while."

"Monogamy, weird..." Tiffany shook her head. "Only in this world."

"Hardly monogamy," Stone argued. "They banged. That's it. Not even sexual fluids were swapped because I know Nyx would have worn a rubber, they're not supposed to go down on the bitches, and unless..." She hummed. "I guess these bikers are dumb enough to think they can't catch an STD if they get a blow job from one of those skanks. Do you think I need to do an STD workshop?"

Giulia choked out a laugh. "If you decide to do that, then please, I want to be there. I might even pay you for a ticket."

Lily laughed. "Me too."

"Me three."

"What's an STD?" I asked, even though I could pick it up from context.

"Sexually Transmitted Disease." Stone frowned. "Maybe we should all get tested. I really don't think I could handle chlamydia right now on top of everything else."

Giulia grumbled, "Already been stuck with more needles for blood work than I have with Nyx's dick, and I've only known about being pregnant for three goddamn weeks. I don't need any more tests."

"Your guy wasn't a manwhore though," Stone rumbled. "Ours were."

"Maverick wasn't." Despite myself, a shy smile curved my lips. "He hadn't had sex in five years until..." I cleared my throat. "This morning."

Giulia released a whoop that had me jumping in surprise. "Finally, you did it!"

A thought crossed my mind. "I should be tested though," I whispered, my pleasure disappearing in the face of this conversation. "I could have anything!"

Stone shook her head. "I ran bloodwork on you all when you got back. You probably wouldn't remember. You came back clean."

A shaky breath escaped me. "Really? You're not just saying that to make me feel better?"

"You have met Stone, haven't you, Alessa?" Indy joked. "She doesn't pull her punches."

Stone grunted under her breath, but got to her feet and stormed off. Indy watched her go, evidently surprised her teasing hadn't gone down so well, but when Stone returned a few moments later, satisfaction creasing her expression, Indy warily asked, "What did you do?"

"Had Brick, that new prospect, go to the on-call pharmacy to get some stuff."

"Stuff?" Lily queried, her eyes wide.

"So I can take blood samples and get us tested." She narrowed her eyes. "If they've given us something, I'm going to chop their dicks off. Steel said he always used a rubber, but—"

"Don't you think they'd rather hurt themselves than hurt us?" Tiffany questioned, her tone uneasy.

"I'd prefer to be safe rather than to be sorry." She frowned. "Although, your blood tests would have shown something at the hospital—" Stone looked at Lily. "Yours too." She heaved a sigh of relief, a thought evidently occurring to her. "Mine as well. If you feel like a pin cushion, Giulia, that's nothing compared to what I've been through the last couple of months. So, Indy, it looks like you're the only one who needs bloodwork."

"You don't need to look so happy about it!" Indy retorted with a scowl, shoving her friend again with a pout.

Stone just snorted. "Consider it payback for not telling me *everything*. And I mean *everything*, do you hear me? You said you had, but it was BS. So, hoes before bros and all that shit from now on."

Giulia snorted. "Seeing as you're pricking everyone all the time, Indy, it'll be nice to see you shed blood."

"Gee, thanks, *sister*."

"You're welcome, *sister*." Her eyes twinkled for a second

before that gleam was doused like water on a fire. "That reminds me though... hoes before bros? That's exactly right. So, we're here tonight because of what Alessa told us, but also... I'm uneasy about this situation with Cyan and Keira. Neither of them seem to be doing all that well. Whenever I see them around Rachel's place, they're always really—I guess the word is sorrowful." She shrugged.

"I hate to prioritize, especially with the situation being as it is, but Tink's an active threat," Indy pointed out softly. "If she can help someone try to bomb us, then she's a danger to us all."

"Especially since Lodestar's still convinced that Martin London isn't a pedophile but a retired pastor," Giulia said grimly.

Indy shook her head. "I don't see it. Not from the way he was looking at her."

"As far as I can tell, Cyan has no means of contacting him. Keira limited her time on the laptop she uses for school, and she doesn't have a phone or a tablet anymore," Giulia informed us as she moved over to the wall beside the ornate fireplace, leaned back against it, and crossed her legs at the ankle and her arms at the waist—free to move now that she'd been freed from her sling yesterday. Somehow, she looked so effortlessly cool that I wasn't sure whether to be amused or not.

It was like looking at a female James Dean.

Pre-crash.

I cleared my throat. "If she has no means of communicating with him, then is he still a threat?"

"Don't you remember what it's like to be a kid?" Lily asked. "If you want something, there are ways and means."

"That's true," Indy replied, her tone edgy. "And after what I saw... she isn't scared of London. That came across loud and clear. She wants to please him, but not out of fear."

I shuddered. "This is disgusting."

"Bet your ass it is." Indy grunted. "Lodestar has to be wrong. I know the way he was... I recognized it. But it happened when I was stressed and under stress, so I mean I could have been wrong. I doubt it, but it's a possibility."

Giulia sighed. "Before we go, we'll speak with Lodestar. I tried to talk with her earlier but she's napping."

Lily nodded. "She's doing that a lot."

"If she's not one hundred percent, then maybe that's why she hasn't found anything yet? Maybe she's too sick to—"

A part of me was ridiculously jealous of Lodestar, even after what Maverick had revealed to me this morning, but I couldn't allow them to disparage her name or her work when I'd seen for myself how dedicated she was.

Not just to finding out the truth but to unraveling the group of *horobtsi* that targeted women in my country and brought us over to the States like we were merchandise to import and export.

"That isn't fair," I interrupted softly, keeping my gaze trained on my knees. "She works hard. She's just slower than she usually is. Needs more rest."

"Trouble is, we have no time for rest," Giulia said uneasily. "We need to move fast."

"Innocent or not, we can still teach the fucker a lesson," Indy replied, and Stone reached over and squeezed her shoulder, which told me the memories were hitting her hard tonight.

Who could blame her?

Sharing a secret that old with a close friend had to be hard, so if it made her bloodthirsty, I considered it cathartic.

"Until we can talk with Lodestar... Tink knows who the sniper is," Lily pointed out. "You said she got into the truck with him after she opened the gates for him, Alessa?" At my nod, she hissed under her breath. "How did she even access the gates without anyone knowing?"

"They weren't manned that night," Stone admitted. "Steel told me that. Rex wanted everyone to party. Said we needed to let our hair down…"

"Jesus, I'll never be able to do that again," Giulia grumbled, rolling her eyes. "Especially not at a party."

"They'll figure it out so that we're safe," Stone replied, her lack of concern surprising. "There must have been a loophole to the gate system Tink figured out, that she overheard or something. She was one of Rex's faves, so maybe that's how, but she messed with the wrong people. You know what they're like. Tangle with them once and their enemies might as well pray to Satan for salvation because once they have someone in their sights, they're not getting away."

"But first," Indy tacked on dryly, "they have to find that someone to set their sights on."

Stone winced. "True."

"We need to find Tink," Giulia said firmly. "We need to get her to talk."

"The other clubwhores will know where she is," Tiffany remarked. "We should ask them."

I reached up and rubbed my bottom lip. "By that logic, I knew what Tatána was doing, and I didn't. I had no clue what was going on. Amara only knew she was sneaking around, not why or with whom."

"You're not close at all, are you?" Lily asked, her voice soft like she was trying not to cause offense but was curious enough to ask anyway.

"I guess we should be considering what we went through together, but that isn't enough to bind people into friendship. I've known you for far less time than I knew them, and I'm closer to all of you than I ever was with Tatána and Amara." I hitched a shoulder. "On top of that, the… masters didn't want us to be close. They worked hard to turn us against each other. It made it less likely that we'd try to band together and escape, I suppose."

A soft whimper escaped Lily, and I turned to look at her, seeing the tears in her eyes, the horror etched into her features, and I understood and empathized with her. Maybe she should have been the one to comfort me, but I was the one who clambered off the sofa and met her on hers.

Huddling close to her, I sat by her side, both sets of our feet digging into the plush down cushions, and murmured, "It isn't your fault, Lily."

"I-I know, but I just... I'm sickened. I can't believe—" She shook her head. "No, that isn't right. I *can* believe it. After what Luke did to the maids, how he hurt them, I know that was in his nature. But it just makes me feel like I could puke. I should have done something. I should have—"

"What could you have done?" Giulia asked quietly, her tone lacking her usual aggression as she peered down at her shoes. "Truthfully, Lily, what could you have done? You were young yourself, abused yourself, terrorized yourself. It wasn't like you were in any position of power, was it? Plus, your family was influential. It made it twice as unlikely that people would believe you."

"I-I don't care," Lily whispered bitterly, her hands forming tight fists that she bounced against her knees. "I should have done something. Even if it only cast doubts on their reputation, it might have helped."

I curled my arm around her shoulders. "There's no point in thinking this, Lily. What's done is done." And I couldn't stop myself from smiling. "They're dead now. They can't hurt us anymore."

When she turned her face into my shoulder and wept, I felt the palpable relief mingling with the sour tang of bitterness that came with regret. But I held her through it.

As I stared around the room, at the hodgepodge of women who couldn't have come from more different walks of life if we'd tried, who came from rich backgrounds and poor, I recognized that somehow, the Sinners had done this.

They'd brought us together.

They'd created Giulia's Posse.

I had to wonder if they were ready for the repercussions of that...

THIRTY-FOUR

MAVERICK

WHEN REX WHEELED Lodestar into the room, neither of them looked very happy.

In fact, shove two wet cats into a bag, throw them into the trunk of a car, then let them out again, and those pussies were probably less pissed than my Prez and my ex right now.

Still, it didn't matter.

It was time for Lodestar to stop being such a sneaky cunt and for her to share all the intel she had on this situation with Rex. The Prez needed to know, and to be honest, I knew he'd avoided me because he hadn't visited me in the hospital today.

That meant he knew his ears were about to be blistered for the colossal clusterfuck that had gone down yesterday.

With Steel, Sin, Nyx, and Link in the know about this meeting, I'd requested that I deal with both friends alone because getting Lodestar to open up was like trying to get molten gummy bears back into shape again. Leaving her with Rex was a disaster waiting to happen.

"Why the hell am I here, Maverick? I'm supposed to be

napping. In fact, this prick woke me up." She heaved a massive sigh. "This is really inconvenient timing."

"She's got more claws than a goddamn cat," Rex grumbled.

Because that was too much like my own analogy, I had to stifle a laugh. "You both deserve the inconvenience, because you're a pair of closemouthed lunatics." If Rex didn't love the hell out of Rachel, I'd wish Lodestar on him as an Old Lady. Jesus Christ, that would be a hoot. "What the fuck was that about yesterday, Rex?" I demanded.

"If you're going to have this conversation, I don't think I should be here."

I scowled at Lodestar. "You said it yourself last night—*our* HQ was bombed. You're a Sinner, whether you like to think you are or not."

Her chin tipped up, but though I saw the usual attitude etched into her features, more than that, I saw a strange warmth that I only registered because I'd seen this woman in all kinds of states. Orgasming, crying with laughter, sobbing with tears over fucking puppies in a commercial, joyful as she dove into a pint of Häagen-Dazs, bitter with grief, distraught with the lives she'd had to take as part of a mission.

I knew her, whether she liked it or not, and I knew that my words made her happy.

She huffed, which was confirmation I was right, and I had more confirmation when she stopped bitching and just sat there, in a wheelchair, her arms crossed.

In fact... "Is that my wheelchair?"

"Wasn't like you're fucking using it, prick," Rex grumbled as he placed his hands on the footrail of the bed and leaned over it by resting his elbows on it next. "Anyway, it isn't. Yours didn't survive the accident." He squinted at me. "What the fuck is going on with you anyway? You're back to being the pain in the ass we know and love?"

"As if you'd know anyway," I retorted. "Wasn't like your ass visited me all that much while I was sick."

He winced. "I was with Dad."

"I know. I'm just giving you a hard time because you deserve it for yesterday's stunt. What were you thinking, man?"

He released a breath but gave Lodestar the side-eye, which told me he was about to keep quiet when the pair of them really needed to start sharing more. If they did, maybe we'd get somewhere and we wouldn't end up dead before we all hit forty.

"No side-eying her, Rex. We gotta start sharing. As it stands, I'm semi in the loop, but not totally because of how I've been... but there are things you have to share so we can survive this attack."

"We're safe for the moment. If any cunt thought we were weak, they know differently now."

Over the course of the day's treatment, I'd spent a lot of time on my phone, discussing shit with Steel and Sin so I knew the state of play. Knew that Rex had gone into a summit, a meeting that hadn't been called in decades, and with the Irish on his side, had taken out the two men who were vying for the position of head of the *Famiglia* as well as the *consigliere* to Don Fieri. A man who, after those two, could have slipped into the position of power with ease.

Talk about a goddamn home run.

How his ass wasn't dead was something we owed to the Irish, but I was pretty fucking pissed at what he'd done because, Jesus fuck, if that wasn't suicidal, I didn't know what was.

I rubbed my hand over my chin at the thought and rumbled, "Safe or not from outside attacks, that doesn't take out the *main* offender, does it?"

Rex's eyes narrowed. "Maybe we should start at the beginning?"

Lodestar heaved a sigh. "The beginning goes way back when, Rex. You can't handle how fucking far it goes back."

"Don't be a bitch, Star. Explain it to him. Exactly how you did to me."

"You mean when you didn't believe me?"

"I listened enough to let you make me a ghost, didn't I?" I snapped, and my statement caught Rex's full attention.

"What?" he boomed. "A ghost? What the fuck are you talking about?"

Lodestar's mouth tensed, but she rumbled, "Back in the seventies, when it was a mobster's wet dream to be alive, this group of law enforcement agents got together to try to level down the corruption in NYC. That's how it started. As with everything, it came from a good place. The Italians and the Irish especially were butt-fucking the city, and what with the president's ties to the mafia hinted at... well, they were concerned. Rightly so.

"They worked together to stomp out crime. Using each other's agencies to get the information required to pin crimes on specific criminals to take them out of play."

"They Caponed them," Rex replied, his eyes wide with interest. I should've figured he'd find this shit fascinating. Something he only validated by moving around the bed to the seat Alessa had vacated earlier. As he slouched back in it, he waved a hand. "Go on."

"Yes, fucking, sir," Lodestar retorted with a scowl, but when I growled under my breath, she rolled her eyes. "They took a lot of bad people off the street, but over time" —she shrugged— "as it does, corruption infected them too.

"By the mid-eighties, they weren't doing shit to fight corruption. They were at the top of the tree because they ran their own rings and did so in silence. No one knew about them, not until a couple of Italians realized what was happening. They did the dumb fuck thing and tried to take out who they thought was at the top of the group, because they believed this body of people was managed like theirs was—with leadership at the top. But that isn't how the Sparrows work.

"They're nesters. They work together, they build and grow together, and keep each other's asses safe from jail and from danger. It's fascinating if you think about it. The only true communist body of power in the fucking world, one that's ruled purely by knowledge and money."

"There has to be a leader," Rex countered. "How the fuck does anyone make a decision to move on? Especially with their pasts—they came from positions of power. Some had to have higher ranks than others."

"They did and do, but to them, a judge is only as important as a prison officer for what they can do for the 'nest.' Look, it doesn't have to make sense to us. It's how they work it. Money is their commodity. If anything, that's what influences opinion.

"A bit like with the government, they petition for business deals and work as a cohesive unit toward that goal."

"I know it sounds insane, Rex, because when she told me about this shit, I thought she was nuts," I remarked, "but I think she's right. Coming off of what happened this past month, I know you might not put much faith in my cognitive abilities—"

"Shut the hell up," Rex grumbled. "Whether you're stuck in the past or the present, either way, you're smarter than most of the council put together. I trust you, Maverick. You know that."

Relief soared through me, because if he trusted me, then this would go a lot easier.

"Carry on, Star."

With no sass this time, she started fiddling with the wheelchair's armrest. "The Italians fucked up big time by targeting the leadership, and essentially the Don at that point, Benito Fieri's father, Giovanni, had to come under their umbrella otherwise the Sparrows vowed to annihilate the *Famiglia* piece by piece—"

"That's impossible. No one could do that," Rex countered.

"Remember I told you it started in NYC? Well, by the mid-eighties, that was a thing of the past. They were everywhere. They'd infiltrated every level of government, every level of the justice department. I wouldn't be surprised if they're in the fucking Pentagon or in the Oval Office. Their taint has spread, and their power knows no bounds. Back then, they could remove the *Famiglia* without even breaking out into a sweat. Now? They could decimate half of Europe if they wanted."

Rex released a sharp breath. "You can't be serious?"

"I am. Deadly," she muttered grimly, for the first time looking him straight in the eye. "I wish I wasn't, but it's true. Somehow, for some fucking reason, you've caught their eye, and that's who was behind the attack on the compound."

"The Sparrows?" he repeated. "What kind of fucking name is that?"

She shrugged. "Their full name is the New World Sparrows. It's a play on words. Back in the days of the Illuminati, members were called the 'passers'...from the word *passeridae,* which is the genus for the Old World Sparrows..."

"Everyone's a fucking genius," I sniped, rolling my eyes. "What do they think they're on? An episode of *Jeopardy*?"

"If they weren't as dangerous as they are, then sure, maybe Alex Trebek would have been able to solve the world's woes right now, but as it stands, real life bites." She shrugged. "I mean, that's what they say. Maybe they just worship at Aphrodite's feet."

Rex shot her a blank look, so I explained, "Sparrows represented Aphrodite in classical lore."

The Prez shook his head. "Where do you two come up with this shit?"

Lodestar muttered impatiently, "The fucking past? It's called history, Rex."

"I'm not a walking fucking Google."

Reaching up to rub the bridge of my nose, I muttered, "If they're as massive as you say, then how the hell can we stop them?"

She shrugged. "You can't. But you can tear them down brick by brick. Why do you think I've been trying to destroy the *Famiglia*? They're a major part of the game. They're the Sparrows' front. By taking them down, you're going a long way to solving things."

Rex raised a hand, and she stunned the hell out of me by actually refraining from speaking, as he questioned, "How did you get tangled up in their web?"

"It was by accident. I was supposed to be helping guard a museum in Iraq. It was going to be ransacked, so we were deployed there to protect the antiquities. I came across something I shouldn't have. They caught me—"

"Cut the BS, Lodestar," I retorted. "Tell him the truth."

Her mouth tightened, and she turned her face away from me. "That is the truth."

"You and I both know you were working for Langley."

"You were in the CIA?" Rex rasped, his surprise clear.

"For a few years."

"Long enough to piss off some powerful people," I remarked. "Enough to get your ass sold into the white slavers market."

She hissed at me, "Shut the fuck up, Maverick."

I just hitched a shoulder. "I told you already, no more lies. No more crap. We need to be on the same page. It was different before. I just thought you were fucking nuts, and I was okay with that because I was okay with being a ghost, until our house was blown up, until people were hurt and we lost loved ones. Things have changed. We need to change with them too."

Because I knew that appealing to her sense of decency wouldn't work, instead, I appealed to her need to belong. She'd always had that issue.

If I was a shrink, I'd have said it was because her father had died when she was young, but who the hell knew why the brain worked the way it did?

Glumly, she muttered, "The premise of the story wasn't bullshit. I *was* assigned to a museum, but it stopped showing antiquities a long time ago. It became a kind of unofficial traders market for information.

"I went there, trying to find a name for an agent who we believed was selling out his people, but when I got there..." She shrugged. "It ended up with me being sold as a fucking slave."

"And what? You believe these Sparrows are the ones who sold you?"

"I'm pretty sure they were running the traders market, Rex. More than that, I'm sure the fucker who I was looking for was a Sparrow too." She pulled a face. "I've spent every moment since I killed my fucking owner trying to figure out ways to destabilize their operations. Targeting the human trafficking side of things was, as I'm sure you can understand after yesterday, a way of fulfilling a personal grudge."

Rex pursed his lips, but his fingers started to tap the armrest in a rhythmic manner that told me he was processing what he'd learned. "How do you know yesterday was about a personal grudge?"

She snorted. "Because I'm not an idiot."

"You been keeping her in the loop with our secrets, Mav?" Rex queried, his tone still as soft as silk.

"Haven't you figured it out yet? You don't have to tell Lodestar anything. She has ways and means of finding shit out."

"Yeah, I heard about my cloned phone."

Lodestar muttered, "Fucking Old Ladies. Treacherous bitches."

"You said it, they're Old Ladies," Rex retorted. "To *Sinners*. Their loyalty belongs to me. I needed to know, and I'll need you to un-clone my phone, even if it's for my safety."

She sniffed. "Having all the facts, getting them by any means necessary is why I'm so good at what I do. You'll be handicapping me—"

"If you were so good before, then how did you get caught?" he countered, changing the subject.

Her smile was tight. "Because I was sold out by someone above me. Someone who knew my reason for being in Hillah and wanted to stop me before I discovered the truth."

Wanting to bring things around again, I cleared my throat and asked, "Rex? You want to share exactly what the fuck made you go to the warehouse?"

"Revenge," he said easily. "Pure and simple."

He explained about the folder that had been dropped off at the compound, explained about the conversation he'd had with Declan O'Donnelly and with Finn O'Grady too. It all led to him admitting, "I was dumb doing what I did. But I don't regret it. Mom might not be the woman the Italians killed but they took away someone who mattered to us."

He pulled something out of his cut. The piece of paper in his hands looked to be the thick kind—not notepad paper but the stuff used for drawing pads.

Reaching for it when he passed it over to me, I opened the folds to reveal a face I hadn't seen in too fucking long.

"She's dead?" Pain floored me as the recognition of who was dead was instantaneous. "Where's her body?"

His jaw turned to stone. "I don't know. We might never find out."

"Fuck!" I rasped, grief for her loss choking me.

"Who is it?" Lodestar asked, sitting up straighter like that would help her see the drawing on the paper.

My voice was hoarse as I muttered, "It's a woman who was raised with us—Storm's sister, Scarlet."

She narrowed her eyes at that. "I wonder why they had to kill her. What is it about the Sinners that has them coming back for more?"

"It's funny you should say that," I rasped uneasily. "Although I don't know if funny is the right word." Gritting my teeth, I explained, "Lodestar, I got the DNA results from the sniper's nest in the field."

"What sniper's nest?" Rex demanded, his anger beginning to throb once he realized what I'd been holding out on him.

"Lodestar heard chatter there was going to be some kind of attack on the compound. She set herself up on the roof, and when she was there, she saw the laser light of a sniper."

I let Lodestar explain about the camera footage, and when she trailed off, I muttered, "I heard back from my buddy about the sniper, Rex. The same person who took the shot from that nest was the same fucker who was involved in a hit and run eight years ago."

Rex's jaw turned white, and he lowered his head, his gaze drifting off mine. "Don't do this to me, Maverick. Please, man. I already thought I was gonna die yesterday, and it was worth it because I thought I was fighting for Mom, but... fuck."

"I'm sorry, Rex. I'm so goddamn sorry, but it was Rene. The same guy who detonated the bomb at the clubhouse and almost killed Bear was the guy who killed your mother."

Silence fell at my declaration, but it was broken a few moments later by Lodestar, who repeated in a whisper, "What the fuck did the Sinners do to get onto their radar?"

"I have no idea," I rasped, and though I shot Rex a look, mostly I could see he was shell-shocked. So totally fucking out of it that I didn't think he'd be much use.

Of course, this was my Prez I was talking about, so underestimating him was dumb of me. "It has to be something to do with Banks. With my uncle. There's a reason I got that package... and how I got it was shady as fuck. A truck dropped it off then high-tailed it outta there. Maybe you can find out how?"

"Of course," I told him. "What day did you get the package? What time was it dropped off? Roughly?"

He gave me the info I needed as he clambered to his feet. "There's a reason all this went down—we just have to figure out what that is. Lodestar, I'm going to take you home now. Maverick, I'll talk with you and the council tomorrow. I expect you at Rachel's place, do you hear me?"

"I hear you, brother."

He grunted, and as he rounded the bed, Lodestar and I shot each other troubled glances.

We were all on the same page now, all aware of what we were up against, but that didn't mean we were any safer. Which made me feel worse when I thought about how I'd let Alessa leave the fucking hospital without me, just so I could have that conversation with Ken, and ultimately, this discussion with Star and Rex.

A few hours later, when Alessa sneaked into my room, I had to smile, because the relief I experienced was acute. I'd had text messages from the prospect who was protecting her that she was on her way, but I only felt better once I set my eyes on her.

And what a fucking sight she was.

"Couldn't stay away, huh?"

She giggled. "No need to be so cocky."

My brows rose at the giggle, because she wasn't exactly a giggler by nature.

"From where I'm sitting, darlin', I'm no oil painting, and neither am I much of a prize. Must have got you hooked on something else. Let me guess, it's my fingers. Can't be my brain considering that ain't worth all that much now," I said dryly, watching through the lights from the hall and from the window as she slipped out of her shoes, then tiptoed over to the bed where she joined me.

The sweet scent of wine hit my nostrils, and my lips twitched as I reflected on how drunk she was and whether it was bad form if I kissed her now.

The way she curved into me reminded me of one of my mother's cats—it was like they were boneless. Damn, it felt good though.

After the last couple of days, just for her to be here with me, to lay at my side, to know that she wanted me as much as I wanted her even though I wasn't exactly a prize was a revelation.

"What you mean you're not worth much now?" she mumbled, fumbling with some words, losing others, and dropping a hiccup in between a few. She patted my chest on a sigh. "You're worth a lot to me."

I smiled into her hair as I turned my face to give her a kiss on the brow. "How much?"

"More than Canada."

"How much is Canada worth?"

"I don't know, but Giulia showed me some memes of Justin Trudeau today. It makes Canada worth more."

"Him alone, huh?" I had to laugh because I'd never heard her talk like this before.

"Uhhhhuh. Then there all are those players."

"Players?"

She hummed. "The ones with the sticks. The ice sticks?"

My brow furrowed. "Ice hockey players?"

"Those are the ones." She snapped her fingers. "You're hotter than all of them. Even Trudeau."

"Christ. I really *am* prime real estate then, huh?"

"Nope. You're *my* prime real estate." She paused. "What's prime real estate?"

"Never mind."

She clucked her tongue. "Everyone speaks in riddles sometimes. How can a room be a salon and also somewhere to get your hair fixed? And what does maverick even mean?"

Hiding my smile again, I murmured, "English makes no sense."

"You're right. It doesn't." She muttered something in Ukrainian. "What is a maverick?"

"Me. Prime real estate, remember?"

"Nope. That's no answer. Why are you called it?"

I grunted. "For two reasons."

"Tell me."

Sighing, I rested my hand on her bicep, loving it when she took the gesture to mean she wasn't close enough to me. She went from lying on her side to raising one leg and cocking it over my lap, her hand slipping over my waist to cling to me, and her head settling in the nook where my arm met my chest.

I'd have worried about needing a shower, but I figured she was too far gone to care, and if she did, she'd just move.

"When we were kids, pre road names, I used to get into a lot of shit, trying things out I shouldn't have. Doing stuff that was bad."

"Like what?"

Wincing at the memories, I muttered, "Stupid things really, but it used to get me into trouble."

"You're talking but not speaking. Why is that?"

"Stop being philosophical."

"I'm Plato."

"You're too cute to be a dead Greek."

"I shall take that as a compliment."

"It was meant to be one."

"I'm glad you think I'm prettier than an ancient skeleton."

Snickering, I murmured, "It's my charm that had you flocking to me, isn't it?"

"Yep, and your eyes." A sleepy sigh escaped her. "They're sooooo beautiful. Like coins. They gleam as if they're treasure. I look into them and..." She paused. "Did you have that cereal with treats in the bags?"

"Before they started to worry kids would choke on the toys, yeah."

"We had them. That's what your eyes remind me of."

"Plastic toys in bags of cereal?" I queried wryly, laughing when she hummed her agreement.

"Yes. Well, how I felt when I found one." Her lips drifted over my chest—I'd tugged off the hospital gown earlier on and had been lying in a pair of boxer briefs ever since. I was damn glad for it now. Especially when her hand rested on my stomach and she started to make circles against my skin. "We didn't have much, and that kind of cereal was expensive, so I didn't have it often. Those were treats I looked forward to."

My brow puckered as I reached for her hand to still it. "I'll give you the world, Alessa, if you'll let me."

She laughed. "You don't have to anymore. Lily gave me ten million worlds. I'd like to spend them with you on things that matter. But I'd also like to buy a house. A little house of our own, where I can never be made to leave it. Where I can live until we're old and gray, and we can see our babies grow up and they can bring their families there for the holidays and..." She sighed. "Yes. A house."

She didn't just mean a house though. She meant a future.

I swallowed, because as much as I wanted everything she'd said, how could I give that to her? Tomorrow wasn't promised to me. Not when tomorrow could shove me back to yesterday. And not just yesterday either. But ancient history.

On top of that, the statistics weren't pretty.

What if I hurt her?

What if this injury I had, this fucking CTE, made me—

No.

I couldn't think that. Not with how much she meant to me.

But kids?

The house was one thing, but the kids? A family?

I stayed silent because I was incapable of words on that matter, so even though the story always made me want to groan, I told her it to get her off the topic.

"There were a lot of books that were banned in our school," I started roughly. "Seemed like anything good that came out wasn't allowed in the library. So, one day, Rex created a distraction in there, I sneaked into the office, managed to break into the server and ordered every single book that we weren't allowed.

"They didn't stock anything like *1984* or *Brave New World*... nothing that made us question the way society worked. Said it was communist propaganda like we were back in the McCarthy era." I heaved a sigh. "It pissed us both off enough to act. I'm not sure how, there must have been CCTV footage of my breaking into the office, but they found out it was me, and I was shoved in detention for eight months. Bear called me 'Maverick.' Said it was fitting."

"Why was it fitting?" she whispered.

"Because a maverick is an unbranded calf, but it also means someone who'll go out on a limb to do something most people won't. Then there's the whole *Top Gun* thing. A character in a big movie over here was called Maverick too." My lips twisted. "You know who Tom Cruise is, right?"

She snorted. "Yes, you're not that old that I don't know who he is." A laugh escaped her at my grunt. "So Bear meant you were all three?"

"That day I was, yeah. He said I had to learn a lesson that the perfect crime didn't exist, and that I'd be ready when I knew how to offset the risk factor so I didn't get caught." My lips twitched. "He always used to come out with stuff like that. Little words of wisdom."

"Wisdom to future criminals," Alessa muttered sleepily.

"I guess," I agreed with a laugh. "I never thought of it that way."

"Why would you? That was your life." She heaved a sigh. "I wish we could sleep like this morning."

Because I wanted that more than I could fucking say, I tensed up. "With me inside you?" I asked cautiously, praying to Yoda that she really meant that and not just me wrapped around her like the cookie around an Oreo cream stuffing.

"Yes," she whispered. "That felt good."

"Until I pulled out of you after," I teased.

"Well, that was different." She patted my chest. "It didn't feel like I thought it would."

"No? In a good way?" Christ, that it might have been in a bad way hit me harder than the prospect of her wanting my kids.

A laugh escaped her, and her hands slid along the divots of my abdomen and down to cup my dick over my boxer briefs. If I hadn't smelled the wine on her, heard it in her voice, I just had confirmation.

Alessa was many things, but confident wasn't one of them. Hesitant, *sure*. But for her to have the *cojones* to go for my dick like that, well, it was definitely courage of the liquid variety that was getting her through.

And as much as my cock wanted to be inside her like we hadn't been together this morning, I reached down and tangled my fingers in hers to stop her before she could turn me on too much.

Wasn't sure what it said about me that my wife's hand around my cock got me harder than a lap dance from a bunch of club-whores, but this little lady, with her heart of gold, her kindness, her warmth, somehow, she managed to break me and put me together again all at the same time.

She pouted. "Don't be mean."

"I'm never mean. And in the future, when you're not drunk and you put your hand on my dick, then I'm going to take that as game on. But, baby, you need to sleep off the wine you had." My lips twitched again. "Did you have a nice evening with the girls?"

"Giulia calls us her posse."

Her mutter had me snickering. "Why doesn't that surprise me?" I sighed as I buried my face in her hair. "I hope you know what that means."

"Posse?" She shrugged. "I assume it's a group of some kind."

"Yes, it is, but it means something more. Especially where she's concerned. Posses were a group of men that a sheriff used to call up to enforce law, and we both know what kind of law Giulia wants to uphold."

"I'm down with that," she mumbled around a yawn. "Sinners' law."

A stillness overtook me at her statement. A statement she made with ease, with no fear, with no shame...

She accepted she was a Sinner, and I didn't think that was because her husband was one, but because she *chose* to be.

And that made all the fucking difference.

THIRTY-FIVE

ALESSA

HOSPITALS WERE NEVER SILENT.

The main reason my mother had sold herself was so my grandmother could afford treatment for a sickness that had ultimately taken her life.

We hadn't known it was cancer, not until the official diagnosis, but after Mama had married, she'd sent money over to fund the treatments and I'd ended up spending a lot of time in the hospital with my *babusya*, the rest of my days being fractioned between school and working on the family farm.

With no one else to look after me, when she'd been sick enough to spend the night, I'd stayed with her, and in the mornings, I'd had to help clean her, and throughout the rest of the day, help her eat when she was too sick to feed herself.

I knew hospitals, but Ukrainian ones were different than American ones. I remembered seeing older people being tied to beds to keep them contained, puddles of innocuous fluids on the floor that were left to stay there until things quieted down. I'd been in a tiny hospital though. Maybe in Kiev it was different—at least, I hoped it was. And I hoped that in the fifteen years since that time, things had changed.

But this place, with the slight scent of chemicals, the scratchy fabric of the blanket covering Maverick and me, the beeps from the machines, the squeak of the nurses' sneakers on the linoleum, the traffic outside, the rush of sirens every now and then, it was alive. Which was strange considering how I associated hospitals with death.

Maybe I was introspective because of the bottles of wine Lily and I had consumed this evening, both of us being silly by finding comfort in a drink that would only give us a sore head in the morning, or maybe I was just not capable of rational thought because this bed, this man, this life, this world, it resonated with me in a way that it hadn't before.

Seeing Lily's tears, her shame, her guilt, I'd never looked at it like that, so when she'd given me access to the account with her gift to me in it, I guessed I'd seen it as blood money. As someone who was as poor as me, I supposed I should have snapped at her fingers rather than questioning things. But seeing the agony in her face tonight had settled something inside me.

The need to forget.

The need to move on.

Without meaning to, I found myself in the middle of some kind of turf war that had my new home exploding into a million pieces, and that was taking precedence over my past.

Was that a good thing or a bad thing?

My priorities were shifting.

I was starting to belong.

Instead of being flotsam, floating here and there, never really settling somewhere, I'd already started to set down roots, something Maverick's desertion had triggered.

Before the blast, I'd started to make friends with the Old

Ladies, and we'd taken to sitting together at parties and such. Mostly, I thought, in self-defense against a lot of the disturbing things that happened at those events, but tonight? And the other day at Rachel's home? Things were changing for all of us.

That blast, which should have ripped us apart like it had our home, was bringing us together.

I *was* a Sinner.

Tonight had been fun. Even after Lodestar had wheeled in to bitch at us for making too much noise and we'd gotten answers from her, it had been a real laugh.

Giggling over shots of tequila and glasses of wine, snacking on Chile and Limón Doritos that had Giulia coughing with every bite and Lily munching on them like they weren't as hot as hell, over smores the women had made in the fire and had practically shoved down my throat, we'd come up with a plan of action.

One our men wouldn't approve of.

But we didn't need their approval.

And that was the most liberating thing of all.

In fact, it was like all my life I'd lived with a man looming over me, his booted foot on my throat. But tonight, my throat was released from that prison, and I could move around once more.

Whether or not Maverick approved, I had the women I'd left snoring away their drunk at Lily's home.

Whether or not Maverick approved, *this* Maverick wouldn't leave me. He wouldn't hurt me. Or punish me. He wouldn't chain me to the wall and leave me outside like a bad dog. He wouldn't piss on me or rape me.

He might snap at me, might grit his teeth and storm off, might even shout, but he wouldn't hurt me.

And in my life, I'd learned that sticks and stones were far more painful than words.

I felt giggly and overheated, flushed with hope, with a promise of a future that was so much more jubilant than the past. I'd been fed drugs and alcohol during my time as a slave so I had a higher tolerance level than the other women, so when I'd discussed children with Maverick, the need for a home, I knew he'd tensed up. I knew he wasn't enamored of the idea. But I also knew he wanted me to be happy.

My happiness mattered to someone.

It actually mattered.

The thought was enough to make me release a gust of air, because a few short months ago, I'd been left to rot in a basement in a cabin in the woods. I'd been left to dehydrate. Left to starve. Left to die.

I'd been an animal.

Now, I was a woman once more.

And this woman wanted her man.

A doctor could come bursting in, someone might walk past the corridor and peer in, someone might call, someone might, someone might, someone might.

I'd been raped in a hall full of men, I'd been choked and abused and hurt one-on-one.

I had no inhibitions.

I wasn't shy.

I was shell-shocked.

I was traumatized.

But I was tired of that. Tired of that boot on my throat. And tonight, I'd taken a step toward changing that. Tonight, I wanted to end it as my day had begun.

With joy.

I wanted more of that. More of the heat, the intensity, the power, the pleasure.

I wanted wet kisses and breathless moans, I wanted wetness and slick juices and sweat.

I wanted Maverick.

No one else.

No other.

Forever.

Just him.

So I shrugged the blanket down, leaving it to cover our upper thighs before I pressed my hand to his abdomen, appreciating the rough flesh of his torso. He was scarred here, the tainted flesh where he'd been injured as a soldier was just proof of the level of sacrifice he was capable of.

What a man.

Muscular if a little lean, scarred and inked, rough and ready, dark and dirty, he was everything I needed.

More, I needed him to know that, and because that boot was away from my throat, I could.

I was free to do what I needed.

For the first time in my life.

So I spread my fingers, letting each tip absorb and appreciate the strength in him, the feel of his sacrifice, the depth of his devotion to his country, and I slid them down over the slightly furred flesh that led to his dick.

I moved over the tight underwear that covered him, the fabric not as pleasing to me as his skin, and I turned my face into his chest where I'd been held close all night like I was a precious thing to him and not someone's cum depository, and I gifted him with the only purity that was left inside me—my heart. My soul. My love.

Letting my tongue peep out, I swirled it around his skin, teasing as I moved to his nipple which I lathed with the tip of my tongue before I started to suck on it. Beneath my hand, his dick twitched, and I carried on, moving higher until I was nestled in his throat where the scent of him was strong and clean and intoxicating. As I nipped him there, I sucked down on his throat too, knowing I'd leave a bruise and wanting to see it tomorrow. Needing to remember this night.

As I teased the area, I moved, rolling from my back and onto my side so I could straddle him, only I stayed high, not letting my weight connect with him. I was wearing too many clothes to tease myself with his bare body, so I kept my distance, just using the freedom to kiss him where I wanted, to touch his hardening length as I slipped my hand beneath his waistband so flesh could collide with flesh, while my other hand moved to his nipple.

Letting my tongue slide over the sinews of his throat, I moved to the other side, going higher and higher until I could nip his earlobe, where I breathed, "I know you're awake."

His hips rocked up, confirming what I already knew and he growled, "Why are you teasing me then?"

"I'm worshipping you," I countered, nipping his earlobe in punishment.

"Baby, if anyone needs worshipping, it's you." When he made to roll us over so I was beneath him, I tutted and squeezed his dick in warning.

"Stay where you are. I haven't had my fun yet," I grumbled, and I wasn't sure why, but that had him obeying.

For all that he was a soldier, Maverick didn't seem like the most obedient of types. For all that he was loyal and smart, capable and strong, I imagined he'd been a nightmare to his superiors. The thought had a smile dancing on my lips as I let our mouths collide, let him taste my smile. My inner peace. The joy that came from the freedom I felt in doing this.

There was no force. There would be no pain. Only pleasure.

Only love.

He did taste it, because he groaned and his hands came to my hips. I let him, squeezing his dick which was soft and hard at the same time, the flesh like silk, the steel core of him throbbing against me, and I loved as he rocked his hips against me again, grinding my pussy into his hardness.

"You can't want to do this in here," he rasped as I pulled back to flutter my tongue along his bottom lip.

"Why wouldn't I?" I countered in surprise, my breathing starting to turn a little husky as that strange excitement overtook me.

I'd felt it this morning. It came with a tightening of my chest, a flood of heat between my legs.

One owner had used a vibrator on me, so I knew what arousal felt like, but he'd often teamed it with a whip studded with metal. There'd been no pleasure/pain for me. If anything, the pleasure from the vibrations had been consumed by the agony of the studs tearing flesh apart. That was why I never wore shorts, because my buttocks, upper thighs, and lower back were scarred.

If he'd seen that or felt that this morning, he hadn't complained, and because he was scarred, I knew he wouldn't see me as some kind of gross creature that he had to pity.

His scars were honestly earned.

Mine were from dishonestly inflicted torture.

But even as the thought dampened my mood some, it stirred something else inside me, prompting me to leap off the bed even though his hands tried to keep me close.

I'd seen before that there was a small bedside light that puddled around the bed so a patient could read, and I switched it on. Maverick winced and used his forearm to shield his eyes, which made me regret the abrupt move because I'd come to see how sensitive he was to light and had forgotten that in my haste.

Annoyance at my lack of care filling me, I moved over to him and whispered, "Sorry."

"It's okay," he rumbled, but I could tell it wasn't. I bit my lip, unsure if things could carry on the way I wanted, then he groused, "You better be stripping. I need to see that fine ass of yours as a reward for blinding me."

Guilt warred with amusement, and I crinkled my nose even as I moved over to the window that overlooked the hall. The blinds weren't closed, so I took care of that before I turned around and found him peeking at me with his forearm still shielding his brow.

Seeing I had his full attention, I went to work on the simple dress I wore with a pair of leggings beneath it. It floated around my knees, bobbing with every move, and it made me feel like I was in a black and white movie, one of my favorites—*Sabrina Fair*. The thought had me smiling, just as the dress did since Lily and I had gone shopping and had changed my wardrobe.

It was understated, with a cinched in waist and a heart neckline that moved into thick straps which pressed my breasts together. It was feminine and elegant, even if I knew it had to be crinkled from sleeping the way I had.

I didn't care.

I knew Maverick didn't either.

Even with his eyes in shadow, I saw his intent. Felt his need.

Drifting closer to the bed so I was in the light, not the dark, I reached for the buttons which lined the center of the dress and began to unfasten them. One by one, slowly, I revealed my body beneath. My breasts bounced free, the skin on my stomach was marred with gooseflesh from the sudden rush of air, and finally, I shrugged out of the dress, kicking it to the floor.

Because I wanted this out of the way, in a rush, I shoved the leggings down and turned around. Even though it was the first time he'd be seeing my tattoo, I knew it wasn't the ink he saw when he released a hiss.

Moving my hands to my sides, I grabbed my panties and bunched them in my fingers before bending over to roll them along my legs. Once they were on the floor, I slowly stood, letting him see the scars, before I turned around, naked.

Bare.

There wasn't a whisper of fear in me that he'd reject me for my scars, for this part of me that wasn't beautiful.

I just wanted him to see me. Flaws and all. Wanted him to know all of me, even if he'd never know what I went through, never be able to understand, I wanted him to have me. Every part.

He was sitting up by now, and his erection had died. His fists were tight balls resting at his sides, and his jaw was clenched with anger.

"Who?" he snarled as I carefully climbed onto the bed.

"A man called Lawrence," I told him, then, slyly, already knowing the answer and not fearing it, I asked, "Do I revolt you now?"

His eyes flared wide as I effectively dismissed the subject. "No! Hell, no!"

My smile blossomed. "I'm glad."

He growled under his breath before his hands moved to my waist and he hauled me against him. Within seconds, I was on my back, and I spread my legs to accommodate him. His dick was hard again, and it notched against my sex. I could feel the heavy weight, his thickness, and knew he had the perfect dick because it was mine.

"I'd kill every cunt who touched you if I could."

I smiled. "I know you would." And wasn't that delicious?

All my enemies were his enemies now.

More liberation. The gift that kept on giving.

But because I didn't need to wallow on that, I leaned up and nipped his bottom lip like he'd done to me earlier, but this time, I did it hard enough to tug, to pull the flesh from his teeth. I wasn't sure why, but that had a snarl escaping him, and out of nowhere, the hands that had been gentle earlier on dipped into my flesh, holding me in place, keeping me steady as he loomed over me.

But that goddamn boot stayed off my throat, and if anything pinned me against the bed, it wasn't his hands but his cock against my pussy—that was what I wanted.

What he wanted to give me too.

I groaned as he rubbed his dick against me, the soft fabric of his underwear an irritation that was surprisingly satisfying. I loved the slightly abrasive sensation, felt it against my clit and that had shockwaves fluttering up and down my spine as I arched my back, tightening my legs more around his hips.

With a moan, I let my head fall to the side and loved when he treated me to the same caresses as I'd given him earlier. When he sucked down hard, bit down hard, I growled and slipped my hands into his hair.

Tugging at the roots, I hissed in his ear, "I need you."

"I'm gonna die needing you, Alessa," he rasped, his head lifting so he could slip the words into my soul with all the finesse of a master swordsman.

I felt the tear in my spirit, felt him fill it back up again with his statement, and then his mouth was back on mine, his tongue fucking mine, his breath replacing mine.

With my heels and toes, awkwardly, I dragged his boxer briefs down over his hips, knowing it would hurt his cock if he stayed like that much longer, and when he growled, then shuffled about some so he could free his dick totally, I sighed with delight as his hardness met my softness.

I was wet again, slick with it. I could taste it in the air. It was around us like a perfume, and so was his scent too—the essence of him. Of heated man. We were bound together in that one scent, more tightly coiled around each other than we were physically at that moment, and I reveled in it.

Reveled in the truth of it. Of the honesty.

The words spilled from me as I was unable to keep them in as he slipped the tip of his cock against my pussy, and he started to rock into me, thrusting deep so I was filled with him in more ways than one.

"I love you," I whispered fervently, desperately.

His mouth moved back to cover mine, but before he shut me up with a kiss, he whispered, "I'm in love with you, Alessa. Ghost. Whatever the fuck you wanna call yourself. I'm in love with you and I'll love you until the day we goddamn die." Each word was punctuated with a thrust of his hips, a thrust that had me arching against him, groaning and moaning as he filled my pussy like he filled my heart. "And even then," he ground out. "I'll love you. I'll never fucking stop."

I came.

A harsh groan escaped me, hard and needy and loaded with relief. It tangled with his as we both exploded at the same time, both of us caught up in the moment. Tossed around like we were in the middle of a storm of our own brewing.

But my orgasm wasn't just physical, it was, crazy though it sounded, mental too.

Because I believed him.

He meant it.

I believed in him.

He wanted it to be true.

And in the future, when he forgot me, when his condition robbed him from me because I had to face facts that it was likely it would, I'd remember tonight. I'd remember his words, remember the feel of him in my body and in my heart and soul, and I'd find comfort in them because no matter what, I knew Maverick would always find his way home to me again.

I just had to be patient, and I couldn't forget.

THIRTY-SIX

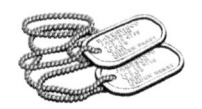

MAVERICK

WE ARRIVED BACK at Lily's mansion early in the morning. So early that my aching head, the disgusting taste in my mouth, and the cricks in my body made themselves even more apparent than before because no biker worth their salt woke up and was moving until at least twelve in the afternoon.

Long ago, I'd embraced that side of the life with open arms—early mornings fucking sucked.

Though I'd had a terrible night's sleep, what had happened in the middle of it was more than enough to make up for it. I was in pain, I knew from Beau's expression that there wasn't going to be much they could do to help me even if he wanted to dose me up with meds, and I was in the middle of a fight I wasn't sure we could win, but I had Alessa.

And she had me.

That meant something. It mattered. It gave me hope, and it gave me a reason to live for. To get up in the morning, to fight instead of rolling over and just doing what I had to to get by.

We parted once we were in the pool house, Alessa going to her bathroom and me to mine. As we prepared for the day ahead, my mind wandered some as my thoughts tangled with her and what I was going to do.

Lodestar and I needed to come up with some plan of attack so I could present that to the council tonight. It'd been a long time since we'd held a church with me attending, so I knew there was shit I had to catch up on. My brain didn't appreciate the thought even if I knew it was necessary.

When I made it out of my room, dressed in jeans, a Henley because it was getting cold out, and my cut, I found Alessa drifting down the hall, Kati at her side. As I watched her move, the innate grace of her had me thinking of when she'd get the chance to be on top of me rather than under me.

The thought of her tits shaking in my face was enough to make me grip my dick and squeeze it into behaving. Not that it'd listen. After the first taste of prime pussy, my cock knew where its bread was goddamn buttered.

It was just a fucking shame that life was going to get in the way because I'd live inside her if I could.

Or, at least, for as long as she'd let me.

Seeing she was wearing a dress again, I noticed she had leggings on once more. What the fabric shielded had any arousal dying. Not because the scars were ugly, but because they infuriated me. They enraged me.

They made me goddamn murderous.

Adding to my to-do list the need to investigate her past owners, I tried to make my expression a little less grim so it didn't freak either Alessa or Kati out when I moved into the kitchen.

Alessa shot me a soft smile which I returned, somehow finding it easy to let go of my wrath when she looked at me like that.

She smiled for me now.

Just like I did for her.

The notion had my heart swelling in my chest. My pulse slowing down. Just like I'd taken a couple of deep breaths or something, the peace that gave me, that she brought to my world, was a gift she'd never be able to understand.

She was a haven in a mad, mad universe, and I vowed to never forget *that*.

Whatever it took, if I had to hardwire my brain with fucking hypnotherapy or whatever BS was required to keep some of my memory functioning, there was something I had to cling to. Something that I had to hold onto with both hands so that she would forever stick with me, even if the CTE took control of me again.

"Maverick?"

She broke into my thoughts with my name, and I was grateful for that, because I didn't have a clue how to do what needed to be done.

"Yes, babe?"

Kati giggled. "Lessie, you're a babe."

They grinned at each other. "I always was one."

"Until he forgot." She pouted, then wagged her finger at me. "Maverick, you were a very bad boy but—" She paused with a dramatic sigh. "I still protected you."

"You did?"

She nodded. "When you fell asleep, I made sure you were safe." Preening a little, she said, "Star told me I did a great job. She even forgave me for setting fire to the microwave."

The words combined with the beaming smile that revealed a gap where her baby teeth had fallen out had me snorting out a laugh. "How did you do that?"

"Star told me to make her some soup."

"And you put the can in the microwave?"

"Well," she said with a huff, "she never told me *not* to do that. It seemed a lot more practical at the time."

"You could have taken it out when it started to flash," Alessa chided, her brow puckering with concern. "You must take more care, Kati."

Her younger sister heaved a sigh. "I knew you'd say that. Where's the fun in being careful, Lessie? It was pretty and so exciting. All those sparks! I loved it."

That was all we needed—a pyromaniac in the ranks.

"Remind me not to shove her and Sin together."

Alessa arched a brow in confusion. "He worked with explosives back when he was in the Forces."

Kati's eyes widened. "He did? OMG, that's so cool! Do you think he'll set—" Her mouth turned down at the corners, and the excitement faded. "The compound... I don't want to feel that again." Her shoulders hunched and then she flinched as if the memory was so tangible, it was enough to make her body remember the sensation. "That boom was terrifying."

Alessa wrapped her arm around her. "Well, best not to ask Sin to set a bomb on something else."

"What about our enemies?" Kati asked solemnly, making Alessa gasp.

"Kati! You can't think that way." A gaggle of Ukrainian escaped her, which I got the feeling Kati half understood because her nose crinkled even if she turned her face away, like that would help her evade Alessa's concern.

I'd like to say she was wrong, but I couldn't. How could I? I didn't even fucking know if there were plans in motion for what Kati just said. Cruz was the go-to chemical man. He could and *had* crafted a bomb with ease. Sin was the more 'traditional' purveyor of destruction. He used what Uncle Sam gave him and set fire to the world with it—legally.

Letting the sisters duke it out because there was nothing I could add to this conversation that wouldn't distress either of them, I grabbed the carton of OJ that was open and drank straight from it. I'd be finishing off the two pints before I left the kitchen, so I saw no point in dirtying more dishes.

When I turned around, I saw Alessa was watching me. Or, to be more precise, she was watching my throat. I'd seen the hickey she put there last night and was pretty fucking proud of the one she was sporting too.

There was no mistaking we were taken—exactly how I wanted to fucking keep it.

"Want anything from the fridge?" I asked her softly.

"A yogurt, please?"

When I saw there was only natural yogurt in there, I didn't ask which flavor, and instead, tried not to grimace as I watched her eat it plain.

Kati, evidently as disgusted, said, "Why do you eat that, Lessie? It's gross. Banana and strawberry is so much better." She smacked her lips. "I think you should keep some here just for when I visit."

Alessa smiled. "I can if you want."

"Duh. I like hanging out with you." She bumped her arm into Alessa's. "Do you think you'll teach me more words in Ukrainian?"

I saw the delight in Alessa's eyes before she could control it. "You'd like that?"

"I would. But only the bad words. That way I can't get in trouble at school when I tell the teacher she's a moron."

I snorted out a laugh at that nearly had me choking on OJ as I did so, but Alessa's disapproving look had me ducking my chin to stay out of this conversation too. In fact, escape seemed the safest route, so I dipped down to give her a kiss which she responded to—Christ, she tasted better than fucking OJ and that was saying something—and left for the secure haven of the main house with the carton still in hand.

As I shoved on the boots I'd dumped by the door earlier on, I nearly hooted when I heard Kati ask, "Did you do it yet?" There was a pause. "Lessie? What is 'it?' Is it nice?"

When her answer was a flurry of Ukrainian, I hazarded a guess that Alessa didn't feel like being truthful.

Laughing as I left the pool house, I made my way down the neat path and smiled as the scent of lavender blossomed around me which, actually, made me think of Alessa. Did she use lavender perfume? As I pondered that, and also pondered where she'd gotten those hot as fuck dresses from, I headed into the house and made my way to the kitchen which I somehow seemed to register was Lodestar's war office.

I wasn't sure how I knew that, just thought that it must be a memory from before. Deciding that was a good sign, I didn't puzzle that hard over it and took another sip of OJ as I rounded the table and took a seat beside her so I could see what she was working on.

The biggest surprise?

She was asleep. Not only was she sleeping, in fact, she didn't wake up as I sat down, nor did she register that I started messing around with her computer.

There were several tabs open, different programs I recognized, a conversation with someone called aCooooig who, twenty minutes ago, had asked if she was there. Evidently, she'd been napping for longer than twenty minutes. I remembered that she'd had a concussion after that nasty flight from the clubhouse roof, so figured she'd be finding it hard to sleep through the subsequent headaches. Didn't stop me from rooting around in her files though.

When I saw a folder titled 'Martin London,' I frowned as I peered through what was, quite clearly, a thorough investigation. I just didn't know why. The man was a retired pastor who, to this day, worked with several charities, most of them children's. He'd traveled all over the States, doing essentially missionary work which didn't exactly make sense by how deeply his bank account was padded. He lived nearby, at an address I recognized as being in a very nice suburb. Upper middle class, definitely.

Why on earth was she interested in him?

Bored, I moved onto another file and realized it was an initial findings report on Donavan Lancaster's financials. I knew why she'd be hunting there too—looking for the house where the fuckers had taken Alessa and the others to rape them in luxurious comfort.

The next folder unveiled a dossier on the information leaked several years ago in what I knew was one of the major reasons behind Cruz's introduction to the MC. He'd helped reveal a shit ton of secrets Uncle Sam wanted to keep hidden... Recognizing some of the paperwork, I scanned through a third of the dossier. When she started to shuffle around, I knew I didn't have much time so I moved onto the final file—Scarlet.

Like she'd done with that London guy, there was a folder on her as well. It wasn't as thorough, no financial check just yet, and though some of Scarlet's movements were traced—her international travel, for one—the files were limited.

Even though I picked up a lot of information, mostly what I learned was that she was definitely under the weather. A workaholic, incapable of taking a chill pill and stepping back from her computer, there was no way these files and dossiers would still be works in progress if she was fully functioning.

This little nap was proof enough.

Feeling the stillness in her that told me she was awake and didn't want anyone around her to know it, I squeezed my carton of OJ and said, "Want a coffee?"

At my voice, she relaxed, and though it was stupid, I smiled, glad she felt she could let her guard down around me. I thought I was probably one of two people she could do that with. And before Kati had come along, I'd been the only one. That was why I'd never understood why she'd fucked around on me.

Who did that?

When you found peace in someone, *with* someone, why wouldn't you try to keep a tight hold of that?

There was no understanding some people, and that was why I'd forgiven her, welcomed her back into my life even though I knew she was a treacherous bitch. Beyond that, beyond the treachery and the lies and the half-truths, I knew she had my back.

Always.

Even if she had a weird way of going about it.

"Please," she muttered, opening bleary eyes to rub them and yawning as she did so. "See you've been hunting around my shit."

"Shouldn't fall asleep with your screen on," I told her unapologetically.

She flipped me the bird but returned her attention to her computer. I had eagle eyes so I saw she replied to aCooooig pretty early off the bat while I set about making her a pot of coffee she probably shouldn't be drinking with a concussion headache, but hell, programmers were the unhealthiest people around for a reason.

All the while the pot of coffee brewed, my mind brewed too. Thinking about what I'd read, what she was investigating, what we'd discussed last night, about the issues we faced, and that was when something occurred to me.

I pulled out my phone and connected a call to Steel. As the secretary, he'd be the one to know this shit. At least, I hoped.

"Hey, bro, what's going on?"

"Steel, man, thought just popped into my mind. What happened with the books?"

"They're with Lily, I think. Why?"

Shit, yeah. I remembered now. She was supposed to start working on them—if she had them, then that meant the brothers had been okay with her just learning the ropes without any input from me. And to be frank, it wasn't like she needed my help with the economics degree she had.

"Not the legit business, the other stuff." I pinched the bridge of my nose. "When I went into the clubhouse, it was to retrieve the computer in the safe." Lodestar and I shared a look. Because I'd been going in for something else too. Something that was missing now.

Fuck.

"As far as I know, Rex had that swept once the fire burned out. Any shit that's in there will be at Rachel's place."

"How did he manage that?"

Steel snorted. "You know that prospect, Brick? His brother works for the fire department."

"Handy."

"Definitely. Anyway, yeah, I imagine Rex has that stuff."

"Great. See you later, bro."

"Yeah, Rex said you called church."

"I did. Lot of shit to discuss, man. Brace yourself."

"Aw, hell, Mav," Steel complained. "You can't leave me with that kind of cliffhanger."

Despite the seriousness of the situation, I had to smirk. "Just watch me."

Then I hung up.

"You think Rex has the USB drive?" Lodestar asked.

I shrugged. "Have to think he does." Rubbing my chin, I queried, "The real question is whether we want him to know that's what we want?" It wasn't much of a question to me, I did want him to know after all, even if it triggered a tidal wave of crap that spewed our way.

"He knows everything else. Well," she conceded, "as much as I can tell him in an hour-long conversation when the information I have on the Sparrows goes back years."

I dipped my chin. "I trust that you told him the pertinent stuff."

"I did. How else would I get him on our side?"

"Good."

"What time's church?"

"When Nyx and Link roll back in tonight. Probably about eleven."

She cast me a look. "The USB drive can wait. I actually need your help with locating the Lancaster property. You always were better at the forensic accounting side of things than me."

That she said it so begrudgingly made it all the sweeter, but it didn't stop me from asking, "That because I'm better at it than you or just because you're feeling like a big pile of horse shit?"

"A small pile," she corrected.

"A small pile," I agreed.

Her nod was just as begrudging, so I sat down, and somehow, as was always the fucking way when I worked with her, the hours slipped by.

And when I said hours, I meant it.

Lily's maids wandered in and out, making us sandwiches we mostly ignored and brewing us coffee that kept us going. The only stops turned out to be bathroom breaks, and when I got the text that Nyx and Link had returned and saw it was eleven PM, guilt hit me because I hadn't even thought about Alessa since that morning, and I knew Lodestar was exhausted too.

I'd pushed her just as she had me, but I'd managed to wend my way through four years of his accounts, which was saying something, while she'd been working on her investigation into Scarlet's background—on the hunt for answers as to why the *Famiglia* would want her dead.

"You should go and get some rest." I yawned. "I'm surprised Kati didn't interrupt us."

"Alessa must have kept her entertained." She rubbed her forehead as she started to go through her programs, slowly shutting them down as she ran a scan on the computer that, I'd bet my goddamn ass on, wasn't hunting for viruses.

The way her laptop sounded like it was about to take off and whiz around the room was clue enough.

Still, as she'd worked, I saw one of the screens I'd noticed earlier, and I murmured, "Who the fuck's Martin London by the way?"

She squinted at me. "You saw. He's a retired pastor."

"Okay, so why are you investigating him?"

That had her pulling a face. "You sure you want to know?"

I sniffed. "Wouldn't have asked if I didn't, and I'm holding the coffee hostage until you give me the answers I want."

"Cruel fucker," she mumbled around another yawn. "It's a guy who—Wait." She heaved a sigh. "You're not to tell Storm any of this."

Surprise had me rearing back. "Storm? What does this guy have to do with Storm?"

"Well, Indy says the guy was bothering Cyan."

"Bothering? In what way?"

That had her bowing her head, and as she tried to hide her expression from me, I wasn't even sure what to say.

Cyan was a kid, after all. How could an adult man pester—

"No." I shook my head, nostrils flaring as I understood her discomfort. "No, Lodestar. Please, fuck, tell me my mind's in the goddamn gutter."

She gritted her teeth. "That's what Indy says. I can't find

anything in his past that would indicate he's that way inclined, but..." She shrugged. "It's not something that he's going to advertise, is it?"

"I'll kill him," I rasped.

"You might not have the chance."

"What the fuck does that mean?"

"There's a posse after him..." Her lips twitched into a smile. "And it's gonna do what a posse does best." The smile turned into a smirk. "Lynch the cunt's ass."

THIRTY-SEVEN

ALESSA

INDY'S CAMARO WAS A DREAMBOAT. I actually preferred it to the cars in Lily's garage because they were so sleek and elegant it was unreal and kind of discomforting to be in them. Not just because we'd be destroying half a million dollars' worth of supercar after our drive, but because of what they represented—a change in my status.

As I bit my lip at the thought, I tilted my head back as the wind streamed in through the open windows. The pressure on my back where my tattoo was, exactly where Maverick had his, ached some, but it was a good ache.

A righteous one.

Just as what we were doing was righteous.

Some things just had to be done.

Lodestar had given Giulia Martin London's address when she asked for it, and that was our end destination. Giulia said Lodestar had repeated that she couldn't find anything on the guy, but that something stank as his bank account was a lot fuller than any pastor, ex or not, she'd ever come across.

That didn't exactly give us answers, but sometimes, instincts were enough. They had to be. Indy's were firing on all cylinders, and she said she *knew* something was going on with the bastard who wasn't as innocent as he was trying to make out.

To be honest, I had more faith in Indy than Lodestar, and seeing how shaken up she'd been last night, I wanted to act, and knew everyone in the vehicle felt the same way.

We were all victims. All of us. And we were trying to stop a little girl from being hurt the same way.

If London *was* innocent, then that was great. Fabulous. *Phenomenal.*

But if he wasn't, then we'd be sending a message while also keeping our family intact.

None of us had mentioned this to Storm. As far as we could tell, Keira hadn't either.

Why we were all intent on protecting a man who hadn't protected his family, I couldn't say. Maybe it was a piece of knowledge that simmered just below the surface of every conversation where London was concerned...

Storm wouldn't have the wherewithal to stalk the man who'd targeted his daughter.

He wouldn't sneak around. Wouldn't try to find a way to kill the pedophile so he wouldn't get caught.

He'd just castrate the man in Walmart or something.

Shoot him in the chest in front of a thousand witnesses.

And that was right.

That was just.

A father *should* do those things. *Should* seek vengeance on his child's behalf.

But that would mean the father would go to jail for a very long time, and that meant the child would never know him—what kind of vengeance was that? Because by the time Storm got out, Cyan would be a woman fully grown, and she'd only know her daddy through visitation times in a prison block.

It went without saying that none of us wanted that.

What we wanted was justice, however.

So we'd take it.

Posse-style.

And it was why the full posse, aside from Stone who was working at the ER, was riding to Martin London's house in the middle of the night, when we knew he'd be in.

The guys were returning from their run tonight, so we'd taken advantage of Nyx and Link's absence to get on with business today. With Maverick and Steel busy, Cruz too, getting around town had been relatively easy.

Fun as well.

Especially when we'd headed to the motel to get answers from the clubwhores about Tink. Just thinking about Giulia breaking Enya's nose had a small smile dancing on my lips.

Tomorrow, we'd sort that bitch out. Today, London was our priority.

When we rolled into a suburb that looked to be the height of respectability, with its neat as a pin yards and the cars that gleamed in the moonlight, with the trees shedding their leaves so that the wind picked them up and they didn't dirty the gardens, alongside the houses that looked like they belonged in a sitcom, it wasn't the kind of place you'd expect a predator to live.

But wasn't suburbia the most powerful of hidey-holes?

Hiding in plain sight enabled a creature such as this one to hunt, and that was what he'd done.

He'd found a vulnerable young girl who didn't want her parents to split up, who was being bullied at school according to Lodestar who'd learned that from Kati and who'd told me, whose father had left and moved to another state… She was a ripe plum to pluck.

But we were going to stop that.

Tonight, we were going to act.

The Camaro's lights turned off as we moved around a bend, and Indy moved deeper into the neighborhood, never revving the engine, always keeping it quiet until we made it to number one-eight-three-four.

We didn't pull up there, instead parked six houses down.

"Now, remember, we go in and we go out," Giulia rumbled, cracking her knuckles. "We don't shed blood and we don't leave bruises. We slip in like ghosts and scare the shit out of him, then we get out of there."

"It won't stop him from pressing charges once he realizes who we are," Tiffany pointed out gruffly.

"You're forgetting… he's a retired pastor, supposedly," Indy remarked. "What on earth would he do if he went to the cops, got you arrested, and you told them you thought he was a pedo? That wouldn't be good for his rep, would it? He'd want to keep it under wraps. Not only that… we're in West Orange, Tiffany. This is Sinners' territory."

Giulia grunted. "Good old corrupt pigs. Always on your side when you need them."

Lily snorted. "That's not supposed to be a positive, Giulia."

"Isn't it? They can at least be on our side when we need them to be," she muttered.

"They weren't on yours," Lily pointed out gently.

"Yeah, but now you're in your father's seat, who's going to pay the cops off?" She smirked, then rubbed her hands together. "I'm looking forward to this."

"You have anger issues," Tiffany countered.

"I wonder fucking why," Giulia snapped, but she didn't say another word as she shoved open the door and climbed out of the car. The rest of us slipped out of the tight fitting Camaro too, and we walked like we had the right to be there. Like one of us owned a place around here, and we were just returning home for the night.

My heart boomed in my chest like a soldier beating on a drum, but I wasn't scared. For once, I felt nothing more than thrilled to be doing something worthwhile. Something proactive.

We were all in on this. All of us ready to do what had to be done to stop this sick man from corrupting Cyan.

London's place was as neat as the rest of the neighborhood. White siding, pretty green trim around the roof, the screens were clean and free from holes, something that was visible thanks to the light of the full moon that was shining down on us.

I peered into its silvery face and sucked in a breath.

Giulia wasn't the only one with anger issues.

I'd realized that before when I'd forced Amara to talk, then when I'd taken such pleasure in helping to destroy one of Lancaster's most prized possessions. Lily and I had wrecked a Ferrari, and we'd bounced on the roof of the car as music piped through the garage until Link, Maverick, and Kati had found us there again.

Old Maverick shook his head and walked off, Kati scampered up there to dance with us, and Link smirked and eyed his woman up in a way that told me what they'd be doing the second he was alone with her.

And I'd been jealous.

As well as angry.

I'd wanted Maverick to look at me that way. To take me away with him...

To no avail.

The anger that desire caused had me gritting my teeth and vowing that I'd fuck my man the second I was home to make up for that impotent rage I'd felt when he wasn't mine, but Nic's. The violence flooded through me in a wave that encompassed what had gone down today with the club bunnies who'd been slow to talk, and I channeled it into what was about to happen.

Indy stepped onto the porch, opened the screen, and then ducked down to pick the locks.

I wasn't sure I wanted to know how she could do this, but only Lily, Tiffany, and I shot each other surprised looks—we'd thought we would have to sneak in through a window. I had to wonder if the Sinners taught lessons like this to kids much as other children would learn morals at Sunday School.

I wouldn't put it past the MC.

The door opened with a gentle snick, and Indy beckoned us forward. We tiptoed in, careful to stay as silent as we could, and the second we crossed the doorstep, a thrill shot through me.

Breaking and entering.

I'd just committed a crime, and I didn't give a damn.

The five of us surged onward, each of us trying to find where the bastard might be.

As I passed the living room, heading for the stairs, as quiet as a mouse even though my heart was still pounding so hard it was a wonder the others couldn't hear it, a strange tang of alcohol burned my nostrils. A bottle lay upended on the floor in a wet puddle, and there were another two on a stand beside an armchair I passed.

Making it upstairs, when I found him, it felt like fate.

The bedroom was neat and trim, and with the moonlight whispering in through the windows that were covered with blinds that were half open, I saw it was also anonymous.

As if the man didn't own much.

But this was a large house.

It was just... empty.

Now that I thought about the hall that led off the door, there'd been a coat rack and nothing more. No table to dump his keys on, no shoe rack to store his dirty sneakers. Up the stairs, there was no rug, and in this room, there was a bed, a dresser, a mirror, and that was it.

But the stench was in here too. Alcohol. And his snores were deep, lusty, like he was unconscious, which explained how I made it in there without him waking up.

I twisted around to head out of the room to get the others, but Tiffany was there, Giulia at her back.

The three of us nodded at one another and moved out, each of us going to the opposite side of the bed.

It was a strange thing to do, but I'd done worse in my time, and I knew it would keep him quiet, keep him from stirring. So I placed my hands on his feet and gently rolled them along his legs, up and up, higher and higher like a lover would. He twisted a little, but it wasn't in distress. As I knelt on the side of the bed, the mattress depressing under my weight, he wasn't disturbed in any way thanks to the caress I gave him that had the other women looking at me like I was crazy.

His legs shuffled apart at my touch, and I used that to my gain, crawling between them to get to his dick.

Exactly what I wanted.

A whisper in the doorway told me the three of us weren't alone, and that the others had joined us, but I didn't turn around, just caught Tiffany's eye. Once everyone was in position, she raised a hand with her ring, middle, and pointer finger standing.

She started to count down, and so did I...

In a flurry of movement, my knee pinned his dick to the bed, just as Tiffany's hand went to cover his mouth and to pinch his nose.

As he struggled, his movements were dulled, slow, confirming the belief he was drunk because a man like this should have been able to overpower us in a flash—this was not the night to have gotten drunk.

Lily and Giulia grabbed his arms, and Indy, a knife in her hands, pressed the tip into his throat.

His movements were almost enough to throw us off him, but I ground my knee into his cock harder, pushing all my weight onto it. I might be skinny, but when it came to the penis, you didn't have to exert much pressure to cause pain. A fact I took advantage of as I imagined grinding his dick into dust.

If I could, I would have.

"You will leave Cyan alone," Indy rattled out from between gritted teeth. "This is just a warning. This is just me telling you to back off. If you don't, we'll be paying you another visit, and I'll slice your dick off."

A moan escaped him, and his head wriggled from side to side as Tiffany worked hard to keep him sluggish thanks to oxygen deprivation. Eventually, he slowed, his movements turning dull with fatigue. At that point, she let go, and as he sucked in a noisy breath, flopping around like a dead fish on the sand, I let my leg rear back and I kneed him.

Hard.

Hard enough that I hoped his balls went into his body.

Hard enough that I hoped he wouldn't get an erection for a week.

Hard enough that I hoped it hurt to piss.

I flung myself off the bed, and the rest of us did the same, fleeing down the stairs, hurrying out of the house. As I made it across the yard, I saw Indy was back there, by the door, and though the others dashed to the car, I waited, not about to leave her behind as she locked up.

When she saw me waiting on her, her eyes flashed wide, gleaming gold in the moonlight with her gratitude, and she shot me a delighted look before the pair of us ran to the Camaro.

My heart was pounding for a different reason this time. Honest exertion and excitement.

God, that had felt good.

And as we hauled our asses into the car, and she took off, we contained our glee until we made it out of the subdivision, but just before we could celebrate, we saw them.

Lined up in a row.

Five of them, their faces revealed in the headlamps.

Maverick riding behind Link, Nyx, Cruz, and Sin, all of them waiting on us.

"Stop the car, Indy," Giulia ordered, but she didn't sound nervous. If anything, she sounded excited.

Frowning, wondering what she was about, I watched as Indy pulled up, and Giulia was out like a rocket. When the door opened, like he knew, Nyx climbed off his bike, and seconds later, she hurled herself at him, her legs coming around his waist, her arms wrapping around him.

When they started to eat each other's faces off, I had to smile, and the adrenaline that was still pumping through me from before, churning through my veins, setting me alight from the inside out...*morphed.*

Twisted.

Formed something else. Something less destructive and something infinitely more powerful.

Lust.

Need.

Desire.

We hadn't slayed our foe, but we'd threatened him and

punished him, and now, like marauding knights who could kill their own dragons, we were ready for our rewards...

An orgasm.

Or two.

Or maybe even three...

THIRTY-EIGHT

MAVERICK

THERE WERE four contrasting emotions rippling through me.

Rage. That she could put herself in danger, that she could be stupid enough to commit a crime when her immigration status wasn't cemented into stone yet.

Concern. That she'd get hurt. Or get caught.

Pride. That she wasn't scared to defend one of our own. That she'd go to bat for my brother's daughter. That she'd do what needed to be done to make sure that little girl was safe.

And lastly, need.

The complicated cocktail made it hard for me to do anything other than stay quiet on the trip home.

Rex, made aware of the situation, had postponed church until tomorrow morning, where we'd been ordered to get our Old Ladies in line because the clubwhores had been whining about some broken noses and black eyes. Rex had apparently used that as an excuse to hide the real truth of why he was delaying church from Storm.

We were protecting the one man who needed to know, but

there was a reason for that. We didn't want him to end up in jail, and that was where he'd be going. Without passing fucking go and without collecting two hundred dollars.

That was his right as well. To defend his daughter, to protect her and guard her from a pedophilic cunt, but there were two issues.

One, we didn't have confirmation yet that London was a pedophile. But we would, shortly, because I'd be heading down that rabbit hole in the AM as well. The second it was sanctioned, London's blood would be painting the Fridge's walls.

And two, because if we got him involved before the bastard was trussed up in the Fridge, he'd do something insane in public. Something we couldn't cover up.

Impotent with rage, need, pride, and concern, I seethed on the ride back to the house in Indy's Camaro. Alessa drove while Indy rode bitch with Cruz, after she'd extruded the promise that Alessa would take it to her place in the AM. It meant that we had privacy, but that privacy wasn't doing much for my mood.

The streetlamps dimmed as we reached a kind of crossroad that would either take us deeper into town or would let us head into the Orange Hills subdivision where Lily's property was located. I fully expected her to drive onto the estate, but she didn't. She pulled off to the side of the road, driving over bumpy terrain for a minute or so until we were sheltered from the minimal traffic that was passing by at this time of the night.

The second she cut the engine, the silence throbbed through the cab, and then she was on me.

I didn't expect it, *couldn't* have expected it. In all honesty, I'd thought she'd be scared about my being angry with her. Never in a million years did I think she'd be fucking horny.

But she was.

Sweet fuck, she was.

She threw herself against me, plastering each of her luscious inches against me. Her hand worked between us to cover my dick with her palm while her other shoved the dainty skirt of her dress up high so she could tunnel beneath her leggings.

When her fingers found gold, she sighed into my mouth, but just for a fraction of a second. Then she was back to thrusting her tongue against mine, fucking me with a ferocity that spoke of an adrenaline high that I was happy to let fizzle out on me.

With my emotions coalescing the way they were, this was the release I needed, but fuck, it was more than that. This was Alessa. And Christ, I needed her as much as I wanted her.

Hands snapping out so I could drag her leggings down, I groaned when I pulled back to see the shadowy motions of her touching her pussy, her fingers slick enough that they made a sound with every caress she gifted herself. I wished I could see that, wished we weren't in the pitch dark of the small copse of off-road trees, but somehow, that pitch black made this all the hotter.

Seeing was hard, but we could hear, we could feel, we could smell, and we could taste. Those four senses suddenly seemed a hell of a lot more powerful than sight.

I wanted that taste on my fucking tongue, and I wasn't about to be denied it.

The Camaro's front seat was too goddamn small, so I pushed open the door and slid out. She squawked at me, but not for long, not when I hauled her out of the car and dragged her to the trunk. At first, I leaned her against it, letting her stand there as I slipped my hands around her bare ass, pulling the cheeks apart with one while I threaded the other between her thighs so I could nudge her slick folds.

The heat of her had me hissing as I explored her mouth, loving that she let me even as she didn't stay passive. She was in this fight as much as I was.

The thought had me pulling back and lifting her so I could wedge her on the small fin on the trunk. As I spread her legs to step between them, I snarled, "You put yourself in danger."

"I'm a Sinner," she snarled back. "It's what we do."

More of that damnable pride filled me.

"You leave it to the men. That's what we're for."

"Some crimes deserve different punishments." She tipped her chin up. "This is bitches' business."

"Fucking Giulia." This had her scent all over it. "It ain't *bitches'* business, it's *club* business. You shouldn't be getting involved in this." I reached up and cupped her throat, forcing her to look at me. "What the fuck would I do if you got deported, huh? Deported and jailed for crimes that we have our own ways of solving."

Her eyes glinted with defiance, and even though it worried me, it also turned me the fuck on.

Alessa, I was coming to realize, was nothing like Ghost.

Ghost was the woman I'd fallen for, but she was a shadow in comparison to Alessa who was more like a full-bodied glass of red. She came with the bitter tang of tannins, and a headache the morning after, but she slipped down your fucking throat like manna from the gods.

Growling under my breath, I pulled her forward so I could kiss her into compliance.

It didn't work.

She fought back. More than before. Harder than earlier. She took everything I had to give and then some, not even faltering when I began to rub her clit then finger fucked her. When she cried out, her cunt pulsing and throbbing around my digits, I didn't stop, just carried on, using orgasms to force her to realize what she was to me.

Mine.

To protect.

To defend.

To love.

As I curled my fingers up against the front wall of her cunt, I pulled back so that our lips hovered above the other's. "You put yourself in fucking danger again, Alessa, I'm gonna make you regret it."

She snapped out, her teeth grabbing my bottom lip. She bit down hard enough to fucking hurt, then pulled back too, taking my lip with her before she let it go. "What are you going to do?" she growled. "Rape me? Slap me? Whip me? Cut me? As if you would."

The words were a dare and a sneer all in one. It spoke of her trust in me, her faith, even as it made me want to go out and kill the fuckers who'd owned her.

Christ, I'd been so busy today that I hadn't even gotten started on that list.

Fuck.

With my lip stinging, I swiped my tongue across it, only to come across the taste of blood.

The metallic flavor filled my mouth for a second until I whispered, "I'll lock you in our bedroom, keep you in our bed, I'll stuff you so full of my fucking cum that it fucking weighs you down and you can't move. I'll keep you so cock-drunk and orgasm happy that you won't know shit about the outside world. I'll fuck you so often and so hard that it'll be hard for both of us to walk, and the only time we do will be to get food so I can fill your stomach to keep you strong enough for the next round."

Her nostrils flared at that, and she dared to state, "Is that supposed to be a threat?"

"It's not a fucking threat," I snarled, "it's a promise."

Her lips flattened, but not in irritation.

In goddamn need.

Want.

Fuck.

My toes curled in my boots, and I was left with no option other than the sanest, *safest* one.

I dropped to my knees, grabbed her thighs so I could pull them apart, and hauled her closer to me. Keeping her mouth busy as she screamed through an orgasm was the only way we'd make it back to the pool house tonight, because if she pushed me anymore, we'd turn into Tarzan and fucking Jane as I showed her I meant every word—whether the bed was under a roof or the night sky didn't matter a damn to me.

Only she did.

Her safety.

Her wellbeing.

That was all that mattered.

THIRTY-NINE

ALESSA

THE SECOND HIS tongue collided with my clit, I felt sure I'd go mad.

Having never experienced this before, I wasn't sure if it was irritating or delicious. It didn't pack the same punch as his fingers, couldn't rub my clit as hard as I needed it, but there was a delicacy about it that caught my breath. And the sounds he made? *Pizda rula.* They added to the deliciousness of what he was doing. He *munched* on me. He slurped me down, tasted me, groaned as he did so. His lips suctioned down around my clit until I was howling, but it was different than the other orgasms he'd gifted me, because it was strong yet also had my toes curling because it had me feeling empty and ready for more.

This was, I realized, an appetizer.

To what he'd promised?

When he'd spoken of punishments, a red mist of annoyance had whispered over me. I'd been punished enough for a lifetime, but his idea was nothing like I'd thought.

His castigation would keep us locked together for hours at a time, and he believed that would be a bad thing? I could think of nothing better.

With my howl echoing around the clearing, ringing in my ears until I felt sure it would deafen me, he finally surged to his feet, unzipping his fly as he moved, and suddenly, he was there. Against me. Between my legs. So close to me I could taste his breath.

When his dick surged into me, I screamed again, my head falling back, my body both tense and straining as his mouth worked its way to my throat. As he sucked down hard on me there, I groaned, my hands moving around to his shoulders, digging into his muscles, holding him close with both my arms and my legs.

As he powered into me, hard and fast thrusts that weren't as gentle as he'd been before, I gloried at his loss of control, something that was founded in his need to protect me.

My pussy clenched at the thought as arousal whirled around me until I felt sure I'd go insane with it. He started to speed up, faster, deeper, he rocked into me, making the vintage car shudder beneath us until finally, he roared out his own release in my ear as I screamed one final time. My entire being pulsing as one big ball of pleasure struck me down like I was ten pins on a bowling lane.

"Tomorrow," he rasped in my ear, having finally let go of his hold on my throat, "when we go to Indy's..."

My breathing was just as fast, just as thick as his. My heart was pounding like I'd been running, and the sensation of his hot exhalations against my tender flesh made it feel even more sensitized.

"To Indy's?" I asked dazedly.

"To drop off her car," he muttered, and I nodded, limply letting my head come to rest against his as my entire body danced with glee at just how wonderful I felt. "We get branded."

"With hot irons?" I questioned, surprised when he tensed up and pulled away from me.

"No!" he shrieked. "Not with hot fucking irons." Even in the dark, I felt him change. His anger transformed into something that gave it wings. "Have you been branded that way?"

Because I was tired, I leaned back so I could rest on the window and I lifted my arm to show him. "Move the cuff," I ordered on a yawn. When he did as bid, his fingers traced over the skin the bracelet had covered.

"Jesus fuck," he whispered. "How did I never see that before?"

"Stone gave me a leather cuff to hide it." I yawned again. "Don't worry about it. It's in the past."

"Sure it is," he rumbled soothingly, moving my wrist so he could press his lips to it. "You're mine now. I want the whole fucking world to know it too."

Because I liked the sound of that, I smiled before flopping forward against him and drifting off to sleep.

FORTY

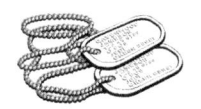

MAVERICK

IT WAS ALMOST pathetic how chirpy we were the next day, making it quite clear for any of the brothers in the vicinity to notice that we'd gotten some.

A lot of 'some.'

From the scowl on his face, I had to assume Rex was the only one whose morning wood hadn't been solved, and as he was staying at Rachel's place, it didn't take a genius to figure out why.

Sure, he could head to the motel where the clubwhores were staying, but A, they'd probably squawk his ear off about Giulia's Posse's 'visit' yesterday, and B, why would he want to fuck those skanks when the woman he really wanted slept down the hall?

So his grouchiness made total sense, and it amused me that not a one of us, not even Link who was the unofficial joker of the bunch, said a word about it.

We didn't have death wishes.

Settling around Rachel's mahogany dining room table was a lot grander than his office back at the clubhouse and I told him as much. "Looks like we've come up in the world."

He stared around the room, which was definitely classy with its terrace doors that overlooked a pool, and which let in a lot of light so the red in the table gleamed like fire, and the greenery from all the plants she had in here made it look all the more savage. I didn't know she had a green thumb, but this room alone made me wonder if she had some kind of weird addiction to plants because they lined every wall, in myriad sizes with different, not matching, pots.

It took the formality down a notch, while still making it feel grand because I recognized one of those orchids by the window from an article I'd read online, and knew they were rare as hell.

"I'd give my left nut to be in my old office," was Rex's grim reply.

As a creature of habit, that didn't surprise me. Plus, as shitty as it had been, there were a lot of memories in that dump. Good and bad. Devastating and amazing.

"Well, don't give up hope on Rachel just yet," Link dared to tease. "You might still need that nut."

Rex shot him a glare. "Fuck off, Link."

"Gladly," was his immediate retort. "None of this sits well with me. Why the fuck are we here and Storm isn't? He needs to know what happened last night and why."

I didn't necessarily disagree, but neither did I fully agree.

It was too complicated to be black and white.

If Storm knew about Martin London, then he'd kill him.

Deservedly so, but he'd act in rage and would repent in a prison cell.

If we took care of shit, then he'd still be around to sort out his kid in the aftermath of what had gone down.

Complicated, see?

Because of the night's events, church was one short. Technically, Storm didn't have to attend because he wasn't this chapter's

VP anymore, but he was our kin. We weren't gonna leave him out totally, we were just going to delay him so we could discuss this shit.

Nyx rocked back on the antique dining chair that creaked under his weight. "We don't want him in a jail cell," he replied. "And I made a promise to Indy that I wouldn't pull those moves anymore."

Sin shook his head. "I don't get it. Why would she make you promise that?"

Nyx's mouth tightened. "Kevin got to her too."

Steel's nostrils flared and horror set his eyes alight. "You're fucking with me?" he demanded, his tone guttural.

"Wish I fucking was, brother, but I ain't." He gritted his teeth. "Quin, when I visited him, said that he didn't get to him, but Christ, just the thought of that cunt with Indy makes me want to —" He released a short, sharp breath, and the tension in him betrayed itself in the bright red flush to his throat, the way the sinews popped out, and the vein that pulsed in his forehead.

I'd never noticed that one before, so it had to be new.

One thing was for sure, if we were going to keep him from breaking his promise to his sister, we'd need to figure out a way to keep him on the straight and narrow. Anger management was definitely in the cards because, otherwise, he'd have a fucking stroke.

"Christ," Sin whispered, which pretty much said it all.

Rex's shoulders hunched as he shoved back his chair, then leaned forward, elbows to his knees as he stared at the floor. "I get the promise you made, Nyx, especially after she told you that she wanted you to prioritize your kid, but this ain't healthy for you, brother."

"It isn't," I agreed. "I was just thinking that you look like you could have a stroke."

His fists settled on the table. "I feel like I'm going crazy," he said rawly. "When I think of it—" His head whipped to the side like he was trying to shake the thoughts away. "Giulia says there are ways of making them pay without killing them, but their deaths... fuck, it soothed something inside me. I don't know if wrecking their lives is enough. I want them to suffer."

The statement had me pursing my lips, especially when all eyes except for Nyx's turned to me. I knew they were looking to me for an answer, and I guessed I had it when I said, "We could dox them."

"Dox them?" Link asked, frowning.

"Yeah. Reveal their identities online. That'll set others onto them. We can torture them without having to get involved."

"That's doable?" Rex queried,

I snorted. "Course it is. Then there are other moves we can pull. To be honest, this would be best discussed with Lodestar because she's a psycho, but you can turn off their electricity, switch off their gas. Cut off their water, crap like that. We could drain their bank accounts. Hell, we could send a SWAT team to their front door. And, depending on what car they drove, I mean if it's new or not, we could probably mess with that as well."

"Long distance?"

Pondering Rex's demand, I nodded. "Don't see why not. Lodestar and I can make magic when we hack together. Just haven't done it in a long while." Since before we split up. "Doesn't mean we can't make an appearance together for a worthy cause," I said dryly. "But I don't know if that's enough. Nyx, what do you think?"

When he didn't say anything, Sin muttered, "I know how that rage feels, Nyx. You know I do. We can work out together, fight, train. There are things we can do to help combat those demons because, God help me, I hear their whispers as much as you do."

That wasn't a lie. For a man to be capable of beating his father to death with his fists, that took a hell of a lot of rage.

"Plus, there's always the Fridge. You could take over those duties," Rex mused. "Maybe help Cruz with clean up."

At that, Nyx pulled a face. "That ain't my scene. Cleaning up after Indy was bad enough. Hacking through limbs isn't how I wanna be spending my Saturday night."

Rex snorted. "I know where to shove you when you piss me off then, huh?"

Nyx rolled his eyes. "You're all heart." He reached up and scrubbed a hand over his jaw. "Look, I appreciate the suggestions, guys. I'm probably going to have to take you up on all of them."

"You thought about maybe doing something on the other side of things, Nyx?" I asked calmly.

"What do you mean?"

"I mean helping the kids in other ways rather than just killing their monsters?"

"Talk," was his brisk reply.

I shrugged. "Kids have to go to court, don't they? Have to look those sick fucks in the eyes as they testify against them? We could do something to help keep them safe. Shore them up, make them feel strong enough to do that."

He was so still I wasn't sure if he'd stopped breathing, then, he rasped, "Yes."

Rex dipped his chin. "Steel?"

The secretary shot Rex a dazed look. "Yeah?"

"Think you can arrange that? Maybe figure shit out? Get Tiff involved, maybe Lily too? I think they'd have the contacts and some know-how. I think Lily told me once she had to help with foundations and charitable organizations before her dad died. Maybe you guys could brainstorm how to make that happen?"

He swallowed. "Can do."

Rex shot me a look. "Good thinking, Mav. You and Lodestar will get to work on the doxing when things are back to some semblance of normalcy, right?"

"That could take a while," was all I said.

"At least it's on the books." He grunted. "With that in mind, you can focus on London. I know Lodestar's research on him pulled up kosher hits, but I doubt your Old Ladies would have gone to that extent last night if they didn't think his shit stank." He rubbed the back of his neck. "You guys are going to have to keep a better hold on them as well. We can't have them rolling around, pulling stunts like that."

"You try and stop them," Nyx retorted. "Giulia's got it into her fucking head she's a Sinner, and that some shit is business only bitches can handle. Those are her fucking words."

"Fucker of it is I can't argue with the logic," Link muttered.

"Course we can," Rex countered. "Whether a traitor is a bitch or a dick, we torture them equally."

"Women have ways about them." Sin shrugged. "Link and I spoke with them about Tink, and not a one of them said shit. Whereas Giulia and her posse managed to worm out the fact she was in Mott Haven."

"You get in touch with the *Demonios Bandidos* and asked them to keep an eye out for her?" Rex asked Nyx who nodded.

"Already done."

"Good." He sighed. "The trouble is you're all fucking whipped. That's why you can't keep your bitches in line."

Nyx snorted. "Yeah, I'll remember that when I see Rachel shoot you down and you keep your fucking whipped mouth closed."

Though he scowled, he didn't reply, just rubbed his chin thoughtfully as the sound of straight pipes rattled in the distance. "Storm's here. We don't mention London in his hearing, but

Maverick, I know you're sick, man, but you gotta find out yea or nay if the creep's a kid fucker or not."

I nodded. "I'm on it."

"Lodestar's been saying that for a while," Nyx complained.

"She's sick, not working at full capacity, and was working on her own," I defended. "Plus, if his front is kosher, then digging deeper isn't as easy as you think. How do you find out a man's secrets without it taking time?"

"He has a point," Link remarked.

"It's going to be a priority, but it could still take me three days of flat out working and I ain't at full capacity either." I shot Rex a look. "We're gonna be slower than I'd like."

"Think the Five Points would help out?" Sin queried cautiously. "One of the O'Donnellys is a hacker. Or so they say..."

"And gossip is always right," Steel rasped, causing me to shoot him a look. The fucker looked strung out, which, after his earlier chirpiness, was weird.

"Not always, no, but we can ask."

"Declan's helpful," Rex inserted. "He's the reason I got out of the summit alive."

"Let's not talk about that today," Nyx muttered. "My blood pressure already feels like I'm close to a coronary."

Rex just grunted. "Either way, yeah, ask, Sin. See if they can help us out with London."

The door surged open, revealing a glowering Storm who ground out, "You started without me?"

"Ain't our fault our asses were early and yours wasn't," Link sniped, earning himself the bird Storm flipped his way as he rounded the table and took the last remaining seat.

"The Musketeers are back together again," I said with a smile, earning snickers all around.

"I'll take Rebecca DeMornay any day of the fucking week," Storm teased.

Most of us grinned, except for Rex, who rumbled, "Okay, now that everyone is *finally* here" —he smirked at Storm— "let's get down to business. There's shit I gotta share with you, and I don't want to. But... first things first, good news." He peered over at Nyx. "The O'Donnellys pulled through for us. The governor has pardoned Quin."

My brows rose at that. "You asked them for that big a favor?"

"Well, I took out their enemies," he said wryly. "I think that's the least they could do."

"Jesus, Rex," Nyx rasped. "Thank you, brother."

Rex bowed his head. "You said he's innocent, said he was framed, and I believe you. Heard from Finn O'Grady, and he said it'll take about a week for him to be released."

"So soon?" Nyx wheezed. "Christ, that's fast."

"We're dealing with mob royalty," was all Rex said, but his gaze drifted to mine. "After our conversation, Maverick, do you have news for me?"

"Lodestar has cameras set up on our perimeter and so do I." Rex scowled at that, but I waved a hand. "She's suspicious of everyone, and in this instance, it works to our advantage. You aren't going to change her," I said wryly. "The driver of the truck who left your uncle's case file at the clubhouse is a woman called Josefa Banks." I pursed my lips. "She's your aunt, Rex."

He clenched his eyes closed. "Fuck, this couldn't be any more convoluted, could it? Why the hell did she hightail it out of there like we were going to hurt her?"

"Maybe she was scared."

"What the fuck are you guys talking about?" Link ground out, his brow puckered as he flashed his focus between Rex and me. A quick glance around the table confirmed everyone looked just as confused.

So I sucked in a breath and said, "You wanna tell them, Rex, or shall I?"

His jaw firmed. "You know more about it than me. Go for it. Blow their minds."

FORTY-ONE

ALESSA

WHEN I WALKED into Indiana Ink, I couldn't hide from how different this visit was to my last one here.

The tattoo in the center of my back was something Maverick had yet to see thanks to the dresses I wore that covered it up, and he'd been more focused on my ass and the scarring there in the hospital to notice, but that one wasn't for him. It was for me.

I was free.

Because of him. His family.

My family.

And today's ink was different. It was for him, and he was getting one for me.

Branded.

I'd experienced that once, and the pain of it had been enough to make me black out. Today's couldn't be more different. Ink was so much less discomforting than molten hot metal searing flesh.

Turning back to look at him, I smiled when I saw that he was watching me. He did that a lot, and when he did, there was a joy to the look like he took pleasure in having his eyes on me. As if I made him happy. And if that wasn't a breathtaking idea, I didn't know what was, because I wanted to make him happy. I wanted his happiness more than I wanted my own.

"Back already?" Indy called out from the desk where she had her feet up.

Giulia laughed, and I saw she was standing by the coffee pot, which had me frowning. "Giulia! You're not supposed to be drinking coffee anymore!"

Her nose crinkled. "I'm suffering through decaf."

Suspiciously, I narrowed my eyes at her before I shot Indy a look. She snorted. "Yeah, it's decaf. Bitch is making me drink that watered down crap too."

"Keeping her honest, huh?" Maverick teased as he strolled over to the desk and perched his ass on it.

"That's one way to look at it," was her dry retort, and she smiled when he tossed her the keys to her Camaro. "Thanks, Mav. What are you guys doing here anyway? Didn't expect to see both of you today."

"It's time," he said simply.

"We're getting brands," was my excited reply when she just arched a brow in confusion.

"You are?" She beamed a smile at us. "That's amazing news." Then, she faltered. "Wait, I thought you already got your version of a brand?"

Maverick shrugged. "I did, but I want a different one."

"You have a brand already?" I gasped.

"I do. The mandala on my back." When I just frowned at him, he lifted up his cut and Henley, then twisted a little so I could see the pretty pattern dancing down his spine toward his hips. "Your name is buried within it."

"That's called a mandala?" I breathed, reaching out to touch proof that this man had loved me for far longer than I'd loved him.

Proof that he'd claimed me before I'd even known I wanted to be claimed.

"It is." His eyes twinkled as he asked, "Like it?"

"I love it." And I did. "Not as much as I love you though."

Giulia snorted. "Pass me a barf bag."

"Like you're not as bad as that with Nyx," Indy sniped back, making me twist around to laugh at them both, even as I kept the flat of my palm against his tattoo.

My brand.

Mine.

And he wanted another.

My heart felt so full of glee, so full of joy, that it was a wonder I didn't burst.

Because Giulia couldn't argue, her lips turned down into a sulky pout as Indy queried, "Okay, Alessa, what's your poison?"

"My poison?" I frowned in confusion.

"She thinks she's being funny," Giulia snarked.

"These two always like this when they're together?" Maverick asked dryly.

"They're worse."

"Christ."

Indy rolled her eyes. "What ink do you want this time?"

"You already got a tattoo?"

Mav's surprise was clear, and I shot him a shy smile as I turned my back to him and murmured, "If you unfasten the zipper, you can see it."

Silence filled the tattoo parlor as he did so, making the sound of the fastener opening all the louder, and his sharp inhalation clearer as he processed what he was seeing.

When his fingers reached out to trace what was a twin to his, just with bastardized lettering, he whispered, "For me?"

"For me," I corrected. "For you. For what you and your family did for me." I peeked at him over my shoulder. "I saw yours and needed it on me because it helped make you the man I love, but I also loved the meaning."

"An oppressed man freed," he parroted, and I saw the understanding in his eyes, felt it even more when, with his other hand, his fingers tangled with the cuff that shielded my brand. One that had been burned into my flesh.

I nodded. "Exactly. I thought it fit perfectly."

"It does." His gaze dropped to the ink. "You're beautiful, Alessa."

Smiling at him, I said, "Thank you."

"Wonder if she thanks him when he tells her he loves her?" Indy said in an aside to Giulia.

"If the fucker *has* told her that yet. Maybe we need to beat him up. Show him how he'd best treat our girl."

At that moment, with Mav's eyes on me, Indy and Giulia in the background, my heart felt too full.

'Our girl.'

I belonged.

Knowing that my full heart was in my eyes, I said, "He's told me. Why do you think we're getting branded?"

"Spill the deets then," Giulia chivvied. "I wanna know what you're getting."

So I told them.

A few hours later, ink completed, a little sore and a lot buzzy from the adrenaline whispering through my system, we finished the errands we had planned for today and returned to Lily's.

I half expected him to head into the kitchen so he could work with Lodestar, only he didn't. With our fingers tangled, our free hands carrying bags from the stuff we'd bought today, together, we walked to the pool house.

As I set my purse on the counter beside the door, he placed the bags carefully on the ground as he closed up behind us.

The second it was shut, I shrieked because his hands were on my hips and he was hauling me back into him. His mouth went to my ear and he rasped, "I wanna feel you and your brand up."

My smile broke loose. "You can't yet. It's still under the Saran Wrap."

"I know," he growled impatiently. "But I wanna."

"Tough," I told him succinctly, laughing when he growled again. Twisting back to look at him, I continued, "I want to bite yours, but I can be patient."

"Well, I can't be," he said with a grunt, and his dick ground into my ass as he slipped his hand over my stomach.

We'd yet to use protection, and I knew that was because he assumed I was taking the pill, but I wasn't.

Wouldn't.

Dolya, fate, had me in its grip, and I wasn't about to mess with it. Not when it had brought me here, to this point.

Even as I wondered if I was pregnant, one hand stayed on top of my stomach, while the other began to lift my skirt higher, higher, until he could reach between my legs unimpeded. I wore no leggings today because the dress I wore danced around my calves, so to feel skin against skin was delicious, especially as he quickly flickered his fingers under my panties.

My hips arched in turn, rocking into him because that felt so good when he aimed straight for my clit and rubbed it back and forth, just how he'd learned I liked it. His breath brushed my ear, the weight of his chin settled on my shoulder, and his front seemed to be pressed against the full length of my spine which let me burn up in his heat and allowed me to feel as if I was surrounded by him.

Nothing could have felt better either.

I groaned, my nipples budding against my dress, skin prickling with the fire he stirred in me as he whispered, "I'm going to fill you up with my cum, Alessa. Stuff you full of it. Your pussy is gonna know me from the inside out, and whenever I'm near, you're gonna start to crave me just like I crave you. Just like I need you."

His words had me tilting my head so I could slot our mouths together, keep them bound as I thrust my tongue against his, needing to unite with him in this one small way.

As he kissed me, he moved us so I was no longer simply staring at the hall ahead, but so I was facing the wall.

Pulling back, he murmured against my lips, "Hands on the wall, sweetheart."

Who was I to argue?

Shivering, I complied, pressing my palms where he indicated, the tips of my fingers curling in as he angled me so I was bent forward.

I heard his zipper retracting, felt his groan like I'd made it myself when he freed his dick and palmed it, then whimpered when his cock, so molten hot I was sure I'd expire from it, brushed against my folds.

"Your pussy is the only pussy I want for the rest of my life, Alessa. No other. Only you. Only yours. You're my woman," he ground out, his dick slipping inside me, filling me full, filling me like no other ever had, ever could. "You're mine. No other's. That brand says it fucking all." His hand moved to gently trace over the Saran Wrap that shielded my ink, and that he could be so tender when I felt as if he was vibrating with tension hit me hard.

This man. A study of contrasts. But he was right... He was mine.

No other.

Ever.

Only him.

"Irreplaceable," I rasped as he moved his hand again, letting his fingers dig into my hips as he started to rock into me. He wasn't as ferocious as he'd been the other night on Indy's Camaro. Whenever he took me, there was something that made me feel as if the air around us was burning up. As if *I* was burning up, and I'd never wanted that more than I did when he was inside me.

His hand held me in place, his forearm banding against my stomach as he started to speed up, and my pussy clutched at him, letting him know I wanted him to keep on fingering my clit, to keep on doing what he was doing, because it was perfection.

With my other hand, I leaned back, gripping him by the nape, and while the natural arch to my spine was even more exaggerated, I felt closer to him, especially when my thumb brushed over the Saran Wrap there.

I thought about being with my friends, my fellow Old Ladies, thought about them watching as I nipped his neck, hard enough to leave bite marks on his throat. I thought about watching Indy trace the marks I'd left behind with tracing paper, and then I shivered as I remembered her tattooing *my* bite onto his skin.

Shuddering at a memory I knew I'd never forget, I groaned long and low, wanting to see that brand as much as he wanted to see the ink on my chest, so instead, I tugged on the ball chain necklace that rattled whenever he thrust into me, and found comfort in our new ritual. A ceremony that was just for us.

Today went deeper than just the act of branding. This went deeper than the marriage ceremony in West Orange's courthouse. This was something that would protect us in the future.

Today, we'd laid down the first foundations for an uncertain tomorrow.

"You're thinking," he ground out in my ear, his breath hot as he nipped my earlobe, hard enough to make me yelp. "Focus on this. On us. On me. On you. Nothing else." The words were ferocious and had my eyes fluttering to a close as his speed increased, forcing my pussy to clamp down around him as he hit the perfect spot with his fingers.

A squeal escaped me, my hips pulsating to a rhythm different than his as I surged my way toward a climax he demanded I have. As I slowed down, my stomach rippling, he sped up, the thud-thud of his thighs against my butt turning staccato as he reached his own peak.

Another squeal escaped me as I heard him grind out a curse in my ear, and I moaned once more as I felt the sharp pulses of his release, combined with the nip to my earlobe and a hissed out, breathless, "Who do I belong to?"

That he asked me that at that moment, when my mind was foggy, dull from pleasure and whittled down to the barest of thoughts, wasn't fair.

But Maverick would never be fair.

Not when he knew tomorrow wasn't promised.

With my eyes closed, I released a shaky sigh, and savoring his gift to me, I rasped, "Me."

Because he did.

And always would.

FORTY-TWO

MAVERICK
THE FOLLOWING DAY

"SIN?"

"Hey, Mav, how's it going?"

Because I knew he wasn't talking about the work we were both doing for the council, instead was meaning on a personal level, I was honest with him. "Had some nightmares last night."

Which was irritating because the way I'd felt when I slept in Alessa's arms, I should have been at peace. Instead, my mind had been turbulent, stormy. And even the sound of a chair scraping on the fucking floor had me rearing back like I was in the middle of a firefight.

"I know how that goes, brother. Wanna talk about it?"

I sighed. "Not really, Sin. I mean, I know I can, and I want you to know you can talk about this shit with me too, but I just—fuck, I'm so used to keeping it inside."

"I get it. I do," he murmured. "It's what we do. But maybe that's why we get the nightmares?"

"Could be." I rocked my head to the side, trying to ease the tension in my neck. "Truth is, this situation ain't helping. All this crap with the Sparrows? It's got me seeing fucking conspiracies left and right."

"Who could blame you? I didn't sleep well myself last night. How many of our brothers are inside on trumped up charges, huh? How fucking many? I can't wait until Quin's out. A week inside is more than I can stand, never mind him."

Because I agreed, I released a heavy sigh. "I'm the same. Be glad when he's home." I pinched the bridge of my nose, needing to get this out because it was stupid, but my brain hadn't been able to see anything but wheels within wheels since I'd woken up this morning, coated in sweat, my chest burning like I'd been running.

Alessa had done the unthinkable—sucked me off until I was calmer, which had turned into a whole other kind of reason for my lungs to be burning—but the thoughts wouldn't go away. They wouldn't leave me.

"Remember how I told everyone in church about the assassin who was behind Rene's death?"

"How could I fucking forget?" he grumbled.

"I just couldn't get this stupid sliver of information out of my mind. It's crazy and dumb as fuck, but... it's too simple to ignore."

"Talk to me, bro. What is it? Where's your mind at?"

That he was willing to listen to me posit a stupid theory had me shrugging my shoulders back as I stared at the water, looking out of the kitchen window into a pool that was slowly turning frigid with fall. "Ken told me how the assassin's surname, or at least, the identities he was willing to burn, were made up of capital cities."

Silence fell on the other end of the line. "You serious?"

"Deadly. He mentioned a Paris, a Moscow, and Madrid."

A hiss sounded down the line. "Can't be a coincidence," he muttered.

"That's what I was thinking." Tension hit me hard, and I

reached up to rub the back of my neck. "London's a more common name than a goddamn Moscow, but still..."

"I'll get Hawk over there. Get him to pick up some DNA samples. See if there's a match." He grunted. "This is too neat, surely?"

"Neat read insane. Whatever the fuck we did to get on the Sparrows' radar..." I shook my head even though I knew he couldn't see me. "I wish we could roll back the hands of goddamn time."

He agreed, told me once more that he'd be sending Hawk out right away as he was in the middle of club business—I didn't ask for more details because, as enforcer, that could mean he was beating the shit out of someone who owed the MC money and I really didn't want to know—before we parted ways and I was left with the ringing silence of the kitchen.

The pool house's situation was such that half of the view from this window was made up of the pool, but the other half led to the yard and the main house, so you could see anything and everything.

At that moment, the pool was still, because there wasn't a lick of a breeze, but Kati was dancing barefoot, her hair a wild cloud around her head and, if my eyes didn't deceive me, some kind of mud on her face. I'd never seen a messier kid, she always had something on her cheeks, a rat's nest for hair, and her clothes were always clean but rumpled to the point where she looked like she lived in a bag.

As I watched her dance though, watched her do some cartwheels and some standing somersaults that had my brows lifting in surprise at her skills, I recognized two things—one, this was why she was always rumpled. She hurled herself from one side of the yard to the other, uncaring if she fell or if she face planted, she just carried on. Getting dirtier and messier as she went.

Two, someone had taught her this shit.

Someone...

The thought had unease unfurling inside me again, and those goddamn wheels within wheels began to churn in my head.

I knew London helped out at gymnastics practice...

Jaw tensing, I stormed out of the house and headed for my sister-in-law who wanted me to act like a big brother. A *protective* older brother.

Was there a reason for that?

Sweet fuck, I hoped not.

***An hour later*
**

MAVERICK

MY STOMACH WAS CHURNING as I headed into West Orange on the back of a hog I shouldn't be riding but really fucking needed to. The last thing I wanted was to eat, but I'd made a date with Alessa and I wasn't about to let her down, especially when nothing was confirmed.

I'd talked to Kati who, I thought, was purposely being obtuse—either that, or I hadn't spelled shit out well enough—so I'd taken her to Lodestar in the kitchen and told them to have a talk about her 'gymnastic' capabilities.

Lodestar being Lodestar had quickly picked up on the situation, but from my conversation with Kati, I didn't fear London had targeted her. I wondered what Cyan had confided in her, because she was the one who'd been instructing Kati who, I knew from Alessa, didn't take goddamn gymnastics.

Cyan's confidences might reveal something about London that

a background check wasn't pulling up. Even with Conor O'Donnelly on the hunt, you couldn't milk blood out of a stone, and if, like I'd laid out for Sin, London *was* a Sparrow backed assassin, he had an army of his own to wipe out his identity and to forge new ones for him.

The blast of the wind in my face was the only thing that was stopping the headache from blinding me. I needed it, needed that air to feel awake, to feel like this nightmare wasn't just an endless circle that we'd never be able to fucking escape.

I needed Alessa, her smiles and her warmth and her love, but I feared for what I was bringing into her world.

She didn't deserve more trouble, more strife.

She deserved a good man, a great life, and what was she gonna get? An MC treasurer who might forget her one moment, and who had brought her into the crosshairs of a cabal that had itchy trigger fingers for us.

Gnawing on the inside of my cheek helped as I made it into West Orange proper, where the noise grew worse and the sun pounded on my head, making me feel like an overripe orange that could burst. My breathing was shallow, my face clammy with sweat, and I knew it was a good thing the MC's diner was around the corner because if I didn't stop soon, I could fucking crash.

What a dumb idea this had been, a dumb fucking move—

Then I saw her.

She was standing by the diner, waiting on me, her attention on her phone, dressed in a slim fitting dress that danced around her knees, black leggings hiding those beautiful legs from the world, a navy shrug covering her arms from the slight chill in the air. She was like a fifties housewife that, for whatever reason, gave me a boner.

Which wasn't really helpful in my current state.

The approach of the straight pipes had her peering at the road, though, and when our eyes caught and held, immediately, I felt better.

As I rolled to a stop, kicked down the stand, and straightened up, I smiled at her as she moved nearer to me, like she didn't want any space between us, which was when a car backfired.

The sound was short.

Sharp.

Staccato.

Nothing in the grand scheme of things.

Nothing to anyone with a normal mind.

But I wasn't normal.

One second, I was looking at the love of my life, the next I was looking at hell itself.

All around me, the COP was in chaos. The sun pounded down on me worse than anything Jersey was capable of even in midsummer, and the weight of my kit on my back, the weight of the helmet on my head, the narrow field of vision in front of me, had me whipping around, trying to find my fucking bearings.

I was standing in the middle of the outpost we'd only just taken back the day before, a grimy piece of shit place that was only useful for a couple of warehouses that stored lethal munitions we didn't want in the enemy's possession. It was barren, blistering with heat, and there were only rocks and very little green anything as far as the eye could see.

What had once been a functioning post was now laid to ruins from several routs.

Men lay dead around me. I saw them, registered their uniforms, saw pools of blood beneath them. There were Taliban soldiers here too, but I only looked at the BDUs for identities of fallen brothers.

The radio sputtered out sound, and I recognized the voice.

Liam. "This is Chaos 7. We need rotary wing gunships. Air support imperative. Over."

"Chaos 7, air support is forty mins away. Use 120mm mortars. Over."

"Mortar pit is pinned down. Over."

I stared around me, trying to figure out the lay of the land and saw the mortar pit *was* pinned down. We were in a kind of bowl, meaning we couldn't reach higher ground.

"We're going to need medevacs. Over."

Before I could process much else, gun fire showered me, but I ducked down, running toward shelter which came in the form of a piece of corrugated iron. As I ran, as the bullets wove and danced between my feet, someone called my name.

"Maverick!"

It was hoarse, a rasp, a splutter.

A death rattle.

Coming from the lips of a man I loved.

I forgot about the bullets, forgot about the heat, the violence, the death, the terror. Just focused on finding that voice.

I darted around corpses, seeing faces of the men I'd served with who were brothers to me. Junkers was down, Samie too, but then there was Nic.

He was on his back, his fatigues puddled with bright splotches of red, and his eyes were glassy as he stared straight up at me. I dove to the ground, my knees spraying up a cloud of dust as I loomed over him. One hand went to check his pulse, the other to put pressure on the gut wound, but he grabbed my wrist with surprising strength and said, "Find Eagle Eyes. Ask him about Dost Mohamet Khan."

My brow puckered. "What? Why do you want me to find Liam?"

In my earpiece, I heard the sudden sputter of, "Chaos Platoon, please be advised. The 10th Mountain Division is delayed. Repeat, delayed. There will be no backup. Pass it on. No medevacs. Over."

"No," I breathed before I howled out my rejection of what I was hearing. Staring down at the blood, so much fucking blood that was draining from Nic's body, killing him, all I could think was—this isn't happening. This *cannot* be happening.

"Chaos 8. We need medevacs. Now! Over," I snarled into my radio as I shoved even more pressure onto Nic's stomach.

His hand reached for mine, and as our fingers tangled, his with that strong grip that belied his weakness, he drew mine away from putting pressure on his abdomen.

"Listen to me, Jameson. Listen well." His eyes were like diamonds that spit fire in the heat of the sun. They compelled me to listen. To never forget. "I want you to live, Jameson. I want you to live and to love. I need you to let me go."

"No!" I moaned, tears burning as they fell, creating dirty tracks that plopped onto his fatigues. "I can't let go, I can't forget you! I can't. I won't."

"You must," he rasped, his urgency raw. "You must. I need you to do what I couldn't—get out. Be free. Live a life that isn't tainted by this hell." He drew me down, dragging me closer so I couldn't avoid or evade him. "I want you to love her. I want you to make babies with her." His smile turned rueful, even as pain creased his brow and dulled his eyes. "If you can't forget about me, why not name one of them Nic?"

A sob escaped me. "I can't. I won't let go." Into my radio, I screamed, "We need medevacs. OVER!"

"Please, Jameson, do it for me. Don't be a ghost. Live your life. Please." He grabbed my hand, pressed my knuckles to his lips, and with his dying breath, whispered, "I love you. Please... promise you wi—"

Mortar fire sent me into a world he'd described.

That of hell.

A blast lifted me off my feet, and when I landed, my knees didn't collide with packed dirt that had a cascade of dust surging around me. They collided with concrete.

A sidewalk.

At my back, horns and traffic whispered into my awareness, and bleary-eyed, deafened by the mortar fire, I stared ahead, once more trying to find my bearings.

A woman was in front of me, fear in her eyes, her beautiful face puckered with terror.

For me?

I shook my head, trying to figure out what was happening. What was going on. But I couldn't understand, couldn't—

"Maverick?" she rasped, a strange lilt to her voice, the intonation on the letter 'E' in my name different than what I was used to hearing. "Maverick, please, look at me."

I gulped, turning my face away because I didn't want to look at her.

Who was she?

Where was Nic?

And then she dropped to her knees in front of me. Behind her, I heard a bell ring out, and booted feet stomped onto the sidewalk. I was surrounded suddenly by men in cuts—the MC?

My MC?

I closed my eyes, unable to deal with this. Why wasn't I in Kembesh? Where was Liam? Why did Nic want me to talk to him? *Dost Mohamet Khan?* Who was he?

I heard a gruff voice grate out, "Not again. Fuck. We need to get him to a hospital."

"No!" The woman's voice was strident, strong with a command. "Jameson, my name is Alessa. I'm your Old Lady.

You're in West Orange, you're not a soldier anymore. You're the treasurer for the Satan's Sinners MC." She tugged on something I wore around my neck that rattled.

The sound urged me to act, and I peered down at the dog tags she held in her hand.

Ellis
Dominic J.
123-45-6790
AB Neg
Catholic

Nic.

Then, she reached for my hand and pressed it to her chest, and as I stared at her, blinking at the fresh ink with shaking fingers, I traced the letters. The shapes. *Felt* the meaning.

She wore dog tags too, but they were forever etched into her skin.

Only, they weren't an identical pair. There were *three* tags.

One was embossed with:

> *Ellis*
> *Dominic J.*
> *123-45-6790*
> *AB Neg*
> *Catholic*

And the other:

> *Ravenwood*
> *Jameson*
> *123-45-6789*
> *O Pos*

Jedi

And the final one was embossed with:

> *Ravenwood*
> *Alessa*
> *O Neg*
> *Catholic*
> *Old Lady*
> *Satan's Sinners MC*

It wasn't like a club to my head, a wallop to my system, but the memories came back.

I remembered.

"Alessa," I whispered, and I broke down. Sobbing.

How could I do anything else?

I shielded my face, unable to deal with what I saw, remembered, felt, heard. But she was there, her hands tracing over me, sliding over my head, drawing me nearer until I was pressed into her in a tight embrace.

The love from her flowed into me, recharged me, regenerated me.

CTE.

PTSD.

An alphabet of abbreviations, all of them destined to take me from her.

"I-I might not always remember," I whispered, because even as I knew I couldn't hold on without her, neither could I put her through this. "It might get worse."

But though my voice was ragged, hers was calm. So calm.

"Worse with you is better than the best days of my life without you."

"You can't say that."

"I can." Then, with a steeliness I felt like she'd slammed a metal bar into my skull, she told me, "I will."

My mouth trembled. "It was a flashback."

"You don't have to talk about it—"

"Nic was there." My eyes seeped more tears as I pulled back to look at her. "He told me to love you. To let him go and to forget about him."

She shook her head. "Then he's dumb. What is it with you men? So self-sacrificing. You don't need to forget him." She pressed my fingers to her chest again, the move awkward as we were so close together. "He's a part of us, Jameson. Forever. And both of us love *you* enough to protect you from yourself. I'm going nowhere, and neither are you."

She was so assured, so strong, so fucking confident where I felt nothing but weak. And stupid, as a thought flashed into my mind. Nic—he'd said he wanted a kid named after him. "What if you're pregnant? We haven't used anything. I can't put a kid through—"

"I hope I am. Life is hard and complicated, and painful too," she conceded on a sigh, "but with you, I'm happy. I'm whole. You gave me a family, you brought me peace, and you made me feel secure. Your child will only add to that. He or she will be one more piece that ties us together. Binds us."

"That's not fair to them."

"It's not fair, either, if a child doesn't have the chance of being your son or daughter, Maverick. You're a good man. The best."

I stared into those eyes that weren't Nic's but were a sharp shade of blue, sharp enough to tell me she meant every word she said. They weren't dazed with emotion, but were hard with reason. Cold, hard reason.

She believed every word she said, and like Nic, she told me, "I love you, Jameson. We will get through this. Together."

And as I murmured the same, told her, "I love you, Alessa," in the background, I heard a cellphone ring.

Then Steel's voice stormed, "What? You're fucking with me, Rain." I tuned him out, but even as I focused on the love in her eyes, on the forgiveness in her beautiful soul for a man whose broken mind would always be fractured but which she'd love anyway, I heard him say, "Follow her. Make sure if he stops, you get to her first. Rain, we believe he's a pedophile. She's in danger. Try to send us your location and we'll be on our way."

And even as Alessa pressed her lips to mine, I registered a hard truth.

The Satan's Sinners weren't like the U.S. Army.

There would never be no backup. No medevacs.

We protected our own.

We killed for them.

We'd die for them.

And that was how it should be.

Forever.

FORTY-THREE

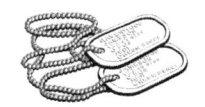

QUIN

FOR SOMEONE who'd recently gained a lot of Irish and Russian friends, the sudden silence came as a surprise. Nowhere was silent in Rikers. That was one of the hardest things about being in here.

There was no peace. Ever.

Serenity wasn't a thing.

Calm wasn't either.

So the sudden silence was proof that a storm was incoming, and when storms made landfall here, they were cataclysmic.

Tension had me backing up, moving out of the common area as I knew that avoidance was imperative, and reversing to my cell where there was minimal safety in my bunkmate's presence.

As I passed an inmate who was notorious for riding correctional officers' legs, I ducked my chin to avoid looking at him and noticed he did the same. Both of us were frightened jack rabbits at that moment, aware a predator was somehow on the loose, and not sure how to survive it.

The walls felt like they were closing in on me. The narrow corridors and the endless sea of bars had claustrophobia hitting me hard, and I knew if I wasn't careful, they'd drown me in brake fluid again.

The hope that'd come from Nyx's visit hadn't lasted long, and I'd ended up with a visit to the ding wing—the psych ward—for my pains. In the aftermath, a fuck ton of Westies and Bratva had started hanging around me, which I'd taken to be a good sign...

Until today.

On the staircase that led to my floor, I darted up and around the bannister, but as I moved down the hall, someone snatched me from one of the cells.

I started to struggle, hitting out in an effort to fend off the incoming attack, well aware that the silence in the unit was for my benefit.

For this moment.

I was the prey, but I was also a fucking predator, and I wasn't about to let anyone think otherwise.

Grabbing my shiv from its hiding place in my fucking underwear, I tried to twist around, tried to make it out of the chokehold the bastard had me in, but I couldn't. So, instead, I struck out, aware from the smell of iron that my aim was true, but it was too late.

I felt his shiv, bigger, colder, and recognized the fucker had a knife.

This was sanctioned.

The COs had turned a blind fucking eye.

A holler went up in the prison, an alarm that triggered lockdown, but just as he twisted me around, shoving me into the wall face first, he dug the weapon deep into my back, and the cunt whispered in my ear, "With love from the Sparrows."

And that was when he let go of me.

When my knees went out from under me.

When I dropped to the floor, my shiv falling from one hand as I reached up to cup the gash he'd made.

As I dropped back, staring up at a grim ceiling that had probably seen many more deaths than just mine, I closed my eyes.

The last thing I thought of?

Nyx and Indy.

As a result, only one word came to mind, powerful enough that I had to speak it out loud.

"Sorry."

EPILOGUE

IF YOUR KINDLE IS IN DANGER OF BEING HURLED AT THE WALL... READ ON. IF YOU DON'T WANT SPOILERS, STOP HERE.

MAVERICK

"NIC! You gotta keep your eye on the ball!"

I grinned at my wife as I shrugged my arm around her shoulder. She was brimming with tension, full of it as she watched our son play his first game of tee-ball. For whatever reason, Nic hadn't inherited my hand-eye coordination. Even though the ball was on the tee, Nic couldn't seem to hit it.

It was funny as fuck, cute too, but Alessa had to go and make a bet with Giulia, which, of course, put more onto this game than usual.

When Nic struck out yet again, I muttered, "Kid's only four, babe. He'll get better."

She heaved a sigh. "You don't know what this means."

I knew the facts.

Giulia was a nutcase, and two sons and a daughter hadn't

made her any more normal than when she'd first found her way back to West Orange.

"What's the bet for?" I asked her, pressing a kiss to her temple. "You wager our house on it? Five mil? What's the damage?"

Aware I was amused, she peeped up at me through those long lashes that still ensnared me all these years later, and muttered, "You won't like it."

My lips twitched. "No?"

She heaved a sigh, reminding me so hard of Nic when he was two and had confessed to putting his kitten, Triskele, in his potty to do her business.

"I'm supposed to teach them how to pole dance."

I cocked a brow. "Why would that bother me? Don't I get a show? Also, how the hell didn't I know that you could pole dance?"

She wafted a hand. "I'm a woman of mystery. You don't know everything about me, Maverick."

I snorted out a laugh, loving her sass. When I'd first fallen for her, she'd been meek, and though my heart had belonged to her since those early days, I loved her more now that she'd gone from being a milk-and-water miss to a sexy, sassy Sinner who had my cock in a clamp and my heart in her hand.

"I just hate pole dancing is all."

"Because of *why* you learned how?" I hazarded a guess.

She pulled a face. "That and you chafe like a bitch between your legs."

I tried not to smile, I really did. "Bad enough to pressure Nic into winning?"

Her scowl was ominous. "I didn't pressure him. I cheered him on."

"You pep talked the kid into being nervous," I retorted with a laugh. "You terrified him."

Her mouth formed the perfect O that, later on, I'd feel around my cock. Shit, it was good to be alive. "I did not!"

"Did too." I pressed a kiss to the tip of her nose. "Just let him be, babe. You know he loves this stuff."

"I didn't mean to make him anxious," she whispered, clearly aghast, but I tapped her tush.

"He'll get over it. We've got fourteen more years to screw his head back on right."

She shoved me in the side. "Mean!"

I grinned. "When he's twenty-eight and still can't hit a ball, I'm sure he'll remember this day and this week where you tried to encourage him to hit paper baseballs with his bamboo straw when he's bitching at his sports shrink about the yips."

Her lips twitched, but before she could reply, Kati, who was visiting, passed us with a squalling Lizzie in her arms. As she lugged the toddler onto her hip, she ground out into her AirPods, at whoever was on the other end of her call, "Oh my God! He's such a prick!"

"Less of the cursing, Kat," Indy groused from a few feet away, as she peered over at the field where her girl, Nevah, was hustling over to bat.

"She's Giulia's daughter. You know that kid already knows what a prick is," I muttered in Alessa's ear which had her laughing, even as she tugged on Kati's hand.

"What's wrong, *zayushka?*" she asked.

Kati looked like she was going to shrug off Alessa's concern, but she didn't. Instead, she replied in Ukrainian, before huffing, "Men!"

Hugging Lizzie tighter, she stomped off, prompting me to ask, "What was that about?"

Alessa just smiled. "Boy trouble."

I rolled my eyes. "Great, am I going to have to go all big brother on some fucker's ass?"

She patted my chest. "Not yet. Things aren't that dire."

"Thank Christ, she's too young for that still."

"She's thirteen," Alessa pointed out with a laugh. "She's plenty old enough for boyfriends."

Though the notion had me grumbling under my breath, I turned and saw Nic heading our way, his shoulders hunched, his face loaded with misery at his—there was no kinder way of phrasing it—shitty game. Still, I squatted down and gently nudged his arm with my fist.

"Little man, you did great."

His bottom lip started to quiver before he hurled himself against my chest.

A sigh escaped me as I felt his tiny form seem to melt into me, and I closed my eyes as I hugged him back. He was starting to get a bit too old for this—wouldn't always let me or his mom kiss him, would run off sometimes, but when shit got real, he wasn't too old for hugs just yet.

If it were down to me, I'd be available for hugs twenty-four seven, except kids didn't always do as you imagined they would. They cried over random shit with such misery and tragedy that wailing over a broken game was as horrendous as there not being enough sweetcorn on their plate, both of which could have my boy sobbing like he'd broken his foot...

Parenthood wasn't how I thought it'd be. It was terrifying, without a doubt, but it was worth it. It gave me a purpose. I knew I had one in Alessa, but together, we'd made this little human that we needed not to mess up.

I hadn't wanted to call him Nic, not with all the memories tangled in the name, but it had been Alessa's suggestion, and as I stared down at the little squalling face, that day outside the diner had come to me.

Nic asking me to name a kid after him in that flashback.

Well, I said flashback, but I knew it was a delusion. Still, that *delusion* had given me peace, and knowing I'd given Nic everything he asked gave me some more.

Staggering to my feet as I hugged him against my chest, I held him close as I turned into Alessa's open arms. When Nic started sniffling as she spoke to him in Ukrainian, I wasn't surprised when he twisted around so he could embrace her instead. I smiled but maintained his weight, not wanting to put pressure on her back. She was so slight still that I wasn't sure if having more kids was wise, not with the health issues she'd had, but she'd insisted on two and who was I to deny her the family she craved?

I'd give her the fucking universe if that was within my power, but it wasn't, so I could make her world right, and she wanted my kids, and I wanted hers. A match made in heaven.

My Ukrainian wasn't that great still, so I switched focus and stared over at the field. The sun beat down, which was messing with my eyes a little, despite the super strength, medical-grade shades I wore, but it was worth it.

The tee-ball team was pretty much made up of Sinners' brats, with only a few locals mixed in. There were two of Giulia and Nyx's boys, because they popped out kids like they were bunny rabbits, Link and Lily's son was there too, and Sin and Tiff's daughter was jumping up and down with excitement as her turn to bat approached. Nevah, Cruz and Indy's kid, finished up making her way around the pitch just as the rumble of straight pipes sounded in the distance.

I turned around to see who was arriving and smiled when I saw Rex make an appearance.

The big, bad biker Prez... at a tee-ball game.

How the mighty fell.

THE NEXT BOOK IN THE SERIES IS NOW AVAILABLE TO READ ON KU!

www.books2read.com/HawkSerenaAkeroyd

AFTERWORD

PTSD.

Not discussed enough.

Not treated enough.

To those who fought for our freedom, to those who are *fighting* for our freedom, I thank YOU. You honor me with your service. You honor us all with the sacrifices you make.

I think Maverick is a book that befits a November release...

#LestWeForget

Please, don't misinterpret the ending of this novel. For each and every soldier out there, be they on active duty or retired, you have my humble thanks.

With that being said, I hope you guys are ready for Hawk. (Now available on preorder here: www.books2read.com/HawkSerenaAkeroyd)

I know, you're wondering why I'm tormenting you. When the hell Rex and Storm will get their story... which they WILL get, but your patience will be rewarded. :P

And in the interim, don't forget to read Filthy Sex. (www.

books2read.com/FilthySex) You'll get a glimpse at what happens with a certain someone who's important to the Sinners in that one. ;)

Each series is standalone, but you'll get a helluva lot more book boyfriends if you read them in order. :P

FILTHY
NYX
LINK
FILTHY RICH
SIN
STEEL
FILTHY DARK
CRUZ
MAVERICK
FILTHY SEX
HAWK
FILTHY HOT
STORM
THE DON
THE LADY
FILTHY SECRET (COMING NOVEMBER 2021)

For your ease, you can just click here: http://www.linktr.ee/SerenaAkeroydReadingOrder

As always, my darlings, many thanks to you for your support.

I know 2020 has been a shitter of a year for the world at large, but I'm sending you all my love.

Thank you so much,

Serena

xoxo

FILTHY

FINN

Obsessive habits weren't alien to me.

They were as much a part of me as my coal-dark hair and my diamond-blue eyes. Ingrained as they were, it didn't mean they weren't irritating as fuck.

As I rifled through the folder on the table in front of me, staring down at the life of one pesky tenant, I wanted to toss it in the trash. I truly did.

I wanted not to be interested in her.

Wanted my focus to return to the matter at hand—business.

But there was something about her.

Something. . .

Irish.

I was a sucker for my own people. When I was a kid, I'd only dated other Irish girls in my class, and though I'd become less discerning about nationality and had grown more interested in tits and ass, I'd thought that desire had died down.

But Aoife Keegan was undeniably, indefatigably Irish.

From her fucking name—I didn't know people still named their kids in Gaelic over here—to her red goddamn hair and milky-white skin.

To many, she wouldn't be sexy. Too pale, too curvy, too rounded and wholesome. But to me? It was like God had formed a creature that was born to be my downfall.

I could feel the beast inside me roaring to life as I stared at the photos of her. It wanted out. It wanted her.

Fuck.

"I told you not to get those briefs."

My eyes flared wide in surprise at my brother, Aidan O'Donnelly's remark. "What?" I snapped.

"I told you not to get those briefs," he repeated, unoffended. Which was a miracle. Had I been speaking to Aidan Sr., I'd probably have lost a finger, but Aidan Jr. was one of my best friends, as well as a confidant and fellow businessman.

When I said business, it wasn't the kind Valley girls dreamed their future husbands would be involved in. No Manhattan socialite, though we were wealthy as fuck, would want us on their arm if they truly knew what games we were involved in.

My business was forged, unashamedly, in blood, sweat, and tears.

Preferably not my own, although I had taken a few hits for the Family over the years.

"My briefs aren't irritating me," I carried on, blowing out a breath.

"No? You look like you've got something up your ass crack." Aidan cocked a brow at me, but his smirk told me he knew exactly what the fuck was wrong.

I flipped him the bird—the finger that I'd have lost by showing cheek to his father—and he just grinned at me as he leaned over my glass desk and scooped up one of the pictures.

That beast I mentioned earlier?

It roared to life again when his eyes drifted over Aoife's curvy form.

"She's like your kryptonite," he breathed, tilting his head to the side. "Fuck me, Finn."

"I'd rather not," I told him dryly. "Now her? Yeah. I'd fuck her anytime."

He wafted a dismissive hand at my teasing. "I knew from that look in your eye, there was a woman involved. I just didn't know it would be a looker like this."

I snatched the photo from him. "Mine."

My growl had him snickering. "The Old Country ain't where I get my women from, Finn. Simmer down."

Throat tightening, I grated out, "What the fuck am I going to do?"

"Screw her?" he suggested.

"I can't."

He snorted. "You can."

"How the fuck am I supposed to get her in my bed when I'm about to bribe her into selling off her commercial lot?"

Aidan shrugged. "Do the bribing after."

That had me blowing out a breath. "You're a bastard, you know that, right?"

Piously, he murmured, "My parents were well and truly married before I came along. I have the wedding and birth certificates to prove it." He grinned. "Anyway, you're only just figuring that out?"

I shot him a scowl. "You're remarkably cheerful today."

"Is that a question or a statement?"

"Both?" The word sounded far too Irish for my own taste. My mother had come from Ireland, Tipperary to be precise—yeah, like the song. I was American born and bred, my accent that of someone who'd been raised in Hell's Kitchen but, and I hated it, my mother's accent would make an appearance every now and then.

'Both' came out sounding almost like 'boat.'

Aidan, knowing me as well as he did, smirked again—the fucker. "I got laid."

Grunting, I told him, "That doesn't usually make you cheerful."

"It does. I just never see you first thing after I wake up. Da hasn't managed to piss me off today."

Aidan was the heir to the Five Points—an Irish gang who operated out of Hell's Kitchen. It wasn't like being the heir to a candy company or a title. It came with responsibilities that no one really appreciated.

We were tied into the life, though. Had been since the day we were born.

There was no use in whining over it, and Aidan wasn't. But if I had to deal with his father on a daily basis? I'd have been whining to the morgue and back.

Aidan Sr. was the shrewdest man I knew. What the man could do with our clout defied belief. Even if I thought he was a sociopath, he had my respect, and in truth, my love and loyalty.

Bastard or no, he'd taken me in when I was fourteen and had made me one of his family. I'd gone from being his kids' friend, the son of one of his runners, to suddenly being welcome in the main house.

All because Aidan Sr.—though I was sure he was certifiable—believed in family.

I shot Aidan Jr. a look. "Was it that blonde over on Canal Street?"

He rubbed his chin. "Yeah."

Snorting, I told him, "Hope you wore a rubber. I swear that

woman has so many men going in and out of her door, it should be on double-action hinges."

He scowled at me. "Are you trying to piss me off?"

"Why? Didn't wear a jimmy?" I grinned at him, my mood soaring in the face of his irritation. "Better get to the clinic before it drops off."

Though he flipped me the bird as easily as I'd done to him—I was his brother, after all—he grumbled, "What are you going to do about little Aoife?"

I squinted at him. "She's not little."

That seemed to restore his humor. "I know. Just how you like them." He shook his head. "You and Conor, I swear. What do you do with them? Drown yourself in their tits?"

Heaving a sigh, I informed him, "My predilection for large tits is none of your business."

"And whether or not I wore a jimmy last night is none of yours."

"If it turns green and looks like a moldy corn on the cob, who you gonna call?"

"Ghostbusters?" he tried.

I shook my head, then pointed a finger at him and back at myself. "No. Me."

Grunting, he got to his feet and pressed his fists to the desk. "We need that building, Finn."

"The business development plan was mine, Aid. I know we need it. Don't worry, I won't do anything stupid."

He snorted. "Your kind of stupid could go one of two ways."

That had me narrowing my eyes at him, but he held up his hands in surrender.

"Fuck her out of your system quickly, and then get started on the deal," he advised. "Best way."

It probably was the best way, but—

He sighed. "That fucking honor of yours."

I had to laugh. Only in the O'Donnelly family would my thoughts be considered honorable.

"If I'm fucking someone over, I want them to know it," was all I said.

"That makes no sense."

"Makes for epic sex, though," I jibed, and he shot me a grin.

"Angry sex is always good." He rubbed his chin, then he reached over again and flipped through the photos. "Who's the old guy to her?"

"To her? Not sure. Sugar daddy?" The thought alone made the beast inside rage. I cleared my throat to get rid of the rasp there. "To us? He's our meal ticket."

Aidan's eyes widened. "He is?"

I nodded. "Just leave it to me."

"I was always going to, *deartháir*." He tilted his chin at me, honoring me with the Gaelic word for brother. "Be careful out there."

"You, too, brother."

Aidan winked at me and, with a far too cheerful whistle for someone whose dick might soon be 'ribbed for her pleasure' without the need for a condom, walked out of my office leaving me to brood.

The instant his back was to me, I stared at the photos again. Flipping through them, I glowered at the innocent face staring back at me through the photo paper—if only she knew.

Hers was a building in Hell's Kitchen. Five Points Territory. One of many on my hit list.

Back in the 70s, Aidan Sr., following in his father's footsteps, had bought up a shit-ton of property, pre-gentrification, and it was my job to either sell off the portfolio, reconstruct, or 'improve' the current aesthetics of the buildings the Points owned.

This particular one was something I'd taken a personal interest in.

See, I was technically a legitimate businessman.

This office?

I had views of the Hudson. I could see the Empire State Building, and in the evening, I had an epic view of the sunset setting over Manhattan. This office building, also Points' property, was worth a cool hundred million, and I was, again technically, the CEO of it.

On paper?

I looked seamless.

The businessman who sported hundred thousand dollar watches and had a house in the Hamptons. No one save the Points and my CPA knew where the money came from. I liked that because, fuck, I had no intention of switching this pad for a lock-up in Riker's Island.

Still, this project cut close to home, and the reasoning was fucking pathetic.

I'd never admit it to any of the O'Donnellys. The bastards were like family to me, and if I admitted to this, they'd never let me hear the end of it.

Extortion?

I usually doled that out to someone else's to do list. Someone with a far lower paygrade than me, someone expendable. But the minute I'd heard of the troublesome tenant who was refusing to sell her lot to us? After not one, not two, not even three attempts with higher prices?

Five outright refusals?

The challenge to convince her otherwise had overtaken me.

See, I liked stubborn in women.

I liked fucking it out of them.

Throw in the fact the woman's name was Aoife? It had been

enough to get me sending someone out to follow her.

If she'd been fifty with as many chins as she had grandchildren, she'd have been safe from me.

But she wasn't.

She was, as Aidan had correctly stated, my kryptonite. All milky flesh with gleaming auburn hair that I wanted to tie around my clenched fist. Her soft features with those delicate green eyes that sparkled when she smiled and were like wet grass when she was mad, acted like a punch to my gut.

Now?

My interest hadn't just been piqued.

It had fucking imploded.

Yeah, I was thinking with my cock, but what man, at the end of the day, didn't?

I'd just have to be careful. Just have to make sure I put pressure on the right places, make sure she'd bend and not break, and the old bastard in the pictures was my key to just that.

See, every third Tuesday of the month, Aoife Keegan had a habit of traipsing across Manhattan to the Upper East Side. There, at three PM on the dot, she'd enter a discreet little boutique hotel and wouldn't leave until nine PM that night.

Five minutes after she arrived and left, the same man would leave, too.

At first, when Jimmy O'Leary had told me that Senator Alan Davidson was at the hotel, I hadn't thought anything of it.

Why would I?

Senators trawled for donations in fancy hotels every fucking day of the week. It was the true luxury of politics. Sure, they made it look real good for the press. Posing in derelict neighborhoods and shaking hands with people who did the fucking work . . . all while they lived it up large with women half their age in two thousand dollar a night suites.

My mouth firmed at that.

Was Aoife selling herself to the Senator?

The thought pissed me off.

I couldn't see why she'd do such a thing. Not when I'd looked into her finances, had seen just how secure she was. But maybe that was why. Maybe the Senator was funneling money to her.

The only problem was that the lot Aoife owned—did I mention it was owned outright? Yeah, that was enough to chafe my suspicions, too, considering she was only twenty-fucking-five years old—was a teashop in a small building in a questionable area of HK.

I mean, come on. I loved Hell's Kitchen. It was home. But fuck. Where she was? What kind of Senator would put his fancy piece in *that*?

My jaw clenched as I studied the Senator's and Aoife's smiling faces as they left the hotel. Separately, of course. But whatever they'd been doing together, it sure put a Cheshire Cat grin on their chops–that was for fucking sure. Jimmy being a dumbass, hadn't put the two together, had just remarked on the 'coincidence,' but I was no fool.

How did I know they were together in the hotel?

Jimmy had been trailing Aoife for four months—told you I was obsessive—and every third Tuesday, come rain or shine, this little routine had jumped out, and when Jimmy had picked up on the fact Davidson had been there each and every time, I'd gotten my hands dirty, bribed one of the hotel maids myself—and fuck, that had been hard. Turned out that place made even the maids sign NDA agreements, but everyone had a price—and I'd found out that my little obsession shared a suite with the old prick.

My fingers curled into fists as I stared at her. Butter wouldn't fucking melt. She was the epitome of innocence. Like a redheaded angel. Could she really be lifting her skirts for that old fucker? Just so she could own a teashop?

Something didn't make sense, and fuck, if that didn't intrigue me all the more.

Aoife Keegan had snared one of the biggest, nastiest sharks in Manhattan.

She just didn't know it yet.

***

Aoife

"We need more scones for tomorrow. I keep telling you four dozen isn't enough."

Lifting a hand at my waitress and friend, Jenny, I mumbled, "I know, I know."

"If you know, then why the hell don't you listen?" Jenny complained, making me grin.

"Because I'm the one who has to make them? Making half that again is just . . ." I sighed.

I loved my job.

I did.

I adored baking—my butt and hips attested to that fact—and making a career out of my passion was something every twenty-something hoped for. Especially in one of the most expensive cities in the world. But sheesh. There was only so much one person could do, and this was still, essentially, a one-woman-band.

With the threat of Acuig Corp looming over me, I didn't feel safe hiring extra staff. I'd held them off for close to six months now.

Six months of them trying to tempt me to leave, to sell up. They'd raised their prices to ten percent above market value, whereas with everyone else in the building, they'd just offered what the apartments were truly worth. Considering this place wasn't the nicest in the block, that wasn't much.

Most people hadn't held out because, hell, why wouldn't they want to live elsewhere?

Those who were landlords hadn't felt any issue in tossing their tenants out on the street. The tenants grumbled, but when did they ever have any rights, anyway?

For myself, this was where my mom and I had worked to—

I brought that thought to a shuddering halt.

Mom was dead now.

I had to remember that. This was on me, not her.

My throat thickened with tears as I turned to Jenny and murmured, "I'll try better tomorrow."

The words had her frowning at me. "Babe, you know I'm not the boss here, right?"

Lips curving, I whispered, "I know. But you're so scary."

She snickered then peered down at herself. "Yeah, I bet I'd make grown men cry."

Maybe for a taste of her. . . .

Jenny was everything I wasn't.

She was slender, didn't dip her hand into the cookie jar at will—the woman had more willpower than I did hips, and my hips seemed to go on forever—and her face looked like it belonged on the cover of a fashion magazine. Even her hair was enough to inspire envy. It was black and straight as a ruler.

Mine?

Bright red and curly like a bitch. I had to straighten it out every morning if I didn't want to look like little orphan Annie.

I'd once read that curly-haired women straightened their hair for special events, and that straight-haired women curled theirs in turn, but I called bullshit.

Curly-haired women lived with their straightening irons surgically attached to their hands.

At least, I did.

My rat's nest was like a ginger afro. Maybe Beyoncé could make that work, but I sure as hell didn't have the bone structure.

"I think grown men would cry," I told her dryly, "if you asked them to."

She pshawed, but there was a twinkle in her eye that I understood. . . . She agreed with me, knew it was true, but wasn't going to admit it. With anyone else, she might have. She had an ego–that was for damn sure. But with me? I think she figured I was zero competition, so she felt no need to rub salt in the wound, too.

I plunked my elbows on the counter and stared around my domain as she bustled off and started clearing the tables. It was her last duty of the day, and my feet were aching so damn bad that I didn't even have it in me to care.

This owning your own business shit?

It wasn't easy.

Not saying I didn't love it, but it was hard.

I slept like four hours a night, and when I wasn't in bed, I was here. All the time.

Baking, cooking, serving, and smiling. Always smiling. Even if I was so sleep-deprived I could sob.

Jenny's actually a life saver.

My mom used to be front of house before. . . .

I sucked down a breath.

I had to get used to thinking about it.

She wasn't here anymore, but just avoiding all thoughts of her period wasn't working for me. It was like I was purposely forgetting her, and, well, fuck that.

She'd always wanted to have a teashop. It had been her one true dream. Back in Ireland, when she was a little girl, her grandmother had owned one in Limerick. Mom had caught the bug and had wanted to have one here in the States. But not only was it too fucking expensive for a woman on her own, it was also impossible with my feckless father at her side.

I didn't want to think about him either, though.

Why?

Because the feckless father who'd pretty much ruined my mother's life, wasn't the only father in my life. My biological dad hadn't exactly cared about her happiness, but once he'd come to know about me, he'd tried. That was more than could be said for the man who'd lived with me throughout my early childhood.

"You look gloomy."

Jenny's statement had me blinking in surprise. She had a ton of dishes piled in her arms, and I'd have worried for the expensive china if I hadn't known she was an old pro at this shit. Just as I was.

We could probably earn a Guinness World Record on how many dishes we could take back and forth to the kitchen of *Ellie's Tea Rooms*. I swear, I had guns because of all that hefting. My biceps were probably the firmest part of my body.

More's the pity.

I'd have preferred an ass you could bounce dimes off of, but, when it boiled down to it, there was no way in this universe I could live without cake.

Just wasn't going to happen.

My big butt wasn't going *anywhere* until scientists could make zero calorie eclairs and pies.

"I'm not glum."

"No? Then why are your eyes sad?"

Were they? I pursed my lips as I let the 'sad eyes' drift around the tea room. I wish I could say it was all forged on my own hard work, but it wasn't. Not really.

"I was just thinking about Mom."

"Oh, honey," Jenny said sadly, and she carefully placed all the dishes on the counter, so she could round it and curve her arm around my waist. "It was only seven months ago. Of course, you were thinking of her."

"I just—" I blew out a breath. "I don't know if I'm doing what she'd want."

"You can't live for her choices, sweetness. You have to do what you think is right for you."

I gnawed at my bottom lip again. "I-I know, but she was always there for me. A guiding light. With Fiona gone and her, too? I don't really know what I'm doing with myself."

This business wasn't something that made me want to get up on a morning. It was my mom's dream, her goal. Every decision I made, I tried to remember how she'd longed for a place like this, but it wasn't my passion. It was hers, and I was trying to keep that dream alive while fretting over the fact my heart wasn't in it.

"I think you're doing a damn fine job. You have a very successful teashop. Your cakes are raved about. Have you visited our TripAdvisor page recently? Or our Yelp?" She squeaked. "I swear, you're making this place a tourist hotspot. I don't think Fiona or Michelle could be more proud of you if they tried."

The baking shit, yeah, that was all on me, but the other stuff? The finances?

I'd caved in.

I'd caved where my mom had always refused in the past.

With the accident had come a lot of medical bills that I just hadn't been able to afford. Without her help, I'd had to take on extra staff, and out of nowhere, my expenses had added up.

Mom had been so proud of this place, so ferociously gleeful

that we'd done it by ourselves, and yet, here I was, financially free for the first time in my life, and I still felt like I was drowning because my freedom went entirely against her wishes.

"Is this to do with Acuig? I know they're still pestering you."

Jenny's statement had me wincing. Acuig were the bottom feeders who wanted to snap up this building, demolish it, and then replace it with a skyscraper. Don't get me wrong, the building was foul, but a lot of people lived here, and the minute it morphed into some exclusive condo, no one from around here would be able to afford to live in it.

It would become yuppy central.

I'd rejected all their offers to buy my tea room even though I didn't want the damn thing, not really. Mostly I wanted to keep mom's goals alive and kicking, but also, it pissed me off the way Acuig were changing Hell's Kitchen. Ratcheting up prices, making it unaffordable for the everyday man and woman—the people I'd grown up with—and bringing a shit-ton of banker-wankers and 1%ers to the area.

So, maybe I'd watched Erin Brockovich a time or two as a kid and had a social conscience . . . Wasn't the worst thing to possess, right?

"Aoife?" Jenny stated, making me look over at her. "Is Acuig pressuring you?"

I winced, realizing I hadn't answered—Jenny was my friend, but she also worked here and relied on the paycheck. It wasn't fair of me to keep her hanging like that. "They upped the sales price. I guess that isn't helping," I admitted, frowning down at my hands.

Unlike Jenny who had her nails manicured, mine were cut neatly and plain. I had no rings on my fingers, and wore no watch or bracelets because my wrists were usually deep in flour or sugar bags.

I spent most of my life right where I wanted it—behind the

shopfront. That had slowly morphed where I was doing double the work to compensate for Mom's loss.

Was it any wonder I was feeling a little out of my league?

I was coping without Fiona, grieving Mom, working without her, too, and then practically living in the kitchens here. I didn't exactly have that much of a life. I had nothing cheerful on the horizon, either.

Well, nothing except for next Tuesday, and that wasn't enough to turn my frown upside down.

The money was a temptation. I didn't need to sell up and start working on my own goals, but that just loaded me down with more guilt and made me feel like a really shitty daughter.

Jenny squeezed me in a gentle hug. But as I turned to speak to her, the bell above the door rang as it opened. We both jerked in surprise—each of us apparently thinking the other had locked up when neither of us had—and turned to face the entrance.

On the brink of telling the client we were closed for the day, my mouth opened then shut.

Standing there, amid the frilly, lacy curtains, was the most masculine man I'd ever seen in my life.

And I meant that.

It was like a thousand aftershave models had morphed into one handsome creature that had just walked through my door.

At my side, I could feel Jenny's 'hot guy radar' flare to life, and for once, I couldn't damn well blame her.

This guy was . . . well, he was enough to make me choke on my words and splutter to a halt.

The tea room was all girly femininity. It was sophisticated enough to appeal to businesswomen with its mauve, taupe, and cream-toned hues, and the ethereal watercolors that decorated the walls. But the tablecloths were lacy, and the china dishes and cake stands we used were the height of Edwardian elegance.

Moms brought their little girls here for their birthday, and high-powered executives spilled dirt on their lovers with their girlfriends over scones and clotted cream—breaking their diets as they discussed the boyfriends who had broken their hearts.

The man, whoever the hell he was, was dressed to impress in a navy suit with the finest pinstripe. It was close to a silver fleck, and I could see, even from this distance, that it was hand tailored. I'd seen custom tailoring before, and only a trained eye could get a suit cut so perfectly to this man's form.

With wide shoulders that looked like they could take the weight of the world, a long, lean frame that was enhanced by strong muscles evident through the close fit of his pants and jacket, then the silkiness of his shirt which revealed delineated abs when his bright gold and scarlet tie flapped as he moved, the guy was hot.

With a capital H.

"How can we help, sir?" Jenny purred, and despite my own awe, I had to dip my chin to hide my smile.

Even if I wanted to throw my hat into this particular man's game, there was no way he'd choose me over Jenny. Fuck, I'd screw her, and I wasn't even a lesbian. Not even a teensy bit bi. I'd gone shopping with her enough to have seen her ass, and I promise you, it's biteable.

So, nope. I didn't have a snowball's chance in hell of this Adonis seeing *me* when Jenny was in the room.

Yet. . . .

When I'd controlled my smile, I looked over at the man, and his focus was on me.

My breath stuttered to a halt.

Why wasn't his gaze glued to Jenny?

Why weren't those ice-white blue eyes fixated on my best

friend's tits, which Jenny helpfully plumped up as she preened at my side?

For a second, I was so close to breaking out into a coughing fit, it was humiliating. Then, more humiliation struck in a quieter manner, but it was nevertheless rotten—I turned pink.

Now, you might think you know what a blush is. You might think you've even experienced it yourself a time or two. But I was a redhead. My skin made fresh milk look yellow, and even my fucking freckles were pale. Everything about me was like I'd been dunked into white wax.

But as the heat crawled over me, taking over my skin as the man looked at me without pause, I knew things had rarely been this dire.

See, with Jenny as a best friend, I was used to the attention going her way. I could hide in the background, hide in her shadow. I liked it there. I was comfortable there. Sometimes, on double dates, she'd drag me along, and even the guy supposed to be dating me would be gaping at Jenny. As pathetic as it was, I was so used to it, it didn't bother me.

But now?

I just wasn't used to being in the spotlight.

Especially not a man like this one's spotlight.

When you're a teenager, practicing with your mom's blush for the first time, you always look like a tomato that's been left out in the sun, right?

I was redder than that.

I could feel it. I could fucking feel the heat turning me tomato red.

When Jenny cleared her throat, I thanked God when it broke the man's attention. He shot her a look, but it wasn't admiring. It wasn't even impressed.

If anything, it was irritated.

Okay, so now both Jenny and I were stunned.

Fuck that, we were floored.

Literally.

Our mouths were doing a pretty good fish impression as the man turned back to look at me.

Shit, was this some kind of joke?

Was it April 1st and I'd just gotten the dates mixed up again?

"Ms. Keegan?"

Oh fuck. His voice.

Oh. My. God.

That voice.

It was. . . .

I had to swallow.

Did men even talk like that?

It was low and husky and raspy and made me think of sex, not just mediocre sex, but the best sex. Toe-curling, nails-breaking-in-the-sheets sex. Sex so fucking good you couldn't walk the next day. Sex so hot that it made my current core temperature look polar in comparison. Sex that I'd never been lucky to have before, so I pined for it in the worst way.

Jenny nudged me in the side when I just carried on gaping at the man. "Y-Yes. That's me." I cleared my throat, feeling nervous and stupid and flustered as I wiped my hands on my apron.

Sweet Jesus.

Was this man really looking for me while I was wearing a goddamn pinafore?

Even as practical as they were, I wanted to beg the patron saint of pinnies to remove it from me. To do something, anything, to make sure that this man didn't see me in the red gingham check that I always wore to cover up stains.

And then I felt it.

Jenny's hand.

Tugging at the knot.

I wanted to kiss her. Seriously. I wanted to give her a fucking raise! As I moved away from the counter and her side, the apron dropped to the floor as I headed for the man whose hand was now held out, ready for me to shake in greeting.

There are those moments in your life when you know you'll never forget them. They can be happy or sad, annoying or exhilarating. This was one of them.

As I slipped my hand into his, I felt the electric shocks down to my core. Meeting his gaze wasn't hard because I was stunned, and I needed to know if he'd felt that, too.

From the way those eyelids were shielding his icy-blue eyes, I figured he was just as surprised.

It was like a satisfied puma was watching me. One that was happy there was plump prey prancing around in front of him.

Shit.

Did I just describe myself as 'plump prey?'

And like that, my house of cards came tumbling down because what the hell would this man want with me?

I was seeing things.

God, I was so stupid sometimes.

I cleared my throat for, like, the fourth damn time, and asked, "I'm Ms. Keegan. You are?"

His smile, when it appeared, was as charming as the rest of him. His teeth were white, but not creepy, reality-TV-star white. They were straight except for one of his canines, which tilted in slightly. In his perfect face, it was one flaw that I almost clung to. Because with that wide brow, the hair so dark it looked like black silk that was cut closely to his head with a faint peak at his forehead, the strong nose, and even stronger jaw, I needed something imperfect to focus on.

Then, I sucked down a breath and remembered what Fiona

had told me once upon a time. When I'd been nervous about asking Jamie Winters to homecoming, she'd advised me in her soft Irish lilt, "Lass, that boy takes a dump just like you do. He uses the bathroom twice a day and undoubtedly leaves a puddle on the floor for his ma to clean up. I bet he's puked a time or two as well. Had diarrhea and the good Lord only knows what else. Just you think that the next time you see that boy and want to ask him out."

Yeah. It was gross, but fuck, it had worked. Her advice had worked so well I hadn't asked anyone out because I could only think of them using the damn toilet!

Still, looking at this Adonis, there was no imagining *that*.

Surely, gods didn't use the bathroom.

Did they?

"The name's Finn. Finn O'Grady."

My eyes flared at the name.

No.

It couldn't be.

Finn O'Grady?

No. It wasn't a rare name, but it was a strong one. One that suited him, one that had always suited him.

I frowned up at him wondering, yet again, if this was a joke of some sort, but as he looked at me, *really* looked at me, I saw no recognition. Saw nothing on his features that revealed any ounce of awareness that I'd known him for years.

Well, okay, not *known*. But I'd known his mother. Our mothers had been best friends. And as I looked, I saw the same almond-shaped eyes Fiona had, the stubborn jaw, and that unmistakable butt-indent on his chin.

At the reminder of just how forgettable I was, my heart sank, and hurt whistled through me.

Then, I realized I was *still* holding his hand, and as he squeezed, the flush returned and I almost died of mortification.

CHAPTER 2

FINN

GOD, she was perfect.

And when I said perfect, I meant it.

I'd fucked a lot of women. Redheads, blondes, brunettes, even the rare thing that is a natural head of black hair. None of them, not a single one, lit up like Aoife Keegan.

Her cheeks were cherry red and in the light camisole she wore, a cheerful yellow, I could see how the blush went all the way down to the upper curve of her breasts.

She'd go that color, I knew, when she came.

And fuck, I wanted to see that.

I wanted to see that perfectly pale flesh turn bright pink under my ministrations.

Even as I looked at her, all shy and flustered, I wondered if she was a screamer in bed.

Some of the shyest often were.

Maybe not at first, but after a handful of orgasms, it was a wonder what that could do to a woman's self-confidence, and Jesus, I wanted to *see* that, too. I wanted a seat at center stage.

My suit jacket was open, and I regretted it. Immensely. My cock was hard, had been since we'd shaken hands, and her fingers had clung to mine like a daughter would to her daddy's at her first visit to the county fair.

Fuck.

Squeezing her fingers wasn't intentional. If anything, I'd just liked the feel of her palm against mine, but when I put faint pressure on her, she jerked back like she'd been scalded.

Her cheeks bloomed with heat again, and she whispered, "Mr. O'Grady, what can I do for you?"

You can get on your fucking knees and sort out the hard-on you just caused.

That's what she could fucking do.

I almost growled at the thought because the image of her on her knees, my cock in her small fist, her dainty mouth opening to take the tip. . . .

Shit.

That had to happen.

Here, too.

In this fancy, frilly, feminine place, I wanted to defile her.

Fuck, I wanted that so goddamn much, it was enough to make me reconsider my demolition plans.

I wanted to screw her against all this goddamn lace, which suited her perfectly. She was made for lace. And silk. Hell, silk would look like heaven against her skin. I wouldn't know where she ended and it began.

When her brow puckered, she dipped her chin, and that gorgeous wave of auburn hair slipped over her shoulder.

If we'd been alone, if that brassy bitch—who was staring at me like I could fuck her over the counter with her friend watching if I was game—wasn't here, I'd have grabbed that rope of hair, twisted it around my fingers, and forced her gaze up.

Some guys liked their women demure. And I was one of them. I wasn't about to lie. I liked that in her, but I wanted her eyes on me. Always.

It was enough to prompt me to bite out, "Can we speak privately?"

She jerked at my words, then as she licked her bottom lip, turned to look at the waitress. "Jenny, it's okay. I can handle the rest by myself. You get home."

Jenny, her gaze drifting between me and her boss, nodded. She retreated to a door that swung as she moved through the opening, and within seconds, she had her coat and purse over her arm.

As she sashayed past—for my benefit, I was sure—she murmured, "See you tomorrow, Aoife."

Aoife nodded and shot her friend a smile, but I wasn't smiling. There were dishes on every table. Plates and saucers and tea pots. Those fancy stands that made any man wonder if he could touch it without snapping it.

Aoife was going to clear all that herself? Not on my fucking watch.

When the bell rang as the waitress opened the door, I didn't take my eyes off her until it rang once more upon closing.

Aoife swallowed, and I watched her throat work, watched it with a hunger that felt alien to me, because, God, I wanted to see my bites on her. Wanted to see my marks on that pale column of skin and her tits.

Barely withholding a groan, I asked, "Do you often let your staff go when you still have a lot of work to do, so you can speak to a stranger?"

Her cheeks flushed again, and she took a step back. "I-I, you're not—" Flustered once more, she fell silent.

"I'm not what?" Curiosity had me asking the question. Whatever I'd expected her to say, it hadn't been that.

She cleared her throat. "N-Nothing. You wished to speak with me, Mr. O'Grady?"

My other hand tightened around my briefcase, and though seeing her had made my reason for being here all that more necessary, I was almost disappointed. There was a gentle warmth to those bright-green eyes that would die out when I told her my purpose for being here. And her innocent attraction to me would change, morph into something else.

But I could only handle *something else.*

Some men were made for forever.

But those men weren't in my line of business.

I moved away from her, pressing my briefcase to one of the few empty tables. I wasn't happy about her having to do all the clearing up later on, and wondered if Paul, my PA, would know who to call to get her some help.

There was no way I was spending the rest of the night alone in my bed, my only companion my fist wrapped around my cock.

No way, no fucking how.

I paid Paul enough for him to come and clear the fucking place on his own if he couldn't find someone else.

I wanted Aoife on her knees, bent over my goddamn bed, and I was a man who always got what he wanted.

In this jungle, I was the lion, and Aoife? She was my prey.

I keyed in the code and opened my briefcase. The manila envelope was large and thick, well-padded with my documentation of Aoife's every move for the past few months.

It had started off as a legitimate move.

I'd wanted to know her weaknesses, so I could put pressure on her and make her cave to my demands.

Now, my demands had changed. I didn't just want her to sell the tea room we were standing in, I wanted her in my bed.

Fuck, I wanted that more than I wanted to make Aidan Sr. a

fucking profit, and Aidan's profit and my balls still being attached to my body ran hand in hand.

Aidan was an evil cunt.

If I failed to deliver, he'd take it out on me. Whether I was his idea of an adopted son or not, he'd have done the same to his blood sons.

Well, he wouldn't have taken their balls. The man, for all his psychotic flaws, was obsessed with the idea of grandchildren, of passing it all on to the next generation. He'd cut his boys though. Without a doubt.

I knew Conor had marks on his back from a beating he refused to speak about. Then there was Brennan. He had a weak wrist because his father had a habit of breaking *that* wrist.

Without speaking, I grabbed the envelope and passed it to her.

She frowned down at it and asked, "For me?"

I smiled at her. "Open it."

"What is it?"

"Leverage."

That had her eyes flaring wide as she pulled out some of the photos. A gasp fell from her lips as she grabbed the photos when she spotted herself in them, jerking so hard the envelope tore. Some of the pictures spilled to the ground, but I didn't care about that.

Leaning back against one of the dainty tables once I was satisfied it would take my weight, I watched her cheeks blanch, all that delicious color dissipating as she took in everything the photos revealed.

"Y-You've been stalking me. Why?"

The question was high-pitched, loaded down with panic. I'd heard it often enough to recognize it easily.

I didn't get involved in wet work anymore. That wasn't my style, but along the way, to reach this point, I'd had no choice but to get my hands dirty. Panic was part of the job when you were collecting debts for the Irish Mob. And the Five Points were notorious for Aidan Sr.'s temper.

He wasn't the first patriarch. If anything, his grandfather was the founder. But Aidan Sr. was the type of guy that if you didn't pay him back, he didn't give a fuck about the money, he cared about the lack of respect.

See, you owed the mob and didn't pay? They'd send heavies around, beat the shit out of you, and threaten to do the same to your family, and usually, that did the trick. You didn't kill the cash cow.

Aidan Sr.?

He didn't give a fuck about the cash cow.

Only the truly desperate thought about borrowing money from Aidan, because if you didn't pay it back, he'd take your teeth, and your fingers and toes as a first warning. Then, if you still didn't pay—and most did—it was death.

Respect meant a lot to Aidan.

And fuck, if it wasn't starting to mean a lot to me. The panic in her voice made my cock throb.

I wanted this woman weak and willing.

I wanted it more than I wanted my next breath.

Ignoring her, I reached for my phone and tapped out a message to Paul.

Need housekeeping crew to clean this place.

I attached my live location, saw the blue ticks as Paul read the message—he knew better than to ignore my texts, whatever time of day they came—and he replied: *Sure thing.*

That was the kind of reply I was used to getting. Not just from Paul, but from everyone.

There were very few people who weren't below me in the strata of Five Points, and I'd worked my ass off to make that so.

The only people who ranked above me included Aidan Jr. and his brothers, Aidan Sr. of course, and then maybe a handful of his advisors that he respected for what they'd done for him and the Points over the years.

But the money I made Aidan Sr.?

That blew most of their 'advice' out of the window.

The reason Aidan had a Dassault Falcon executive private plane?

Because I was, as the City itself called me, a whiz kid.

I'd made my first million—backed by the Points, of course—at twenty-two.

Fifteen years later?

I'd made him hundreds of millions.

My own personal fortune was nothing to sniff at, either.

"W-Why have you done this?" Aoife asked, her voice breathy enough to make me wonder if she sounded like that in the sack.

"Because you've been a very stubborn little girl."

Her eyes flared wide. "Excuse me?"

I reached into the inside pocket of my suit coat and pulled out a business card. "For you," I prompted, offering it to her.

When she turned it over, saw the logo of five points shaped into a star, then read Acuig—in the Gaelic way, ah-coo-ig, not a butchered American way, ah-coo-ch—aloud, I watched her throat work as she swallowed.

"I-I should have realized with the Irish name," she whispered, the muscles in her brow twitching as she took in the chaos of the scattered photos on the floor.

Watching her as she dropped the contents on the ground, so she was surrounded by them, I tilted my head to the side, taking her in as her panic started to crest.

"I-I won't sell." Her first words surprised me.

I should have figured, though. Everything about this woman was surprisingly delicious.

"You have no choice," I purred. "As far as I'm aware, the Senator has a wife. He also has a reputation to protect. I'm not sure he'd be happy if any of those made it onto the *National Enquirer's* front page. Not when he's just trying to shore up his image to take a run for the White House next election."

She reached up and clutched her throat. The self-protective gesture was enough to make me smile at her—I knew what the absence of hope looked like.

There'd been a time when that had been my life, too.

"But, on the bright side," I carried on, "this can all be wiped away if you sell." As her gaze flicked to mine, I added, "As well as if you do something for me."

For a second, she was speechless. I could see she knew what that *something* was. Had my body language given it away? Had there been a certain raspiness to my tone?

I wasn't sure, and frankly, didn't give a fuck.

There was a little hiccoughing sound that escaped her lips, and she frowned at me, then down at herself.

"Is this a joke?"

"Do I look like I'm the kind of guy who jokes, Aoife?" Fuck, I loved saying her name.

The Gaelic notes just drove me insane.

Ee-Fah.

Nothing like the spelling, and all the more complicated and delicious for it.

"N-No," she confirmed, "but . . ."

"But what?" I prompted.

"I mean . . . you just can't be serious."

"Oh, but I am." I grinned. "Deadly. You've wasted a lot of my time, Aoife Keegan. A lot. Do you think I'm normally involved in negotiations of this level?"

Her eyes whispered over me, and I felt the loving caress of her gaze as she took in each and every inch of me. When she licked her lips, I knew she liked what she saw. I didn't really care, but it was helpful for her to be eager in some small way—especially when coercion was involved.

Aidan had called it bribery. I preferred 'coercion'. It sounded far kinder.

"No. That suit alone probably cost the mortgage payment on this place."

I nodded—she wasn't wrong. I knew what she'd been paying as rent, then as a mortgage, before some kind *benefactor* had paid it all off. Free and clear.

"I had to get my hands dirty, and while I might like some things dirty . . .," I trailed off, smirking when she flushed. "So, as I see it, we have a problem. I want this building. You don't want anyone to know you're having an affair with a Senator. Or, should I say, the Senator doesn't want anyone to know he's having an affair with someone young enough to be his daughter . . ."

If my voice turned into a growl at that point, then it was because the notion of her spreading her legs for that old bastard just turned my stomach.

Fuck, this woman, the thoughts she made me think.

Because I was startled at the possessive note to my growl, I ran a hand over my head. I kept my hair short for a reason—ease. I wasn't the kind of man who wasted time primping. It was an expensive cut, so I didn't have to do anything to it. Even mussing it up had it falling back into the same sleek lines as before—a man in my position had to look pristine under pressure. And very few people could even begin to understand the kind of strain I was under.

The formation of igneous rock had less volcanic pressure than Aidan Sr.

She licked her lips as she stared down at the photos, then back up at me. "And you want me to sell the place to you, even though this is my livelihood and the livelihood of all my staff, and then sleep with you?"

Her squeaky voice, putting suspicion into words, had me crossing my legs at the ankle. "We wouldn't be doing much sleeping."

Another shaky breath soughed from her lips, then, those beautiful pillowy morsels that would look good around my cock, quivered.

"This is crazy," she whispered shakily.

"As far as I'm concerned, all of this could be avoided if you'd just sold to me a few months back. Now you have to pay for my time wasted on this project."

"By spreading my legs?"

Another squeak. I tsked at her question, but in truth, I was annoyed at her using those same words I had to describe her with that old hypocrite of a Senator.

I didn't move, though. Didn't even flex my arms in irritation, just murmured, "Small price to pay. And, even though it's ten percent above market price, I'll stick to the last offer Acuig gave you. Can't say anything's fairer than that."

She shook her head, and there was a desperation to the gesture as she cried, "I need this business. You don't understand—"

"I understand that some very powerful and very dangerous businessmen want this building demolished. I understand that those same powerful and dangerous men want a skyscraper taking up this plot of land. I understand that a four hundred million dollar project isn't going to be put on hiatus because one small Irish woman doesn't want to go out of business . . ." I cocked a brow at her. "You think I'm coming in hot and heavy? These kinds of men, Aoife, they're not the sort you fuck around with.

"Take my check, and my other offer, before you or the people you care about are threatened." I got to my feet and straightened my jacket out. "This suit? These shoes? That briefcase and this watch? I own them because I'm damn good at what I do. I'm a financial advisor, Aoife. Take my word for it. You're getting the best deal out of this."

She staggered back, the counter stopping her from crumpling to the floor. "You'd hurt me?"

"Not me," I repudiated. Not in the way she thought, anyway. "But the men I work for?"

Her gaze dropped to the one thing she'd retained in her hand—my card. "Acuig," she whispered. "Five in Gaelic."

My brows twitched in surprise. She knew Gaelic?

"The Five Points." Her eyes flared wide with terror. "They're behind this deal."

I hadn't expected her to put one and one together, but now that she had? It worked to my advantage.

Nodding, I told her, "Any minute now, there'll be a team of housekeepers coming in here to clear up for the night." When she gaped at me, I retrieved the contract from my briefcase, slapped it on the table, and handed her a pen as I carried on, "I suggest you let tonight be your last night of business."

What I didn't tell her, was that my suggestions weren't wasted words. They were like the law.

You didn't break them, and, like any lawmaker, I expected immediate obeisance.

***

Aoife

SO, the beautiful man just happened to be an absolute cocksucker of a bastard.

Still, this couldn't be real, could it?

The dick could have anyone he wanted. Jesus, Jenny was panting after him like a dog in heat. She would have gone out with him if he'd so much as clicked his fingers at her.

But he'd had eyes for me.

Like he wanted me.

He thought he'd bought me. Or, at least, bought my silence, and yeah, to some extent he had. But . . . why buy me, why not just drop the price on the building if he wanted me to pay for the time he'd wasted on me?

The arrogance imbued in those words was enough to make me pull my hair out, but that was inwardly. I was a redhead. I had a temper. But that temper was mostly overshadowed by fear.

Senator Alan Davidson wasn't my boyfriend, my lover, as this dick seemed to believe. He was my father, and as Finn O'Grady had correctly surmised, he was aiming for the White House.

How could I put that in jeopardy?

My dad was a good man. He'd made a mistake one summer when he'd come home from college, one that only some careful digging by his campaign manager had uncovered. Dad himself hadn't known of my existence, not until his CM had gone hunting for any nasty secrets that could come out and bite him in the ass.

This had been five years ago when he'd run for Senator. Now, Dad's goal was the presidential seat, and I wasn't going to be the one who put a wrench in the works.

When Garry Smythe had approached me back then, I'd

thought he was joking. I was out on the street, heading home from work. At the side of me, a black car had driven in from the lane of traffic, just to park, or so I'd thought. As he'd held out his hand with a card, one of the car doors had opened up, and I'd been 'invited' inside.

Had I been scared?

At first.

But when Garry had told me my country needed me, I hadn't been sure whether to laugh or tell him to fuck off. He hadn't shuffled me into the car, though, hadn't tried to coerce me. He'd just asked if I'd voted for Senator Alan Davidson in the elections, and because he was one of the only politicians out there who wasn't a complete douche, and that was the name printed on the card in my hand, I'd shuffled into the back of the car.

Where the Senator himself had been sitting.

Now, when I thought about that day, I realized how fucking naive I'd been to get into the back of a limo for such a vague reason. But I'd been fortunate. Alan *had* been waiting for me. Waiting to tell me a story that still shook me to my core.

I'd made a promise to my dad that I wouldn't tell anyone. He'd offered me money, and I hadn't accepted it. I guess I should have, but back then, I'd been haughty and proud, and because the good guy I'd thought him to be hadn't been so good when he tried to buy my silence, I'd told him to fuck off. I'd been disappointed in him, frightened by the lifelong lie I'd been living, and equally hurt that the man who'd sired me was just concerned that I was a threat to his campaign.

I'd walked out of that car never expecting to see my dear old Dad ever again.

Then, the day after he'd been elected, he'd been sitting in the booth of the cafe where I worked part-time to get me through culinary school.

Seeing him, I'd almost handed that table off to one of the other waitresses, but I hadn't. Not when every time I'd passed the table, he'd caught my eye, a patient smile on his lips, one that said he'd wait for me all day if he had to.

Ever since that second meeting, I'd been catching up with him every three weeks.

And this bastard thought he could use our limited time together against my father? The one politician who could make a difference in the White House? One who didn't have Big Oil up his ass, a pharmaceutical company sucking his dick, or any other kind of corporation so far up his rectum that he was a walking, talking lie?

No.

That wasn't going to happen.

Which meant I was going to have to sleep with this stranger.

Before this conversation, hell, that hadn't been too disturbing a prospect. Because, dayum, what woman wouldn't want to sleep with this guy?

Even with an ego as big as his, he was delicious. Better than any cake I could bake, that was for fucking sure.

More than that, I knew him.

And I now knew that the life Fiona would never have wanted for her son was one he'd been drawn into.

The Mob.

The Five Points were notorious in these parts. Everyone was scared of them. I paid protection money to them, for God's sake. I knew to be scared of them, and having been raised in their territory, it was the height of stupidity to think paying them wasn't just a part of business.

Still, Fiona had never wanted that for Finn, and her Finn was the same as the one standing before me here today. In my tea room, which looked far too small to contain the might of this man.

She'd be so disappointed. So heart-sore to know that he was up to his neck in dirty dealings with the Five Points, and as he'd pointed out, the cost of his shoes, his clothes, and his jewelry, was enough to speak for itself.

If he wasn't high up the ladder in the gang, then I wasn't one of the best bakers of scones in the district.

Like Jenny had said, I had five star ratings across most social media platforms for a reason. I was good. But apparently, this man wasn't.

Before I could utter a word, before I could even cringe at how utterly sorrowful Fiona would be about this turn of events—not just about the Five Points but what her son was making me do—the door clattered open.

Like he'd predicted, a team of people swarmed in.

Finn motioned to the floor. "Want anyone to see those?"

With a gasp, I dropped to my knees and collected the shots, stuffing them back into the envelope with a haste that wasn't exactly practical.

Two shiny shoes appeared before me, followed by two expensively clad legs, and I peered up at him, wondering what he was about. He held out his hand, but I clasped the photos to my chest.

"You're making more of a mess than anything else, Aoife." His voice was raspy, his eyes weighted down by heavy lids.

For a second, I wondered why, then I saw *why*.

He had an erection.

An erection?

I peered around at the staff, but they were all men. Not a single woman in sight, well, save for the seventy-year-old with a clipboard who was barking out orders to the guys in what sounded like Russian.

So that meant, what?

The erection was for me?

The blush, the dreaded, hated blush, made another goddamn appearance, and to cover it, I ducked my head, then pushed the photos and the envelope at him.

For whatever reason, I stayed where I was, staring up at him as he calmly, coolly, and so fucking collectedly pushed the photos back into the torn envelope—it was some coverage. Better than none at all, I figured.

Being down here was....

Hell, I don't know what it was.

To be looked at like that?

For his body to respond to me like that?

It was unprecedented.

I'd had one sexual experience with a boy back in college, and that had not gone according to plan. So much so I was still technically a fucking virgin because, and this was no lie, the guy had *zero* understanding of a woman's body.

Craig had spent more time fingering my perineum than my clit, and every time he'd tried to shove his dick into me, he'd somehow managed to drag it down toward my ass.

I'd gotten so sick of him frigging the wrong bits of me, that I'd pushed him off and given him a blowjob. It had been the quickest way to get out of that annoying situation.

Yeah, annoying.

Jenny, when I'd told her, had pissed herself laughing, and ever since, had tried to get me to hook up with randoms, so I could slough off my virginity like it was dead skin and I was a snake. But life had just always gotten in the way, and I'd had no time for men.

Shortly after *that* had happened, we'd lost Fiona. Then, I'd graduated, and after, Mom and I had set up this place thanks to some insurance money she'd come into after her husband had died. It had been crazy building the tea room into an established cafe, and then mom had passed on, too.

So, here I was. Still a virgin. On my knees in front of the sexiest man on Earth, a man I knew, a man whose mother had half raised me, one who wanted me in his bed as some kind of blackmail payment.

Was this a dream?

Seriously?

I mean, I'd been depressed before Finn O'Grady had walked through my doors. Now I wasn't sure whether to be apoplectic or worried as fuck because he wasn't wrong: you didn't mess with the Five Points.

God, if I'd known they'd been behind the development on this building, I'd have probably signed over months ago.

The Points were. . . .

I shuddered.

Vindictive.

Aidan O'Donnelly was half-evil genius and half-twisted sociopath. St. Patrick's Church, two streets away, had the best roof in the neighborhood and the strongest attendance because Aidan, for all he'd cut you into more pieces than a butcher, was a devout Catholic. His men knew better than to avoid Sunday service, and I reckoned that Father Doyle was the busiest priest in the city because of Five Points' attendance.

"I like you down there," he murmured absentmindedly.

The words weren't exactly dirty, but the meaning? They had my temperature soaring.

Shit.

What the hell was I doing?

Enjoying the way this man was victimizing me?

It was so wrong, and yet, what was standing right in front of me? I knew he'd know what to do with that thing tucked behind his pants.

He wouldn't try to penetrate my urethra—yes, you read that right. Craig had tried to fuck my pee-hole! Like, *why?*

Finn?

He oozed sex appeal.

It seemed to seep from every pore, perfuming the air around me with his pheromones.

I hadn't even believed in pheromones until I scented Finn O'Grady's delicious essence.

It reminded me of the one out of town vacation we'd ever had. We'd gone to Cooperstown, and I'd scented a body of water that didn't have corpses floating in it—Otsego Lake. He reminded me of that. So green and earthy. It was an attack on my overwhelmed senses, an attack I didn't need.

With the envelope in his hand, he held out his other for me. When I placed my fingers in his, the size difference between us was noticeable once more.

I was just over five feet, and he was over six. I was round and curvy, and he was hard and lean.

It reminded me of the nursery tale Mom had sung to me as a child—Jack Sprat could eat no fat, and his wife could eat no lean.

Did it say a lot for my confidence that I couldn't seem to take it in that he wanted *me?* Or was it simply that I wasn't understanding how anyone could prefer me over Jenny?

Even my mom had called Jenny beautiful, whereas she'd kissed me on the nose and called me her 'bonny lass.'

Biting my lip, I accepted his help off the floor. My black jeans weren't the smartest thing for the tea room, but I didn't actually serve that many dishes, just bustled around behind the counter, working up the courage to do what Mom had done every day—greet people.

I wasn't a sociable person. I preferred my kitchen to the front of house, hence the jeans, but I regretted not wearing something else today. Something that covered just how big my ass was, how slender my waist *wasn't*.

Ugh.

This man is blackmailing you into his bed, Aoife. For Christ's sake, you're not supposed to be worrying if he likes the goods, too!

Still, no matter how much I tried, years of inadequacy weighed me down as I wiped off my knees.

"Do you have a coat?" he asked, and his voice was raspy again. "A jacket? Or a purse?"

I nodded at him but kept my gaze trained on the floor. "Yes."

"Go get them."

His order had me shuffling my feet toward the kitchen, but as I approached the door, I heard his strong voice speaking with the old woman with the clipboard: "I want this all cleaned up and boxed. Take it to my storage lot in Queens."

With my back to him, I stiffened at his brisk orders. *Was I just going to let him do this? Get away with it?*

My shoulders immediately sagged.

Did I have a choice?

If it was just him, just Acuig, then I'd fight this, as I'd been fighting it since the building had come to the attention of the developer. But this wasn't a regular business deal.

This was mob business, and it seemed like somehow, I'd become a part of that.

FML.

Seriously, FML.

CHAPTER 3

FINN

SHE WASN'T AS fiery as I imagined.

Did that disappoint me?

Maybe.

Then I had to chide myself because, Jesus, the woman had just been *coerced* out of her business. What did I expect? For her to be popping open a champagne bottle after I'd forced her to sign over her building to me?

Sure, she'd made a nice and tidy profit on her investment—I hadn't screwed her that way. But this morning, she'd gone into work with a game plan in mind, and tonight? Well, tonight she was out of a job and knee deep in a deal with the devil.

Of course, she hadn't actually agreed to my other terms, but when I guided her out of the tea room and toward my waiting car, she didn't falter.

Didn't utter a peep.

Just climbed into the vehicle, neatly tucked her knees together, and waited for me to get in beside her.

Like the well-oiled team my chauffeur and car were, they set off the minute I'd clicked my seatbelt.

The privacy screen was up, and I knew how soundproofed it was—not because of technology, but because Samuel knew not to listen to any of the murmurs he might hear back here.

And if he was ever to share the most innocent of those whispers he might have discerned? We both knew I'd slice off his fucking ear.

This was a hard world. One we'd both grown up in, so we knew how things rolled. Samuel had it pretty easy with me, and he wasn't about to fuck up this job when he was so close to retirement. If he kept his mouth shut, did as I asked, ignored what he may or may not have heard, and drove me wherever the fuck I wanted to go, Sam knew I'd set him and his missus up somewhere nice in Florida. Near the beach, so the moaning old bastard's knees didn't give him too much trouble in his dotage.

See?

I wasn't all bad.

Rapping my fingers against my knee, I studied her, and I made no bones about it.

Her face was tilted down, and it let me see the longest lashes I'd ever come across on a woman. Well, natural ones. Those fucking false ones that fell off on my sheets were just irritating. But as with everything, Aoife was all natural.

So pure.

So fucking perfect.

Jesus, Mary, and Joseph.

She was a benediction come to life.

I wasn't as devout as Aidan Sr. would like me to be, but even I felt uncomfortable thinking such thoughts while sporting a hard-on that made me ache. That made my mental blasphemy even worse.

"Why did you let him touch you? Was it for money?"

I hadn't meant to ask that question.

Really, I hadn't.

It was the last thing I wanted to know, but like poison, it had spewed from my lips.

Who she'd fucked and who she hadn't, was none of my goddamn affair.

This was a business deal. Nothing more, nothing less. She'd fuck me to make sure I kept quiet, and I fucked her so I could revel in the copious curves this woman had to offer.

Simple, no?

She stiffened at the question, and I couldn't blame her. "Do I really have to answer that?"

I could have made her. It was on the tip of my tongue to force her to, but I didn't really want to know even if, somewhere deep down, I did.

"You know why you're here, don't you?" I asked instead of replying.

Her nostrils flared. "To keep silent."

I nodded and almost smiled at her because, internally she was furious, but equally, she was lost. I could sense that like a shark could scent blood in the water. This had thrown her for a loop, and she was in shock, but she was, underneath it all, angry.

Good.

I wanted to fuck her tonight when she was angry.

Spitting flames at me, taking her outrage out on me as she scratched lines of fire down my spine as she screamed her climax. . . .

I almost shuddered at how well I'd painted that mental picture.

"When you're ready, you have my card."

"Ready for what?" she asked, perplexed. Her brow furrowed

as she, for the first time since she'd climbed into the car, looked over at me.

"To make another tea room. I've had them move all the stuff into storage."

She licked her lips. "I want to say that's kind of you, but I'm in this predicament because of you."

A corner of my mouth hitched at that. "Honestly, be grateful I was the one who came knocking today. You wouldn't want any of the Five Points' men around that place. Half that china would be on the floor now."

Her shoulders drooped. "I know."

"You do?"

"I pay them protection money," she snapped. "Plus, I grew up around enough Five Pointers to know the score."

That statement targeted my curiosity, hard. "You did, huh? Whereabouts?"

Her mouth pursed. "Nowhere you'd know," she muttered under her breath.

"I doubt it. This is my area, too."

She turned to me, and the tautness around her eyes reminded me of something, but even as it flashed into being, the memory disappeared as I drowned in her emerald green eyes. "Why are you doing this?"

"Why do you think?" I retorted. "You're a beautiful woman—"

"Don't pretend like you couldn't have any woman under you if you asked them."

I wanted to smile, but I didn't because I knew, just as Aidan had pointed out to me earlier that day, that Aoife wasn't exactly what society considered on trend.

She'd have suited the glorious Titian era. She was a Raphaelite, a gorgeous and vivacious Aphrodite.

She wasn't slender. Her butt bounced, and when I fucked her,

I'd have some meat to slam into, and her hips would be delicious handholds to grab.

If I smiled, I'd confirm that I was mocking her, and though I was a bastard, and though I was enough of a cunt to blackmail her into this when it hadn't been necessary—after all, before I'd told her who I was, I could have asked her out and done this normally—there was no way I was going to knock this glorious creature's confidence.

"Some men like slim and trim gym bunnies, some men like curves." I shrugged. "That's how it works, isn't it?"

Her eyes flared at that. "But Jenny—"

"Would you prefer she be here with me?" I asked dryly, amused when she flushed.

"Of course not. I wouldn't want her to be in this position."

I laughed. "Nicely phrased."

"What's that supposed to mean?"

Leaning forward, I grabbed her chin and forced her to look at me. "It's supposed to mean that you can fight this all you fucking want, but deep down, you're glad you're here. Your little cunt is probably sopping wet, and it's dying for a taste of my dick. So, simmer down. We're almost at my apartment."

And with that, I dipped my chin, and opening my mouth, raked my teeth down her bottom lip before I bit her. Hard enough to make her moan.

***

Aoife

THE STING of pain should have had me rearing back.

It didn't.

It felt. . . .

I almost shuddered.

Good.

It had felt good.

The way he'd done it. So fucking cocky, so fucking sure of himself, and who could blame him? He'd taken what he wanted, and I hadn't pulled away because he was right. My pussy *was* wet, and even though this was all kinds of wrong, I did want to feel him there. To have his cock push inside me.

Jesus, this was way too early for Stockholm syndrome, right?

I mean, this was . . . what was it?

It couldn't be that I was so horny and desperate for male attention that I was willingly allowing this to happen, was it?

Fuck. How pathetic was I if that was true? And yet, I didn't feel desperate for anything other than more of that small taste Finn had given me.

As a little girl, I'd watched Finn. It had been back in the day when his old man had been around and Fiona had lived with her husband and son. He'd beaten her up something rotten. Barely a week went by when Fiona, my mom's friend, didn't appear with some badly made-up bruise on her face.

I was young, only two, but old enough to know something wasn't right. I'd even asked my mom about it, wanting to understand why someone would do that to another person.

I couldn't remember what my mother had said, but I could remember how sad she'd been.

For all his faults, my dipshit stepfather had never beaten her, he'd just taken all her tips for himself and spent every night getting drunk.

Well, Finn's dad had been the same, except where mine passed out on the decrepit La-Z-Boy in front of the TV, Gerry had taken out his drunk out on Fiona.

And eventually, Finn.

Even as a boy, in the photos Fiona kept of him, Finn had been beautiful.

I could see him now, deep in my mind's eye. His hair had been as coal dark then as it was now, and not even a hint of silver or gray marred the noir perfection. His jaw and nose had grown, obviously, but they were just as obstinate as I remembered. Fiona had always said Finn was hardheaded.

When I was little, I hadn't had a crush on him—I'd been a toddler, for God's sake—but I'd been in awe of him. In awe of the big boy who'd been all arms and legs, just waiting for his growth spurt. Sadly, when that had happened, he'd disappeared.

As had his father.

Overnight, Fiona had gone from having a full house to an empty nest, and my mom had comforted her over the loss of her boy.

To my young self, I'd thought he'd died.

Genuinely. The way Fiona had mourned him? It had been as though both men had passed on, except we'd never had to go to church for a service, and there'd been no wake.

As kids do, I'd forgotten him. I'd been two when he'd disappeared, so I only really remembered that Fiona was a mom and that she was grieving.

We'd barely spoken his name because it could set her off into bouts of tears that would have my mom pouring tea down her gullet as they talked through her feelings.

As time passed, those little scenes in our crappy kitchen stopped, yet Fiona hung around our place so much it was like her second home.

One day, my stepfather died in an accident at work. The insurance paid out, Fiona moved in with us, and Mom had started scheming as to how to make her dream of owning a tea room come true. With Fiona living in, I'd heard Finn's name more often, but the notion he was dead still rang true.

Yet, here he was.

Finn wasn't dead.

He was very much alive.

Had Fiona known that?

Had she?

I wasn't sure what I hoped for her.

Was it better to believe your son was dead, or that your son didn't give enough of a fuck about you to contact you for years?

I gnawed on my bottom lip at the thought and accidentally raked over the tissue where Finn had bitten earlier.

"We're almost there," the man himself grated out, and I could sense he was pissed because the phone had buzzed, and whatever he'd been reading had a storm cloud passing behind his eyes.

"O-Okay," I replied, hating the quiver in my voice, but also just hating my situation.

This was. . . .

It was too much.

How was it that I was sitting here?

This morning, I'd owned a tea room. Now, I didn't.

This morning, I'd been exhausted, depressed about my mom, and *feeling* lost.

Now?

I was the *epitome* of lost.

A man was going to use me for sex, for Christ's sake.

But all I could think was: *did I still have my hymen?*

God, would he be angry if he had to push through it?

Should I tell him?

If I did, it would be for my benefit, not his, and why the hell was I thinking like this? I should be trying to convince him that normal people did not work business deals out by bribing someone into bed.

But, deep down, I knew all my scattered thinking was futile.

I wasn't dealing with normal people here.

I was dealing with a Five Pointer.

A high ranking one at that.

It was like dealing with a Martian. To average, everyday folk, a Five Pointer was just outside of their knowledge banks.

Sure, they thought they knew what they were like because they watched *The Wire* or some other procedural show, but they didn't.

Real-life gangsters?

They were larger than life.

They throbbed with violence, and hell, a part of me knew that Finn was cutting me some slack by asking to sleep with me.

Yeah, as fucked up as that was, it was the truth.

He could have asked for so much more.

He'd have a Senator in his pocket, and to the mob, what else would they ask for if not that?

Yet Finn?

He just wanted to fuck me.

My throat felt tight and itchy from dryness. I wanted some water so badly, but equally, I wasn't sure if it would make me puke.

Not at the thought of sex with this man—a part of me knew I'd enjoy it too much to even be nervous.

No, at what else he could ask of me, that had me fretting.

Was this a one-time deal?

How could I protect my dad from the Five Points when . . .?

I shuddered because there was nothing I could do. There was

no way I could even broach any of those questions since I wasn't in charge here.

Finn was.

Finn always would be until he deemed I'd paid my dues. Whether that was tomorrow or two years down the line.

Shit, it might even be forever. If my dad hit the White House, only God knew what kind of leverage Finn could pull if my father tried to carry on covering up my existence. . . .

"We're here."

Something had *definitely* pissed him off.

He'd gone from the cat who'd drank a carton full of cream, to a pissed off tabby scrounging for supper in the trash.

"We're going to go through to the private elevator, and I'm going to head straight down the hall to my living room. You're going to slip into the first door on the right—that's my bedroom."

"O-Okay," I told him, wondering what the hell was going on.

"You're going to stay quiet, and you're going to try to not hear any fucking thing I say, do you hear me?"

"I hear you."

"You'd better," he ground out, his hand tightening around his cellphone. "Coming to Aidan O'Donnelly's attention is the last thing a little mouse like you wants."

A shiver ran through me.

Aidan O'Donnelly was in his apartment?

Fuck, just how high up the ranks was he?

CONTINUE
THE FIVE POINTS' MOB COLLECTION
HERE:
www.books2read.com/FilthySerenaAkeroyd

CONTINUE
A DARK & DIRTY SINNERS' MC SERIES HERE:

www.books2read.com/HawkSerenaAkeroyd

AFTERWORD

PTSD.

Not discussed enough.

Not treated enough.

To those who fought for our freedom, to those who are *fighting* for our freedom, I thank YOU. You honor me with your service. You honor us all with the sacrifices you make.

I think Maverick is a book that befits a November release...

#LestWeForget

Please, don't misinterpret the ending of this novel. For each and every soldier out there, be they on active duty or retired, you have my humble thanks.

With that being said, I hope you guys are ready for Hawk. (Now available here: www.books2read.com/HawkSerenaAkeroyd)

I know, you're wondering why I'm tormenting you. When the hell Rex and Storm will get their story... which they WILL get, but your patience will be rewarded. :P

And in the interim, don't forget to read Filthy Sex. (www.

books2read.com/FilthySex) You'll get a glimpse at what happens with a certain someone who's important to the Sinners in that one. ;)

Each series is standalone, but you'll get a helluva lot more book boyfriends if you read them in order. :P

FILTHY
NYX
LINK
FILTHY RICH
SIN
STEEL
FILTHY DARK
CRUZ
MAVERICK
FILTHY SEX

For your ease, you can just click here: http://www.linktr.ee/SerenaAkeroydReadingOrder

As always, my darlings, many thanks to you for your support.

I know 2020 has been a shitter of a year for the world at large, but I'm sending you all my love.

Thank you so much,

Serena

xoxo

FREE BOOK!

Don't forget to grab your free e-Book!
Secrets & Lies is now free!

Meg's love life was missing a spark until she discovered her need to be dominated. When her fiancé shared the same kink, she thought all her birthdays had come at once, and then she came to learn their relationship was one big fat lie.

Gabe has loved Meg for years, watching her from afar, and always wishing he'd been the one to date her first and not his brother. When he has the chance to have Meg in his bed—even better, tied to it—it's an opportunity he can't refuse.

With disastrous consequences.

Can Gabe make Meg realize she's the one woman he's always wanted? But once secrets and lies have wormed their way into a relationship, is it impossible to establish the firm base of trust needed between lovers, and more importantly, between sub and Sir...?

This story features orgasm control in a BDSM setting.
Secrets & Lies is now free!

CONNECT WITH SERENA

For the latest updates, be sure to check out my website! But if you'd like to hang out with me and get to know me better, then I'd love to see you in my Diva reader's group where you can find out all the gossip on new releases as and when they happen. You can join here: www.facebook.com/groups/SerenaAkeroydsDivas. Or you can always PM or email me. I love to hear from you guys: serenaakeroyd@gmail.com.

ABOUT THE AUTHOR

I'm a romance novelaholic and I won't touch a book unless I know there's a happy ending. This addiction is what made me craft stories that suit my voracious need for raunchy romance. I love twists and unexpected turns, and my novels all contain sexy guys, dark humor, and hot AF love scenes.

I write MF, menage, and reverse harem (also known as why choose romance,) in both contemporary and paranormal. Some of my stories are darker than others, but I can promise you one thing, you will always get the happy ending your heart needs!